PRAISE FOR
ROCK, ROLL, AND RUIN

"Double-crosses, divas, detectives, and divorces—all set against the soundtrack of our lives. *Rock, Roll, and Ruin* takes us on a rollicking musical trip down memory lane with Buddy Holly, Chuck Barry, Elvis, and a host of musical delights. Oh, and a murder or ten."

—Susan Van Kirk, President of the
Guppy Chapter of Sisters in Crime
and author of the Endurance Mysteries

"The clever theme of this delightful anthology leads to a plethora of fine short stories featuring music from rock and roll through gospel, country, ole time rock and roll, and opera. Sleuths range from teachers to physicians to waitresses to musicians. Authors are new and veteran. *Rock, Roll, and Ruin* indeed offers something for any mystery lover."

—Molly Weston, Mystery Writers of America
Raven Award for Meritorious Mysteries

"From self-important bands through a high school sock hop to rabid fans, these twenty-seven stories follow music-obsessed individuals as their lives descend into crime and mayhem. A fascinating look at danger in our music culture."
                                                    —KM Rockwood, author of the
                                                    Jesse Damon crime novel series

"A rollicking good collection of crime stories powered by lyrics, strains, beats, and bop (on the head) malice."
                                                    —Molly MacRae, author of
                                                    The Highland Bookshop Mysteries
                                                    and The Haunted Yarn Shop Mysteries

"When the combination of mystery and music runs amok, the result is *Rock, Roll, and Ruin*—a book you can't put down!"
                                                    —Debra Goldstein, author of the Sarah Blair mysteries

ROCK, ROLL, AND RUIN

THE TRIANGLE SISTERS IN CRIME ANTHOLOGIES

Carolina Crimes: 19 Tales of Lust, Love, and Longing
Karen Pullen, editor

Carolina Crimes: 21 Tales of Need, Greed, and Dirty Deeds
Nora Gaskin, editor

Rock, Roll, and Ruin
Karen Pullen, editor

KAREN PULLEN, EDITOR

ROCK, ROLL, AND RUIN

A Triangle Sisters in Crime Anthology

Down & Out Books
3959 Van Dyke Road, Suite 265
Lutz, FL 33558
DownAndOutBooks.com

Cover design by Margo Nauert

ISBN: 1-64396-274-4
ISBN-13: 978-1-64396-274-0

TABLE OF CONTENTS

Introduction   1
Hank Phillippi Ryan

Songs of an Angry God   3
E Senteio

The Thursday Night All-You-Can-Eat   15
Elvis Everlasting Club
Ruth Moose

Rock and Roll May Take Your Soul   23
James Michael McGuffey

Stevie and Keith for the Save   37
E. B. Davis

Sweet Dreams   47
Gina Lea

All About Evie   63
Polly Iyer

The Vigil   73
Toni Goodyear

A Death at the Opera   87
Judy Fowler

Shaggy Dog, Shaggy Puppy   103
Bonnie Olsen

Delilah   115
Kari Wainwright

With a Side of Star   127
Jennifer Lowry

The Twist   133
Kathy Heady

Morocco Rococo   145
Caroline Taylor

Bitter Truth   155
David Goldston

The Day the Migraine Died   171
Kerry Peresta

Duet   183
Jennifer Riley

Hound Dog   189
Jamie Catcher

Lips Don't Lie   205
Bonnie Wisler

Rock 'n' Roll Never Forgets   219
Karen McCullough

The M and M's Mystery   235
Noelle Granger

The Sound of Murder   251
Marni Graff

Soundtrack to a Death   267
Kate Parker

Fickle Mistress   277
Lawrence Kelter

Past Connections   287
E. J. Murray

A Funny Face   305
Karen Pullen

Falling Star   321
Jacy Sellers

The Day the Music Died   337
Pamela Raymond

About the Authors   351

In memory of Margaret Maron,
inspirational mentor
and generous friend to so many

Introduction
Hank Phillippi Ryan

The key that links music and mystery is marvelously universal. It is the love of storytelling, isn't it? For a good story you need a character you care about. A problem that needs to be solved. You need a good guy and a bad guy. You need emotion. You need to lure the reader along until the irresistible end. Just like in a song.

How many stories are passed down in songs? From the doomed love of "Greensleeves" (Alas, my love, you have done me wrong) to "Miss Otis Regrets" (She pulled a gun and shot her lover down, madam); to "Frankie and Johnny," when Frankie walks into the bar room, and pulls out her old .44. The "Ode to Billy Joe," when Billy Joe McAllister throws something off the Tallahatchie Bridge. In the Cher classic "Bang Bang," it's all about murder. (Isn't it?) Oh, and in the sprightly "Copacabana," right? A murder mystery (and psychological thriller) in three verses and three choruses. And, in *my* teenage years at least, we learned you won't come back from "Dead Man's Curve," and understood that if you dated "The Leader of the Pack," it would not end well. And poor "Teen Angel."

And if you are laughing now, and singing in recognition, that's exactly the point. No matter when and where we grew up, it was the music that brought us together. And it still does.

1

Music is the soundtrack of our lives, isn't it? Think of all those times we turn to music for solace or inspiration or happiness or even…revenge. (When it's "Judy's Turn to Cry"?) How many times have we put on our favorite song before a big event to get us energized, or played a quieting song to sooth a cranky child, or had a song called "ours" with a special friend. It can inspire us, it can move us, it can change us. And when you sing with someone else, all the boundaries fall away.

In reading these oh-so-unique stories, I kept wondering: what was the original inspiration for each one? Did someone wonder if a jukebox could be magic…or sinister? How many Elvis fans contributed to this collection? Favorite songs, too, are hinted at throughout. See if you can find them. And I dare you not to sing along.

And in this fascinating anthology, using the inspiration of a song and the sly skill of a storyteller, these talented authors have created stories that are more than the sum of their parts. These stories come with a ready-made soundtrack—I know you'll be humming "Delilah" or "Hound Dog" or "American Pie" as you race through these stories. In one—I'll leave you to find it— "Piece of My Heart" takes on a whole different meaning. Delilah appears, the irresistible Delilah—and no wonder there are songs about her. And what good is a mystery without "The Twist"?

And as authors, we have certain songs that seem to have been created just for us: "Paperback Writer," certainly. "Misery," sometimes. "It's Only Words," always. Unwritten—Natasha Bedingfield had it right, didn't she? And let's call on the Bee Gees for—in music and in the writing life—the big finale: "Stayin' Alive."

Dip in to this concert of mystery, open to any story, and you'll sing a chorus of approval. I am honored to offer you this brief overture…but now, on with the show.

Songs of an Angry God
E Senteio

I joined the church choir not only because I'm a good Christian and a strong tenor, but because a wicked deed had been done, and now Dolores, my friend of twenty years, was dead, sitting at the Lord's feet singing "Nearer My God to Thee." The evildoer who took her life two weeks ago was still out there, and the Lord had said to me, *seek, and ye shall find.*

As I glided into the chapel with its polished pews and sparkling columns, the chattering and vocalizing stopped. All that remained were the hollow thuds resonating from my short heels with each slow and deliberate step I took across the marble. I came late to rehearsal intentionally. The element of surprise can't be underestimated. I had already donned my designer choir robe, and the weight of it shielded me like the hand of God.

"I Got the Music in Me," as my mother—God rest her soul—used to say. So, naturally, the church had been begging me for years to join the choir. I repeatedly declined; it was too far a fall from the pedestal of my diva days. When I sailed through that door and up the church's long center aisle, swinging the wide gold sleeves of my custom robe with its satin black trim swirling like restless snakes around my wrists and ankles, all I lacked was a flaming sword of vengeance. But God alone knew it was burning high and hot in my heart! As I lifted my voice to those arched ceilings singing "Onward, Christian Soldiers," all eyes

3

were on me. And there I was, marching as to war.

Too bad there was no gust of wind to agitate my curls and give me that Medusa vibe like in the video I did with Prince. He said Medusa needed to be regal, and that only came with age. I hold the honor of being the "oldest fine-ass woman" in a Prince video. Little known fact: Prince's song "I Would Die 4 U" was about Jesus.

And Sweet Jesus it was that set me on this mission. Everyone, including the medical examiner, claimed Delores had died from natural causes, that I was imagining foul play because I *hadn't adjusted well* to her loss, whatever that means. But it seemed that only I could see the serpents in the trees, and although I didn't know who or how, I knew in the crannies of my very soul that Dolores had been murdered.

I went to the police, but those uniform-wearing pups just off their mother's tit called me a crazy old lady. They didn't say it out loud, but I saw it in their eyes. I know crazy old ladies, plenty of them in my family. Even my mother—God rest her soul—started imagining things when she got a bit old and dotty. Daddy used to hum Lennon's "Imagine" to warn me when Ma was having a bad day. But I didn't *imagine* finding Dolores's stiff, lukewarm body two weeks ago in the very pew I just paraded past. If it was natural causes, then dress me in a tutu and call me a ballerina; that would be just about as believable.

"Bravo! Bravo!" The whirlwind that was Tasha blew down from the wooden stage and over to me. The look on my face stopped her just short of making a fool of herself. "We're so happy you're stepping in for Dolores." She took a few advisable steps back. Before I could ask her if Stevie Wonder "stepped in" for a town crier, Trombone darted over.

Dolores and I called the choir director Trombone because he's long and loud. "Oh, 'What A Friend We Have in Jesus.'" He clasped his hands to his chest and shouted like we were on opposite sides of a raging river. "That's the song in my heart as He blesses us with your presence, my dear sweet Caroline."

"Yes, well, I know Dolores would want me to be here with all of *you*," I said. God's eye was on the sparrow, but my eyes were scanning thirteen faces for a cringe of fear, a twitch of guilt. I knew God would give me a sign. Dolores was the one who'd known all their real names, but I never bothered. She and I always used the nicknames we gave them. I rarely saw the other choir members unless rehearsal was running late when I came to pick her up. She didn't like to drive, and it was on my way from water aerobics.

"Your robe is absolutely stunning," Trombone trumpeted. "We must look shabby to you, but we don't usually wear robes during rehearsals."

"I find God worth the effort, choir director." I ran my hands pointedly down the silky material. "And isn't all of life a dress rehearsal? To prove we deserve a part in the final big show?"

I wasn't always holier than thou until the day I realized I was. Well, I certainly was a hell of a lot holier than most. One day, when I was performing at a concert, clear as a bell, I heard God say to me, *Caroline, you are holier than him and her and her and them.*

When I'd found Dolores, it was obvious she'd been sitting in the aisle seat at the end of the fourth pew. She was lying on her right arm as if she'd simply slumped over sideways. Dolores never was fancy. Not much fanfare in life or death. She and I, we balanced each other out. I gave her pizzazz; she gave me placidity. And Dolores always made sure I stayed on track and kept me on the side of the angels.

Supposedly, on the evening she died, Dolores had mentioned she felt lightheaded. When no one saw her after the first half of rehearsal, they thought she'd left early. I wanted to ask them if they also thought she'd sprouted wings. Was she walking around singing "I Believe I Can Fly"? Because that would have been the only way she could have gotten home without me picking her up. Just another reason that I know it was murder. Everyone came and went through the side door except for Sunday and special services, so no one noticed her lying dead in the shadow of the pew. Dolores had become the proverbial tree that fell in the forest and didn't make a sound.

Oh, the devil is crafty. It all sounds so plausible, doesn't it? Except, where were Dolores's knitting needles? Why were her eyes wide open when I found her?

See, I'd known for sure Dolores would never let those knitting needles out of her sight. She always claimed they were the very ones Audrey Hepburn used in the film *Breakfast at Tiffany's*. And if you watch the scene, they sure do look like them: smooth and wooden with big knob ends. Sure, a person could buy replicas, but Dolores was a straight shooter—and she was leaving them to me in her will. To use a clichéd but apt vulgarity: she wouldn't pee on my leg and tell me it's raining.

I had to go through a baker's dozen of potential suspects, the exact number of people at the Last Supper, if you count Jesus. So, like The 5th Dimension, "(Last Night) I Didn't Get to Sleep at All." I prayed God would give me direction, and He'd sent me here to this rehearsal. I've known for a while now what I wish I'd understood long ago; if you really listen, you hear the melodious voice of God sliding between the notes and strains of all kinds of musical compositions, drifting in the melody, thrumming in the rhythms, beating through the bass. Even bad music can spread The Good Word.

But ever since Dolores died, all I hear are songs of an angry God.

Last night, I'd kept "The Eye of the Tiger" blasting on a loop to keep me focused and alert as I ran through the list of suspects. I considered and dismissed Bozo, a grown woman who dyed her hair orange; the Twins, self-explanatory; Jennie, I remembered her actual name because it was the same as my ill-fated aunt's;

and Headband, she always had one that matched her outfit. The others I also dismissed had only recently joined the choir, or Dolores had said so little about them they hadn't warranted nicknames.

My focus was on the three remaining prime suspects: the Ram, the Biscuit Baker, and Grace. They each had a selfish, petty reason to want to do away with Dolores.

The Ram—with her gray hair parted directly down the middle, combed flat against the sides of her skull, then ending in huge, hairspray-hardened flips just over her ears—looked like a Dorset sheep just wandering in from a hillside graze. She made the list because she'd always wanted Dolores's knitting needles. My mother—God rest her soul—used to say, *If you see a cat walking down the street wearing a top hat and tap shoes, he's not an ordinary cat,* meaning some things were obvious. Dolores would never give them up, not for anything. I remember her joking that they'd have to be pried from her cold dead hands. Not so funny now, is it? Not with the image of the Ram bending back Dolores's lifeless fingers to snatch away her prize.

The Biscuit Baker brought a basket of buttermilk biscuits to every rehearsal for the last year. (Alliteration is a cappella rap.) He always made a show of them being freshly baked. I could smell the full-fat butter melting in a warmer and saw the covered basket everyone would gather around greedily at break.

Well, as it turns out, Dolores was in Apex about a week ago, and who does she see coming out of the Bowl & Biscuit Boutique carrying the big bakery to-go box? Dolores had mimicked the Biscuit Baker's wide eyes and frozen stance, and I imagined Elvis belting out "Suspicious Minds" as their eyes locked across the small back alley. "That faux Biscuit Baker was looking for a Florida sinkhole to swallow him whole in North Carolina. Ha!" Dolores's eyes disappeared when she laughed. And I was laughing right along with her. She was always a good mimic.

Last on my suspect list was Grace. Proverbs says, "The woman named Folly is loud; she is naive and knows nothing." That's a spot-on description of Grace. That she thought only she should sing the solo of "Amazing Grace" *because her name was in it* tells you all you need to know. Dolores did her funny snort-laugh, imitating how Grace's voice kicked into high-whine: "But *her* name is *Dolores*, why does *she* get to sing it?" What Grace lacked in logic, she made up for in persuasiveness; she had talked Trombone into including "All the Single Ladies" in the Christmas music program, using the "logic" that it was anti-premarital sex. It's not. He's just an idiot with a secular soul. Now, with Dolores in Heaven washing Jesus's feet, Grace was next in queue for the solo.

Oh, they like to sing about how "The Devil Went Down to Georgia." What you rarely hear is that he was only on vacation. He lives right here in Crooked Fork, North Carolina. One of these choristers was guilty. I could feel it all the way down to the coil of the curl of the hair on my big toe, and it was up to me to figure out which one killed Dolores, so her soul could rest.

Trombone started rehearsals with a joyless rendition of "Make a Joyful Noise." I begged off, claiming I wanted to listen to them as a group before I joined in. It gave me an opportunity to move around the stage and observe as I circled the three-tier riser the choir performed on. I searched the cluster of faces for some indication of guilt.

They had fooled the police and the medical examiner who said that sometimes when people die, their muscles relax and their eyes open—and it was more common than you would think. Well, I don't *think*. I have *faith*. And I didn't believe that Quincy wannabe, not for one second. My soul was humming with the awareness that Dolores had an up-close and personal "Dance with the Devil."

I listened hard as the choir bumbled through hymns and soft

seculars. But God remained silent.

As I circled, I went over everything in my mind: the motives, the inconsistencies, the open eyes, the missing knitting needles, the biscuits, the solo. God alone knew of any other nefarious goings-on that Dolores hadn't mentioned. I remained vigilant, ears perked for an illuminating lyric from the Lord.

Oh, I've lived long enough to trust that if you have the ear and heart to hear, God will make His will known. Today, the Twins were His messengers. As they harmonized on the throwback hymn "Into Your Hands," God joined in on the second chorus, writhing in the riffs, whispering *Vengeance is Mine.* Well, He didn't have to hit me over the head with a cleaver like my Uncle Bert did to Aunt Jennie.

When Scruffy—he always dressed like a hobo—stopped playing the piano to search through his disorganized sheets of music for the next song, I saw the three people most likely to have killed Dolores grouped together for a secret confab. They only separated when Trombone clapped his hands and shouted: "Let's take our break a bit early and give Bennet time to track down the new songbook." How they didn't flinch every time he opened his mouth, I'll never understand.

Like parking lot crows spotting a french fry, the choir swarmed the basket of buttermilk biscuits, cawing and squawking their way to the side table and scent of warm butter. The Biscuit Baker's voice rose above the din, his eyes flashing toward me as he snatched a biscuit: "I picked this batch up in Apex. They're almost as good as mine. You probably can't tell the difference."

Was that God telling me the Biscuit Baker had done it? Or that he hadn't, since he almost came clean? Was there a clue I missed?

I didn't have any time to think or pray about it before Grace came over in a puff of butter and crumbs and asked me if I'd consider singing the "Amazing Grace" solo. "I talked it over with some of the others, and they think we would all be blessed if you'd agree." The only reason I hesitated in answering was that I'd assumed from the moment I'd walked in the door that was a given. Grace had to know that too, so was this empty gesture an attempt to deflect from her original motivation?

They were wily. I'll give them that. By then, I thought I would've been belting out a righteous and rousing rendition of "Praise the Lord I Saw the Light," and the miscreant would be nabbed. If my name were Jane Marple or Aloysius Pendergast, I would have already spotted the culprit by an accidental slip of the tongue, a telling whiff of almond, a stray strand of hairspray-hardened hair.

Just by thinking about her, I'd conjured the Ram. For the first time, I noticed her sitting on the single chair at the back of the stage, elbows on knees, head in hands. Guilt is heavy. *Carrying guilt*, my mother—God rest her soul—always said, *is like carrying two cows over your shoulders. One will be kicking you in the gut, the other will be kicking you in the ass, and in the end, it will bring you down.* When I walked over to her, the Ram raised tearful eyes and offered a quivering apology for not greeting me properly. "Oh, Caroline, seeing you and hearing your voice— like an angel from the Lord—makes me miss Dolores even more. She talked about you all the time."

"Well, Dolores loved to talk." No way would I offer succor when I didn't know if it was guilt or pain that caused the Ram's tears. Truth be told, I probably wouldn't offer it anyway. I baited her: "She mentioned how you two were in the knitting circle together last month."

"Oh, 'Bless the Lord/ Oh, my soul.'" She dabbed at wet eyes and stood up, touching my shoulder with moist fingers, "Stay here for one second, please."

Surprisingly, while I contemplated how to get her to confess, the Ram moved like a gazelle, dashing through the side door and back. She reached into the large tote she was carrying and pulled out Dolores's knitting needles. "I was planning to drop these by, but since you're here." She shrugged and handed them to me. "I know how much she loved them. No matter how much I offered her, she always said they were meant for you when she went home to God. I found them on the edge of the stage." Before wandering off for her biscuit, the Ram made a sad face that made her look more like a cow than a ram. "I realized if she had been sitting—well, you know, where you found her—she would have been looking right at them, and you know she never let them out of her sight."

When God spoke to me, especially through music and song, it wasn't always exactly clear. He made me work for it. I thought He would have shown me a sign, something obvious that would lead to my "AHA!" moment; one look at Dolores's killer and Kenny Loggins's "This Is It" would blast out of pores in the air. I had high hopes that I would be clever enough to avenge Dolores's death. But my gift is not detection; it is loyalty and faithfulness.

And! *He is faithful who promised*: "I will shortly pour out My wrath on you and spend My anger against you." It made me think of how Dolores was a big comic nerd. She used to remind me that God is like David Banner (aka the Hulk)—you won't like Him when He's angry. That's why, when I finally heard the almighty Lord slip between the chords that vengeance was *His*, I knew I was only a spectator.

So, just as the Twins were wrapping up their harmony and everyone was buoyant over an early biscuit break, I poured the potently distilled poison from the angel's trumpet plant into the melting butter. Scripture says, "They shall take up serpents, and if they drink any deadly thing, it shall not hurt them." On faith, I trusted God would sort the chaff from the wheat as I started singing loud and clear, "Jesus, Take the Wheel."

My voice filled the vestibule and flowed like a river of retribution down its arches.

Trombone was just calling everyone back from break when I saw Grace grab her flat stomach and double over. But before I could shout, *"Hallelujah, the Devil's been revealed!"* the Biscuit

Baker stumbled then fell flat, his face bouncing hard on the sideboard. Well, well. They were a team. "God moves in a mysterious way, His wonders to perform."

Still, I admit I was a bit surprised when Bozo and Headband started looking queasy because I had taken them off my suspect list, but the thud of Trombone's head hitting the marble floor when he fell backward off the stage distracted me. On the other side of the platform, Scruffy's face took the brunt of it as he slumped forward tinkling a few piano keys that set off the mellow voice of Boy George singing "Karma Chameleon" in my head, then bridging smoothly into "Do You Really Want to Hurt Me" as if God were checking to see if I would stand fast. Tasha stumbled toward me with her hand outstretched like a pop idol reaching beyond the footlights for a swooning groupie. I side-stepped just as she fell, and it was at that moment I realized I was wrong.

The twang of Patsy Cline's "So Wrong" filled my head, drowning out everything else. Time went a bit wonky, caught up on discordant notes ricocheting around my brain as the Ram and the remaining nameless choir members tumbled, plunged, and collapsed in slow motion. One by one, they fell at my feet or not far off—except the Twins. They fell together in the aisle not far from the fourth pew where Dolores sat shaking her head in disappointment, maybe shame. Dear Lord, forgive me. I've been such a fool. Call me Icarus and dip my wings in wax.

I'm no detective or smooth-talking gumshoe. Tell the truth and shame the devil, I'm not even usually very inquisitive. That I ever thought a diva like me—although blessed with this voice and the ear to hear God—could solve Dolores's death and point the finger at the *one* guilty party was the height of hubris. But this was proof from God that *I* certainly wasn't crazy.

As I watched the final twitches, the gasps and gags, the last sighs a symphony of "How Great Thou Art," I understood that never in a month of Sundays would I have ever figured out that Dolores's death had been a conspiracy. They were all in it together. They were legion.

I joined the church choir because a wicked deed had been done. Now that God has revealed the transgressors that snuffed out her light, Dolores, my friend of twenty years, was sitting at the Lord's table singing "It Is Well With My Soul." I smoothed down my pleats and hiked up the serpent-trimmed hem of my gold robe as I stepped over and around the bodies of the Deceiver's murdering minions.

His truth was marching on. "Glory, Glory Hallelujah!"

The Thursday Night All-You-Can-Eat Elvis Everlasting Club
Ruth Moose

In line before me, at the salad bar, in Golden Sands's Thursday night all-you-can-eat buffet, is a fat Elvis. And I do mean FAT. I can't guess the poundage, but I bet he'd flatten any scale. Elvis. True. Right in front of me. He's got the hair, black as asphalt and dyed I'm sure, or a wig; but can a wig have sideburns, long and wide sideburns? He has a rope of thick gold chains that jingle jangle and a belt buckle big enough to hold in the world. When Fat Elvis reaches for the mixed greens, I see a ring on each of his ten fingers, some with glittering stones big as ice cubes. Not one of them real. Can't be real.

I didn't realize I had said that out loud until Joyce Ann flounced by and said out the side of her red, red lipsticked mouth, "Well, it takes one to know one." Then she sashayed off swinging and swaying, clicking her fingers.

Oh, so tacky.

But who am I to judge? I'm here at the monthly meeting of Elvis Everlasting Club, not by choice, please understand, but by order of my daughter-in-law, sweet Joyce Ann McClain, leader/organizer and forever president of this "club." This "club" is Joyce Ann's baby, her fame and glory. I call it her obsession. She's been over the top on this thing, this Elvis obsession, for years now. Years! I mean, it's sick stuff. Sick, sick, sick. She's got one whole room in their otherwise lovely and very nice house (built and mortgaged by my own precious son, William the patient, William the trod-upon, William the conquered) filled with "Everything Elvis." Online she's bought life-size, stand-up, cut-out movie cardboard figures of Elvis; one in his all-white outfit, another in blue. In that Elvis room, it's spooky. You walk in and bump into one and she, Joyce Ann, nearly has a heart attack. "Did you scratch it?" Then she rubs the cardboard thing all over saying, "Baby, are you all right? Are you hurt? Did the mean old lady scare you?"

(MEAN OLD LADY, MEANING ME?)

On shelves in that room, shelves my son had to build and sand and paint, she's got Elvis stuff from salt and pepper shakers to something somebody told her was shoe polish that belonged to Elvis. Who knows? Who knew? It's sick. Like anything anybody told her or sold her had been touched, breathed on by the E god himself. Of course, she's got tapes and CDs of every song he ever recorded. Some in Japanese. Some in French. Some in Farsi even. My lord, it sounds like the UN in there.

"You can't understand a word of any of those," I told her.

"I already know every word," she flounced back at me. "I know every word of every song he ever sang. And where he sang it. Elvis is more popular than God." Then she teared up. "He was too good for this world. Too big. Too wonderful, and we lost him." Then she bawled. A grown woman crying her heart out.

She's got aprons and potholders that say "Love me Tender." She's got mugs and to-go cups from The Heartbreak Hotel. She makes our darling little Richard carry an Elvis lunchbox to school, and I bet he wanted and cried for a Spider Man or Star Wars. She even puts peanut butter and banana sandwiches in it.

She's got an Elvis snow globe and a music box that plays "Love Me Tender." Then there are the T-shirts, sweatshirts, and yoga pants that read "Never Let Me Go."

As if anybody would want to. I mean wear them. She does. She's a walking, singing, talking billboard.

AND...that's not all. Instead of spending time with her precious family, she buries herself in that room binge-watching all the movies Elvis ever made.

One time she said with a handkerchief to her eyes, "That Ann Margaret didn't know how good she had it. Skinny ferret couldn't dance. They had to dub in her voice. I know they did."

"Joyce," I said, "you don't know that. Did you read it somewhere?"

"You," she screamed at me, started pushing me toward the door. "You don't know anything Elvis. You, in your narrow-minded self won't let anything wonderful in. Out. Just go."

So, I left, only to have her email me in all capital letters, *IF YOU WANT TO EVER ENJOY THE COMPANY OF YOUR SON OR GRANDSON AGAIN IN THIS LIFETIME...*

What? I wrote back. *What do you mean?*

Then she called me on the phone. "You need to stop being ugly to me about my Elvis collection. For years I have been patient, but you have been putting me down every chance you get. In this town, things have gotten back to me that you have said. You have made fun of the one thing I enjoy in my life. You have to join my Elvis Everlasting Club and come to all the meetings, or I will cut you out of our life. I mean it. No Christmas, birthdays, and don't even think about Mother's Day. You will not be present. We will move across the country. We will move across the world. You will never see your weakling son or sniveling little snot grandson again."

She knew she had me, had me by the hairs on my chin.

William and Little Richard are all I have since Hilburt committed suicide five years ago. A suicide takes over your life forever. You never get away from it. And though Hilburt did it, I have to go on living in a town where everybody knows and maybe half of them are always asking or thinking it was my fault. I knew he was depressed after losing his job at the meat-packing plant, but I didn't know he was depressed to the point of suicide. If the man hadn't owned a gun, I think he'd still be alive to this day. It was awful. Sometimes I still wake up in the middle of the night thinking I heard the shot and have to go find him in the barn. I'll never get what I found and saw out of my mind if I live to be a hundred.

"Okay," I said. "What can I do?" So here I was, with my arms filled with a bouquet of roses (thank you, Aldi, $3.99) to present Joyce Ann after she's installed as the "new president." Ha, she'd been the ONLY president for the ten years of "the club." Oh, I can be most gracious, and I will do anything to keep my son and grandson in my life. They are the only life I have, and she knows it. Blond witch in a gold, skin-tight dress. Blond witch who will be gone, not in a puff of smoke, but with stinking green streaming out her vitals.

Now in the line at the salad-serving station, I fill my plate with one of each thing here. Bean salad, macaroni salad, tuna, crab, chicken, fruit...I love it all.

But this Fat Elvis with his spoonful of mixed greens doesn't fool me. His plate may be scant, but when nobody is looking, he'll come back, go to each of the stations, and load up a plate from each. Mixed greens, my foot. He is bigger than big. He's Macy's Parade balloon big. He's blown-up plastic yard decoration big. Those Santas and sleighs, reindeer on rooftops, have nothing on him. He out-bigs them all.

Then I see, right in front of him, Mrs. Fat Elvis, and she's all in black with gold jangles and rings and things, guitar strung across her back, helping herself to the salad bar. Are they a duo? They move wide and slow as tanker trucks.

I want to boost them along a bit, but my arms are loaded with the red rose bouquet still in its cellophane cone and the little jar of my special honey that my bees have made from yellow jessamine which grows in my garden and is poison, poison, poison. *Gelsemium sempervirens* the books call it, but I just love all that golden yellow when it blooms. My garden glows gold.

Joyce Ann has said I spent more time in my garden than God ever did in Eden. And she laughs when she says it. I belong to three garden clubs, two of which I started, but have never been president, not that I haven't been asked. Some of us don't like to call attention to ourselves, which is more than I can say about Joyce. And she doesn't stop with her Elvis Everlasting business but has to make my sweet William and Little Richard the butt of all this. She paid to have Elvis costumes made for them, and they have to come to the meetings dressed in the mess. They would be here tonight except Little Richard had a fever of 102, and William was taking him to the First Alert Emergency Clinic. She, Joyce Ann, got so mad the boy was sick, said he was faking it, doing it on purpose to mess up her special night.

I said, "Joyce Ann, with this awful virus going around, I don't think you should take any chances. I mean a fever is a fever, and he's not faking it."

She screamed that I was always taking up for the two of them.

I said, "If it would make you feel better, instead of going to the emergency clinic, though I'd worry myself sick the whole time, I'll go to your wonderful meeting."

"Fine," she said and left, slamming the screen door enough to warp it.

So here I was, bouquet and all, though I'd stopped by Aldi first. Would not cut a single bloom from any flower in my yard to give to somebody who didn't deserve them. Wouldn't appreciate them. Aldi for $3.99 was all I could do. And that was more than I wanted to do, but I can humble myself for the sake of my son and grandson, the loves of my life. Real, honest-to-gosh living and breathing family, not some cardboard and on-the-screen addiction which is sick. Crazy sick. Like maybe here in the salad bar line like these two Elvises, the specially invited, long-awaited guests of this "cause," which is dear Joyce's heart and lifeblood. The cause she devotes herself to when she should be home with William, my sweet son and his own darling boy, little Richard, the precious child. But no, here's Joyce Ann sweeping around the room in her gold satin (adorned with sequins spelling out *Elvis*) floor-length gown, and it's six o'clock on a Thursday, not a dance floor in sight, nor a red carpet, though if she could have rented one, there would be. This is her night, her club, her premier program. So here she is in prom festivities with matching eight-inch-high pumps. She's got her bleached blond hair piled beehive tall and, tucked in here and there, small rhinestones like raindrops. She's a winner, that dear sweet Joyce Ann, who waggled her hips and leaned down her bigger-than-normal and heavily enhanced boobs, that lured my innocent son, William the serious and scholarly, into a life of servitude and woe. For her, he took a job so far beneath him a basement is a high rise. He, with his fine computer mind and sensibilities, left the life I wanted for him, scrimped and saved to send him to the best IT school in the country. But she flounced her curvy self right up there to Boston, got herself PG; and of course since I raised him right, he came home and married her. O, the shining bitch of the hour.

I warned him, O, I warned him, no good would come of a life wedded to a woman who ate, slept, and breathed Elvis, Elvis, Elvis. She didn't, couldn't, wouldn't, open her mouth, but one of his song lyrics rang out. And Lord, she was no singing bird, but had the screech of a red-tailed hawk.

I follow the others into the already packed room with a small stage up front. The stage is stacked with speakers and enough electronics to send a person to another planet (and I will wish they would when the godawful music starts).

Dutifully, I take a seat at a table near the front, hope the music (ha ha) won't be so loud when it's upfront and personal.

As soon as everybody is seated and before they start their forks, Joyce Ann takes the stage, picks up the microphone, and announces a small business session. "Only five minutes, folks," she says, "and then the eating and music can begin."

An elderly man in black, guitar strapped to his chest, wig (I'm sure) trying to look like Johnny Cash, steps up beside her.

"Why, it is our own Johnny Cash all in person," she exclaims. "Let's hear it for our guest...one of our very special guests."

There is applause, loud with some cat calls and foot stomps, plus another person has gone to the stage and begins beating a drum. Boom, boom, boom. The room rocks with each boom.

I know I can't get out of this place fast enough. I dig into my macaroni salad, which has too much mayonnaise.

He, whoever he really is, takes the microphone from Joyce Ann, and says he'll ask the blessing with every head bowed, every eye closed.

So I close my eyes and bow my head, but pray my own prayer that this whole hell-of-an-Elvis mess will be over soon. That my grandson gets well and goes on to live a long and successful life. Maybe he and William will move in with me after they sell that house full of Elvis stuff.

There has to be a market for it, someone as looney and crazy as Joyce Ann.

Then Johnny Whoever (?) plucks a guitar string, waits, announces that officers of the club are to be installed and he has the honor, as usual, for the tenth year in a row.

So they do the treasurer, and some skinny pole of a tall, beautifully dressed, very intelligent-looking dark-skinned guy stands up and is applauded. He waves to the audience.

Secretary. A woman who could be a lookalike Joyce Ann, steps toward the stage, but there's no room, so she stops, turns to the audience and waves.

More applause.

Vice president. A girl in short shorts, red and purple hair in a top knot, stands at the back of the room and waves. There is a boom boom from the drummer.

"And finally," the Cash man with the microphone almost screams, "our own, our not to be equaled for the tenth time, our Joyce Ann will once again be president."

Joyce Ann, beaming, bowing Joyce Ann, even does a little dance there on the stage while the music and applause get so loud I can only hear the roaring in my head. She is so full of herself, of the moment, she takes my bouquet and doesn't even see who handed it to her. It could be a golden dagger for all she sees.

While the beat goes on, Joyce Ann, with my Aldi bouquet, bows and waves her flowers. The audience stands, applauds, and hoots, keeps on and on hooting and applauding. These are HER people.

I quietly step beside Joyce Ann's chair, quickly open her purse that is black, of course, and big as an overnight suitcase, leave her the little jar of honey and one of my homemade butter biscuits. She DOES love my biscuits.

I quietly slide from the room.

Nobody notices.

And nobody ever will.

Her obituary will read/gush/mush that she died suddenly of "heart arrest after a night of celebrating her reelection as president of the Elvis Forever club. She was one of a kind and loved by all far and wide."

Except maybe one.

Rock and Roll
May Take Your Soul
James Michael McGuffey

After his last stop on a northwestern Iowa sales trip, Jack Smith felt he had to have a break from his routine. Instead of going straight back to his home base in Omaha, he decided to detour along the Outlaw Trail. Highway 12 across northern Nebraska had been designated a scenic byway to attract tourists who liked to get off the major highways. He passed through small towns—Wynot, Crofton, Niobrara. Population in the hundreds, all similar, with a two-block downtown and a few craft and artist stores filled with trinkets themed on the outlaws, Indians, cowboys, and buffalo that had populated the area.

He tuned the car radio to an Elvis Sirius XM channel, old-time rock and roll. Music he loved, music that lifted his spirits. His spirits needed a lift. Two months ago, Gina, his wife of two years, left him to go back home to North Carolina where he had met and married her while in the Marine Corps. Couldn't take the Nebraska winters, she said. Divorce papers followed soon. She wasn't returning his calls.

As he approached a town named Valentine, he saw an unusual one-story building with a large model of a guitar on the roof and a sign that said *Old Time Rock and Roll*. The walls displayed a life-sized mural of guitar players, topped by strings of lights that would illuminate the whole front of the building at night. A sign on the door said *Open from 7:00 Until.* Old time rock and roll. My kind of place, he thought. He'd find a place to stay and get a bite to eat then check it out.

Just beyond the bar was an old one-story roadside motel, the Valentine Ranch Motel, set back farther from the road. It looked well-maintained, with a nice lawn. He guessed the bar and motel were owned together, since their parking lots connected. He saw only one car at the far end near the office, so he should have his choice of rooms.

When he entered the office door, a buzzer sounded and an elderly but spry woman came out from a back room. He could hear a TV running in the back. "Room for one," he said.

She placed a registration card on the desk. "How many nights?"

"Just one. Tell me about the rock-and-roll bar next door. Is it a busy place at night?"

"Not on weeknights. It picks up on weekends when a lot of locals show up to dance and do karaoke. But it's worthwhile, to see a lot of memorabilia the owner collected from the late fifties and early sixties."

"I loved that music growing up."

She gave him a big smile as she handed him a key.

"I bet you could bop with the best," he said.

"Maybe," she said over her shoulder as she walked into the back room.

He went to his room, dropped his suitcase and briefcase on the bed, and drove down the road for a quick supper. Back in the room, he put on a pair of jeans, a knit shirt, and a pair of loafers. He looked at his watch, 7:15. Time to check out the bar, hear some good music, relax with a drink.

A fully restored 1957 Impala with a beautiful emerald green paint job and sculptured rear fenders was parked in front of the building. Inside, a long bar ran along the wall on the right. The room was empty, not even a bartender. In the far-left corner was a small stage where a person or duo could perform. He remembered the woman at the motel had mentioned karaoke.

As his eyes adjusted from the bright light outside to the dimness of the bar, he noticed old posters covering most of the walls. Many of them were signed by the artists. They must be originals, he thought, advertising rock-and-roll shows from the fifties and sixties. Some featured legends like Elvis and Johnny Cash, and others were performers who'd had one hit record and played it over and over across the Midwest. When he was a teenager, he had seen some of them in person. Above the posters were old guitars, each signed by a performer and described with a plaque.

On the wall at the end of the bar was a large framed photograph of a group of eight young people sitting on cars from the fifties. He recognized a Thunderbird, an Impala like the one outside, and a Corvette. The picture had been taken in front of the bar. Though the cars were over fifty years old, the men and women in the picture wore modern clothing. Eight of them, too many for a band. Perhaps a group of friends who frequented the bar because of the music theme, he thought.

As he pulled out a barstool, a door at the end of the bar opened, and a lanky man came out. He had black hair and a short-cut beard, both showing a lot of gray. He called out, "What can I get you?"

"A shot of Jim Beam and a cold beer. Any kind," Jack replied.

The bartender pulled a shot glass and a fifth of Jim Bean off a shelf, opened a cooler and got out a bottle of Coors. "Cold as it can be," he said.

Jack took a long drink of the beer and then downed the shot. He felt good. His depression was lifting. "This is some collection you have."

The bartender smiled. "I spent a long time finding them, from all over." He opened his arms wide. "Then I got the idea for this bar."

"I saw a few of these bands in person," Jack said. He looked around. "Business a little slow tonight?"

The bartender shrugged. "It's like this on weeknights. Just a few people passing through. We'll get a few locals in later. On the weekends, people of all ages come in to drink and dance away their cares."

"That's what I want to do," said Jack. "Drink away some cares. What's your name?"

"Jesse," the bartender replied. He looked down and saw a wedding ring on Jack's finger. "Are you in town alone?" he asked.

Jack followed Jesse's glance down to his finger. He took off the ring and put it in his pocket. "Just about divorced," he said. "I don't know why I'm still wearing it. That's the reason I'm here, to forget why." He signaled to the bartender to pour another shot. Then he heard a humming sound and looked across to the far side of the room. An old jukebox had lit up and the humming was coming from it. Odd, he thought. How had he missed that when he walked around the room? "Does that old thing still work?" he asked.

"Takes quarters," the bartender said.

Jack pulled some money out of his pocket, peeled off three dollars and put them on the bar. "Change them out for me." The bartender stacked twelve quarters on the bar and Jack took them over to the jukebox. He read down the play list—Jerry Lee Lewis, Buddy Holly, Elvis, Chuck Berry, Johnny Cash, and many others. He knew most of the songs, had played them over and over as a teenager and danced the night away to the music with Gina in beach clubs in North Carolina. He fed the quarters in and punched buttons for twelve songs. His mood lifted again as the first song came up, "Peggy Sue," by Buddy Holly.

As he sat down, he heard the door open. Two men about his age walked to the far end of the bar and took a seat. The bartender placed two shot glasses filled with bourbon in front of the newcomers. Another song came on the jukebox—Chuck Berry's "Maybellene." A group of six young people entered the bar, dressed casually. Jack glanced at the picture on the wall to his right. They must be the same people in that picture. This was their hangout. Two couples started to swing dance right away. The other couple came up to the bar where the bartender was setting out beers. The music was irresistible, and Jack wished there was someone he could dance with, twirl around.

They'd left the door wide open. It looked dark outside. Strange, he thought, it's too early to be dark this time of year. Then a beautiful young woman walked through the door. He had not been able to see her in the darkness beyond, and it seemed to him she just emerged suddenly. Long black hair, ivory skin, and ruby lips. She looked straight at him with dark blue eyes. She walked over to him and put a hand on his shoulder. A tremor went through him. She looked straight into his eyes and said, "You must be a real man."

His heart jumped but he felt his mojo rising. "Um, yeah, I'm real," he replied.

She took his hand, and he felt a shock of energy. "Come dance with me." He had not danced in a long time, but he felt confidence somehow flowing from her touch. They hit the floor, and everything came natural to him. He twirled her around. The other dancers gave them room and cheered them on. He brought her in close to him when he spun her around. He felt the heat from her body driving him to fancier moves. The records changed over without stopping, and they danced on and on.

A slow song began, Elvis's "Love Me Tender," the last song Jack had punched in. He brought her close to him and felt her breasts against his chest. She looked up into his eyes and said, "Let's go outside now."

He didn't have to be asked twice. He took her hand, and they turned toward the door, toward the darkness outside. But suddenly a young man emerged from the darkness. He raised his hand and said, "Connie, you need to stop doing this!"

The woman yelled, "Tim, not now!" She tugged on Jack's arm, but the young man stood in his way. Then, as the music ended, and the final guitar chord faded, the woman vanished. In an instant, he was alone in a dead-silent room, empty except for the bartender. He stumbled back to the bar. What the hell was happening?

The bartender placed a beer in front of him and poured a shot of Jim Beam. "You said to keep them coming," Jesse said, looking at him intently, with a strange curl on his lips. "Would you like some more quarters?" he asked. "For the jukebox?"

The jukebox hummed and twinkled. Jack sat stunned. Then a smile came over his face, and he knew what he wanted. He reached into his pocket, pulled out some bills and put a five on the bar. "Give me twenty quarters and another shot of Jim Beam."

Sheriff Lars Holden picked up the sandwich his wife Jan had just served him. Chicken salad meant it was Thursday. For the past year, since the awful accident, he had been coming home for lunch as often as he could, for ham salad, egg salad, tuna salad, or occasionally a grilled cheese with an apple. He realized she was talking to him.

"I got a call from my sister today," Jan said. "She has found the perfect spot in Florida for us. A pristine trailer with a large deck in a well-maintained community. Not on the waterway, but there's a marina where you can keep a fishing boat. She says it's very nice and she can get it at a very good price for us."

Lars looked up at his wife of thirty-five years. His heart sank a little at the thought of this conversation she kept returning to. "We can't leave."

"We have to leave. To get away from the memories. Start new ones," she said in a determined tone. "Lars, she's up in the cemetery with our family and her friends. She doesn't need us nearby. We need to move on. You can't keep blaming yourself. It was an accident."

"An accident? Six dead. Two suicides after that. All her group gone. I let them race around these roads. I could have put a stop to it."

"Lars, quit it." He could see her spine stiffen. "We spoiled her. The other parents did too. We didn't want them to leave Valentine, to go to Denver or Portland. That's our fault. We need to move past it, and we can't do it here. I'm booking a flight to Florida. I want you to go. I am not spending another winter here."

His phone buzzed, and he picked it up. His lead detective, Tom Rivers, said, "I need you to come to the Valentine Ranch Motel. Important."

"I'll be there shortly," he replied and closed the call. "Jan, that was Tom. I've got to go. We'll talk tonight."

Jan turned her back and started rattling dishes and utensils around in the sink, "I'm booking a flight. Let me know if you want to be on it."

He went out the door without saying another word. He loved Jan. The thought of her leaving without him was too much to bear, but he wasn't ready to join her. He got in the car and turned on the lights and siren. He wanted to go fast.

Ten minutes later he turned into the old motel. He saw a cruiser, his lead detective's car. Tom approached him as he got out. "Lars, remember four weeks ago I told you the manager here contacted us? A man checked in for one night. The next afternoon his clothes and car were still there, but he didn't come back. They needed the room for the weekend and put his things in storage. They called us after the weekend asking what they should do with his car.

"I remember," Lars replied. "And then the same thing happened two weeks later. Both guys last seen in the bar next door."

"Right. I had my assistant try to track them down. The first man—she couldn't find anyone who knew him. She did find a neighbor of the second man, who said he lost his young wife to cancer, quit his job, sold his house, and left on a road trip across the country. Didn't have any family he knew of."

"So, now we have a third, I take it."

"That's right."

"And you think that's too many coincidences." Lars paused, squinting as he looked toward the motel in the bright afternoon sun. "Well, so do I."

"There's one thing different." said Tom. "This one's fresh. I told them to call me right away if something like this happened again."

Lars started toward the motel. "Let's take a look."

The room had two twin beds. On one was a briefcase and an open suitcase. Beside the suitcase was a nice pair of pants and shirt; a pair of boots was next to the bed, on the floor. Neither bed looked slept in. The kit with a man's toiletries was in the bathroom, but only the toothbrush and a tube of toothpaste were on the counter.

"Looks like he quickly changed clothes and went out," Tom said. "The manager said he was interested in the rock-and-roll bar. It's likely he went over there."

The sheriff walked out of the room and looked toward the bar. The restored Impala was out front. "Let's go over and have a talk with Jesse."

Tom hustled to keep up with the long strides of the tall lean Lars. "Do you want me to take the lead on this?" he asked. He knew Lars carried some resentment toward Jesse, for serving alcohol to Connie and her friends the night of the accident.

"I've got this," Lars replied.

The front door was unlocked, and they went in. Jesse came out of the back room with a mop and bucket.

"You're in early today," Lars said.

"Just cleaning up and getting things ready for the weekend," Jesse replied. "What's up with you being here, Sheriff?"

"You tell me, Jesse. I'm sure you saw the police car next door."

"I'm not one for guessing games."

"Any new customers in here yesterday?"

"One man, early. Had a few drinks. Looked around at the collection. Thought it was great. Left about eight thirty. No other customers except Al and Jacob, as usual, shortly after nine."

"Did he say anything to you about meeting anyone?"

"He didn't talk much at all. Just some questions about the posters and pictures."

The sheriff scanned the room. When he noticed the photograph of his daughter and her friends, he froze. When Tom saw the sheriff stiffen up, he moved to occupy the space between Lars and Jesse. "What are you thinking, putting those kids on the wall?" the sheriff said.

"You haven't been in here in a long time, Sheriff," Jesse said. "We hung that picture up after the accident. Everybody loved that group, especially Connie."

The sheriff turned back toward Jesse with a hard look on his face. "You didn't hear anything outside, after the guy left?"

"No. I couldn't hear anything from outside. I had music on."

The sheriff, still fighting to hold his temper, looked around the room and saw the jukebox. "From that old jukebox over there? Does it still work?"

"No. Not for a long time. I have play lists from my phone over a wired system."

"And you just had to come in early today to clean up?"

"I always set things up for the weekend on Thursday."

Based on their history, the sheriff knew that Jesse was lying about something—or everything—how much the guy drank, who he talked to, danced with, the jukebox, why he was here mopping on a perfectly fine Thursday afternoon. You never could get a straight answer out of him. "Well, you can go home now. And stay away from here tonight. This whole area will be blocked off as a crime scene."

The sheriff signaled to Tom, and they walked outside. "This man may be on a bender somewhere, but three's too many. Call the dog tracking experts in. We have the guy's clothes for a scent article. Canvass the whole area. It's possible there are some bodies back in the gullies behind this place. Talk to anyone who passed through here last night."

At seven that night, Lars stood with Tom in front of the motel. "The only thing the dogs picked up, after five hours of work, is that he walked into the motel office, over to his room, then from his room to the bar," Tom said. "We contacted his employer. The last they heard from him was two days ago. He's due back in the office Friday. We got his cell phone number from them and ran the number. No activity the last two days."

"So, he just walked out of the bar, got into a car with someone and went on a bender. Or maybe he just walked away and left no scent trail or just maybe he never walked out," Lars said. "Do you find it suspicious that Jesse was cleaning up this afternoon?"

"Hard for me to see it, Sheriff. Jesse's been around a long time. Everyone knows him. He's just an old rock and roller."

The sheriff surveyed the bar. "Pack it up and go home. We start again tomorrow. We may have to notify the state police."

"What are you going to do?" Tom asked.

"You don't need to know. See you in the morning."

The sheriff got in his car and drove to a diner for a bite to eat. He didn't want to go home and then have to explain to Jan why he was going out again. He also didn't want to hear any more about Florida right now. He texted her he was still working, don't hold dinner.

Three men walk into a bar...It had to be the bar. He drove back there. It was dark. Jesse had stayed away like they asked. He drove around to the back and got out of the car. He stood listening for a couple of minutes and only heard a few cars pass on the highway. He opened his trunk and found the crowbar. There was a platform off the back of the building for unloading kegs and cases of beer. He went up the steps and the crowbar made easy work prying open the locked door. He turned on his flashlight and surveyed the room.

To the right was a door to a cooler. He went there first. Inside were several kegs of draft beer and a stack of bottled Coors cases, nothing else. Next, he saw a chest cooler. He opened it and saw lots of different beers on ice. He pushed ice and beer aside but found nothing there. There was a big sink with a cleaning board. He shined his flashlight all around and down the drain but saw no signs of blood. Well, maybe there is nothing to find, he thought.

He went into the bar area and started shining his flashlight around on the floor but could not find any stains. A humming noise startled him. Turning around, he saw that the old jukebox was lit up. He walked over to it and the humming became louder and his heart started racing. Jesse had told him it didn't work anymore. He put his right hand into his pants pocket and pulled out some quarters. He picked one out and put it in the slot. His eyes ran down the playlist and he saw an old Roy Orbison favorite, "Pretty Woman." He punched it in and stood back.

As the song filled the room, he heard a noise behind him and turned around. The front door was open but there was only darkness beyond. Suddenly his daughter Connie walked through. She ran to him and clasped him in a big hug. She was solid, alive, beloved. He felt her heat, her energy. It was a miracle. Fantastic. Unreal.

"Daddy, I've missed you so much, but I knew my plan was good and you would work it out and come to me." The jukebox wailed, the song soared as the pretty woman turned and walked back.

Overwhelmed, he could hardly breathe. "I've missed you, sweetheart," he said.

She looked up into his eyes. "Come with me now, Daddy. We can be happy and together forever." She took his hand and tugged.

He didn't move. He fought through his emotions. Was this real? He wanted it to be but knew it couldn't. Then, what she said—my plan was good—broke through his astonishment and set off alarms. "Connie, did you take the men that are missing?"

"I didn't take them, Daddy. They wanted to come of their

own free will. They were depressed about life. I helped them, and I knew it would bring you to me." She pulled on his arm urgently. "We need to go now!"

He followed her toward the door but stopped short. "What about your mother?"

"Daddy, she's going to Florida to be with my aunt. She doesn't need us. We need each other here."

"She loves you too."

She pulled his arm, but suddenly the song ended, and she was gone. He looked around. The door was closed and the room was like it had always been and he was alone. Was she real? A hallucination? As the jukebox began to hum, a shiver ran down his spine. That's how it worked. You put quarters in the jukebox. He put his hand in his pocket and pulled out several quarters. He stepped toward the jukebox but hesitated, remembering the missing men. Connie's plan. He wanted to live. Jan was alive. Connie wasn't. Connie was dead. Buried in the ground. So what was that, that thing he hugged, that thing with Connie's flashing eyes? It wasn't his daughter, and he didn't want to go where she would take him.

He turned away from the jukebox, went into the back room, and came out into the bar again. The jukebox was humming loudly. He walked toward it. In his hand was a heavy, long-handled ball-peen hammer. The humming grew louder, becoming a fearful throb. He raised the hammer and brought it down, shattering the glass front. As the humming stopped the jukebox let off a mournful sound almost like a wail, but he kept raising the hammer, bringing it down and smashing all the records over and over until he had worn himself out.

Exhausted, he dropped the hammer and pulled out his phone to call Jan. When she answered, he said, "Jan, book me on that plane too. I'm ready to go."

"No, Lars. You need to come home now. The most fantastic thing has happened. You won't believe it." He could tell from her voice that she was happy, exhilarated.

And also, in the background, a string-bending guitar solo. Chuck Berry. A chill came over him. "What's that music?"

"Oh Lars, I was cleaning out the hall closet and came across that old box of rock-and-roll albums. I've been playing the best hits from the fifties. But that's not important." She laughed. "You won't believe it, but you need to come home right away."

"What is it?"

"It sounds crazy. You need to come home and find out for yourself."

His apprehension grew. "What is it, Jan? Tell me."

"I know this sounds crazy, but Connie came walking through the door. It's her, Lars. She's solid, alive. Come home right away. She wants me to go out for a walk around the neighborhood, but we'll be back before you get here."

Lars yelled out, "No, no." He started running toward the back door, stumbling as he screamed over the phone, "Turn off the music! Turn off the music!!"

Stevie and Keith for the Save
E. B. Davis

I'm trying not to freak out. The police interrogation room looks like a dungeon. The pond-scum green walls are closing in on me. Metal door. Cheap particle board wooden tables. They threw me in the back of a stinking panda car. At the station, I called my attorney, then they stuck me in this room. I'm waiting and hoping she'll have me out of here soon. At least I wasn't locked in a cell.

Of all the nerve. Scott the Rot, as I now refer to him, stole from me and destroyed my property. And that was after breaking up our fifteen-year marriage for an Evelyn Sue cosmetics rep. I ended up moving out of our house because he refused. I knew when I left that he'd get the house, but by then I didn't care. Who wanted to live with the memories?

The doorknob rattles and in pops my attorney, Roxy Miller. Literally, pops like an explosive. Topping five feet in height, she always wears four-inch designer heels and a woman's business suit so sharp it can ricochet bullets. Seeing her, my tense shoulders sink like the chairs at the salon when they finish your hair.

Her stern expression doesn't change when she sticks out her hand to shake mine. I expect her to say something. Instead, she whispers and points, "Jenny, you need to sit with your back to that window."

I scooch around the gross table to the opposite side and sit down. Thankfully, I wore my old jeans, sweater, and sneakers. My hair is still in a ponytail. The only good thing is it's high and doesn't touch the chair, but earlier it sure worked against me. I clasp my hands together on the tabletop even though I doubt they'd washed it this year. "Why?"

"That's an observation window. They're not supposed to watch or listen into our conversation, but I don't trust them." Roxy sits in the chair opposite from me and pats my hands. "Let's talk. You've been charged with breaking and entering, burglary, and assault and battery. I would have handed this over to another lawyer, but it just happens that in addition to divorce, I also represent women against unfair treatment no matter what the situation, and I have a feeling those charges might be just that. Divorce related, perhaps? Talk to me. What happened?"

"I moved into my rented townhouse a month ago. No pets allowed. I hated leaving Hendrix, our Airedale, but when I find a house to buy—"

"I know that part—we're going for at least joint custody. Focus on today."

I breathe in and then out. "Scott called me a week ago. He had to go out of town on business." I pause, looking her straight in the eyes. "Or so he said. He asked if I would take care of Hendrix while he was gone. I agreed immediately. I miss that dog so much, and he knows it, too." I try to refocus and get to the point. "Roxy, he set me up. I know he did."

"Tell me what happened—today, Jenny." She looks at her watch. I have to get every detail right.

As I lifted the pot of geraniums I planted earlier this year, Hendrix started to yowl. Dogs' hearing abilities always amazed me. The key to the house sat on the concrete under the plant where Scott said it would be. The exterior of the colonial two-story used to make me feel warm and happy. Except for Hendrix inside, it held nothing for me now. Scott had the house rekeyed after I moved out. I pocketed the key in my pea coat and followed the sound of barks to the kitchen.

Scott had left Hendrix crated there, which ticked me off. He isn't a destructive dog. Being crated for an entire weekend seemed like punishment to me. Why? Maybe because Hendrix liked me better than Scott.

I opened the crate. Hendrix shot out and wagged his entire body. We hadn't seen each other for a while. After giving him hugs, I said, "Come on, boy. Let's go walkies!" I found his leash hanging from the usual hook by the front door, attached it to Hendrix's collar, and closed the door behind us. We walked for a good half hour. By the time we got back, the sun was setting and the temperature was dropping.

Hendrix ran right to the kitchen and started nosing his bowl around the floor. He knew how to communicate his needs. I followed slowly through the foyer to the kitchen. The house felt creepy. Maybe it was being in the house without my stuff in it, but I felt like a stranger here. I also felt as if I were being watched, but I shrugged that off. I was acting paranoid. And yet, once I'd found out about the Evelyn Sue rep, the gloves had come off. I hadn't trusted him since. Our divorce couldn't be described as amicable. To make myself feel better, I envisioned Scott in the passenger seat of a two-tone peach and gold Malibu.

In the kitchen, I turned the light on over the stove. The house was dark now. But since I had no intention of wandering around the house, I didn't turn on any additional lights. I opened the pantry to find the cheapest, nastiest dog food the big box store sold and wrinkled my nose. That stuff was nothing but overcooked nitrates. I wouldn't feed that to my dog. On the counter, I found the container we used to store dog treats in. It was full, thankfully. I took two out and fed him the treats to hold off his hunger.

I had bought some of Dr. Gary's nutritious freeze-dried dog food and left a bag in the garage hoping Scott would use it. I opened the garage door from the kitchen and turned on the garage light. Cartons lined the back wall. Rummaging through cartons, I found the dog food, right on top of a box of my albums. I had packed them, but they never made it to my new place. I opened the box and looked through them. Oh wow, my X-pensive Winos albums! I'd gone to a concert, and Keith Richards had signed two albums on the inside sleeves. *To Jenny, Keep on rocking, Love, Keith.* As soon as I saw those albums, I knew I had to take them with me. I looked through the stack, smiling at the memories and great music, but the garage was cold and Hendrix was waiting. I quickly sealed the rest of the albums back into the box and grabbed the dog food.

Back in the kitchen, I placed the albums on the counter and then measured out the amount of food Hendrix was supposed to have, opened the tap, ran a bit of water over the food, and mixed it. It was supposed to sit for a few minutes before serving. While I had the tap on, I figured I'd heat some water for tea. It might warm me up. I'd taken the kettle, so I opened the cabinet and took out a small saucepan. To my surprise, I also saw my grandmother's small cast-iron skillet that Scott must have stolen from one of my kitchen boxes. I held it up. It smelled of the greasy sausages he loved. I abhorred them and would now associate the skillet with Scott, but I left it on the counter. I'd decide before I left if I wanted it or not. I filled the saucepan with water and turned on the burner to medium high.

Hendrix nudged me with his nose. "Okay, already. Here you go!" I bent down and placed his filled bowl on the mat next to his water. He dove in, loving the better food. "*Bon appetit*, good buddy. I've missed you so much." I wanted to hug him again, but I also knew eating was a lone and sacred time for him.

So...I did something I knew I shouldn't do, but using Scott's tactic against him felt like justice. And I wanted my dog! I went to the back of the house toward the powder room and Scott's den. When I got to the powder room, I turned on the water in the sink, scooted into Scott's den, got two items, and went back to the powder room, flushed the toilet, and turned off the faucet. I don't know why I did that. I was covering my actions. It was wrong, but then no one would know, and Scott deserved it. I still felt as though someone were watching me. The creepiness made me shiver.

While Hendrix ate, I grabbed my albums off the counter and went out to my car. I placed the albums in the trunk and went back inside, slamming the front door shut, and found that the water on the stove was boiling. I found the tea bags and poured water into a mug. Hendrix had finished eating. He lay down on the rug in front of the sink.

A noise came from the foyer by the front door. I heard it again. Footsteps! Scott was out of town. Had I locked the front door? I couldn't see into the darkness of the foyer.

I picked up the skillet and snuck into a dark corner of the kitchen near its entrance to the foyer. A dark shape moved past me. I whacked the shape with the skillet and winced at the thump of a hollow-melon reverberation.

"Ow! What the hell are you doing, Jenny?"

"Scott! What are you doing here?"

The dark shape snapped on the overhead kitchen light. Scott clutched his head. "I live here. This is my house now."

"I knoooow that, stupid. You told me you were going out of town. That's the reason I'm here—to take care of Hendrix—remember?"

"You stole two albums." He turned his back to me and walked farther into the kitchen.

"I did not," I said, following him.

Scott walked past Hendrix without a greeting or glance and opened the garage door. He went right to the box of my albums, like he knew where they were located. He ripped open the box, took out a few albums, and walked back into the kitchen. "You took two albums out of this box. I think you took them to your car, but the camera didn't capture you outside of the house."

"Camera?" My mouth dropped open for a second until I regained my momentum. "You asked me to come here to help

41

you. You must have heisted a box of my albums from the others I'd packed. Then you set up cameras to catch me stealing my own albums?" I put my hands on my hips and squared off with him. "That's not only nasty, you're nuts."

"This is what I will do to your precious albums if you don't stop with the demands from your lawyer." Scott lifted the Rolling Stones's *Sticky Fingers* album, the one designed by Andy Warhol, the one with the working zipper on the cover, and cracked it on the edge of the counter. The album ripped down the zipper and the vinyl record cracked in half. He held one-half of the album out to me as if he were being reasonable. "Here's your half of the album, Jenny."

I bonked him in the head with the skillet again—just couldn't help it. I'd had that album for as long as I remembered, and it had been in pristine condition. "You are a creep. I'm leaving. You'll hear from my lawyer."

"Oh no you don't." With one hand, he grabbed my ponytail holding me in place. With the other hand, he put his phone on the kitchen counter and dialed 911.

By the time I finish telling Roxy, my fists clench. I'm shaking. "He asked me to come take care of Hendrix. I didn't break in. The albums I took are mine. He destroyed my property. And he told me he was going out of town. I hit him thinking he was an intruder."

I pause in the moment, remembering how scared I'd been. "In retrospect, I should have known if Hendrix wasn't growling, he knew who it was. Then, Scott told me he'd seen me take albums out of the garage."

Roxy gasps. "He set up live-feed cameras?" Her eyebrows lower, and she clenches her jaw.

"Yes, I think he positioned one at the front door, but another one must have shown the garage area where he stashed my box of albums. That's why I think the whole thing was a setup, to catch me going into that box."

"Can you prove he asked you to be there?"

"I told my whole office. I was so excited about seeing Hendrix again. Besides, he's the one who told me where the key would be hidden. He rekeyed the house. It's not like I can get in using my old key."

"Okay, I think we can prove you didn't break and enter the house unlawfully. Technically, it's still your house, too. Your name is still on the deed. But I'm not so sure we can prove that the albums you took and put in your car are yours."

"But I can. They're X-pensive Wino albums. Keith Richards signed the inside sleeves using my name."

"Lovely. That's pretty good proof." She stopped and thought a while. "Look, I'll talk to Scott. Did he know those albums were signed?"

"Nope, totally clueless. He always thought I loved Mick Jagger. But I was always a Keith chick. That assumption could have been the original problem with our marriage. He pegged me as the wrong type."

"Oh yeah, big difference."

"But men don't know about that."

"Nah, clueless."

I hesitate. This is blackmail, and I don't want to involve Roxy, but to get out of jail, I have to play the hand I'd given myself. I look her in the eye and say, "But here's the thing, Roxy. When you talk to Scott, tell him if he doesn't drop the charges, he'll never see his Stevies again."

"What?" She put her hands out, palms facing me. "No—don't say another word. I don't want to know. Let me call him, and then I'll talk with the police."

I beam at Roxy. "You do that. You'll let me know what he says?"

"If I'm correct in assuming what you did, I'll have you home tonight."

"Roxy, wait a second. I want more. Tell him he can keep the

skillet. But not only does he have to drop all charges against me, he'll only get the Stevies back if he gives me full custody of Hendrix."

"You're sure it's worth it to him? That's driving a hard bargain."

"He doesn't really care about Hendrix. He's just using him to negotiate a better divorce settlement. I can prove I didn't break in. I can prove that the albums are mine. And no one can prove I took his precious Stevies. The only thing he's got on me is assault. I had reasonable cause to protect myself since he told me he was traveling. I told everyone at the office about his call asking me to take care of Hendrix. He'll deal."

"I'll do what I can." Roxy leaves the room, closing the door behind her.

I hope it won't take long. After I found my albums, I figured I might need leverage getting custody of Hendrix. I hadn't known about the cameras, but my creep meter was going crazy in the house. Maybe I suspected he'd installed security cameras, but I knew he wouldn't have put them in his precious, sacrosanct man-cave den where he kept his records and sound system. I stuck *Bella Donna* and *Rock a Little* into the waistband of my jeans and covered them up with my pea coat. Those albums I locked in my trunk, too. Both had been signed by Stevie Nicks to Scott with personalized messages he treasured. If he didn't drop the charges and give me Hendrix, he'd never see his Stevie albums again. I envisioned Frisbeeing them into the river.

About a half hour later, a cop comes into the room to tell me I can go. Roxy waits for me by the station's front desk where they return my purse. Outside, she says, "I'll drive you back to pick up your car. Before we do anything, I want him to sign a statement about Hendrix. You stay in the car. Only then will I give him the Stevies back. In return, he'll give me the rest of the albums."

Once we were in her car, I ask, "Can he renege on the signed statement?"

"He can try. Nothing is ever a done deal."

"Then tell him he gets one album now. I'm pissed he smashed my *Sticky Fingers* album. When I find a house and can move Hendrix in, he'll get the other album." In the long run, I'll be plus a great dog and minus one lousy husband.

Roxy shakes her head. "I'll put this one in my memoirs."

"And Roxy, I want to change back to my maiden name. The less of him I drag around, the better." It felt good to use Stevie's ideas against him, too.

"Consider it done." Roxy winks at me, puts the car in gear, and pulls out, on her way to negotiate my new life.

Sweet Dreams
Gina Lea

It should have been an early night. A simple case of recovering stolen hi-fi records. Instead, Cara found herself trudging down the docks near dawn, swatting at the no-see-ums buzzing around her face and biting her arms. What she wouldn't give for a fly swatter, baseball bat, or flamethrower to get the miserable creatures to cease and desist. After this long, wet, fruitless night, all Cara wanted was a hot shower and to crawl into bed with Zuzu, her furry bedmate. Unfortunately, the little peke-pug would want her walk, treat, and a twenty-minute snuggle before sleep.

Cara hurried down the gangway toward her boat. In the darkness, she tripped on something, stumbled forward, and landed hard on her hands and knees just inches from the edge of the dock. Staring up from the water were the milky-glass eyes of a woman floating face up, hair adrift.

Oh, crap.

Cara's gaze slid toward the object that had tripped her. A bloody arm draped on the edge of the dock.

Still pining for that hot shower, Cara sat on the deck of her houseboat watching the police scour the dock. Sunlight danced across the water, while the marina swarmed with men taking pictures and snatching evidence into plastic bags. Two men carted the body away in a black bag, the gurney making a sad thudding noise as it traveled across the docks.

A tall sandy-haired man waited next to her transom deck. He reminded her of a young Bill Pullman with his blue eyes and sheepish grin, or was it snarky? "Permission to come aboard, Miss McKnight?" he asked.

Cara shrugged, waving him aboard and rising to greet him. "Sure. Doubt you need it."

"I'm Detective Adams. Do you know who owns this house-boat?" He held out his badge-holder, shield on one side, photo ID on the other.

"Me." She suppressed a smile as his eyes grew wide with surprise.

"I see," he said. The doubt in those words made Cara want to kick him in the shins. She looked down at Zuzu, who was standing at the ready for any petting the detective offered. He reached down to give her a good scratch. Zuzu wriggled happily against his hand. Traitor.

Cara pointed to a chair as an invite.

"No thanks. The officers tell me you found the body?"

"Yep." Cara flopped down in a chair. "Guess you want to look around."

"That's not necessary. I just have a few questions. I understand you were out most of the night?" His tone said it all.

"Yep." Cara decided she liked frustrating him.

"Because..." His eyes said, *two can play that game.*

Cara sighed. "I recover things. Find things for people."

"You're a private detective?"

"I don't have a license, if that's what you're asking."

"Okay, I'll bite." He gracefully fit his six-foot frame into her best deck chair and crossed his legs, like a trained dancer. Cara knew this, since at one time, she was one. Long before she stumbled onto her current career. Before college and her dad's death. After Harry.

"I told you. I find things for people."

He waited.

She tossed him one of the business cards she kept in her jacket.

"Cara McKnight. Recovery Specialist." He turned it over then looked up at her. "Interesting. What causes a young woman to go into recovery work?"

She bristled at his tone then gave herself a shake inside. *Stop it, Cara, the man is just doing his job. For all he knows, I could have killed that poor girl.*

"Started in college," she replied. "A friend needed to get his grandmother's engagement ring back from an ex. I managed that, and then the word spread. I've recovered all sorts of things in the last five years. That's how I ended up getting this boat."

Adams studied the mahogany sign above her head. "Andrew's Chandlery." He whistled. Cara could almost see the wheels turning. He looked down at the dog. "So, this is *the* peke-pug?" He jerked his head toward the sign. "The million-dollar pup stolen from Andrew Callahan. You're the mysterious rescuer. I heard he died last year. Then left you the dog and this boat?"

"Uh, huh," she acknowledged, shutting down. He didn't need to know that poor Andrew's wife died not long after she found Zuzu and how quick Andrew went after that. She hated sharing her own past, let alone someone else's misery.

A familiar voice called from the docks. "Cara?" Her best friend was making her way gingerly onto the transom. Sully's wide girth navigated the step up with care. She huffed. "I had to arm wrestle one of those men to let me get past their army. Finally resorted to lying and telling them I was your aunt."

Adams unfolded himself from the deck chair and stood. He towered over Sully. "I take it you aren't?"

Sully aimed her stormy dark eyes at the detective. She pulled back graying strands of hair with one vicious snap. "And you are?" The ice in her voice could have frozen all the water in the marina.

Once again Adams pulled out his badge and ID. Sully examined it, then handed it back like it held germs. "I am the nearest thing this girl has to a relative, and I am staying with her till my lawyer arrives." Sully's teacher mode was in full gear as she defended the helpless girl from the bad boy pulling her pigtails. But since Cara had never been helpless, she decided to intercede.

"Don't need a lawyer, Sully. It's not like they suspect me. I just found the body."

"Well, we do need to ask a few questions." Adams said. "What were you doing on the dock at five in the morning?"

"Like I told the other cop, I was coming home from an all-night stake-out. My client had his prize collection of hi-fi records stolen by an ex-employee."

"Do you have siblings, cousins perhaps?" Adams watched her closely. "A sister, maybe."

She turned her back on him to adjust a dock line. "No. Only a brother, long gone."

"Look, you had to notice the resemblance?"

She turned back with a frown. "What are you talking about?"

He looked at her with sympathy. Cara closed her eyes slowly and was back on the dock, shocked by what she saw in the water. The woman had been tall and slender, that was clear even in her bloody state. Hard knees, elbows, long hair that was knotted and tangled with kelp. The face, slack and milky-eyed, partly obscured by shadows.

"This is the victim." Adams held up his phone with a photo of a young woman with a guitar. She was smiling, a wide, open smile with firm jaw. Long, strawberry-blond hair, swept back from her forehead. Wide green eyes with glints of gold. She was pretty.

The woman could have been Cara's twin. "This is really, uh, weird." Cara's voice sounded strangled in her head. "That's me, but it's not."

Sully took the phone and moaned when she saw the happy face smiling at her. "What does this mean?"

"Sure is a coincidence, you're not-twin is killed right here on your dock." Adams's voice softened a touch. "There has to be an explanation. Someone out to hurt you, Cara?"

"No. I avoid people." It came out before she could stop herself. "I mean...I prefer to be on my own." Cara turned to Sully, pleading silently for a moment's respite from the questioning.

Sully held Cara's memories safe. Easier for her to tell the detective about the missing brother, taken at four years old from the grocery store that Cara's mother went to every Friday. Harry's disappearance took all the wind out of their mother's world.

At fourteen, Cara came home to find her mother packed up and gone. Sully, her school guidance counselor, helped her dad raise a daughter he didn't know what to do with, until he passed away from a heart attack while Cara was in college. Harry, her parents, everyone she cared about, was gone.

Cara felt herself distancing from Sully and Adams's voices, sinking into the safe place where the bad memories couldn't find her. Including the rain-soaked day those detectives knocked on the front door and told her parents, in their condescending tone, that they had done all they could to find Harry. Her parents needed to move on with their lives. Try to forget. Easy words for those men with their worthless badges she'd come to despise.

This was why she didn't take on cases involving people. People broke your heart. Like birth moms who abandoned their babies, adoptive moms who split the scene. Little brothers who left you and never returned.

Sully tugged on Cara's arm. "That's enough, Detective." She looked at Adams with that firm, no arguing tone. "She needs to sleep. Is there anything else?"

Adams snapped his notebook closed. "Is there someplace nearby you can stay?"

"Cara and Zuzu will stay with me." Sully put the question to bed, and Adams nodded like he got what he wanted. Cara close enough to poke. Ask more questions. Tear into her past.

Cara's fatigue was setting in as Sully helped her pack everything that she and Zuzu would need for the next few days. By the time they climbed onto her friend's boat, the sun was peeking through clouds high in the sky.

Zuzu flopped in her bed, while Cara dumped all her stuff in a corner then followed suit, collapsing on Sully's sofa. Dreams haunted her sleep. The shadow at the end of the grocery aisle. A glimpse of the man who lived at the end of the lane. Maybe? The glimpse melting away, leaving only Harry's shoe lying on the ground. Her mother crying after Harry went missing. Dad in the stands at a dance recital, alone.

"Hey, girl." Sully shook her shoulders. "You were moaning in your sleep. You okay?" She held out a mug of hot tea.

Cara sat up and rubbed the fog from her eyes, then took a grateful sip of tea. "Yeah. Just bad dreams."

"The old ones?" Sully sat down across from her with a martini and a bowl of nuts.

"Yep."

"Been a while." Sully sipped and ate nuts as Cara pulled her hair up into a ponytail. "Want to talk about it?" she asked, pretending to contemplate her next nut.

"No, I wanna do my run." Cara looked at the clock. She'd only slept an hour. "I'm not gonna let the past ruin my life. Anyway, it's still daylight. I'll be careful."

She donned sneakers and headed out. She thrived on routine. Up half the night, which was okay since she never slept more than a few hours at a time. Rise at dawn, make breakfast for her and the dog before a daily run on the beach. If it was a good day, back at the boat, work on her tan and sneak in a power nap, read and research before a light dinner.

At least once a week she liked to tinker on the boat. The trust Andrew left her covered maintenance and upkeep as well as the expensive dock fees, but Cara liked the work. It made her feel like the boat was really hers, even though the final probate had not come through yet. Once a month or so, she thought about selling the boat and building a home up in the mountains surrounded by tall pines. But just like here on the coast, some hateful developer would come along and plow down her side of the mountain. Progress was stealing all the peaceful places she loved.

She was back at Sully's in an hour with a plan. But down in the salon sat Mr. Detective, making himself at home, with Sully serving him his own bowl of nuts and a glass of sweet tea.

"Cara." He scooped up a handful of nuts. "I have a few follow-up questions."

She barely tilted her head. This guy was becoming a pain. She grabbed a towel out of her bag and scrubbed the sweat off the back of her neck.

"When your brother disappeared all those years ago, did you see who took him? The lead investigator seemed to think you might have."

Cara froze.

Sully sat up tall. "Now listen here, that's cutting it too close!"

"I need to know." Adams kept his eyes locked on Cara.

Cara pulled the tie out of her ponytail before replying, "No, not really."

Adams's eyebrows lifted. He dropped the nuts back into his bowl. "Not really?"

"I mean, I saw a shadow but that was all. Kind of looked like this loner that lived in the creepy house down at the end of the lane. But he had moved away the week before. One minute the shadow was at the end of the aisle where Harry had been standing, and the next he was gone. I looked away for a moment. Only a moment." Cara felt the tightening in her chest. The bad feeling was back. It was her fault. She was supposed to watch Harry.

She dropped the towel. "So why all the questions about my brother? Does this have something to do with him?"

"Maybe." Adams scrubbed his hand through his hair in frustration. "We're digging into everyone she knew, including where she was that night and why she was on this dock. Coroner says she was hacked up with a sword, around midnight, when you were waiting it out in that bar. Bartender confirms you were there during the killing. Lots of questions without a lot of answers so far. I can tell you what I think. I think the fact that she looks like you is not a coincidence."

"So?"

"So, maybe whoever did this thought they were killing you. Maybe it goes back to your brother's kidnapping all those years ago."

Sully cracked a nut with a loud bang. "Why would you think that?"

"New information on the case—"

"What?!" Sully and Cara sounded like barking seagulls.

"A prisoner up for parole has come across the radar of the Ft. Lauderdale PD." Adams's voice seemed to come from a long hallway. "They saw your name on the report we filled out today."

Cara took in a sharp breath and closed her eyes.

"You okay?" Adams rose abruptly, spilling nuts all over the floor.

"Yep. Sorry, Detective. Haven't eaten today and well, the world went tilt there for a minute."

"Understandable. You need a moment?"

"I'm okay, really." She took a deep cleansing breath. "I don't get what this prisoner has to do with the dead girl."

Adams huffed in disgust. "I'm not sure it does, but Ft. Lauderdale PD believed this guy has information about your brother's disappearance. This guy is a lifer, and he's trying to cut a deal in exchange for his testimony. He swears the real kidnapper confessed to him right before he was let loose and will be coming after you."

Cara snorted. "So, they think this guy is trying to cut a deal, and my brother's real kidnapper is lurking around here trying to kill me so I can't testify against him someday. Sounds like a movie of the week to me." She tried to smile.

Adams cocked his head but let it go. "I'd like you to be extra careful. Until we find our suspect. You need to sit tight."

Sully set her jaw. "Agreed, Detective. She'll stay here until we know for sure."

Cara grabbed her backpack. "No can do. I have some research to do at the Destinybay Pier." At his frown, she added. "I've still got a case to solve."

His frown deepened to a scowl. "I don't think that's a good idea."

Sully nodded her agreement with Adams.

"Hey, it's easy money, and I promise I'll be extra careful." Cara sprinted down the steps to the head before the two of them could talk her out of it.

When she came back up, the detective was gone and Sully was nursing a cup of coffee. "Listen, Cara. I think you should stay in."

Cara dug out her laptop. "I'm not going after the records; I want to find out about our mystery girl. My supposed twin." She searched through Google for the news story about the dead woman. Lara Miller, an up-and-coming singer. Following the links, she landed on a publicity page. Cara clicked on a link and music filled the air. "Oh, I've heard this version of 'Sweet Dreams.' Do you recognize her, Sully?"

"Well, she certainly looks like you. Wait." Sully leaner in closer to read the bio page. "Lara Miller? I know her father. He lives one dock over on that big seventy-five-footer. He moved in six months ago after the death of his wife. We've bumped into each other a few times at the clubhouse. Exchanged the little niceties in life. Told me he has a daughter in Riverdale who's a singer. He knew I had a 'niece' who worked salvage." Sully sipped her coffee slowly, buying time to see how Cara felt about bits of her life being out in the ether.

Cara waited quietly. Part of her wanted to run. But another part wanted to know more about this unknown doppelganger.

55

"Can you get him over here?"

Sully picked up her cell phone.

Mr. Miller sat down like a man who had aged twenty years overnight. Cara had seen him on his houseboat a few times and thought what a fit man he was, but all his energy had washed away with his daughter's life. He looked over at her and tears filled his eyes. "You didn't lie, Sully. They could be sisters."

Sully patted his back and handed him a glass of iced tea. He shook his head and stared at Cara hungrily. Quietly he said, "Maybe twins. Now don't that beat all. Sully tells me you recover things?"

Cara nodded mutely.

The man struggled to speak. "So, the deal is, whoever killed my girl took her guitar, and I want it back."

"You want the guitar?" Cara was surprised. "Not your daughter's killer?"

The old man waved away her protests. "Police'll find her killer and then he'll rot in Hell. That guitar...that's like a part of her." His voice broke. "Me and my wife adopted Lara when she was a baby. Lara loved music from the beginning. Do you like music? Figure you might."

Lara was adopted too? Cara felt her heart swell and break at the same time. Could they really be sisters like Mr. Miller says? "Dance," she said. "I loved to dance at one time."

Miller rose and looked out the porthole. "We adored that girl. Music lessons, Vanderbilt, whatever she wanted. After my wife died, I spared no expense, including getting her a rare Martin guitar. One rumored to have belonged to some hit singer."

Miller sat back down. "Funny thing was, that guitar made her a star. The first song she recorded on it was 'Sweet Dreams,' that Patsy Cline hit. After that, Lara broke out. She'd just been offered a record deal and tour."

Cara felt sad as she remembered the girl's haunting version.

"I loved what she did with that song."

Sully agreed. "You and everyone else, honey."

Miller handed Cara a sheet of paper. "Here are the guitar specs. I don't pretend it will make any sense to you, but that guitar's special. I think my daughter's spirit is tied to it."

Cara put the paper down and leaned toward Mr. Miller. "I want to find your daughter's killer. Maybe because I found her body, maybe because we might be sisters. No matter, perhaps finding her guitar will lead me to whoever did this."

The old man let out a breath. "Good girl. I'll pay you handsomely."

Sully asked, "But is this safe? What if the killer has the guitar?"

"Do we know she even had it with her when she died? And you heard that detective. He doesn't think Lara was the target." Cara grew thoughtful. After a moment she asked the old man, "What do you think?"

"She always had it with her." Miller struggled to go on. "I figure it was grabbed and sold to a pawn dealer. Lara's cash and credit cards were missing from her wallet. Sounds like robbery to me."

Zuzu jumped into Cara's lap and began to lick her face. "I'm gonna catch this bastard," Cara said. "And I'll get her guitar too."

"Where will you look?" Sully asked.

"At the bar, of course." Cara grabbed her pack and headed out.

At five p.m., at the Pelican's Bar and Grill, Cara picked at a basket of crab and seafood dip. The sea salt tortillas were not on her diet, but then neither was the dip. A margarita sat in front of her for staging. She never drank on the job, but sometimes one needed the right props to convince folks she wasn't working.

Her target was Donovan King, a sleezy shop owner who was known to trade and sell questionable goods. He showed up here most nights. But as soon as her drink arrived, she spotted a fly in the ointment. Across the room lounged Detective Adams, smiling like a crazy fool as he munched on the "bait pail," a pile of fried fish, shrimp, oysters, gator, fries, and slaw. Cara wondered how he kept in such good shape.

He sipped sweet tea and pretended to look at his phone now and then. He wasn't fooling Cara. Mr. Detective was there to keep her out of trouble. Like she needed help. Cara had been recovering things for five years and had yet to break a sweat, let alone need a sidekick! He winked back at her cold glare.

"Need another?" She turned and stared into the face of her target. Donovan had the gray pallor of a chain smoker. He smelled like the moth balls his goods came packed in, and his breath reeked of old alcohol. But that did not stop him from hitting on a pretty girl. He looked over her shoulder, saw the detective grinning, and scurried off his stool and out the door.

Detective Adams stood, throwing some money down. "Guess you can head home now."

"No chance, cowboy," Cara said. "Nick has poured me a lovely drink, and I intend to enjoy it."

Nick, the bartender, stood nearby with his arms crossed, backing her up.

Adams held his up hands in surrender. "Just make sure she gets to her car, okay?"

"What was that all about?" Nick asked. Nick was one of the few she called friend.

"Just a little overzealous protection. Hey, Nick, you know everybody in this town. Do you know any high-end pawn dealers?"

Ten minutes later, Cara stepped into a pawnshop filled with the refuse of other people's lives. Behind the counter, instead of the old gaffer she expected, was a young man with long greasy hair and a few scrubby whiskers dusting his jawline. He looked more at home in a comic shop until she saw his popping muscles as he hoisted a heavy ledger.

"Can I help you?" he asked, without looking up.

"I'm looking for a special guitar. A Martin D-28 made in 1957. Has anyone brought one in today or have you heard of anyone selling one?"

The young man slowly raised his head and looked at her, his face flushed and sweaty. "Who's asking?"

"Just me," Cara said.

"Yeah, someone tried to pawn one earlier today, but I passed."

"Why?"

"No pedigree. This is a classy shop. We don't buy anything that could be hot." He looked her up and down.

Cara had no time for this greasy kid. "Well, thanks anyway."

"Better be careful. That guy looked creepy."

"Sure." As she stepped out of the shop, Cara muttered under her breath, "Says the creepier one."

The night air was muggy and hot. One of those nights when Cara wanted to sleep on the deck, just feel the cool breezes coming off the water.

"'Bout time." Detective Adams stood waiting for her at the top of the docks.

She sighed and fell in with him as they walked down to Sully's boat. "Thanks for the escort."

"My pleasure, ma'am." Adams tipped his ball cap. "You are in for the night, correct?"

"Yes, sir." She saluted mockingly, willing him to leave. Something was nipping at the corner of her memory. Something just out of focus.

"Good, 'cause that informant down in Ft. Lauderdale turned out to be a dead end. Just a con trying to lie his way into a get-out-of-jail card." He headed back up the docks.

"That you?" Sully called from her salon.

"Yes'm."

Zuzu danced around her feet then ran toward the stairs going up to the deck.

"I know, I know. You have to pee. But I need to check something out."

Waiting for her laptop to power up, Cara snapped on Zuzu's leash. She clicked through the photos on Lara's web page, landing on the one she remembered. Zooming in, she gasped and grabbed her phone.

"Adams?" she asked when he answered. "I think I have a lead on our killer."

"I've stopped for gas, so I'll circle back in ten minutes," he replied. "Don't go anywhere without me."

Cara looked down at the dancing dog. "Right."

"C'mon Zuzu. Stop sniffing every blade of grass." Cara loved the pug, but she always picked the worst moments to dally about her business.

"Grrr." A low growl came from her furry friend. Cara's skin prickled. She rarely heard the little peke-pug growl.

"Zuzu," she called. "What's got you all riled up?" Zuzu's hackles stood on end as Cara tried to pull her back.

Cara sensed movement out of the corner of her eye. She ducked so the blow to the back of her head was a glancing one. Stars burst in front of her eyes, but she tucked and rolled, a move from her dancing days.

Zuzu was growling around a piece of the man's pant leg. Cara rolled down the gentle slope, using gravity in her favor, then stood up on unsteady legs and groped for the only weapon she could find, a heavy branch that had been a favorite stopping point on Zuzu's walks.

The dark form became clearer, and Cara felt a shock when she saw the pawnshop keeper, bounding toward her with a weapon in his hand.

"I killed you once, Lara, and I can kill you again." He raised a powerful arm in the air and she saw a gleaming sword. A shadow crossed between them as a small torpedo lunged up and sunk her teeth into his thigh. He screamed in shock, dropping the sword and landing a kick at the little dog.

Cara dove for the sword, but he got there first and swung wide, slicing her shoulder into red-hot flames. With no time to cry, Cara drop-kicked him in the stomach, which plunged him to his knees. She lunged for the branch, grabbed it, and twisted around to let it fly. She heard a sickening crunch before he went down for good.

Zuzu lay in a small heap nearby. Cara crawled toward her and cradled her in her arms as she stumbled to her feet, limping down to Sully's boat, alternately hollering for help and whispering soothing words to the dog. Every inhabited boat on the dock lit up as Cara collapsed next to a confused Sully standing on the dock in her nightgown.

"I called that detective as soon as you started yelling." Sully gasped at the sight of blood pouring down Cara's side, then held her arms out for the still bundle.

Suddenly dizzy, Cara sank to her knees. "Please, don't let her die."

Sirens grew louder. From what sounded like a long way away, Detective Adams barked orders to his team converging on the dock. People appeared out of boats to gawk.

Mr. Miller hunched down and took her hand. "Don't you die either. Never should have sent you after that guitar. Stay with us, you hear."

Adams leaned over her. "Couldn't wait, could you. You are one stubborn lady."

Cara tried to smile but the world was spinning.

"Cara. Cara." She heard her father's voice. That couldn't be right. She opened her eyes to Detective Adams sitting next to her bed. Sully sat on the other side.

"Zuzu?"

Sully's eyes brimmed with tears. "That precious dog is alive. The folks at the animal hospital are treating her like a hero, as are we all! You'll be fine too. You have some stitches but the doctor says you're gonna be fine."

"The creep that attacked me?"

"In jail. He's facing murder and attempted murder." Adams's voice was grim. "He confessed to killing Lara. Seems he was obsessed with her, and she wouldn't give him the time of day. He finally confronted her on the docks carrying his favorite katana sword and confessing his love. When she laughed at him, he killed her in a fit of rage. Then you showed up at his pawnshop, like the ghost of Lara haunting him."

"I saw him in many of her concert photos. The guitar?" Talking was painful. Her shoulder felt like it had ten thousand and one stitches.

"We got it," Adams said. "Along with steroid pills, scrapbooks full of photos and articles about the victim. Our perp went to all her concerts. Sent her love notes. He was convinced that Lara loved him too. When you came round, all cool as a cucumber, he was sure you were her ghost come to haunt him."

Cara sighed. "Or maybe a sister." She hoped DNA would confirm that.

"You okay?" he asked, his voice dropping low.

"Yep." Cara smiled at Sully who had pulled out a bag of nuts and opened her book. "I will be. Tonight, I intend to sleep. And dream sweet dreams."

All About Evie
Polly Iyer

MOLLY

I couldn't believe it when Deke, our group's manager and my boyfriend, called to tell us that our all-female rock-and-roll band sold out the five-thousand-seat Charlotte Metro Credit Union Amphitheatre tonight. I knew the tickets were selling well, but sold out? Wow. More importantly, Deke sent a tape of our Charleston performance to a producer from Universal who'd be in the audience to see us, in person.

I remember when everyone said that no one would pay good money to see four twenty-something "girls" play rock music in the style of the 50s, 60s, and 70s, but Deke thought we had something special. He took us on and proved the naysayers wrong, guiding us to bigger and better venues. We hit it off, and he'd been my boyfriend ever since.

We imitate the female superstars of the rock-and-roll era like Grace, Aretha, Tina, Stevie, and Janis. I write most of the songs to avoid singing their biggest hits and paying licensing fees to do so. I do Tina—wig, high heels, and gams a'plenty—and rock Janis, slugging on a bottle of Southern Comfort filled with sweet tea. We call ourselves The Anachronistics. Deke said the guy from Universal wasn't interested in the impressions as long as we keep writing and singing the rock-and-roll music he heard on our audition tape. *Yikes, he loves our songs.*

I started the group, all music majors, at the University of South Carolina in Columbia. I chose the best instrumentalists and voices for the group. It took a few changes before we got the sound right, but we did. When we graduated, we played the small clubs around Myrtle Beach and Charleston, but as our fame grew, Deke got us gigs in Charlotte and Columbia.

I play keyboard and sing most of the vocals. Evie on lead guitar, Tess on bass, and Samantha on drums rounds out our foursome. We can all play each other's instruments and sometimes switch during our performances. The crowd loves when we do. Everyone sings at least two solos during the show. We do six sets, one for each superstar, and finish off with a group finale. Our audiences are filled with boomers, but they have the money, and they love the music. Lately, we've noticed millennials populating our shows, which gives us a whole new fan base. Maybe millennial interest in good old rock and roll is why Universal thinks we're on the right track to the best new thing. Isn't everything old new again?

I'm so excited about tonight, but I won't count on anything until the ink is dried on the contract, if we're lucky enough to be offered one. Meanwhile, we need to stay calm until showtime. We rehearsed this morning and planned to meet for dinner at five at a nearby diner. That gives us enough time to get ready for the opening number, which is Janis without Big Brother and the Holding Company. Big sisters will have to do.

EVIE

Why didn't Deke tell me about the record producer in the audience tonight before announcing it to everyone at rehearsal this morning? I told him to keep me in the loop. I thought he was on my side. Guess I was wrong. He and Molly knew a couple of days ago, but they didn't want to make us nervous, they said. Good thing I always plan ahead. With everyone at the restaurant, this is the perfect time. Then I'll rush to join them. Tonight will be my night.

I grasp the small bottle from my backpack. It takes about thirty minutes for this to work. Molly'll slug the Southern Comfort tea during the first song, like she always has. Like Janis did. I'll have to take over the second set when Molly can't continue. Tess and Samantha will never forgive me, and Molly will want me dead, but this is my chance to make a solo impression without Molly, with her saucer-size blue eyes, stealing my thunder. I'm not going to miss the opportunity.

I open the small fridge backstage where we keep our drinks. Molly's Southern Comfort bottle is right where she left it after we finished rehearsal. I uncap the open bottle of fake whiskey and pour half the contents of the vial inside, just enough to make Molly incapable of continuing after Janis. But never fear, Aretha will take over. Mouth dry, I lift my water bottle and take a big slug, then close the fridge door and hotfoot it to the restaurant.

SAMANTHA

Poor Molly. Her head's in the clouds. In every interview she's told journalists how we all get along, how things are hunky-dory. She's right, except for Evie, who thinks she should be the star of the show. Why can't Molly see Evie's machinations? Evie commandeered the last interview, pimping herself for the article. "No one sings Aretha like I do, except Aretha herself," she said. Molly agreed. She's clueless. Really clueless.

Tess and I tried to tell her, but she got testy when we did, as if we were trying to break up the group. Why would we do that? Why isn't Molly's red hair on fire and her ears burning off her head for all the backstabbing that comes out of Evie's fake plump lips? She's as sugar sweet as Molly's tea in front of her, clever and manipulative in ways that get Molly to do what she wants.

Evie's a good musician, no doubt about it, and when she plays Tina in rehearsal, she's almost as spellbinding as Molly;

but she doesn't have that extra something that Molly has. Molly connects with the audience because she appreciates the people who come to our shows. Evie calls them geezers. I call them boomers, and Myrtle Beach is filled with them. Tons of shag clubs and shag weekends draw the crowds into the area. Though we don't play beach music, we tap into those music lovers in a different way.

My stomach is in knots. I can't eat the wings I ordered. Evie struts in late, preening to the diners like she's the star of the show. I catch Tess's eye. We have the same thought. I wonder where Deke is. If we get picked up by Universal tonight, it's all because of him.

I'm a wreck. Big show. Record producer. What could go wrong?

TESS

I've had a bad feeling all day. Evie's quiet at the table. What's she hiding? I don't trust her. Samantha's eye roll told me we're on the same page where Evie's concerned. If she's got something planned, I hope it's not for tonight.

When Deke told us about the producer from Universal being in the audience tonight, I felt like exploding with joy. He didn't want to tell us, but Molly made him. She wants us to give our best performance.

Universal has a huge share of the industry and represents some of the biggest stars, like Billie Eilish and Lady Gaga. If this guy likes our show, tonight's sellout concert would be nothing in comparison. They put big money behind their acts, and they're betting our music is ready for a resurgence. That's what Deke says. So why does Evie look like the cat that ate the canary? What's she got up her sleeve? Good gawd, how many clichés can I get in my thoughts? I release a nervous chuckle and hope no one notices.

On top of Evie's weird behavior, didn't Molly notice she's

been making a play for Deke these last few weeks? Another thing, why was Molly's sister, Jenny, hanging around? She sat in on our rehearsals from time to time, even played backup, but she never came backstage. Something's going on. After dinner, I ask Molly why Jenny is here. She shrugs and says she just showed up and not to worry about it. Yeah, I'm worried. This could be the biggest night in the band's career. I don't want anything bad to happen.

SHOWTIME

MOLLY

The crowd is raucous. I'm at the end of the first song. I don't mention Joplin's name, but the audience knows who's singing. Big glasses, wild hair wig, and chunky necklaces, drinking away at my Southern Comfort. I pause before going into the next Janis number while we all take a bow and revel in the applause. Evie leans over and grabs her water bottle, watching me like a hawk. It's almost like she's expecting me to do something. She's freaking me out.

We finish up Janis, and the audience is wild when we leave the stage to prepare for the next artist. This time it's Evie's turn to do Aretha, but when we get backstage, Deke is standing there talking with a cop, and my sister Jenny is dressed like Aretha.

"What's going on?" I ask as Tess and Samantha dress for our version of Big Brother and the Holding Company backup, cautious and watchful of Deke, who offers no explanation other than to say, "Ask Evie."

Evie's face is blood red. "Ask me what?" she says.

Deke holds up a vial. "You put some of this in Molly's tea. I saw you."

The cop stands there, stone-faced, eyes on Evie.

I don't know what all this means, but we have to get back to the show for the next performer, Aretha. I look at Deke.

67

"Jenny will finish out the night," Deke says.

I don't have time to find out more. The audience is clapping for us to get back on stage. Tess and Samantha, exchanging glances, get out there. Jenny—playing Aretha—follows. Feeling slightly sick with apprehension, I hurry and change into one of Aretha's backup singers and join my band. Evie's left backstage with Deke and the cop. The look she gives me sends daggers into my heart.

TESS

The show goes off without a hitch. Jenny rocks the crowd. She's played backup for us at rehearsal a few times, but I didn't know how good she is until tonight. Her Aretha is far better than Evie's, full of raw emotion and deep resonance; in fact, she kills both of Evie's songs, and her raging guitar solo juices the audience up out of their seats with cheers. Molly, Samantha, and I have never been better. No tension for the first time in ages. No upstaging.

Our combined sound is tuned to perfection for the rest of the show. We get a solid five-minute ovation, with three encores. We're ecstatic. The audience is happy. We are happy.

The cop is still backstage at the end of the show, but now there's a suit with them. This guy's almost as tall and good looking as six-foot-four-inch Deke. Evie's in handcuffs, arguing with the cop. She shuts up when we gather round. We're still confused, but we let things play out.

BACKSTAGE, AFTER THE SHOW

MOLLY

I take one look at Evie's red eyes and say, "Why is a cop here, and who's this guy?" I point to the suit. He's tall with a no-nonsense demeanor.

"I saw her doctor your Southern Comfort bottle," Deke says. "I saved the contents, then refilled the bottle with more tea, before I called the police. I told them what I suspected, and the officer came, but he called for this man when he figured out what Evie had done." Deke introduces Agent Will Harold from Charlotte's DEA office.

Evie's arguing is over. She remains quiet. No denial, nothing. I'm shattered. "Why? This was our big night. Why would you do that?"

"It was just supposed to make you sleepy so I could finish the show."

I'm unable to speak.

"I took a preliminary test, and I'm sure it's GHB," Agent Harold says. "A date-rape drug. Odorless, colorless, tasteless. I'll send it to the lab for confirmation." He looks at Evie. "You know the drug is illegal. Where did you get it?"

"I'm not saying another thing," Evie says. She points at Deke. "He searched my things. Isn't that illegal?"

"Not if there's cause," Harold says, "and after he saw you doctor her drink, that's cause."

I know she's already said too much when she admitted that whatever she put in my drink would make me sleepy. She's in a world of trouble.

"You flip on your supplier," the DEA cop says, "and we can go light on you, maybe with probation. Where did you get it?"

Evie still doesn't say anything, but I can see her mind working.

"I don't understand," I say. "You risked screwing up our chance with a big record company. Big bucks, a contract. What were you thinking?"

"I know," Tess says. "It's all about Evie looking for a solo contract. It's always been all about Evie."

Evie still doesn't say anything. Tears fill my eyes.

"Tell me who sold it to you and how you found him," Harold says. "If I can stop this person from selling it to someone else, I promise I'll make sure you won't do time."

"Time? Like jail?" Evie says.

"Yes, jail," Harold says. "Besides being illegal, enough of it can kill someone."

"I didn't know." Evie is crying now. Big, fat, wet tears. Her whole body is shaking.

"You need to go with the officer," Harold says. "Think about what you want to do, on the ride." The cop takes Evie by the arm.

"You have the time it takes to get to the police station," the cop says, "but no matter, you're spending the night in jail."

"You can't let them do this to me," Evie pleads, rising shakily. "I made this group what it is. Me. I'll sue you."

"We'll take our chances," Deke says.

Evie unleashes some unladylike words as the officer leads her out of the room. Agent Harold says a few words to Deke I can't hear, then tips his head toward us, says, "Ladies," and follows them out.

I start to say that I can't believe what just happened, but I'm so shocked, again nothing comes out of my mouth. I'm devastated. From the looks on everyone's faces, they feel the same.

"I suspected she'd do something like this one of these nights," Tess said, "but I hoped I'd be wrong."

"When I saw what she did, I called Jenny," Deke said. "I knew she was in the audience."

"Yes, Jenny," Samantha says. "You were beyond fab. You saved the night."

"You know my kid sister's always known the routines, but she was in college, and I wanted her to get an education," I said. "I also wanted her to be twenty-one, which she is now. If Evie had stayed honest to the group, I would have asked everyone to vote on a fifth member, but...Evie's out. There's no coming back. I'm proposing Jenny as our new member. What say you?"

"No problem here," Tess says. "You were terrific."

"Nor here," Samantha chimes in. "Welcome aboard."

"Thanks," Jenny says. "Glad to be part of the group and

that it's okay with y'all."

"And just so you ladies know," Deke says, "I got a text from Dan Lauter, the producer from Universal. He wants to meet with us tomorrow to discuss the contract. Is that okay with everyone?"

Everyone shrieks some form of yes at the same time.

"Why do you look so down, Molly?" Samantha asks.

I know she's trying to lift my spirits, so I wrap my arm around her shoulder and pull her close. "I'm happy about the meeting, but I'm sad that Evie felt she had to take such drastic measures to be the star of the show. I could have been sick, maybe worse. It really *was* all about Evie."

"All about Evie," Deke says. "Why does that ring a bell?"

The Vigil
Toni Goodyear

Our escape from the Anawahi casino was like my first marriage: riddled with potholes and hairpin turns, with two semi-humans bleeding out in the front seat. If I hadn't been busy trying not to die, I would've laughed.

Thomson, riding shotgun, groaned as he tightened his fake leather belt around his left thigh. Even with the makeshift tourniquet in place, a thin rivulet of blood dribbled toward his shoes. He'd taken the slug from the security guard's pistol like a Hollywood stunt man, swan diving from the second-floor balcony into the hotel pool, his ruined knee drawing bloody swirls in the chlorine like chum for sharks.

I'd almost made it out of the casino unscathed when another fat fuck of a guard put a round into my lower intestine. The eerie thing about this kind of wound is you can still drive a getaway car while your lights dim. I wasn't in as bad shape as that *Braveheart* guy who stayed conscious while his executioner yanked out his bowels. My insides were still inside; kicking off could take me a while. So here I was, twisting around mountain roads, one fist crushing the steering wheel, the other jamming a wadded-up towel into the yuk below my stomach. My brain felt lighter, like a breeze was blowing in one ear and out the other.

"Maybe we should use Brock's disaster plan, park the stuff at the old borrow pit in Swenson," I said. "In case we don't...you know…"

Thomson leaned back against the headrest. "In case we don't make it back to Brock's. He would love that, wouldn't he? He'd get it all. Puts us right where he likes us—between a Brock and a hard place."

He laughed like hell on a Saturday night at that one, then cried out and fainted. I wiped a new tide of spittle from my lips with my sleeve. Truth was, I had no intention of parking the money anywhere Brock could find it, never mind his prearranged drop point for emergencies. Simple as that. The agreement was clear: his plan, his contact on the inside, our execution. And we'd pulled it off. We'd had a couple of bad breaks but we'd held onto the prize as we bled and fled. That kept us equal. *More* than equal. Question was, could we still trust him to stick to the deal?

Somehow, I had to stay conscious for another thirteen miles. I had to descend the mountain, get the hell off Indian land, point the SUV toward Conway, find the first traffic light in Benstown, make three rights and two lefts, and tuck this baby into a waiting bay at Brock's InTown Garage as agreed. All before I passed out or dropped dead. Like dutiful soldiers, we'd apprised Brock of our situation as we made our fucked-up getaway—two wounded men, booty in hand, headed your way. He is therefore *supposed* to have someone ready to patch us up. He's also *supposed* to remain committed to sharing equally the million and a half bucks we've got crammed into custom-built compartments under the car floor, even if two of us happen to be unconscious.

I blasted up the corkscrew roadway, over Okana Ridge, and started down the other side of the mountain. A mile later the pine forest parted briefly, revealing the valley below. I hugged the side of the mountain, concentrating on keeping the car on the road, trying not to stare at the panorama. I had a quick image of the car soaring over the cliff edge, gently rocking from side to side like a leaf in the wind, down to the valley floor where it was reduced to the size of a toaster.

A short straightaway and another hair-raising, descending-radius curve brought to you by the serial killers of the WPA led to a pullout called the Honaklee Valley Scenic Overlook. I tugged the wheel sideways and ground to a sloppy stop on gravel. The upcoming town was laid out below. Behind us were brief glimpses of the highway we'd just traveled—no cars visibly in pursuit. At least I could say amen to that. The vista should've been inspiring but wasn't. The purple rays of late afternoon seemed to foretell more of hell than heaven.

I took a quick peek behind the towel at my gut. The bleeding had slowed, things were holding. I could see that the wound was off to one side; maybe I'd gotten lucky. A welcome numbness helped with the pain. I felt Thomson's pulse. His heart was still beating. So far, so good. I closed my eyes and gave myself two minutes for self-indulgence. Then I slapped myself hard and threw the car into gear.

I was still awake when I hit Conway. I reached the Benstown city limits half an hour later and spotted the sign for Brock's InTown Garage. Hope surged; maybe the Indians were about to lose another skirmish to the white devils after all. My head was clearer, either from the adrenalin rush of having made it this far or from the supernatural clarity poets say you feel just before your living soul departs your body.

The left bay door stood open as promised. I pulled the car all the way in and saw Brock in the rearview, grinning as he hit the button to bring down the door. I killed the ignition, felt again for Thomson's pulse—yup, still there—and laid my head back against the headrest. It was the last thing I remembered for quite a while.

The alleged doctor had a face like a cow, an expressionless expanse of flesh with big doughy eyes and a ruminating mouth movement that chewed a toothpick while he worked. He needed to go on a serious diet, that much was clear.

"Well, hello there," he said, backing up a step when my eyes opened.

My hands went to my wound, bandaged now. A mild burning sensation. The kind I could already tell was not gonna be mild once whatever was pumping into my arm wore off.

I looked around slowly, getting my bearings. Brock's house probably, though I'd never been in this room before. Suburban type furnishings. A bedroom of the nondescript "guest" variety.

My lips felt glued shut. I had to consciously pry them apart. "Where's Thomson?" I finally got out.

"He needed some patching up, but he'll keep his leg. He's sleeping down the hall."

I tried to raise my head but quickly gave up the idea. "Me?"

"Stitched like a stuffed bird, antibiotic-ed, de-pained. Piping reconnected." Geez, where the hell did Brock get this guy? "You lost blood, but it'll build back up fast enough. No arteries punctured. Nothing to worry about."

I cringed. *Nothing to worry about.* A curse if ever there was one. An ironclad guarantee that a major shitstorm is on the way. I wanted this stupid doctor to take it back. Crooks are mega-superstitious; we throw salt, dodge cracks in the pavement, turn around three times to ward off misfortune, spit on the sidewalk. It's vital we stay on friendly terms with the Fates.

Right on cue, Brock appeared in the doorway—a potential shitstorm on the hoof. "Well, well, look who's conscious."

I tried to nod but failed. "How long?"

"About a day and a half. Thomson too." He jerked his head at the doctor who wordlessly took his leave. "We thought it best for you guys to get a little rest. Helps the healing."

He dragged an armchair closer to the bed and sat, smiling like we were about to have tea. "So where is it, Johnny?"

I moved my gaze toward the window. A day and a half out cold. A little imposed vacation for me and Thomson while Brock searched for the money. I had no doubt that if he'd found it, he would already be gone—and so, I suspected, might we.

I blinked a few times as if having a sudden attack of drug-induced muck-brain. It wasn't a far stretch.

But he wasn't buying. "It's not in the car, and it's not at our prearranged stash point. So where, I wonder, has it gone?"

I dug up a weak smile. "Just a little insurance, Brock. Make sure we got fixed up. I put it in a safe place just before I hit town. A temporary precaution."

"I see." He held my gaze a long time; he looked like a crocodile tucking in a dinner napkin. "Then there should be no problem. You've gotten medical attention, though I'm wounded to the heart that you didn't trust me to play this out according to Hoyle. That offends me, Johnny. But we'll let it go. You tell me where the money is, and I'll go get it."

"No."

His eyes narrowed. "You leave it with someone?"

I grunted. "I'm not crazy, just shot."

He hesitated. I could see the crossroad in his eyes. Push it? Leave it?

Decision made. He patted my leg. "Same old Johnny. Believing in no one. Okay, we'll do it your way for now. How long a delay did you have in mind?"

"Until Thomson and I can move around without falling over. You would've done the same thing, Brock. Admit it."

He reset the charm meter. "You're right, I probably would have. Given the circumstances, we'll give things time to settle."

"What about the car?"

"Already history. How good was my plan?"

"Like you said. Light staff on Sunday." I sucked in a breath and nudged my torso a little to the right; the damn bandages pulled. "They couldn't organize fast enough to mount a good chase. And the weekend take was still on site."

"Bad luck about the guards," he said. "Money truck's supposed to come around seven. Thomson says the extra muscle just happened to come early to gamble."

"Yeah." My head felt heavier; sleep was calling. "Tell

Thomson not to worry about the money, okay? He was out cold, I had to make a decision. Anything on the scanner?"

He flashed his reptile smile. "They finally put out a BOLO about thirty minutes after your exit. Guess it took them a while to get the white cops to give a shit."

"There was no one following us. Nothing linking us to here."

He looked thoughtful. "Okay, smart guy. For now, we'll stand watch on the scanners, the TV, and the internet and see what shakes out. Let's hope we get lucky."

I could feel my strength sliding down a rabbit hole. "What about the doctor?"

"Nasty man. Don't worry. He'll be taken out of the equation."

I relaxed back against the stacked pillows. "In that case, I think I'll take a nap."

The media exploded with the news. Turns out there's a very low incidence of Caucasian bad guys raiding Native American casinos. We'd worn masks of course, but white skin still flashed, and a lot of white words too. I couldn't tell which generated more outrage: racial indignation or financial loss. I figured the former. A million and a half couldn't be more than a small bite for a casino, right?

A TV was already in my room, and I had my cell phone. Brock brought in a laptop. Thomson was given the same setup in his room, and there was a police scanner in the kitchen. The idea was to keep all three of us looking and listening round the clock to give us maximum warning if things went south. Thank god for pushy reporters. They work their asses off to give us outlaws way more information than we should have. Imagine what Butch and Sundance would've given for the late-breaking news that half the Bolivian army was just outside their hiding place, waiting for them to stick out a toe.

In the media circus of blame-throwing and wild speculation on how such a heinous crime could've been pulled off, it was music that captured our attention. College students had mounted a protest vigil in support of the Native American community. They were camped out in the town park, a couple of hundred overprivileged Gen Z'ers swearing to maintain a hunger strike until law enforcement brought the reservation desecrators to justice. The local twenty-four-hour cable news channel was providing near-continuous coverage. The face of the vigil was right out of central casting: "native chanting" delivered badly by white wannabees, "smudging groups" burning what was probably supermarket rosemary and sage, "spirit circles" clustered around fire pits, and ceremonial "dances" that consisted mostly of stomping and drumming in a weird cross between Buffalo Bill's Wild West Show and Tiger Lily. The native garb looked like it came from a hippie Goodwill store.

On the fringe of this bizarre display was a small pocket of a couple dozen young people who seemed to ignore the greater hubbub. These—it gradually dawned on me—were the real deal: actual Anawahis. They were dressed simply, in T-shirts and jeans, with here and there a pendant or headband, staving off night chills in Columbia fleeces and hoodies. They sat close together, cross-legged, in two circles on the grass.

And they made music. Low, haunting music from wooden flutes, a sound that flowed with a sense of inevitability, like a river along a course that had been carved out long ago. A plea, a mystical warning, a plaintive cry. The cry was there beneath the drumming and the angry protesters yelling into microphones. It was there when the larger crowd momentarily spent itself and paused to rest. Sometimes the Anawahis played together, sometimes individually, in a relay pattern that denied silence a fingerhold, even in the wee hours. The relentless, ghostly tone worked itself into my brain, rolling in like a mist, inescapable. It conquered without intention, pulling us into a natural cavern of human breath, notes from a hidden depth, hour after hour, entraining the nerve cells, hypnotically stroking the mind. The music was there as we slept, as we woke, as we changed our bandages, as we peed, as we limped to the kitchen and tried to eat.

"Those flutes are driving me crazy," Thomson groaned on day three, closing his eyes and breathing deeply. "They hurt my head." He'd been reasonable about my stashing the money. He said he not only trusted me but would've done the same.

"Ignore them," Brock said. "We've got to keep monitoring." He'd been stuffing his ears with cotton balls and trying to capture TV conversations by reading subtitles. Neither had worked very well. The music still got through, and the captions were mostly incomprehensible. He finally gave up.

For the next two nights no one slept much. Brock developed excruciating pains in his back. Thomson said his heart was suddenly flopping around with an irregular beat. We all started to look bleary eyed, a bit like zombies—the kind that never changed clothes.

On day five of the vigil, a cable newsman interviewed an Anawahi spokesman. Thomson and I dragged our asses to the den and joined Brock for a beer as we watched. The flutes went mournfully on in the background, our never-ending underscore.

"The flutes call upon the ancients to help the tribe in times of trouble," the spokesman said when asked the meaning of the music. "We play to rouse our protectors to come forth and speak with one voice, to help right this wrong and deliver justice to our enemies. We will play on until justice is served."

The vigil, and the music, continued. The wannabees got more hungry, more desperate, more threatening. Some fainted and were carted off in ambulances; others replaced them.

The day after the Anawahi spokesman, Thomson's good leg spasmed so bad we had to knock him out with a half pint of rye. That night, Brock reported a strange numbness in his shoulders and chest; the next morning he spent two hours seeing double. "I should've kept the goddamn doctor," he grumbled. "In the ground, he's no good to anyone."

The music played on as I loudly complained about headaches and pains in my stomach. By day seven, I was openly beset by dry heaves. Still the music went on, expanding and thriving, until finally it burst free, free of the town park, free of the state, free of the boundaries of the galaxy, maybe even the known universe, and maybe all the universes there ever were and ever would be.

"We're fucked!" Thomson cried. His leg wound, which had been healing well, had again begun to throb, he said. His eyes had that kind of panicky quality you get when you hear a police siren coming closer.

Brock sat holding his left hand in his right. "My fingers have gone stiff. I can't close my fist. Damn, damn, damn." He tried unsuccessfully to grip the handle of his coffee mug.

"We can't explain this, but it is what it is," I said, then bent over for another vigorous bout of dry heaves. When I came up for air I added, "Maybe we should give the damn money back. We can't spend it if we're dead."

Like I said, thieves are ultra-sensitive to things like curses. But we're also greedy as hell; that's why we're thieves. I watched my partners wrestle with the impact of what I had just proposed. I saw them laying it out on their mental pool tables, lining up the balls, gauging the possibility of making a rare banana shot, the one you need to use if you want to hit a ball that's plainly unhittable. A shot only the very best can pull off. I saw their eyes dim as they realized the odds were against them. I let that simmer.

Brock became sullen and still, like an aborted insult choking in an unfriendly throat. His eyes were angry slits.

"Sometimes the breath leaves my body like it's never coming back," Thomson said to no one in particular.

Thomson was the first to spy our Anawahi accomplice on the news that night. "Hey, isn't that Tahoma?" He pointed at the television.

We looked. There he sat, sure as shit, his lips to the blowhole of a big daddy flute. Our contact inside the casino. The man who worked in the money room, the guy Brock had cut in for a share of the profit in exchange for leaving a few things unattended and keeping his mouth shut.

"Son of a bitch," Brock said. "I should've followed my instinct and took him out after the job. Call that bastard right now, tell him to get all this bullshit stopped."

I held my stomach and shook my head. "Hell, I think it's genius. We told him we wanted him to stay on good terms with the tribe, right? He's just capitalizing on what the kids started, putting on a great face, showing his utter devotion to his people in their hour of need. It's okay, Brock."

He looked at me the way kids look when their mother tells them they'll wind up a stunted dwarf if they don't finish their broccoli, eyes squinted as he weighed the odds of it being true.

"Anyway, Tahoma's sincerity is not our main challenge," I said.

"No? Then tell me, what the hell is our main challenge?"

Thomson turned in his seat and threw up into a bucket. "We're gonna have to give the money back." He wiped his mouth on his sleeve.

I nodded. "Yes. We have to give it back. We're all getting worse by the hour."

Brock grunted an *over-my-dead-body* kind of grunt.

Next day, with a strange new paralysis creeping up his left arm, he conceded. "I can't fucking believe this," he said, trying—and failing—to pick up his shoes.

Now we had a new problem. We were the first casino thieves in history who wanted to give the money back. And, as Brock pointed out, we needed to do it soon, before none of us could walk, see, or inhale.

It was decided that I would drive away, call the casino from one of the last remaining public phone booths in the state, and tell them where the money was. "I'll tell them the spirit of the Anawahi has been victorious. We've seen the error of our ways." I punctuated the thought with another bout of heaves. "And I won't be lying. I don't want to touch that damn money."

"Me either," Thomson said.

"Then we're agreed. We go our separate ways," Brock said. "I'm a respected businessman in this town. You two get the hell out of Dodge. In different directions. I've got two rebuilds in back of the shop, no trace on them." He threw car keys on the table. "I'll take you to the garage. Then you get in them and go."

Thomson's head bobbed up and down like a piston, like he could already feel the pains in his body lessening with every mile away from his ill-gotten gains. To call him spooked would be like calling Darth Vader grumpy.

We spent the next few hours getting organized: meds, water, bandages, clothes, a bit of food, the cane Thomson had borrowed from Brock. Then Brock used his good arm to drive us to the garage.

Thomson was already gone with a hurried wave when Brock turned to me. "I want you to know this, smart guy: I'll be watching the news to make sure you do the right thing. I'll be coming after you if you don't."

"That's fine, Brock, you do that. But remember it might not go down that way. They might decide not to publicize the return of the money. I wouldn't. You know, for insurance purposes."

Brock looked smug, like he'd caught me in a bear trap. "I'll also be talking to Tahoma. No way they can pull off that kind of thing without him knowing. So, you see, I'll know. Either way, I'll know if you don't do the right thing."

I shot him a hard look, then decided it wasn't worth my time. I gave the brim of my baseball cap a tug. "Nothing to worry about, Brock."

He glowered. "Get the hell out of here."

The car he gave me was an old straight drive Toyota Corolla with peeling paint and almost three hundred thousand miles on it. I said a little prayer, shifted into first, and headed out of town. Thomson had agreed to go east; I went west. Back up toward the hills, to the little crossroads called Conway, the first sign of civilization I'd encountered coming down off the mountain. Conway consisted of a mom-and-pop gas station and a greasy spoon grill. Half a mile past the grill was the entrance to a small state-run campground, the kind that had no rangers, no attendants, just a shed with a site map and a bunch of envelopes for honor system dollars and a door slot for depositing them.

I parked out of view of the one and only surveillance camera, pulled out my cell phone, and sent a quick text. Then I walked into the pines, far enough to be invisible from the parking lot but not far enough to attract most campers, to an in-between patch of forest close enough for a gut-shot man to drag his haul and hide it under rotting logs, covered with layers of leaves. Today was a weekday in early November, same as when I hid it. No lake, no hunting, no special attractions. No one would be camping.

I dragged out the bags and started re-sorting a million and a half dollars in banded bundles of one hundred hundred-dollar bills evenly into two large vinyl duffels. It took a while.

I had just finished the count-out and zipped up the loot when I heard the crunch of footsteps. Tahoma saw me and grinned wide, his dark eyes dancing. "Johnny Wiles, I do believe. Nice office you've got here."

I laughed and pointed to a bag sitting on a log. "There you go, my new friend. Three-quarters of a million bucks in sweet little C-notes, double what Brock promised you. Go ahead, open it."

"No need. I'm pretty sure I can trust you."

He could, for two reasons. Not only could he fry my ass if I stiffed him, but guys as competent as Tahoma were hard to come by. When I called him from my recovery room, I'd asked him one simple question—got any idea how we can make lemonade out of college protesters and weak criminal minds? He not only didn't laugh, he'd made the idea soar.

"Look forward to working together again sometime," I said. "We make a great team. And you play a mean flute."

He chuckled. "How are the invalids?"

"Like my dry heaves, miraculously cured by the decision to

84

give the money back, two walking examples of the psychosomatic power of superstition. We should send the guard who shot me and those college kids a thank-you card for showing us the way. Oh, and you'll probably be hearing from Brock soon. Just to make sure I did the right thing."

"I'm sure I will." He stuck out his hand and we shook. "Nice doing business with you, Johnny. Give me a call anytime."

"Will do. You take care of yourself."

He touched his forehead in an Anawahi gesture of friendship, Then, in the finest tradition of his ancestors, he disappeared silently into the forest.

A moment later I, too, was gone.

A Death at the Opera
Judy Fowler

From her seat in the balcony of Norfolk's Theatre for the Performing Arts, Eleanor Grant applauded the conclusion of Mozart's opera, *Don Giovanni,* a character who enjoyed ignoring other people's boundaries. She was there to review the performance for the *Ocean Gazette*, but her eyes were on her friend Lewis, who'd been hired to conduct this final performance when his predecessor fell ill. Long-ago sweethearts, they'd split up after graduation from music school. Recently he'd moved to Norfolk, and they both were eager to renew their relationship.

Her stocky sweetheart bounded onstage to join the cast for a group bow. His hair looked damp, but his smile was broad. He pointed to the orchestra in the pit to share the applause.

The audience gathered their wraps and got in line to descend red-carpeted stairs. Balcony patrons generally waited for lower tiers to get out first. Tonight's wait went on uncommonly long. Eleanor used the time to draft her review on her phone. Michelle Frazier, who played Zerlina, a peasant bride, had made a strong impression on Eleanor. Don Giovanni's *droit de seigneur* allows him to sample Zerlina's assets before her wedding to the peasant groom, Masetto. *Don Giovanni embodies the statement "when you're famous, they let you,"* Eleanor typed. *Ms. Frazier has a golden future.*

"Hey," a man in line said. "My friend says the police are questioning everyone trying to leave the building."

The police?

Eleanor spotted her friend Barbara Curry off to the side, shining her usher's flashlight onto the carpeted stairs. Eleanor wriggled through the line to reach her former choir mate.

Barbara's face changed from fearful to cheerful at the sight of a friend.

"The pitfalls of live theater!" Eleanor whispered.

"Makes our choir loft seem roomy," Barbara quipped back.

"Any idea why the police are in the lobby? I told Lewis I'd meet him outside the stage door."

"I didn't know the police were here," Barbara answered. "This way. I'll get you to him."

She pulled aside a black curtain to reveal a metal emergency staircase. They used Barbara's flashlight to guide them down.

The stairs ended on the stage level near the left wing, where they were met by a frightening scene.

Not ten feet away, the singer who'd portrayed Don Giovanni lay on the floor, face up and motionless. His partially detached black wig revealed the baritone's actual gray hair.

A sword stuck out of his chest.

The women gasped. Eleanor grabbed Barbara's hand. Was this really happening? Cast members and stage crew milled about, their faces reflecting shock and concern, some in tears. Police had cordoned off the area around the body.

"You two! Step back." The sharp command came from a lanky man in a jacket and slacks, a detective, clearly in charge.

They did as they were told. When Eleanor saw Lewis approaching them from the stage, she felt such relief.

"He's dead, Lew. Murdered," she said.

"A stagehand found him and called 911," Lewis whispered. "The police aren't letting the cast go."

"Looks like someone waited for this man to come off stage," the detective said. "Who was backstage after the curtain call before my victim left the stage? Step forward."

The first one to step forward was Zerlina, then the tenor playing her bridegroom, followed by Donna Anna, Donna Elvira, and finally Lewis.

The answer was so simple that Eleanor blurted it out. "Everyone but the victim was backstage before your victim, Detective—?"

"Hardy. Who are you?"

"Eleanor Grant. I was in the audience. Don Giovanni took his solo bow after everyone else went backstage right. He was alone in front of the curtain." *And milking the last of the applause for all it was worth.* She kept that to herself out of respect for the corpse. "He exited stage right."

Cast members still gawked at the body on the floor. Hardy spoke firmly to them. "Each of you stays in costume until my photographer gets photos. Provide your contact information so we can schedule your written statements, then you can leave." He turned to Eleanor and Barbara. "You two stick around for a few minutes." He walked over to the metal staircase, looked at the black fabric around it, and called for someone on his team to dust the railing for prints. "Someone who wanted to attack the victim could have used these stairs." He looked at Eleanor and Barbara when he said it. "Explain to me why you were on the metal staircase. Were you avoiding my officers?"

Barbara spoke up. "The line wasn't moving, and Ellie wanted to meet her friend Lewis. I'm an usher, so I led her down the emergency stairs."

Hardy studied their faces. "These stairs may well have been a killer's entrance and exit strategy. Who knew about them besides you?"

Eleanor saw her friend's face turn red and tried to help. "There's an emergency sign on each level of seating in the theater. We all saw Giovanni exit stage right. Why lie in wait stage left? The only advantage Barb had was easy access and the flashlight."

She saw Barbara imploring with her eyes for Eleanor to stop

defending her.

"Take it easy, Ms. Grant," Hardy said. "No one's accusing anyone yet."

Barbara's explanation of their action, though true, had sounded weak. "Detective, we don't know anything," Eleanor said. "The stage manager has a book with everyone's exits and entrances, and the prop master can tell you which of his swords was sharp enough to puncture the barrel chest of a baritone."

Hardy looked at Eleanor with a twinkle in his eye. "You seem to think, Ms....?"

"Grant," Eleanor said.

"You seem to think this is my first murder at the opera, Ms. Grant."

"Isn't it?"

"I'm messing with you. Give us your phone numbers, then you can leave." He rejoined his team onstage.

Barbara hurried off to hand in her remaining programs. Eleanor went to the dressing rooms to look for Lew.

Costumed performers smoked, talked, and toweled off their face paint. One cursed that he'd just missed his flight to New York. An employee of the theater passed out hastily assigned hotel room numbers.

No one even spoke of, let alone mourned, the production's leading man, except one soprano, the cast's Donna Anna, who looked distraught and had been weeping.

Eleanor found Lew talking to Michelle Frazier at her cluttered dressing table. The soprano had exchanged Zerlina's peasant dress for tan suede vest and pants, accenting her cleavage and curves. She held out her hand to Eleanor.

"Michelle Frazier," she said, in the honeyed voice that stirred the audience to bravos during her curtain call. "Lewis says you worked together when you were younger."

The catty remark wasn't lost on Eleanor, who was wondering how Lew, in such limited time, had made a friend. Unless they'd worked together before? After all, she didn't know everything about Lew's life before he came to Norfolk.

Michelle stashed some hairpins in a pale blue clutch. "I got to change into my street clothes, but not to leave. Lewis advises me not to despair."

Enough was enough. Eleanor claimed her territory by planting a kiss on Lew's cheek and telling him what a great job he'd done and that she'd see him later, as planned.

"I don't think I'll get out in time, Ellie," he said. "How about a rain check?"

She left the two and went to find the detective. Hardy was onstage with the medical examiner, who instructed the EMS workers to take the bagged body to the morgue.

"Did you want something else, Ms. Grant?" Hardy asked.

"I want to go home. May I?"

"Yeah. Keep your ticket stub. We'll call you for a formal statement."

Eleanor posted her review—minus the grisly encore—before going to bed. She checked the urge to delete her praise for Michelle.

Monday dawned. Apart from her close encounter with a dead body and competition emerging for Lew's affection, Eleanor woke to a familiar world. Traffic distracted her as she drove to the courthouse for her day job, educating defendants about their rights in court.

At the end of the day, she checked her messages. There were two. Lewis left a non-message: "Oh. Not there? Okay. Later."

Then Barbara Curry. "Eleanor, I have to talk to you!"

She called Barbara first.

"Eleanor, I'm in trouble."

"Why?"

"It's something I saw before the show last night that I left out of my statement today."

"Tell me."

"How can I say this? I always use the stage door to get into the theater. It saves time because it's less crowded than the lobby."

"So?"

"When I walked past the men's dressing rooms, I saw that gorgeous sword outside Jake's dressing room and wondered why it wasn't on the prop table at thirty minutes to curtain." Barbara explained that she'd been a prop girl once at a summer theater, and when owners lent good things, she hated that she'd have to return them damaged. "I picked it up to take it to the prop master before I remembered it was a union show, and I put it back."

"Your fingerprints are on the sword that killed Giovanni?"

"That's what I'm saying."

Eleanor looked out her kitchen window at the full moon. "Hang up and call Detective Hardy, Barb."

"I'm scared."

Eventually, Barbara agreed to call Hardy if she could call back if she needed further support. An hour later, a text arrived, saying Barbara had amended her statement and was going to bed.

In the morning, Eleanor drank coffee and planned her day. The doorbell rang.

"Hey, Nancy Drew." Lewis held two newspapers.

"Oh, Lew, I'm sorry," she said. "I didn't call you back to hear about your reviews. Read them to me while I eat breakfast."

She got out another bowl and spoon in case he wanted to share her cereal and berries. As she placed it on the table, Lewis held out his strong arms and gathered her to him. "No cornflakes right now," he whispered.

She wasn't due at work until ten. Relieved to have the conductor's full attention, Eleanor let him lead.

By nine thirty, Lew had left to teach music at a middle school, and Eleanor was on her way to the courthouse. At the end of her workday, she got a call from Detective Hardy. "Can you meet me in the parking lot of Rallyburgers?"

He was leaning on his car under the cloud-filled coastal sky when she arrived.

"Your friend's fingerprints were on the sword," he said.

"She told me."

"I'm still waiting for all my forensics to come back, but I need your help while I wait."

"How can I help? The only people I know from last night are one usher and the last-minute replacement conductor."

Hardy looked at her through blue eyes she hoped had seen more restful days. "I believe you, but—"

"You've got the stage manager's book and the prop list, I'm sure. And the crew boss's assignments for breaking down the final set?"

"The prop sword was the victim's, and its blade actually cut. And, yes, I've been faxed paperwork about who should have been where…"

"Only?"

Hardy stretched and yawned. "Only who wasn't where they should have been? We didn't find scuff marks near the victim. No one admits to seeing him cross over to stage left."

He's a quick learner, she thought.

Hardy pointed to the drive-in window. "I'm buying dinner. How about coming back to my office for a half hour?"

At the station they divvied up their fast food. A fry dipped in ketchup reminded her of blood on the dead man's chest. "Look at those union crew guys," she suggested. "A crew member at the Met in New York was responsible for the death of a pretty violinist during intermission a while back."

"The conductor said you had a passion for crime stories," Hardy said.

Yup, her dear Lew knew she couldn't close a book until she knew whodunnit and why. "I guess murder stories are like tragic opera plots. How can I help here?"

Hardy pointed to a whiteboard with names on it. "So far,

without all the forensic evidence in, I have three persons of interest and one question mark."

"Is Barbara a question mark?"

"Her fingerprints on the weapon, plus access? What do you think?"

"What motive could she have?"

"She's on the board as a suspect," he said, wiping mustard off his dimpled chin.

"Every usher in the house had a flashlight and is trained to use the emergency stairs," she mused.

"The question mark is your friend, the conductor."

"Lewis? He got the job two days before the performance!" She wondered if Lew had told her everything about life before Norfolk. "Who else is on your suspect list?"

"That's where I need your ideas. Three people might have considered the victim to be a threat."

"Male or female?"

Hardy stared at her over a curly fry. "Male. Why?"

"In the world of opera, it's hard to know who finds who attractive."

"Three males, all close to Michelle Frazier." Hardy put down his burger to write the names of two teamsters: Ed Walker, and Walker's cousin.

Nepotism in the crew? What a surprise. "Who's the third?"

"A big guy who played a soldier. He's also Don Giovanni's understudy." He wrote the man's name on the board, then dropped the chalk to concentrate on his fries.

Eleanor let out her breath. "She was in relationships with three men in one show?"

"That's what they bragged about in their statements. Ed Walker said each of them knew about the others and that she also had a thing with the dead man." He reached for one of her fries after finishing his own.

Eleanor handed him the whole sack. "Too greasy for me," she said. "Just an aside, but sex often leads to death in opera.

Both subjects get a lot of play."

She thought Hardy looked at her with new appreciation. An idea came to her. "Did any of them share an address in New York?" she asked.

"They're all here for another day or two, but we entered their permanent addresses." He wiped his hands before opening a window on his desktop. "Tell me why I'm looking for addresses?"

"There's a joke about starving artists—"

"Give me a break!"

She laughed. "I thought you wanted me to educate you about theater people?"

"Only what's necessary to my case, Ms. Grant."

"You can call me Eleanor."

"How would you feel if I reeled off the things police say in locker rooms, Eleanor?"

"I'd find that extremely interesting," she said. "So, the joke is, what do you call a performer without a girlfriend?"

"What?"

"Homeless," Eleanor replied. "If one of these suitors is sofa-surfing at Michelle's apartment, he'd be worried about home-lessness if Jake started crashing there, too. It may not sound like motive down here, but rents in New York are impossibly high for newcomers in the arts. And Michelle's not just pretty. With her talent, she'll always have rent money. I'd look closely at the guy playing the nameless soldier. Those crew guys have mothers in New Jersey or the boroughs. They wouldn't need Michelle's sofa."

Hardy sucked down the last of his soda as he made notes.

"And his motive could be he's tired of being Jake's understudy. But why kill him when it's the final performance? Unless they had the same arrangement for an upcoming role that the soldier wanted." She bit into her burger. "Yum. Add a strawberry shake from Doumar's, and I'll fall into a coma."

"Got fifteen more minutes? You're a big help."

After Hardy assured her that no one else shared Michelle's

address, Eleanor learned that Jake had been married with two grown children. She told Hardy that such facts wouldn't usually impede romance on the road.

The detective told Eleanor to go home, promising to get in touch if he needed more opera advice.

The classical music station played Maria Callas singing *Tosca* on Eleanor's drive home. Both divas had jealous flare-ups like the one Eleanor had avoided by leaving Michelle's dressing table. Eleanor had felt her jealousy go from zero to sixty when she saw Lew look at Michelle as if he knew her well. Eleanor wondered if Hardy had miscounted the number of suitors the singer had, or if that was why Lew was a question mark on the whiteboard.

Hardy called and asked if Eleanor would meet him after work at the theater.

The building was dimly lit outside. A cop conference between two officers through their driver's side windows stopped long enough to point her to the door Hardy had gone in.

He sat on the stage, studying the chalk outline of his victim.

"Hey, Eleanor." A second chair was next to him.

She sat.

"I got the coroner's report. I'm not going to show it to you, but it clears one guy."

Let it be Lewis. "Who?"

"The dead man. He didn't fall on his sword accidentally."

"Very funny. Why am I here, Detective?"

"Joe."

"Who?"

"Joe's my name. Feel free to use it."

Eleanor wasn't ready to call a police detective by his first name. "Maybe at some point, thanks."

"These singers are driving us nuts. They're whining about losing auditions in New York."

"Actors," Eleanor said. "They call themselves actors who

sing."

"Not helpful to my case, Eleanor."

"I assume you reached Jake's wife. Is she coming down?"

"She didn't have to."

"Why?"

"She's already here. She's in the cast. Sherice Cantrell."

"Donna Anna?" The hair on the back of Eleanor's neck stood up. Donna Anna was among those who had taken a step forward at Hardy's request. What she didn't do was cry out that it was her husband lying dead in the wings. "Were his wife's fingerprints on the sword?"

"No. Only my victim's and Barbara Curry's. I hoped you could try to remember exactly how she got you to come down the stairs with her, like an alibi."

So Barbara was first on the suspect list even if Joe—Hardy— didn't say it outright.

"Sure, I'll think about it and let you know." Did Barbara have a motive? No. Was her meek friend capable of murder? No. Instead, on her drive home, Eleanor thought about costumes.

She had experience wearing them and knew how they oriented audiences to a production's time and place. They also helped performers get the feel of a setting or custom, like Zerlina's peasant costume and bonnet. A country bride's arms and hands were bare. Characters with wealth, like Donna Elvira and Donna Anna, were dressed in fine fabrics and wore refinements like scarves, large hats, and gloves. She tried to remember whether Jake's widow Sherice, who played Donna Anna, had worn gloves. She recalled only the character's elegant shawl.

At home she texted Barbara for a favor and in the morning got a text back while she toasted a muffin. Armed with the text, she left for work, but around ten she punched in the number Barbara gave her for the stage manager. The woman answered on the second ring. She was nasty and curt at that hour, but informative. Eleanor thanked her for the service she'd agreed to, and for the costume information.

At the stroke of five, Eleanor left work for the day.

She drove to the theater where a policeman guarded yellow crime scene tape. He remembered seeing Eleanor meeting with Hardy the evening before. After confirming that the stage manager and Hardy were okay with it, the officer let Eleanor go inside. The stage manager had left a door open for her.

Eleanor felt along the walls until she found the hall light switch where the stage manager said it would be. It lit the women's dressing room as well. The rented costumes were suddenly in view. They'd been left in plastic bags to be picked up by a vendor when the investigation was over.

Accessories were still on the actresses' dressing tables—fans, scarves, hats decorated with feathers. And gloves. A pair of long gloves had been tossed on Michelle's table, where there should have been a peasant girl's bonnet.

She called Hardy on her cell phone.

"Yeah," he answered.

"Joe, it's Eleanor Grant."

His tone changed. "What's wrong?"

"I'm in the women's dressing room at the theater. You said I couldn't take anything out of here. But I'm looking at gloves with bloodstains on them."

"Don't touch them until the officer outside joins you—"

"It could be a smudge of rouge—prop gloves get all kinds of things on them."

Someone grabbed her phone. A hand pulled at her hair.

"Give those to me!"

Donna Anna—Sherice Cantrell—had Eleanor by the throat.

Unable to get free, Eleanor kicked at Sherice without luck, but it allowed her to breathe for a moment. The singer was strong and determined and eventually wrestled one glove out of Eleanor's hands. Eleanor saw a chance to strike at Sherice's throat and took it.

"Argh!" Sherice grabbed her own throat to protect it.

Singers.

98

Eleanor ran for the door with the one glove, followed by Sherice. Outside, when the police officer saw her, he dove between Eleanor and her pursuer. By the time Hardy arrived, the officer had Sherice in cuffs in his squad car.

Hardy locked Eleanor in his car to give her time to breathe normally again. She refused to go to the hospital but wanted to talk about Sherice. "She wanted those gloves. Did she kill her husband?"

Hardy shrugged. "We'll wait for the tests on the gloves."

"Jealousy is a terrible thing." Eleanor might have been talking to herself. She was no murderer, though. She rubbed her bruised throat.

Sherice's attorney notified Hardy the next morning that she wanted to make a full confession. Hardy called Eleanor in the evening. "She'd been waiting for an opportunity to return to the theater for her bloodstained gloves. She got her chance when the stage manager left the door unlocked for you, Eleanor. When the night officer replaced the day shift, they chatted with their backs turned and she got inside. But, unlike you, she didn't know where the light switch was for the dressing rooms, and the theater was too dark for her to find the gloves where she'd put them. When you turned on the lights, Sherice hid, until she heard you telling me that you'd found the gloves."

"And she attacked me to get evidence of her crime back."

"She and Jake had a nontraditional marriage," Hardy said. "She'd stopped performing to raise their kids. Donna Anna was her comeback role. They agreed to keep their marriage a secret during the production because she wanted separate names and separate reviews."

"Then Michelle came along," Eleanor said.

"Sherice said nontraditional was easier in theory than watching Jake cat around in rehearsals. When Michelle was onstage, Sherice texted Jake from Michelle's phone, asking him to meet her backstage left where no one would see them."

"I bet I know the ending," Eleanor said. "In the dark backstage, Jake thought he was whispering sweet nothings to Michelle, only he had his wife in his arms."

"That's exactly what she told me. She threw her gloved arms around him, begging him to leave Michelle behind. He drew back, and she saw the glint of the sword."

"The switched-identities thing is straight out of Mozart's *Marriage of Figaro*," Eleanor said. "Opera's getting too real. I'll stick to my jail job."

The following week, Lewis and Eleanor tried out a salad bar restaurant in town. Dinner was relaxing after all the tension of a murder mystery.

Eleanor waved her hands around to convey to Lewis the theatrical text message Sherice used to lured Jake over to stage left after the show. "And she said she kissed him just before she killed him."

"*Otello*, Act Four," Lew jumped in. "Divas."

Eleanor hadn't ever asked Hardy why Lew was a question mark on his whiteboard. Maybe she'd ask Lewis, but not tonight. She tasted her sweetheart's feta and eggplant salad, and he offered up bites of tuna sushi on frisée lettuce with lemon dressing. Background Muzak came as a welcome relief to both of them.

Eleanor buttered a slice of French bread. "Sherice and Jake were leaving for home after the show. She hoped to shame him into dropping his affair with Michelle before they got back to New York where it might continue."

"And when he expressed his love for her rival, she lost it."

Eleanor asked a waitress for ice water before she answered. "Right. Then the police frisked the whole cast and she had to get rid of the bloodstained gloves. She threw them into the clutter on Michelle's table. Somehow the police ignored them in their costume sweep. She was feeling around in the dark for them when I threw on the lights, forcing her to hide until I left."

The waitress brought water, one Black Forest cake to share, and two spoons.

"Then she heard you tell Hardy you'd found her bloodstained gloves." Lew reached for Eleanor's hand. "She could have killed you. I could kick myself for telling that detective you liked murder mysteries."

"Blood spatter and lipstick," Eleanor said. "Hard to get out." She sighed. "Ahh. This cake is delicious."

Later, parked in her driveway, they looked up at an enchanting harvest moon. Lewis pulled a box with a ring in it out of his jacket pocket and asked if he could put the ring on her finger.

"Wait," Eleanor said. She put her hand on his.

"Be my wife," Lewis said. "I love you, Eleanor. And you love me."

"Why now?" Eleanor said. She still didn't know why Hardy suspected Lew of knowing something about Jake's death, or if it had to do with the charms of Michelle Frazier.

"If not now, when?" Lewis asked. "You held off when we were twenty. Without you, I nearly died of loneliness. I gave up music for a while and joined the Navy. Too many wasted years. I'll be thirty-nine soon. Ellie, you and I are meant to be."

"What about the way you looked at Michelle, Lew? You looked at her the same way...the way you looked at me when we first met."

Lewis didn't let bucket seats stop him from tenderly reaching for her. He tried to kiss her but recalling that look caused Eleanor's jealousy to flare up again. "You always did like new works, Lewis." *Ugh. Now he's seen the real me.*

"I was looking at her because she reminded me of someone."

"Who?"

He sighed and put his hands on the wheel. "You, at nineteen. Beautiful, full of energy and enthusiasm, and...joy. That's what she brought back. And I couldn't believe I'd let us deteriorate into this bland friends-with-benefits thing."

Her heart softened. "I don't want a ring because you remember me when."

They sat in silence until she knew what she did want from him. She took his warm hand in hers.

"Get back to me with that ring when you're desperate for Eleanor now, not Eleanor once upon a time." She kissed his cheek. "'I sang the '*La ci darem la mano*' duet in a workshop performance once." She sang the English translation for him. "'There I'll give you my hand, there I'll say yes. See? It is not far.' And I'm glad you sent the detective work my way even when you knew it would distract me from being with you. That was generous."

"It killed me to let that handsome detective near you." He put the ring back in his pocket.

"He's probably tone deaf, Lew," she said. "What's a duet if one of the parties can't make music?"

Shaggy Dog, Shaggy Puppy
Bonnie Olsen

I eased myself onto a kitchen chair. "What you got cooking there, Sweetpea?"

She gave me one of her *isn't it obvious?* looks. "Cookies, Grandpa. Want a cup of coffee?"

I'm a decrepit old man with aches in every joint of my body; I always want a cup of coffee. "So why the cookie-making? Nothing to do with Girl Scouts, I'm guessing."

She handed me a brimful cup. "Nope, raising money for our local chapter of SinCPYS."

I took a sip—weak, but drinkable. She'd been learning to make the brew but wasn't allowed to drink it yet. "Okay, Sweetpea, I'll bite. What's SinCPYS?"

"Stands for Sisters in Crime's Pesky Younger Siblings."

"And you like this pesky sisters group?"

She moved the coffeepot to where I could more easily reach it and plugged it in. Thoughtful child.

"Do I like the SinCPYS, Grandpa? Heck yes. We learn all about crime and detection and drugs and things." She made sure the pot was switched on. "Get this, Grandpa, last week we learned the four classifications of illegal drugs." She counted them off on her fingers. "Uppers, downers, opiates, and hallucinogens."

I took another sip. "And you're raising money for what, dare I ask?"

"Field trip to the body farm in Tennessee—see how corpses rot. We already got the tickets—fly out and back out of JFK—but we need spending money for when we're there."

I had to ask. "This isn't another of your shaggy dogs, is it?" Shaggy dog stories are a specialty of hers—learned, of course, from the master, yours truly. Now, a shaggy dog story isn't just any drawn-out tale. You have to lure your victim in, fascinate him, tantalize him, meander through countless details, some of which are relevant, some not, and throughout this whole long story, you can't once lose your listener's attention. At the very end, you usually give your tale a crashing anticlimax—and your listener realizes he's been suckered.

There's not many can pull off a really good shaggy dog. My granddaughter's got pretty darn good at it, but I'm still the champ.

As if she just now needed to hunt for something cold, my granddaughter stuck her head deep into the refrigerator. "Tell *you* a shaggy dog, Grandpa? I wouldn't dare."

This SinCPYS *was* one of her shaggy dogs—or would be if one smart Grandpa didn't head her off at the pass. The thing about my shaggy dogs is, I'm an old man with a colorful past, so the stories I tell are—or could be—true.

I took another sip of weak-ish coffee. "I ever tell you, Sweetpea, about the time I got sent to JFK, 'Go pick up your cousin and stay out of trouble'?"

She unwrapped a cube of butter, dumped it into her mixing bowl, and discarded the wrapper into the under-sink garbage pail. Then she picked up a spoon and started mashing the heck out of that stick of butter. Her bowl was the right size, but her spoon was way too small. I know quite a lot about cookie-baking, having loved to watch my mother back in the day, rest her sweet soul.

"Go pick up your cousin and stay out of trouble? Not that I remember."

I took another sip, and Sweetpea kept mashing her stick of

butter. I had her nibbling my bait, but not hooked—yet. "So, my cousin was due in at 3:40—"

She stopped mashing. "A.M.?"

"P.M."

She started mashing again, indifferent, yet attentive.

"And he wasn't the first passenger off the plane, but he wasn't the last, and when he got closer, I could see he looked like death warmed over..."

She kept on mashing. "Like what?"

"Dull gray pallor, honey, red-rimmed eyes, shaking hands..."

"Like he was on uppers?"

She was hooked, by golly, hooked! "Well honey, uppers is exactly what I thought, so when my cousin and I got to the luggage carousel, I wasn't at all surprised when he walked right by it, because I'd already noticed he was wearing a knapsack—"

"They call them backpacks nowadays, Grandpa." Her mashing had got slower, an unconscious routine.

"—though when he left, he'd been pulling his mother's powder blue roll-along—"

"With the leather strap and wonky wheel?"

"The very one. But I didn't say anything, because I was pretty sure..."

She looked up. "Sure that he was carrying drugs, right? Because with a backpack, you just board the plane wearing it and shove your backpack under the seat, no questions asked."

"Right." I took a sip of coffee. Thank you, SinCPYS. "One way to steer clear of the narcs."

"Narcotics investigators, Grandpa." She'd given up on mashing, and now was digging cupfuls of sugar out of a canister and dumping them onto her mashed-up butter. One, two, three— these were going to be some awfully sweet cookies—four...this cookie-making project of hers was a disaster waiting to happen. I couldn't look away...five, six.

I took another sip of coffee. "So there I was, following my cousin and his knapsack through that crazy maze of JFK, and after a while, I realized that my cousin wasn't heading for the subway like any regular New Yorker." Now she was dumping the sugar—at least whatever sugar wasn't firmly stuck to her mashed-up butter—out of her bowl and into the sink. My mother's cookie-baking talents sure didn't run in the family.

My less-talented granddaughter brought her mostly sugar-free bowl back to the counter. "So your cousin wasn't headed for the subway. Go on."

I helped myself to fresh coffee, plenty left in the pot. "My cousin was headed for the taxi stand, and I was thinking, *one thing's for sure, I am* not *paying for any airport taxi*, when he walked right past the waiting taxis and slid into a shiny black limousine. 'Go pick up your cousin,' they'd told me, 'and stay out of trouble.' Well, my cousin didn't need picking up, and those shady drug dealers who'd sent this limousine were for sure getting us into trouble. But all I could do was slide in too."

She started measuring sugar again, only two cups this time, thank goodness.

I took another sip. "So there we were, riding along, and I kept checking to see if our limousine was being followed, and the limousine driver kept checking too, and my cousin was playing it cool, but *too* cool, if you know what I mean."

"Except he's shaking."

"Except he's shaking. And then I realized, this limousine wasn't taking us back to town, but out to the suburbs, and Sweetpea, you know how your grandpa feels about the suburbs."

"Yeah, I know. Fish out of water."

"We had to be headed for some shady illegal handoff, maybe something worse, but when the limousine got to where all the houses were small and clean like the pictures in Dick and Jane—"

"Like *what*, Grandpa?"

"—all I could do was follow my cousin across the lawn to this house with flowerpots all around. Some pots had red geraniums, some white, but my cousin headed straight for the only pot with flowers striped red *and* white. He took a key from under it, and..."

She broke two eggs into her butter, mashed them up with too much sugar, fished out some shards of eggshell, and flipped them into the under-sink garbage pail. "Okay, so your cousin knows this place."

"Or he knows about it. Anyway, I checked around to see if the neighbors were watching, and of course they *were* watching, had to be, probably dialing 911 already."

She fished out one more shard of eggshell. "I would too, Grandpa. I mean, even without drugs. In a neighborhood like that, big black limousine, couple of nervous-looking city boys, it's got to look suspicious."

"The limousine had already driven off, but my cousin, cool as a cucumber—"

"—except for the shaking—"

"—opened the door, and I couldn't think of a thing to do but follow him into..." I took a long, steady pull from my cup of coffee.

"Into *what*, Grandpa?"

"Into a perfectly empty house."

"Oh." She started beating the eggs into her mashed-up butter and too much sugar. Both eggs. My mother had always beat eggs in one at a time.

I set down my cup. "Except this house wasn't *perfectly* empty, because rugs and carpets were everywhere: on the floors, on the walls, over the windows, tacked to the doors, everywhere."

My granddaughter's tone was pure condescension. "That would be soundproofing, Grandpa, nothing illegal about soundproofing—though," and here her tone turned hopeful, "though, I guess there *could* still be drugs."

I tried not to smile. "Anyway, I knew my cousin, and I could tell he wasn't happy about something, because he started mumbling under his breath and racing around this crazy carpet-house, opening carpet-covered doors to room after room, looking in, then racing to the next room, and now his mumbling was getting louder, not in any language I knew, and I started trying to remember the first aid for overdose—"

"You keep the victim warm, Grandpa." She got out a second bowl, a sifter, and a canister of flour.

"So he's still running around the house, and knowing this cousin the way I did, I could guess what he was looking for, and me, I was wishing I could just keep out of trouble like I'd promised, and then he opened the very last door at the end of the very last hallway, looked in, and…" I took a judicious sip.

"So he'd found the drugs?" She was scooping from the canister, one, two…

"His mumbling stopped, so I looked into the room too, and what I saw was…" I took very, very long pull of coffee.

She stopped scooping and turned. "You saw *what*, Grandpa?" I swear, she looked ready to dump that flour over my head.

"Boxes," I told her quickly. "Boxes is what I saw, Sugarplum." I tried for a restorative sip of coffee but found my cup strangely empty. I helped myself to a refill. "So this whole room was packed full of big cardboard boxes, like the kind kids use for building forts. But of course my cousin wasn't building forts, and I was pretty sure simple cardboard boxes wouldn't be good for shipping drugs."

She scooped another couple of scoopfuls into her sifter. Three, four…"Because of sniffer dogs?"

"And by now, my cousin's hands were shaking so bad, he couldn't open the yolk on a fried egg, so I opened the nearest, biggest box myself, and I couldn't be more surprised when I saw…" Coffee-sipping time again.

My sweet little granddaughter threatened me with a flour sifter. "Saw *what*, for Pete's sake!"

I leaned away from the sifter. "It was the big bass drum from this drum set he'd had back in high school days when me and this cousin and a couple other guys were on our way to being the next greatest rock-and-roll band in teenage history."

"The Bushpokers?"

"No, that was later. So I helped my cousin unbox his entire set and carry it into the living room where I arranged it like he said, the bass here, the snare, the cow bells, the sleigh bells, the wood blocks, the first tom, the second tom, the high-hat, and then I noticed—"

"The Muffinthumpers?"

"We did come up with some wild names in those days, but no. What I noticed is that he wasn't setting up in the middle of the room, but off to one side, as if he expected our old bandmates to show up and—"

"The Pussybumpers?"

"—and then there was a knock on the front door and right after it, another knock on the back door, and I wasn't surprised because of all those neighbors and their 911 calls."

"That was fast."

"I was sure it was the cops, but my cousin just told me to go ahead and open the back door, and I looked over at that knapsack he'd left in a corner, right out where anyone could spot it, and so far as I was concerned, opening the back door, any door, was the last thing I wanted to do, not after I'd promised to keep out of trouble. What I really wanted to do was go hide in a closet."

Now she was measuring spoonfuls of assorted non-flour ingredients into her sifter, seemingly careless of which spoons she used or how many spoonfuls of what. "Oh, Grandpa, it wouldn't do any good to hide in a closet, not if it's cops. I mean, cops have these ram things and hydraulic door blasters and—"

"But I went ahead and opened the door, and in walked two fat Eskimos."

She looked up. "You're kidding."

"And when I turned around, I saw that my cousin had let two other fat Eskimos in through the front door."

She started sifting her floury concoction into the butter and eggs bowl. "We say Inuit now, Grandpa."

I took a sip of coffee to show that I understood about saying

Inuit.

"What then?"

"So then my cousin, calm as could be, he tells me to go get chairs from the garage."

She tapped her sifter as if to clean it and returned it—unwashed—to its place in the cupboard. "So that's what you did? There's a bunch of strange Inuits in the house, and you went to go get chairs from the garage?"

I shrugged. "It was one of those attached garages, which, being a city boy, I'd never seen before and thought was awfully nifty—"

"Grandpa, nobody says 'nifty' anymore."

"But for the life of me, I couldn't find the light switch, and there I was, bumbling around in the gloom, and it took a while, but I finally discovered this card table all folded up and leaning against a wall, spider webs and everything, and I figured it had to be part of a set, folding table with folding chairs you know, and those chairs were just bound to be..." I refilled my cup that didn't really need refilling.

"And?" She was beating that dough to death.

I gave another shrug. "And then I found the chairs."

"That's it?" She disappeared for a while, crashing around in a lower cupboard, then emerged with two battered old cookie sheets I remembered from my mother.

Oh, how small things from the past do hit us. I had to take a good long sip of coffee and not, this time, for dramatic effect.

I cleared my throat. "By the time I showed up lugging those chairs, sure enough, a drugs deal *was* going down, my cousin dispensing pills from his knapsack, taking in wads of cash, and helping himself to the goods—more than once—but that was the least of my worries."

My granddaughter spoke from under the kitchen sink, and I knew why. She'd be rummaging through the garbage pail for that butter wrapper she'd discarded. Mother had always greased her cookie sheets with butter wrappers.

Sweetpea's voice came out muffled. "How on earth can that be the least of your worries?"

I wondered if she'd remembered to preheat the oven. "It was the least of my worries, because those Eskimos had removed their disguises."

Sweetpea stood, garbage-y butter wrapper in hand, and set to smearing it over my mother's nice, clean cookie sheets. "I never thought they were Eskimos, Grandpa."

Now she was gouging out spoonfuls of dough and depositing them onto the garbage-greased cookie sheets. I had to take a breath to refocus. There.

"I looked and looked again, and then the Eskimo-used-to-be's started talking, and I knew those voices and I knew those accents, pure Liverpudlian, and..."

She ducked down out of sight again to slip her sheet of maybe-cookies into the oven. Then she stood tall and turned to face me, hands on hips. "You're telling me, Grandpa, the Beatles and your cousin had some kind of secret drugs meeting way out in mildest suburbia?"

"Not exactly the Beatles."

"What exactly do you mean by 'not exactly'?"

"Well, there was John—"

"He was still alive then?"

"Obviously. And Yoko, and George and Paul."

"But not Ringo."

"Not Ringo. And I was trying to peel back a corner of window-carpet so I could see if Ringo was coming, when I was just about blasted off my feet by one heck of a guitar chord with the amp turned high."

"Where'd the guitar come from and the amp?"

"I wasn't worried about that, because I'd just realized what was going down, and it wasn't only a drugs deal."

"But you saw—"

"—what I'd seen was Yoko and the others paying for drugs, sure, but what was really going down was an audition. You know how Yoko—"

"How it's Yoko's fault the Beatles broke up. Yes, Grandpa, everyone knows that."

"But it *wasn't* Yoko's fault."

"No?"

"No. Because what I now realized was, the problem had to be Ringo. In fact, Yoko was as eager as anyone to keep the band going."

"And your cousin was auditioning to become the Beatles' next drummer?"

"Right. And I was worried because—"

"Because your cousin wasn't all that good?"

"Oh, he was better than good."

"Okay then, you were worried because of those drugs he took?"

"Not just any drugs, Sweetpea."

She gave me that look. "So what was it, Grandpa? Beans? Blue Boys? Babydolls?"

Thank you, SinCPYS. "Back in the day, what we called it was creamed spinach."

"Yuck."

Oh, how I love it when she gives me that yuck face. "I know. And I was worried because I remembered what happened back in the day with the Beaverticklers, and—"

"And?"

"And I noticed that John, Paul, George, even Yoko, they were all looking happy and hopeful, like not only had they got a maybe-good-enough drummer to replace Ringo, but they'd also discovered this brand-new drug."

"And you were worried because the Beatles might fall prey to this creamed spinach stuff?"

"That didn't matter."

She turned her back, pretending to be loading the dishwasher, pretending she didn't care.

"It didn't matter, because the minute they started playing,

my cousin started in doing what he'd always done whenever he played amped up on spinach, that same darn thing he used to do with the Snatchcatchers."

She fit another dish into the washer. "I thought it was the Beaverticklers."

"You want to hear this or not?"

"Yes!"

"Okay. Do you remember what I unpacked from the boxes: the bass, the snare, the toms, the high-hat—"

"—the cow bells, the sleigh bells, the wood blocks."

"Right." I took a last sip. "And back in the old Snatchcatcher days, my amped-up cousin just couldn't lay off the sleigh bells."

"So?"

"So, Sweetpea, there's just no sleigh bells in rock and roll."

She looked at me, head cocked, an *is that really true, Grandpa?* expression on her face.

"Gotcha!"

We were still laughing and pointing the way we do whenever one of us has entrapped the other in a shaggy dog, when the oven timer buzzed—surely too soon—and she withdrew from the oven...and set before me...my mother's three-tiered, ivy-patterned serving dish. And there on each tier lay a cluster of perfectly baked, golden yellow, sugar-butter cookies, baked, no doubt, according to my sainted mother's recipe. They must have been hidden in the oven until just this moment.

"Gotcha, Grandpa."

She'd said she wouldn't dream of telling a shaggy dog, and she hadn't. She'd *acted* one. From that first cube of butter, she'd lured me in, and then, no matter what she'd done or how off-base it was, I hadn't once been able to look away.

Cookies on a dish, or just no sleigh bells in rock and roll—either tale was a winner.

This time, I poured out *two* cups of coffee: one for me, and one for my Sweetpea. She'd earned it.

Delilah
Kari Wainwright

Poor Tom Jones: Delilah was his woman, but she was bad for him, *and* she was a hussy.

I met the Delilah in my life at The Come-Hither Bar, a country-western saloon I passed every day on my way to work at a new job in a new town. Friday night rolled around, and it was time to see what the local environment had to offer.

Delilah wore a bright red off-the-shoulder peasant blouse and the tightest black leather pants I'd ever seen. I wore a totally stunned expression on my face.

She laughed at something the bartender said, then turned and saw me. Her flashing dark eyes beckoned, but I resisted. Why would such a gorgeous woman want me?

When this beauty on a barstool crooked a finger at me, it might as well have been a fishhook with a brightly colored lure. I pointed to my chest to make sure she meant me. She nodded. I wove through the dancers doing the scooty-boot, or whatever, and took a seat next to her.

She held out her hand. "My name's Delilah," she said in a husky whisper, so that I had to lean in closer to hear her. "What's yours, big guy?"

"Harry," I stammered.

"I don't think I've seen you here before, Harry."

"I just moved into town, and I'm learning my way around."

She swung her long black hair in a feathery arc. "You've come to the right person. I definitely know my way around."

My breath caught, first in my lungs, then my throat—until I forced it out my nose in one long exhale.

A woman like this was normally out of my league. I was tall and lean, but certainly not hunk material. I wasn't ugly, but I'd been told that my facial features were as bland as vanilla ice cream. At one point I grew a mustache and thought it added a dash of panache, but my then-girlfriend didn't like it, so I shaved it off. A week later, she ran off with an artist with a full beard. I should have dumped her instead of my mustache. Something to remember for next time.

Delilah wrapped a crimson-tipped hand around my arm and pulled me closer until I could smell the perfumed scent of her shampoo. I no longer cared what she saw in me. I was too busy becoming entangled in her web of beauty.

The bartender rapped on the wooden bar to get my attention, but Delilah silenced him with a glance and a glare. "You don't need to drink *here*, Harry. We can go to my place."

How could I refuse? *Why* would I refuse?

I started to lead her outside when the bartender said, "That'll be eighteen bucks, my friend. Delilah never pays for her own drinks." I flung a twenty on the bar and walked out with my prize.

Once in the parking lot, she brushed a wisp of a kiss on my lips. "Thanks for picking up my tab."

I couldn't answer through my tingling lips.

"Which one is your car?" she asked.

I pointed to my green Subaru. Would she think that too pedestrian? "Do you have a car here?"

She shook her head. "A friend dropped me off but couldn't stay." She studied the parking lot as if expecting somebody. When a black SUV turned into the lot, she grabbed my arm and pulled me toward my car. "Let's go."

I didn't hesitate. After we were buckled in, Delilah sank

down in her seat and told me to hit the gas. As we exited the parking lot, she gave me her address and directions.

Searching my mind for something captivating to say, I asked, "What do you do for a living?" Sigh! I was no Cyrano de Bergerac.

"A little of this, a little of that," she said with a vague smile. "And what do you do in town, new guy?"

"I'm the office manager of the Wakefield Medical Center. It's quite an advancement in my career. And now I can help my mother with some of her assisted living needs." I glanced at her. She busied herself twirling a curl of her hair. Probably bored. "I suppose that's more information than you wanted to know."

"Is the center the one near the mall?"

"That's it."

"Now I know where to go if I get hurt." She directed me to turn right into an apartment complex lot.

Her apartment was on the ground floor. I barely had time to look around before she pulled me to her. She placed her hands on my shoulders and stood on tiptoe to offer me a fiery kiss that sent flames dancing throughout my body. My finger in a socket couldn't have been more electrifying.

As my hands tangled in her glorious hair, a car, its lights on bright, pulled into a parking space outside her window and momentarily blinded me. I felt relief when the headlights shut off.

The intrusion made me think of a song my dad used to sing—"Delilah" by Tom Jones. In the tune, Delilah was Tom Jones's woman, but she done him wrong with another man. He found out when he passed her house one night and saw shadows on the window blind. They flickered, doing the dance of love. It hadn't ended well.

Delilah pulled herself from my embrace and lowered the window shade. "Now, where were we?"

I forgot about the song and returned to her embrace.

A few minutes later, we heard the car leave. She gentled herself out of my arms and straightened her blouse. "Harry darling, I am so sorry, but I just remembered an appointment I have in the morning. Would you be a dear and go now?"

Dazed and flustered, I sputtered, "But will I see you again?"

She caressed my face with her soft hand. "Of course, Harry. Come to the bar this Friday night. We'll get a booth in the back and make out like crazy." Then she hustled me out the door as if I were stale bread. With mold on it.

Friday was three days away, but the way I felt, it might as well have been three years. One moment I was flushed with excitement about seeing Delilah again. The next, I remembered the way she ushered me out of her apartment like a whipped dog, one that had been rejected by his favorite bitch in heat.

Damn the woman!

Still, Friday night started with a shower, a shave, and a splash of my muskiest cologne. Then came new jeans and a new cowboy shirt, complete with horses galloping around my chest and back. I still needed to buy boots if I was going to continue drinking at that saloon.

I arrived early, but the parking lot was already three-quarters packed. Smoothing back my hair, I walked across the lot, taking deep breaths with every stride. The door swung open, surprising me, and a couple exited the bar, wrapped up in each other's eyes and arms.

I looked at the bar area. No Delilah. Studied the dancers and didn't see her weaving across the floor. Red vinyl booths held no dark-haired beauty. I took a barstool facing the door and nursed a Budweiser.

Until it was gone.

After an hour I decided she was worth one more slow beer.

About halfway through my drink, there she stood, silhouetted in the doorway. Wearing a hot pink top over ripped jeans. All that tawny flesh peeking through made me want to howl like a wolf, then rip those jeans right off her.

I staggered off my stool, more drunk with lust than I was with booze.

Delilah slipped her arm around my waist, and we found an empty booth near the restrooms. I didn't care about the location. Any place with this gorgeous woman next to me was paradise.

She drank vodka tonics; I consumed more frothy mugs of beer. My arm around her shoulders, I stared into her glittering eyes that sparked even more desire in me. She wrapped her hand around the side of my neck and drew me into an intense kiss. Heaven!

With a jolt, I was yanked from the Promised Land by a huge hand and thrown onto the floor of the Come-Hither Bar. A bulky barbarian loomed over me.

"Get your hands off my woman, you scumbag."

"Anton," Delilah crooned as she edged out of the booth and sidled up to him. "He's just a friend. Don't hurt him."

"Is he the same friend from the other night—the one I saw at your place?"

Oh my god. Was I one of the shadows on the blind in the Tom Jones song?

"What were you doing there?" she asked. "Spying on me?"

"Apparently you need to be spied on, woman. Why were you kissing this so-called friend?"

"*You* kissed my friend Elise."

I struggled to my feet. I wanted to get the hell out of here. Just like the song, this wasn't going to end well.

It didn't. The brute's fist broke my nose with a painful crunch, slamming me backward to the hard floor. Mercifully, that knocked me out, and I didn't remember the rest of the beating or the ambulance ride.

I woke up later in the ER of the Wakefield Medical Center. As I studied the faces surrounding me through one less-swollen eye, I realized I knew most of these people. They were my coworkers. I felt mortified. I recalled the smug look on Delilah's face as she snuggled up to the barbarian's side. I had simply been her tool to make Anton jealous.

I'd been humiliated by her manipulation, humiliated by the brute's strength, and now humiliated by the pity of my cohorts. Anger arose in me like lava in a dormant volcano exploding to life. The lava overflowed when my boss strode into the room. He questioned a nurse, then came closer to study my damaged face.

Then he fired me. For hurting the reputation of the medical center because I got into a drunken brawl.

Delilah would pay for this!

I spent the weekend at home, worried about being unemployed while nursing my wounds and my pride. I wasn't sure which hurt more. Until I got a phone call from Delilah. Then I knew it was pride.

"I'm so sorry that Anton assaulted you," she said. "How are you?"

Right. As if Anton's attack wasn't just what she wanted. I was so stunned, my voice croaked out an answer, "Peachy keen."

"I know that's not true. I've been hit by Anton, and I know how much damage his jackhammer fist can cause."

"Then why do you stay with him?"

"I love him," she said, as if it should be obvious.

I knew very little about battered women, but I did know how Delilah had treated me. "To me, it's stupid to stay with a guy like him when you could have a decent man who loves you and doesn't beat you."

"You mean like you?"

"Yes," I said. "Like me. And yet, you've treated me like dirt."

"I'm sorry, but you just aren't my type."

"I was good enough for you to use me," I said. "You purposely led Anton on until he was ready to kill me. I was your pawn. And I don't see the need for this call."

She started to say "sorry" again, but I interrupted her. "I don't want an apology from you. Because of you, I lost my job." I hung up. She thought she could maneuver me into forgiving her? No way. I'd been enslaved by her, but I was no longer going to be her puppet man.

No woman was ever going to use me again. No more Mr. Nice Guy, no sir.

On Monday, I felt lost. No job to go to. But even with my pain, I was too restless to stay at home.

I drove to the parking lot for the trailhead of a rugged mountain path. I'd heard about the Lone Wolf Trail, a difficult footpath that ended with a glorious view of the valley below. I wanted to see if it would serve my purpose.

Even on a weekday, there were other hikers enjoying the spring weather and wildflowers. My bruises were as colorful as the latter but didn't qualify as pretty. Other people on the trail took one look at me and quickly moved on.

At first, the path through the forest was gentle, weaving through the trees. Then it steepened, and rocks littered the trail. The tree-covered mountainside sloped upward on my right, but as the path narrowed, the drop-off on the left rapidly deepened, as did my nervousness. At one point I stopped and hesitantly peeked over the edge. A rushing river ran through the bottom of the ravine, a humming burble of water. Large boulders and sharp rocks lay in wait for the errant misstep of a clumsy hiker. I moved back and hugged the rough mountain, my face plastered to its side. I didn't care if it hurt my injuries; I needed to feel safe.

After several deep breaths, I crept carefully up the trail. Once I reached the top, the vast view of the valley, surrounded by rugged mountains, looked like a postcard. I crawled to the rim and found a different type of view, one that vibrated with danger. Down below was a stronghold of punishing stones. No one could survive landing on them from this height.

I inched back to a rounded boulder, where I sat and pondered my scheme. Alone at the top of the trail, I visualized the terror on Delilah's face when she realized I planned to push her off the edge.

Silence surrounded me now, but in my mind, I heard a terrible scream from Delilah. Yes, this was the way to do it. In the song, Delilah had been stabbed by her lover, but my Delilah merited a worse punishment. After the way she abused me and cost me my job, she deserved to be treated like the garbage she was and tossed away.

How could I lure the vixen to her death? I thought about that every waking moment. The next weekend, I decided to follow her. I caught up with her as she left a nail salon, her talons freshly polished.

She looked up from her smartphone when I blocked her way. Startled, she took a step back. "Oh, you poor dear, your face looks just awful."

My bruises had reached the yellowish-green stage. Not my best colors. "Yeah. Someone used me as a punching bag."

She flinched. She reached out her fingers to touch my face.

My turn to flinch. I drew back as if her touch was toxic, then realized I needed to make her think all was forgiven. Otherwise, I'd never get her up that mountain trail.

"I'm sorry, Delilah. Guess I'm still a bit touchy."

"I understand." She moved as if to go around me.

I blocked her. "I've been thinking. Remember the night we met?"

She nodded.

"I thought you were the most beautiful woman I'd ever met."

That earned a slight smile from her.

I continued. "You promised to show me around. Now, I know you have a man in your life, but my birthday is Friday, and I hoped to spend one last time with you."

Wariness clouded her face.

"Nothing sexual," I promised. "I want to trek up Lone Wolf Trail. I hear there are some gorgeous views from the top. I'd love to see them with you. It would make the day more special."

"And are you saying you want me to go hiking with you?" She looked down at her blinged-out high heels. "Really? This is my usual footwear. I don't even own hiking boots."

"You're the one who said you could show me around." I lightly touched my bruised face. "Plus, I think you owe me a favor. A really big one."

She hesitated, looking conflicted.

I touched her arm. "I'll buy you some shoes." That seemed like a waste of money since they'd only be worn once, but a man's gotta do what a man's gotta do.

"These boots better be the sexiest ones you can find."

I agreed to that, and she finally said okay, as long as she was back by five to get ready for her evening at the Come-Hither Bar.

We made the arrangements, then parted—until next Friday, six days away.

For the next few days, time might as well have been traveling on the back of a tortoise. As Friday grew closer, my doubts increased. Could I really carry through with my plan? And even if my conscience didn't stop me from killing Delilah, what if my scheme didn't work? What if other people were at the top of the trail? There were too many ifs, but not enough to dissuade me from trying. If this didn't work, I would go to plan B. Maybe a sharp knife like the one used in the Tom Jones song. Too bad I couldn't stand the sight of blood.

Thursday night, sleep eluded me, and worry left me in a pool of sweat and dread. I tried to shower it all away. Even clean, I swore I could smell fear oozing from my pores.

Empowering myself with strong coffee, I dressed, packed water, and drove to Delilah's apartment. She wasn't ready, too busy dithering about what jeans to wear. Eventually, she appeared wearing too-tight jeans, too much jewelry and too much makeup. What was the woman thinking? Finally, we made it to the nearest shoe store where she dithered over which boots to get.

Dithering done, we headed to the trailhead. The parking lot was almost empty—probably because a rare, eerie fog had drifted in. It shrouded the trees, turning them into ghostly shadows. I wasn't sure if this was a good thing or a bad thing, but this was going to be my only chance to get Delilah up that trail.

"I'm not sure this is such a good idea," she said.

"It'll be okay," I said. "Most likely, the fog will dissipate as we go higher."

"Dissipate. My, my, aren't we educated."

A snarky dig if ever I heard one. Funny, she didn't feel the need for sarcasm when she was seducing me. All the more reason to hate her.

We headed carefully along the path, enveloped in wet pine scent, the mist separating only a foot or so in front of us. A slew of mountain lions, bears, and wolves could have been waiting for us a few feet away, and we would not have known it.

As the trail started upward, the haze lessened. Thank goodness, because now we could see and avoid the slippery rocks in our path.

We reached the part where the mountain rose on one side and the dangerous drop-off deepened on the other.

"Harry, I don't like this," Delilah said. "And these new shoes hurt my feet."

Oh, please! I wanted to tell her if she'd picked the right size for her stupid feet, the shoes wouldn't be hurting her already. But I didn't think that would further my cause. I held out my hand. "Come on, I bet the view's incredible."

She took the offered hand, and I was disconcerted by the electric frisson of sexuality that surged through my body. I thought about pushing her off here, but wanted to feel her magnetism a little longer, one last time.

Our backs practically melted into the mountainside as we skirted the cliffside and cautiously made our way to the top of the trail. I was ready to distract Delilah with the all-encompassing view, but fog blanketed the valley like a heavy cloak.

"Oh, my," Delilah said in a resounding voice. "There's not much to see, is there?"

"Why are you talking so loudly?"

"To scare away ghosts." She giggled.

"And what if I were to tell you that you're about to become one?" I stood behind her and raised my hands to push.

A huge hand grasped my shoulder. A booming voice vibrated my eardrums. "Don't touch her."

The barbarian, Anton. He must have been waiting for us on the other side of the boulder. Apparently, I wasn't the only one with a plan.

Delilah turned to face me. "Surprise, Harry. Anton decided he wanted you out of our lives." She raised her eyes to mine. "It's so sad. A newcomer to town takes on more than he can handle and falls to his death."

I looked around. I didn't see a way out. But I wasn't going alone.

With Anton still holding my right shoulder, I grasped Delilah's upper arm with my left hand and thrust her toward the precipice. I leaned forward, my equilibrium shifting. Anton's hand left my body, and out of the corner of my eye I saw him reach for Delilah. He grabbed her wrist at the last moment. But the weight of our two bodies as we started to fall was too much for him. The barbarian joined our descent, creating a doomed unholy triad.

This wasn't the ending I'd planned. Now, I wished I'd stuck with Tom Jones's song lyrics and stabbed Delilah to death.

I'd have to remember that for next—

With a Side of Star
Jennifer Lowry

A strong smell of jasmine and cinnamon fills my nostrils. A pipe has an owner. A sadistic someone who's strapped a helpless woman to a captain's chair. It starts to come back to me. Ripples of cognition. Slowly. *Why am I here?*

I try to piece together the timeline. The last moment I remember was walking off stage after one of the best performances of my career at Walnut Creek Stadium. I am still wearing the fishnets and Madonna gloves from my final set. The last call was a throwback 80s tribute to all the talented women that paved the way for me. It was my favorite part of every evening, singing ballads by Ann and Nancy Wilson of Heart.

My head struggles to clear itself from the fog, to remember the journey from the stage and screaming fans to this room, this chair, dazed and paralyzed. My vision blurs, and I blink cobwebs away. I don't recognize this ornate room with rich tapestries and furniture fit for royalty, but clearly someone knows me. On the dark mahogany wall, a screen shows a clip of me, center stage, hair wild and blowing, sequins flashing. Whoever has captured me has a need for me to relive that particular performance. Last spring, a concert in Philadelphia. Was that night the moment when he locked in on me? I remember the costume well. A low-cut Simmons's black leather jumpsuit with white platform boots for a throwback "Rock and Roll All Nite" tribute to

Kiss. I looked amazing, if I might add that observation.

The recorded clip comes to an end and the screen goes black as my memory searches for meaning. What was it about that night? *There you are.* The gift of recognition arrives right on time. My head slightly tilts now, neck waking from a long nap, as I see his portrait on the wall. If I had facial movement, maybe I could smile at this. The fog machine in my mind spurts its last smoke and clears. My captor had been at that spring show. I remember him so vividly. Felt him before I saw him. He stood in the wing of the VIP ticket section, silent, stoic, in a gray pinstriped suit and derby hat. He was a dark stranger who gave me the ultimate creep vibes and set me off on my new exploit.

The presence of darkness rubbed my spirit the wrong way. I had my trusted man find everything there was to know about him. I learned more than I ever bargained for. He was a seeker of youthful vibrance but not to promote. He only served to demolish every dream with his demonic affairs, snatching lives before their time as he evaded the police.

It became my turn to carry out justice behind the veil.

Years on the road caused me to become calloused and desensitized to life's daily pleasures. I had to heighten the thrill. There were new goals before me, a hobby with a vigilante flair. Paparazzi or my crew did not see the work I did in my off time. I could blend into shadows, too. What I did would panic the faint-hearted, but for me, the adrenaline of it was enough to fuel me for moments like this. So close to death. Whose would it be? How will all of this end? I will soon find out and pray I'll be the one left to see the dawn of a new day.

But I'm strapped to a captain's chair, helpless, with my eyes feasting on a full gourmet spread at the dinner table as if this dark stranger is expecting a party.

My phone buzzes. My eyes glance down at the tabletop. Beside the golden place setting, my phone taunts me, but my arms are dead weight at my sides.

Frantic texts from my publicist pop up on my home screen.

Where are you? Why aren't you answering? Return my call or I'll track your whereabouts.

I stare up at his oil portrait. He is a peach, this one. Millions in old money and a name that affords the connections to escape suspicion.

I learned a lot about his masquerades over the past year. How could one lead such a double life? A rich oil tycoon like this fine fellow could be a killer, too? It seemed at odds with the stereotype of having it made, as if no sin could touch the rich. How naive I was, asking why would anyone risk their freedom when they had all that money? Was it not enough? I now know the truth of the matter. Dark is dark and doesn't discriminate.

Those were questions that plagued me until I, too, took on that role. I could live with this new pursuit in secret. I had all the lights, riches, and glory in an inhale, and with an exhale I could wipe out darkness with darkness. I could taste and relish both: the dark and the light. I could have fame and fortune yet slip into shadows and crevices of the night where only the soulless roam. I could do those things to answer the rising passions within me, to fulfill the hunger, the need for quiet justice. Not the loud banging justice of bars and court gavels. Of sentencing. No one would know. I would be sure to keep it that way.

A voice startles me, interrupts my thoughts. I did not hear him enter. "Picture this," he says. "A fine piece of art. You will become part of my collection."

Art...I follow his voice to the long wall to my right and take in the paintings, avoiding his stare. Glass cases line the walls with priceless sculptures, interspersed with jars containing not cookies but body parts—organs, bones, eyes, nameless bits of once-living tissue. I could be touring an exotic museum for the criminally insane, if I could only move, but my legs are twisted unnaturally underneath me. My legs do not work, but my fingers flex, my hands clench. Movement returns to my arms. Perfect timing.

"Tiny finger sandwiches?" I ask, as he approaches the table

and places a silver plate under my nose. He can do better than this. His reputation on the dark web is beyond such quaint pleasantries. He is a vile one, yet with duplicity, delicate in disposition. I know I shouldn't be fooled or drop my guard. He is a criminal and clearly psychotic. I am a hunter. We have set roles. He isn't aware of his part.

I whisper, as helpless as I can force my voice to drop, "What's going on? Why can't I move?"

The gentleman in the fine suit says nothing. He only nods toward the plate. I glance down again, and my eyes focus. My arms are plastered to my side, yet there are no more constraints. Lovely. Is he expecting me to eat this? To gobble like a dog?

Tears sting my eyes. I can fake it easily by now. Years of practice in getting what I want. My body is not in pain, and my emotional state feels strangely in check for the peril I am in. Fear can come at times of uncertainty. This is one of those times, but I don't feel the fear. I see a flash of wonder and curiosity in his eyes. Maybe he smells the light on me, like I feel darkness on him.

I cry, trying to deflect any sense that I am not a victim. "Something's not right. Why can't I move my arms? What have you done to me?"

"Why sound incredulous?" he replies. "It is a miracle I stumbled upon you in the dark, dear. Couldn't let that opportune moment pass me by. Here, have one. It's a delicacy."

My eyes catch his soulless gaze, and no longer am I dizzy. Dark pools of murky waters stare at me. This is exactly what I'd been hoping for. Planned for. It took months to track him. If I wasn't careful, I'd be in the next sandwich.

Not today.

My confidence swells. I give him a small smile. "They'll find you. I'm always tracked. Did you know? Check the phone if you don't believe me. Surely you wouldn't be that stupid."

He lets out a soft chuckle. "Let them try. I have prepared a place for you at my table. Please. You need your strength. Eat before the end. It's satisfying to me when there are contents I love in your stomach. Double the pleasure." He pauses, then takes calculated steps toward me. "Oh, I forgot. Here. Let me feed you, my pet."

I stare at him, refusing to allow time for the fear to settle in. Think. Think of a song. A lyric. Anything. "You Can't Get Me" by Joan Jett would do. Focus on what he won't be able to do. Regardless of his plan. He won't get control. I knew him before he fully knew me. Remember that. It's part of the composition. My song back to the world.

Tingling sensations. I feel them coursing. Slight movements in my thighs. Twitching. Toes thawing out after an ice bath, stretching. *Limit your movements. Don't let on, girl. Hold on. Your time is coming.*

He places the tray down and moves with a grace that would fool the world. He stops by each jar along the wall and gives me a brief rundown of how he's collected either a foot bone or an eyeball or a cranium. How many lives has he taken? Just like this? In this very room. Evil in a suit. I keep him talking. I keep questioning, preying on his narcissistic tendencies. Let him draw out his stories of how he sliced and diced. Let him take center stage for now.

When he returns to my side and is so close I can smell his spearmint breath, I am getting full feeling back. He sees me as a helpless victim. I can see the excitement in his eyes. He is unaware. I am the hunter. He is the prey.

"You will eat this," he says. He opens the sandwich and my stomach lurches. What appears to be skin peelings and knuckle bones are topped with chopped cucumbers. "For you are surface. You are superficial. You will eat parts of others to grow into more of yourself."

Time for the show to begin.

I grab a knife and plunge it into his chest. He slumps forward. Blood pours over the tray, soaking the bread, filling the enormous platter. Easy to clean, though. Just throw it in the dishwasher. Cascade clean.

Just then, my cell rings.

What now? Can't a girl create a new music video without interruption? Could I at least have time to write lyrics or get a catchy line for a chorus?

I answer the phone. "Hello," I say, wiping my hands on his fine linen.

My manager belts, "Have you heard? You've got that nomination for Female of the Year in the bag! How are you going to top last night's performance? You are only as good as your last show."

I speak loudly to cover up the cannibal's gurgles. "I've got an idea for a new album. Working on a thematic concept now. It's a little dark, but I think the fans will expect that of me as I evolve."

My impatient manager demands, "Details."

I laugh. Tickled I will get away with this again. And again. And again. "It's not ready to share. Not yet. Hope you're hungry. I'm getting us a fine piece of filet cut this evening."

I know he'll be as exquisite as his taste in art.

The Twist

Kathy Heady

"I wonder how many of these girls will be pregnant before the end of the year?" Ruby Jenkins asked.

I looked at her, unsure how to respond. Ruby laughed. "You'll see," she said. "Especially now. Look at the way they dress, and the dances and the music. Elvis Presley was bad enough, but now it's only gotten worse. All they do is show off their bodies."

It was my first year of teaching. I had married my high school sweetheart and was back at the school in rural Illinois where I had graduated, teaching junior and senior English and sponsoring the yearbook. The yearbook always attracted the popular crowd, so they could make sure that they were featured prominently. I had not been part of that crowd when I was a student, but now I could enjoy the status of being a teacher.

Ruby looked me up and down. I was dressed much like the high school girls, in a straight plaid skirt and a short-sleeve white mohair sweater. My only concession to adulthood was my short, unteased hair.

Ruby Jenkins had been teaching when I was a student, although I had never had her for a class. She was probably in her early fifties, and she and her husband lived on a farm a few miles outside of town. She had a daughter a few years older than I was, who had gone out of state to college and stayed there, someplace in Ohio, I thought.

I had raised my hand at the faculty meeting to volunteer as a chaperone for the first sock hop of the 1962–63 school year. It was my chance to get to know my students on a friendly basis, not just as teacher and student. The seniors at Jefferson High School were just four years younger than I was, as I had zipped through college at warp speed and graduated in three years.

The sock hop took place in the gym after the first football game of the season. It was a warm September evening, and the home team had won, beating Jerseyville 26–10. I had fallen into step with Ruby Jenkins as we made our way from the football field to the high school gym.

"This is so exciting!" I said.

"You'll get over it," she answered.

A swarm of kids surged around us, talking and laughing. The girls wore skirts and sweaters, many with scarves around their necks. Their hair was teased and sprayed into unmoving helmets. There were boys wearing their letter jackets, although the evening was really too warm for a jacket, and the gym would be even warmer once the dancing started.

"Remember, you are a teacher, not a student," Ruby said to me in that superior way she had. I didn't know if she was trying to be helpful or insulting. Then she quickened her stride to walk ahead, calling out to students as she went. "Form a line please. No cutting. If you want to get in, you must follow the rules."

I lost track of Ruby as we crowded into the gym. Orange and blue streamers, our school colors, festooned the doorways and hung from the basketball hoops. A couple of boys had a stack of 45 records and a phonograph and were setting up on the stage. Soon Rick Nelson was singing "Hello Mary Lou." Someone called out, "Play something we can dance to!" "Hello Mary Lou" ended abruptly, and Chubby Checker came on. Students jumped to their feet and gyrated to the twist.

The dance floor was soon crowded. I could see Ruby Jenkins on the other side of the gym, standing with another older teacher. The disapproval on Ruby's face was obvious. Clearly, dancing the twist was a sure route to teen pregnancy.

"Mrs. Garrett, are you going to dance?" Lenora Connelly from one of my junior English classes smiled up at me. She was only about five feet tall, but the top of her dark hair was teased to add at least two inches of height.

I returned her smile. "I'll dance if Mrs. Jenkins does." I glanced over where the other two teachers stood, studying the crowd for any misbehavior.

"Ha!" Lenora laughed. "You know that will never happen!" She moved away with her friends.

I circulated around my side of the gym, avoiding Ruby Jenkins. I spoke with another teacher I knew slightly and made small talk with some of the students. The music warmed up the room as they danced to "Quarter to Three," "Blue Moon," "Who Put the Bomp?," "The Twist," and "Let's Twist Again." After an hour or so, the disc jockeys put on some slow songs, and the romantic couples took the floor. The Lettermen were crooning "The Way You Look Tonight," and I was wishing my husband was there to dance with me, when Mr. Parnell, the principal, came up to me.

"Mrs. Garrett," he said. "Would you do me a favor? It's time to start serving the refreshments and Mrs. Jenkins usually takes charge of that. I haven't seen her in a while. Would you mind seeing if she's in the ladies' room?"

I knew she wouldn't be in the student restroom, which was crowded with gossiping girls and air thick with hair spray. I checked the faculty restroom on the second floor. No Mrs. Jenkins. I saw someone in the distance down the corridor by the library, but just caught a glimpse of the swirl of a teal blue skirt. Definitely not Mrs. Jenkins.

Then, outside the faculty lounge, I saw broken 45 records scattered on the floor, along with a long strand of teal blue angora yarn. The girls who were going steady wore angora yarn to hold their boyfriends' rings in place on their fingers. Without thinking, I picked up the yarn and put it in the pocket of my skirt. Taking a deep breath, I pushed the door open to the faculty lounge. Ruby Jenkins lay sprawled on the floor, her legs unglamorously splayed, exposing her garter belt. Her eyes were open and unmoving, and her head lay in a pool of blood. I backed out of the door, running right into Mr. Parnell.

"Did you find her?" he asked.

I shoved him out of the way and vomited into a nearby trash can. Wiping my mouth inefficiently with the back of my hand, I turned around. Mr. Parnell and a couple of senior boys were staring at me. "She's..." I pointed to the faculty lounge door. The three of them continued to stare at me, the new teacher with vomit on the front of her fuzzy sweater. I'm sure they thought I had been drinking.

After a moment, Mr. Parnell pulled his gaze away from me and pushed open the faculty lounge door. "Oh, my God!" The boys started to follow him in, but I had the presence of mind to tell them to wait.

Mr. Parnell ended the sock hop. The students were told there had been an accident, and everyone had to go home. But word soon got around that the "accident" had something to do with Mrs. Jenkins...and me. And as the police and ambulance arrived just as the students were clearing out of the gym, it was obvious to everyone that it was a serious accident.

Monday was a somber school day. The students knew that I had found Mrs. Jenkins, but everything else was speculation. When the yearbook group came in at the end of the day, all that was on their minds was what kind of a memorial should appear in the yearbook. Mrs. Jenkins had not been a popular teacher. Her classroom standards were high, and she made no exceptions. She had once had a very popular junior boy suspended for chewing gum. The students' jokes were cruel, and I didn't have the energy to deal with them.

I was in my car five minutes after the school day ended. My husband and I lived in a newly built ranch-style house on the edge of town, and I was home changing into jeans and a sweatshirt in ten minutes. I collapsed on the sofa with a Coke, and was sitting there, minus the Coke, two hours later when Jack arrived home. He took one look at me and said, "I'll go pick up some burgers from the Dog and Suds, and then you're going to bed." No argument from me. He was a good man.

When I arrived at school the next morning, the door to the guidance counselor's office was open. The office had been turned into a temporary faculty lounge since the room upstairs was still a crime scene. Cigarette smoke drifted out of the open door, and I heard subdued conversation and an occasional bark of laughter. I reached the door as another new teacher was coming out, her eyes wide and clearly eager to share news. "You heard what happened?" she said.

I shook my head.

"Lenora Connelly—in the junior class? always has a book in her hand?—the police called her in for questioning. Someone saw her in the hallway by the faculty lounge that night."

She started to say something else, but students were pouring in the front door as the first buses arrived, and we could tell from the buzz of conversation that they knew about Lenora.

Again, my answer to the students' questions all day long consisted of "I don't know" and "I have no idea." I announced a quiz for the next day. The juniors were reading *Macbeth,* and the seniors were finishing *The Scarlet Letter.* I could easily come up with a few questions to keep them on their toes, and maybe distract them a little with literary murder.

The yearbook group shuffled in last period, half of them after the bell rang. There were eight girls and two boys in the class, and they lounged in the chairs and perched on the tables and desks, eager to chat.

"My dad says someone strangled her," a husky senior boy in the back announced. "He's friends with the sheriff."

"Who do you think will get killed next, Mrs. Garrett?" The question came from Jake Eisley, who sat on the arm of the only easy chair in the room, which was occupied by a blond girl who spent most of the class period adjusting her hair and checking her lipstick in her compact mirror.

"I hope no one," I answered. I took a deep breath. I wanted to teach, not deal with a murder.

"I heard there were broken records scattered in the hallway," added Joanne Bauer. Joanne was popular, probably because she was pretty with dark brown hair, short like mine, and green eyes, but she kept to herself. Word was that she had a boyfriend in the Air Force, and she seemed to be always writing letters to him.

"Maybe that's because she sounded like a broken record when she droned on and on in class," Jake interrupted, meriting a laugh from the rest of the class.

Joanne glared at him and continued, "Mrs. Jenkins hated rock and roll." She looked over at the usually talkative Mike Henderson. "What's wrong, Mike? Betty Lou giving you a hard time? I saw her crying again this morning."

Mike looked up. "Aw, she's just mad because I can't see her this week. She knows I have to help my dad get the soybeans in after school. It's that time of year."

Lenora Connelly came into my classroom just after the bell rang, and her serious face told me she wanted to talk. Jake was still gathering his books and seemed in no big hurry to leave. He had a girlfriend, Susan, but he trailed after Lenora like a puppy dog, while she ignored him.

"I think someone in this school knows who killed Mrs. Jenkins," she said to me. She gave Jake a challenging look. "And it wasn't me, and I didn't see anyone in the hallway. I told the police that."

"Who do you think did it?" Jake asked.

"I don't know," Lenora answered. She shifted her armload of books from one side to the other. "But I've got a hunch. My mom isn't picking me up until four, so I'm going to do some investigating."

"Jake, let's go," Susan called from the classroom doorway. "Betty Lou and Mike are waiting for us." And Susan wanted to get her boyfriend away from Lenora, too, I was sure.

"Be careful, Lenora," I said. Whether I was referring to snooping around, or interfering with Susan and Jake's relationship, I left up to her.

The school was closed the day of the funeral. All of the teachers attended, and a fair number of students. The Jenkins daughter had returned from her job out of state and stood solemnly with her father. I saw Lenora Connelly, dressed in a teal blue skirt, with her mother talking with the Jenkins family, and remembered that Lenora's mother was active in the PTA. Betty Lou Miller and Mike Henderson were there, too, with their parents.

I paid my respects and then went home and started laundry, which I had neglected after the chaos of the last few days. I had learned to check all the pockets after once finding a twenty-dollar bill in my husband's pants. No such luck this time, but when I slid my hand into the pocket of the skirt I had worn to the sock hop, I found the piece of teal blue angora yarn.

I turned on the washer, left a note for my husband, and drove to the police station. I had already talked with them once since I had found Mrs. Jenkins's body, but I knew the yarn could be important. I explained to the officer where I had found it, but I honestly had no idea whose it was. Who was wearing a teal blue skirt that night? Lenora had one on at the funeral, but she wasn't going steady with anyone. I had to explain to the police officer the significance of going steady and the girl wrapping a class ring with angora yarn to match her outfit of the day.

The next day the mood at school was subdued, but the students' conversations were returning to normal. A substitute teacher had been hired to fill in for Mrs. Jenkins until a permanent replacement could be found. Students had come up with their own bizarre theories about what had happened to her. Many thought it wasn't murder at all, that she had been angry and broken the records out of spite, and then simply fallen and hit her head. The police had allowed the teachers access to the faculty lounge again for lunch and smoke breaks. Someone had removed the record player and records that we had listened to from time to time. Too much of a reminder of what had happened in that room.

When my yearbook group came in at the end of the day, they were strangely silent. Joanne Bauer sat alone writing a letter. Susan and Jake sat together, whispering quietly to each other. After checking attendance—everyone was present—I made an effort to start the class. "Shall we get to work? Sometimes that's the best way to forget your troubles."

About half the class looked at me blankly. Then Jake spoke up. "Could we put on some music? You have a record player, don't you?"

Not a bad idea. I opened a cabinet door and took out a small phonograph I sometimes listened to after school. I had a small stash of 45s and a new Beach Boys LP I had just bought. Mike pulled some 45s out of the back of his school binder and added them to the collection. Soon everyone was working on their yearbook assignments and singing along to the music, Del Shannon's "Runaway." I looked up after about half an hour and realized someone was missing. "Where's Mike?" I asked.

"His girlfriend stopped by, and he left, but his stuff is still here," Joanne answered quickly as she looked up, chewing on the end of her pencil.

Just then Mike walked back into the room, looking a little sheepish. "Sorry, Mrs. Garrett," he said. "Betty Lou wanted to ask me something." There was lipstick on the front of his shirt. He sat down next to Jake and began work, so I said nothing.

The next morning, half my junior class was late to third period. They pushed through the door together, talking loudly as they found their seats, bumping into each other and the students already seated, who glared at them. "Fight in the girls' bathroom over by Mrs. Lane's room. She went in and pulled them out." The boy laughed as he spoke. "But I love to watch girls fight. All that hair pulling and scratching."

"If they were going to fight, they should have gone to another part of the school," another boy chimed in. "Not between Mrs. Lane's room and the main office."

"Who was it?" I asked.

"Betty Lou Miller and that girl who reads all the time. Lenora something?"

"Lenora?" I was shocked. Lenora was not the kind of girl to fight. "What were they fighting about?"

Darlene Meyer flipped her wavy brown hair and laughed. "I didn't think teachers were interested in what kids fight about." She recrossed her legs, causing her narrow black skirt to move up an inch or two, while she smoothed the matching black angora yarn that was wound around her boyfriend's class ring.

The first boy, who had taken his seat next to Darlene, answered. "It was something to do with Mrs. Jenkins. When Mrs. Lane was dragging them out of the bathroom, Betty Lou was saying, 'I didn't kill her!'"

"Who was she talking to?" Darlene asked. "Lenora?"

"Maybe. I couldn't tell. Everyone was yelling."

I had my hands full focusing the class on the work at hand. We were supposed to read an Edgar Allan Poe short story, "The Tell-Tale Heart," but the drama in the school was much more exciting to my students, and to tell the truth, it was to me as well. My mind wandered as we struggled through the story. As soon as we finished, I assigned a three-paragraph reflection paper, due at the end of class. I needed them quiet so I could think. The class shuffled around finding loose-leaf paper. "Can I borrow a sheet of paper?" was whispered several times. I collected the students' papers as they filed out of the classroom.

I had lunch duty that day, and the jukebox was blaring when I walked into the cafeteria. "Pony Time" was playing, and a few kids, mostly girls, were dancing next to the jukebox. Mike Henderson and Betty Lou Miller stood in the lunch line. He had his arm around her, and she was crying. *The drama of young love*, I thought.

Suddenly the music stopped, and I looked over to see that

Mr. Parnell had unplugged the jukebox. He waited for quiet, which took only a few seconds since two of the town's police officers stood next to him. The students who had been dancing immediately took their seats. Lenora Connelly sidled up next to me. "Have a seat, Lenora," I said. "You okay?"

"I think so," she said. Her eyes were red and blotchy, and I squeezed her hand.

The principal cleared his throat. "These officers have something to say." He turned to his companions. More throat clearing and the senior officer began to speak. "We had a tragedy happen at this school just a week ago. The police department of Jefferson swore we would get to the bottom of the tragic death of Mrs. Jenkins. This isn't the kind of town where crimes like this happen." He paused. "And it was a crime. We are here to take into custody the parties we believe were responsible." He looked around the room and then the two of them walked the length of the cafeteria to Mike and Betty Lou. "Michael Henderson, I am arresting you on suspicion of murder in the second degree, and Betty Lou Miller, I am arresting you as an accessory to murder."

Betty Lou slumped to the floor as Mike's wrists were encased in handcuffs. Mr. Parnell and the policewoman helped Betty Lou to her feet, and she was handcuffed. Betty Lou screamed. Mike started to sob.

The cafeteria remained silent as the police led Mike and Betty Lou away. Then it erupted in an astonished roar. I put my arm around Lenora's shoulders. "You knew, didn't you?" I asked.

"Yes," she whispered. She looked around the cafeteria, but no one was paying attention with the commotion and talk about Mike and Betty Lou. "I suspected something when I overheard Betty Lou at her locker yesterday. She was swearing at Mike, saying Jenkins was dead cause he overreacted. They were in trouble, big time, because she ripped her skirt and lost the matching yarn. So, in the girls' bathroom this morning, I said to her, 'Who killed her? You or Mike?' She burst out of the stall and grabbed me, and that's when the fight started."

When the police report was finally released, the autopsy revealed that Mrs. Jenkins had been choked before she was pushed against the filing cabinet. Tell-tale finger marks on her neck confirmed that fact. And Mike admitted to the police that he had attempted to choke the teacher and to shove her against a filing cabinet, where she hit her head. A piece of teal blue fabric had been found caught on a corner of the table in the faculty room, fabric torn from Betty Lou Miller's skirt, as well as Mike's class ring, which had fallen from his girlfriend's finger and rolled under the table.

"She told me I would be pregnant before the end of the school year. That I was a failure," Betty Lou said in her statement. "She even took the records I had with me and broke them into pieces. I was so angry."

All in all, it was a rough start to my first year of teaching. My goals had changed. I no longer cared about being a part of the popular group I had envied so much when I was in high school. And, as a twist of fate, it was not Betty Lou Miller who became pregnant that fall, it was me. I finished out the first semester and then left the school to stay home and prepare for the birth. My husband was thrilled and supportive and agreed I should stay home as long as I wanted and go back to teaching when I was ready. As I said, he is a good man.

Morocco Rococo
Caroline Taylor

"I'm tellin' ya, Marty, we gotta get him outta here." Looie stared down at the cigarette in his hand, thinking Marty had to have some bright idea on how to rescue the situation.

"What the...is...on there?"

Jesus, he hated this fucking country. Phones in Morocco never worked when you needed them to. Always breaking up. Nothing worked like it was supposed to. "It's a big fuckin' mess, man."

"What now, Looie?" Marty's voice had a tone of weary resignation, or was it him not being awake yet? It was three a.m. back in L.A. "I swear, the...needs a goddamn nanny, and he's, what? Thirty-one?"

"Twenty-nine. He's got himself in big, big trouble, Marty." Why the hell did Danny think this sand pit would be the ideal place to unwind after that shitstorm divorce from his gold-digging bitch of a wife? Oh. Right. The hashish. According to the kid, Tangier offered "supreme-o, top-of-the-line stuff."

"What kind...trouble?"

"Danny could go to jail, which means he'll be a no-show at the Rock the Dock festival next week in Wilmington."

"Shit." Looie heard a match being struck, and then Marty said, "Let the...embassy handle it. Isn't that...they're for?"

"Uh, Marty? It's a consulate here in Tangier."

"Whatever."

He didn't get it, but how best to enlighten the guy? "Geez, Marty, lemme think…Yeah. I can see it now: tomorrow's headline in the *New York Times*. 'Moroccan Authorities Arrest Teen Idol.' That'll be a big boost to Danny's career."

"Shit."

C'mon, Marty. Work with *me.* "Can you send the plane?"

"To *Morocco?* You kidding me? It's not a Triple Seven, for…sake. No way can it…that far."

Take a deep breath. Try not to yell. "We gotta get him out, Marty. I could put him on a commercial flight, first class, natch, but it means him having to go through passport control, and these guys, they might think he's on the lam."

"Well, duh?"

Do not *punch a hole in the wall. Remember, it often takes Marty a while to grasp matters of urgency.* "They think he killed a guy."

Silence, stretching out so long Looie wondered if he'd lost the connection.

"Looie. Remind me again why we're managing this asshole. I mean, really. Danny Z might be the…eye candy for the teenyboppers, but the guy can't sing…a damn. He's been trouble from the…he inked the contract."

It was *you* wanted to sign him. The kid did play a mean guitar, though. He wasn't quite up there with Eric Clapton or van Halen but way better than Neil Young. "He's making us a ton of money, Marty. A *ton.*"

"Okay. Right."

Another long silence. Looie hoped that meant Marty was thinking, which could go either way, in his opinion. It would be a brilliant outside-the-box solution to the current problem or a totally fucked-up plan that would land the kid in a Moroccan jail. Looie shuddered.

"Any other way out of the country, Lou? Like by train or car?"

"Sure, Marty. Only there's this thing called a border that you gotta cross. To do that, you have-ta maybe get a visa, show them your passport. We don't have—"

"I know that," Marty cut in. "I wasn't thinking along...lines. So...ditch the...sarcasm."

Looie gritted his teeth, took another deep breath, crossed his fingers. "What lines were you thinkin' along?"

"Monsieur Cuomo. Are you, by any chance, related to the former governor of New York?"

The Moroccan policeman who'd just entered Looie's hotel room seemed friendly. Would a little lie help? "Naw. I'm from L.A." As though that hardly answered the man's question.

"Ah. Well. Your client, Monsieur Zee, appears to have left his hotel. Is he perhaps staying here with you?"

Shit. Where was the little fucker? Probably some hash den. "He ain't here. You don't believe me, go ahead, search the fuckin' place."

Looie hadn't really meant it literally, but two hours later, the police finished a thorough toss of his room, and the lead detective emerged with a small folded knife that Looie had forgotten was in his dopp kit.

The cop handed it over, saying, "Your airport security in the United States is perhaps not so good, sir."

"You don't know the half of it."

That got a puzzled look from the guy, so Looie explained, "Means we got security like a sieve." That didn't seem to enlighten the guy, either. But at least they let him keep the knife.

No point hanging around the place. He'd let the hotel maids put things back in order while he undertook yet another search of Tangier's hashish hot spots. He had to find the fucker and put Marty's lunatic plan into play before the kid wound up arrested for murder. There were other suspects, thank God, but still...

* * *

147

"Danny. We gotta go. Now." Typical of a lot of hashish dens, the place was black as a moonless sky. From what little Looie could see, the kid looked stoned out of his gourd. His long, greasy hair hadn't been washed in days, and he smelled like a sewer. What his teenage fans saw in him was baffling. Looked like a fuckin' girl with those puffy lips and curly blond hair. What was the word for it? Andro—andromeda? Some fancy-assed word like that.

"Who the fuck you think you are, Lou? I'm havin' a good time here. Feelin' really fine, ya know? I tell ya, this stuff is…is…yeah."

"Danny. *Now*." Looie hauled the kid up off the sofa and marched him out onto the street where Danny shook his arm free.

"No need to get physical, man."

Looie led Danny to a café and ordered strong Turkish coffee for both of them. Maybe it would cut the hash haze enough for him to get through to the kid. "Why aren't you in your hotel like I told ya?"

"Got bored, Lou. Place is like a tomb. Plus, all that gilt and those swirly rugs on the floors and scrolly Arabic writing on the walls and ceiling was freakin' me out big time."

"Danny. You are in big trouble. Big, big trouble. If you don't do what I say, you're gonna land in a Moroccan jail."

"Quit messin' with my head, Lou. I've done nothing wrong. Hashish is legal here, you know."

"No, it ain't. The only reason you aren't up on drug charges is 'cause the Moroccans know it would cause a big stink back home." Or at least that's what Looie hoped was the reason. Maybe they didn't care about the drug thing when they were lookin' at murder.

"Excellent. Knew it was a good idea to come here."

Looie ordered another Turkish coffee for Danny. The stuff was really strong but came in itty-bitty cups for some weird reason. "Murder is also against the law, case you were wondering."

"Whoa, man. What're you talkin' about?"

"Don't bullshit me, Danny. They know you was in the hotel room where the man was found dead yesterday. The one that had his throat cut? You mighta been the last person to see him alive."

"You talkin' about that raghead I was buyin' from?"

"Danny. Keep your fuckin' voice down. I don't guess you know it's also a crime here to diss the locals. That means you don't call 'em ragheads."

"Whatever. The stuff he was sellin' wasn't near as high quality as—"

"For God's sake," Looie broke in. "Get your head on straight. Either that, or I'm leavin' you to deal with the cops yourself."

"Not in the contract, Looie. You're supposed to be my bodyguard. So do your fuckin' job."

"Excuse me, gentlemen."

Looie looked up to see a young man wearing that long dress-like thing you saw on a lot of Moroccan men. He was smiling.

"Are you Danny Z?" the man asked the kid.

"You bet."

"My daughter Safiya loves your music."

"Rockin'!"

"Would you—? That is, could you autograph this for her?" He held out a cloth napkin, accompanied by a marker pen, and Danny slashed his unreadable signature on it, beaming up at the man.

"Would you put her name on it, too?" he asked. "Dear Safiya?"

"Sure." What with the man having to spell out his daughter's name in that thick French accent, it took as long as it would an eight-year-old for Danny to form the right letters. He handed the napkin and pen back to the man, saying, "Tell your daughter I'll

149

be thinkin' about her the next time I sing 'Rock Me, Baby.'"

Kids seemed to love the spin that Danny put on the B.B. King oldie, not that the Moroccan man knew any of this. He didn't look too happy, either. In fact, he looked disgusted.

"Thank you, monsieur, but, no," the man said, "I don't think that would be something she should listen to."

"Hey! Lighten up, dude!"

The guy walked off, his shoulders stiff like he regretted the whole thing.

Danny sat there, scowling. "Shit, Looie. What's wrong with these people?"

"We got bigger problems than that, kid. If there's any proof you were in that man's room..." Looie ran a finger across his throat. "It's time to go home."

"Aw, hell, Looie. I'm still chillin' here. I've been workin' on a song called 'Morocco Rock,' about how everything here is so...so...whatever." He broke into song:

Gimme more, more, more, more Morocco rock.
Lemme dance, dance, dance, dance around the clock.

Danny shrugged. "Still workin' on it."

Yeah. And likely would be doin' that when Looie was moldering in his grave. Danny Z had one talent: playing the guitar while swiveling his hips. No way could he write a decent song, let alone the words to it. No fuckin' way. He had the looks, the physique, and the moves. Period. Couldn't hardly hold a tune. Nothin' but showbiz. "Good. You can work on it while we're on the road." He stood up and waited for Danny to realize it was time to go.

"You want me to *what?*"

"Shhh," said Looie. "We take the ferry to Spain. Day trip, like everybody else."

"I ain't gonna dress up like one of them Ay-rab women. No way, man. Think what people will say when they find—"

"Nobody's gonna know nothin' about this," said Looie.

Jeez, the kid was dumb. "Nobody's gonna know it's you. That's the whole fuckin' point."

"But why? I mean, what's the big deal?"

Do not hit the kid. Do not yell. Deep breaths. "The big deal is—that call I just got from the police? Seems they got video of you comin' and goin' from the murdered man's hotel room—like I warned you about—and they are lookin' for you everywhere, including other cities like Casablanca and Rabat. I figure they'll be watching the ferries to Spain." Actually, it was Marty who'd warned Looie about it, but no need to spook the kid.

"I was only there five minutes, Lou. The guy was alive when I left."

Tell that to the judge.

No. That would be a really bad idea. "You want, you turn yourself over to the police, tell 'em what you just told me, see if they believe the infidel, hashish addict who, I only just learned, totally trashed that hotel room where you was stayin'."

"Aw, man. A rocker can't be a goody-good. It's part of the image, you know? They expect it. It's why I pay more than ordinary people."

No, you pay more because you always demand a suite. "It's only an hour, two, tops. Think of it as material for your new song."

"Shit. Dressed like a girl? You better not be shittin' me about the publicity."

"I am not shittin' you, Danny. Now, here's the dress thing you gotta wear. I made sure it was big enough for a guy your size." Actually, not hard to do since Danny Z was way short of six feet. "We take a taxi to the ferry. Get on board, go to Spain, get off, take a taxi to a hotel, and you're home free." And hope to hell his ploy with the passport was gonna work. Marty's ploy, that is. Might work; might land both of them in jail.

Right before the taxi pulled up at the ferry terminal, Looie opened the two passports. Lewis Vittorio Cuomo, nationality USA, date of birth 10/9/76, place of birth New Jersey. Then there was the one issued to Rosslyn Jeremiah Franklin, Danny's real name, nationality USA, date of birth 5/12/91, place of birth North Carolina. That photo showed a blond with shaggy dark eyebrows over light blue eyes and a pouty smile—totally andro-whatever, you asked Looie—so maybe, just maybe, it would work. And it did.

They were on their way in no time, with Danny complaining nonstop about the kaftan and how he could hardly walk in those shoes—"How do chicks manage it?"—and gnawing fiercely at his lipsticked mouth with Looie constantly reminding him to keep his voice down—or use what little falsetto he could manage—and not to screw with the lipstick. Shit. Marty's plan was working, and yet the dumbass kid was still doing everything he could to derail things.

"We heading back to the States?" asked Danny as the Spanish peninsula came into view.

"You bet your ass. I ain't never goin' abroad with you again."

"Why not, man?" Danny giggled. "I had a great time, fabulous hashish, even did the hookah couple of times. Plus, I got away with murder. Sonofabitch deserved it too, trying to sell that totally crap hash."

Holy fuckin' Christ. Looie was sittin' next to a goddamn murderer. Who was laughing at him.

"Scared ya, didn't I?" the kid choked out between guffaws. "Just kidding, man."

"Excuse me, monsieur."

Looie looked up at the familiar uniform of a Moroccan policeman. His stomach lurched into his throat. "Y-yes?"

"Are you Lewis Cuomo?"

"Ya got me. What can I do for ya?"

"And this is…?" The man gestured at Danny.

"My, uh, lady friend. Rosslyn." *Don't you say one word, kid. Keep. It. Zipped.*

"May I see your passports?"

With sinking heart, Looie handed them over. "They've got the right stamps," he said.

The policeman scrutinized Danny's passport. "Jeremiah. It is a boy's name, no?"

"Family name. The mother's family are the Jeremiahs from Durham, North Carolina." Jesus. If Looie didn't get control of his bowels, there'd be a major disaster here.

"Ah." The cop pulled a crumpled napkin out of his pocket and compared the signature on it with the one in Danny's passport. Then he squinted at Danny. "You are perhaps a transgender person?"

"No fuckin' way, man. This get-up was Looie's idea."

The handcuffs came next.

Bitter Truth
David Goldston

Emily Morgan saved the paperwork for her fifth patient of the morning and headed to her office for a bite of lunch. She was dying to sit in blessed silence for an hour. But when she checked her phone, she found a voicemail left by Dixie, her Uncle Frank's wife.

Dixie sounded hysterical. "Emily, Frank has shot himself. He's dead, and I don't know what to do. Please come quickly!"

Emily couldn't believe it. Uncle Frank killed himself? She saw him only two days ago, in his study, to discuss how long he might expect to live. His last scan showed that the kidney cancer had spread to his brain. "Whatever you do, Emily," he'd said, "don't say anything to Dixie. She'll panic. She won't be able to cope. And don't tell Malcolm. I don't want my son lurking in the corner, watching and waiting for me to die."

"Don't worry, Uncle Frank," Emily had said, "I'll look after you." She'd prescribed medicine to control seizures. He had been in good spirits. They'd walked outside to the lake, and he'd shown her his new camera, a Blackmagic 6K Cinema Pro. They'd spent over an hour together while he, like a kid with a new toy, described the features of the cinema camera and talked about a photography trip, maybe to the mountains. "I don't have a lot of time, Emily, so let's plan it soon." She'd wept onto his shirt and promised. Yes, very soon.

Dixie didn't pick up her call, so Emily ran past the front desk and told them to reschedule all her patients for the afternoon. She drove to her uncle's house, trying to control her sobs. Uncle Frank was practically a father to her, and she'd thought she had weeks, maybe even months, to spend with him.

When she arrived, Dixie met her at the door. Emily opened her arms and Dixie fell into them, jittery and trembling. "I heard a gunshot. I came downstairs. It's horrible." Her body sagged against the wall. Dixie was Frank's second wife and Emily's friend from high school. It had been almost fifteen years since they'd graduated, but Dixie had managed to keep the flat abs and toned butt from her cheerleading days and hadn't aged a day.

"Did you call 911?" Emily asked. She struggled to keep her voice from breaking.

"Yes, right after I called you and Malcolm."

Ugh, Cousin Malcolm. Frank's son and heir apparent to the Morgan empire. He was the worst version of an elitist frat boy. Captain of their high school football and baseball teams, prom king to Dixie's prom queen, and silver-spooned devil. He and Dixie had dated through high school; they'd even been engaged before Mal broke it off when Dixie decided to skip college. Not good enough to grace his arm. Yep, an all-around ambitious ass.

"Is Mal on the way?"

"He's coming from Raleigh; he should be here in about a half hour. I don't know why Frank did this," Dixie wailed. "We were happy. He was happy."

"Maybe he didn't do it." The gruff voice belonged to Alice, Frank's six-foot-tall right hand and factotum, aka estate manager. She'd come into the hallway from the kitchen, wearing her usual uniform of white blouse, plaid skirt, and jacket. Alice's face was red and blotchy from weeping. Emily's heart ached for her; she'd been with Frank for over thirty years.

"What do you mean, he didn't do it?" Dixie practically

shrieked. "Oh, this is the worst day of my life." She stumbled away, into the kitchen. Shaking her head, Alice followed.

Good. Emily could have a private moment with Frank— Frank's body—before Mal and the police descended. She went into the study.

Frank Morgan was slumped in the oversized leather chair behind his desk, head thrown back, jaw slack, mouth open wide. Below his chin, she could see a clean entry wound. Blood had dried across his chest like a burnt sienna bib. This doesn't make sense, she thought. Even with all he was going through, he never spoke of suicide as an option he'd considered. He'd seemed ready to fight to the end.

She turned on her cell phone's video camera, entering what Frank had called the Zone, a trance-like state where time disappeared and nothing could break her focus. She felt compelled to capture the outrage before her but was glad of the distance the lens provided. The pain and shock would wait, like eyes glowing from the darkness around a campfire. If she let it, grief would drag her into a black hole. Focus, she told herself.

She began a methodical documentation of the room, careful not to brush against the antiques and artwork, especially the portrait of Frank in all his Scottish finery that hung over the desk. It reflected the awful event, with shards of bone embedded in the canvas, and blood droplets, looking like measles, spread across his face.

Frank's right arm dangled toward the floor. She zoomed in on the handgun still hanging from his trigger finger—*Glock G30* stamped on the slide. Suicide? Why? She thought Frank had always seemed to love life too much for that. He'd asked her to hide his diagnosis from the family and the public for fear of what it would do to the business he'd spent a lifetime building. Surely, he would have thought through the effect that suicide would have on the business.

In the middle of the desk, otherwise empty, lay a folded paper. Emily eased it open with her phone and saw block printing: *I'm ending my life before old age takes my pleasures, my energy, and makes me a burden to others.*

This made no sense. Frank had not been a morose man. He hadn't seemed to fear growing old. Although he'd been devastated when Aunt Mary died, he'd found new life with Dixie. Why kill himself now? She studied the note. Was that even Frank's handwriting? His firm printing always slanted left. In this note, the printing was shaky and wobbled right. Of course, she was no handwriting expert and if you're about to kill yourself, your hand might have a tremor.

She returned to the doorway and captured the rest of the room. Floor-to-ceiling bookcases filled with the classics. Windows on either side of the portrait with views of the gardens and Lake Wheeler in the distance. A case containing Uncle Frank's prized camera collection sat below a large flat-screen monitor. There was the Sony Handycam they'd used the summer before her senior year at Appalachian State University.

"The best time ever, our ten days in Africa," she whispered. She closed her eyes to relive the good memories. They'd taken thousands of digital photos and hours of video. Together they'd created a documentary of the trip. She wrote the script. Frank, who was fond of saying that without "Tara's Theme" there was no *Gone with the Wind*, created the soundtrack and served as narrator—Sir Richard Attenborough with a Southern accent. "You were my best friend, did you know that? You shouldn't have left me this way."

Emily returned the phone to her pocket and went into the kitchen to wait with Dixie and Alice for Sheriff Taylor. The too-young widow sat at the breakfast table staring out the window, her eyes dull, face slack, not at all the vivacious woman who'd drawn Frank out of his shell after Mary died. They had celebrated their tenth wedding anniversary only three months ago, Dixie's thirty-third birthday a month after that. Frank had turned sixty-six only two weeks ago.

"Tell me about this morning," Emily said.

"Frank was up early. He headed to the study while I made coffee for him. After I took it to him, he told me he was preparing for an important business meeting and didn't want to be disturbed until lunchtime. I swam, then went through my yoga routine." Dixie shivered, like a cat shaking off water. "He said he'd always take care of me. What will I do now?"

Well, for one thing, you'll have to learn to stand on your own, thought Emily. "You'll get through this. I'll help."

"Mal will be so mad. He'll blame me." Dixie clasped Emily's hand. Her eyes widened and filled with tears. "He'll say it was my fault. That I should have been a better wife. That's what they always say when someone commits suicide."

"No one will say that. And what did you do after yoga?" Emily asked.

Dixie glanced to her right. The movement niggled at Emily. Then she realized why: she recalled the now-debunked theory that people look to the right when lying and to the left when telling the truth. It'd be nice if life were so simple.

"I went upstairs to change. I stayed there and sank into my book. Life in books is so much better than this one, don't you think? Have you read *Station Eleven?* It's so awesome."

"Dixie, focus. What happened next?"

She looked again to her right, out the window. Emily shook off her unwarranted suspicion. "I had just gotten to the end of a chapter when I heard a gunshot. It scared the bejeezus out of me. Then nothing. It was so quiet. I went downstairs to the study. Frank was leaning back in his chair. He was dead." Daisy looked at Emily, tears ruining her mascara. "I called you and Mal."

Alice listened to this recital of events with a dull expression. She had never liked Dixie, Emily knew, thinking her much too young for Frank and an unsuitable replacement for his beloved Mary. Emily turned to her. "Where were you, Alice? Did you hear the gunshot?"

Before she answered, the doorbell rang.

Emily accompanied Dixie to the front door where they found

Sheriff Taylor and Malcolm. The sheriff removed his hat, "Morning, ladies. Malcolm has given me the gist of the situation. Let's get this done so we can get Frank settled."

"Malcolm, I'm so sorry," Emily said, hoping this tragedy would allow them to put aside their mutual antipathy. He'd always been jealous of her close relationship with Frank; she'd always thought he was rude, entitled, and even cruel to his father. She opened her arms to give him a hug, but he turned away, a dark look on his face. Okay, be like that, she thought. Despite his tailored suit and polished shoes, underneath his fragrant aftershave she could smell his sour sweat.

Sheriff Taylor paused at the entrance to the study and scanned the scene. "Dixie, darlin', how about you walk me through the events leading you to call me this morning?" He began inspecting the study as Dixie recited her and Frank's movements since rising.

The sheriff looked up at Emily. "I understand that you were the first responder on scene. Is that right?"

"I was first here but not as a responder. Dixie called me."

"Family then. You go on back to the kitchen and I'll talk with you later. Dixie, why don't you join her." Emily started to protest; the sheriff raised his hand, forestalling her efforts. "Go on now." Malcolm gave her a crooked smile as she backed out of the study.

She lingered in the hallway trying to catch Malcolm and the sheriff's conversation.

Sheriff Taylor asked, "Do you know any reason your father would kill himself?" He squatted at the side of the desk examining the pistol in Frank's hand.

Malcolm, leaning against the bookcase, responded to the question while watching Emily through the doorway. "He's been under a lot of pressure lately. Taking time away from the company and going off on unexplained trips the past couple of months. I thought he was looking for a way out but I wouldn't have expected this. I guess he wasn't as strong as we all thought we was." He leered at Emily and motioned her away with his hands. "Go away now," he mouthed.

Fifteen minutes later, the sheriff entered the kitchen. "Okay, this is clearly a suicide. Dixie, darlin', I'm sorry for your loss. I'll do everything I can to expedite the coroner's report and get the body released to the family. Malcolm tells me that Frank wanted to be cremated and his ashes spread along the lakeshore." He looked out the bay window behind Emily. "A beautiful place to rest for eternity." Malcolm stood behind the sheriff smirking at Emily as if to say, *gotcha!*

She tried to follow the sheriff to the front door but Malcolm stepped in front of her, blocking her from speaking. "Sheriff Taylor understands the need to resolve this quickly," he hissed. "Keep your opinions to yourself."

Emily left the house, frustrated. The scene had played out as she feared. Mal and the sheriff would whitewash the scene to "spare the family any further pain."

She started her car and then sat back to read her texts. Harrison Daniels, Uncle Frank's lawyer, had sent: *Reading Frank's will; main house; 11 am tomorrow.*

Emily went home and changed into her running clothes. She needed to run hard, to get out of her head and forget how her beloved uncle ended his life. Two hours and a half-marathon later, after stretching and a shower, she curled on the couch, pulled a throw pillow in close, and cried for her loss.

Twenty minutes early and the driveway was already filled with cars, pickup trucks, and SUVs. Many were decorated with Confederate symbols, stickers, and flags. Looks like most of the family is here, Emily thought. Frank had used his money to control the family, so she wasn't surprised to see the mice scurrying for any crumbs.

She parked behind the horse barn: easier to stay out of the line of fire when people started leaving. Charlotte Llewelyn met

Emily at the dining room entrance. They'd gone to college together and stayed friends. They ran together at least once a week. With shoulder-length red hair and her green eyes, Charlotte caught the eye of every guy when they went for drinks. After college, she'd become a paralegal for Harrison Daniels, Frank's lawyer. "Hi, Emi, you're the last to arrive. They're back there—" she gestured over her shoulder—"grumbling at Harrison for keeping them waiting."

"Thanks, Charlotte." The dining room was large enough to seat sixteen guests with standing room for another twenty—lackeys, her uncle would have called them. The room had been reconfigured for the reading of the will: five rows of six chairs, three on each side of a central aisle. The chairs faced a large flat-screen monitor. Daniels, a man of small stature and graying hair, in a neatly pressed gray pinstripe suit, stood at the front of the room, behind a lectern. He motioned her forward. "Miss Morgan, please take your seat." One chair on the front row remained open.

Emily walked up the aisle, feeling daggers from family members who expected to be rewarded for their tolerance of her uncle and his peccadilloes. She noticed Dixie and Malcolm standing by the windows, looking out over the back meadow, heads close together, whispering. She was surprised to see Mal appearing to comfort Dixie. Their breakup after high school had been legendary. Five years later, Dixie had turned up as Frank's wife, a development that Malcolm had famously opposed. Now, incredibly, they seemed to be supporting each other.

She sat and composed herself to listen.

Daniels cleared his throat. "Welcome. We're gathered here for the reading of the last will and testament of Franklin Morgan, Esquire. His instructions were quite specific. First, I have a video prepared by Mr. Morgan."

The screen lit up and Frank appeared, seated at his desk, his portrait looming behind him. He looked like the president speaking from the Oval Office.

"I, Franklin Morgan, being of sound mind and body, etcetera, etcetera, la-de-da. I know you're all here to learn what you're getting from me. Well, here it is: not one of you is getting a red cent."

Ashley and Tom, Emily's second cousins twice removed, stood up, exclaiming, "You son of a bitch!" Daniels paused the video, raised his hands, and gestured for people to sit. "Let's continue, please." Others in the family stayed in their seats, looking hopeful. Maybe this was a joke. He pressed play, and Frank continued.

"Originally, I planned to have my estate liquidated and the proceeds given to those organizations supporting the conservative values we all share, mostly Republicans. Then the Southern Republicans lost their way. Somewhere in the swamps that pass for their brains, they decided the only way to remain in power was to end our democracy."

Frank stood and, reminiscent of Rex Harrison from *My Fair Lady*, began talk-singing the Yankee version of Dixie. "Away down south in the land of traitors, rattlesnakes, and alligators, right away, come away, right away, Dixieland…"

"How dare he! Sacrilege!" Emily heard behind her. "He always was a controlling SOB," someone yelled.

Daniels stopped the video and raised his hands again for silence. He pressed play once again, and Frank continued, "Anyone left in the room? If you're there, here's the good news. I'm not liquidating my estate." Emily heard a collective sigh from those behind her. She could feel their anticipation, like kids at Christmas getting ready to open presents.

"Instead, I'm putting my assets into a foundation to maintain my legacy, forever. And don't bother contesting the will. It's ironclad, and I've included a clause where anyone disputing it will trigger the release of all humiliating information about them from my little black book. Try to break my will, and the feds will have your gonads for breakfast. Now, everyone get the hell out of my house. Malcolm, Dixie, Emily, and Alice: you four come back after lunch." The screen went dark.

You go, Uncle Frank, Emily thought. She wondered what he considered his "legacy." Maybe Daniels would tell them later.

The assorted family members seemed stunned. One by one, they rose in obvious disappointment. Another cousin flipped the bird at Harrison and left. The occasional snippet reached her. "What a prick." "Just wants to screw with us." "This is BS!"

Daniels sat at the table shuffling papers. Ashley was the last to depart, with a final parting jab at the lawyer, "Guess you're going to enjoy controlling all that money." Daniels studiously ignored her and, after a minute staring at the top of his head, she left.

Charlotte sat next to Emily. "Sorry about Frank," she said.

"Thank you. It's been a whirlwind twenty-four hours." Emily paused. "No point in hanging around here. Better do what Frank asked. Have you got time to join me for lunch, or does Mr. Daniels need you?"

"Actually, he asked me to take you to lunch. We need to talk," Charlotte said as she gathered her briefcase.

Ten minutes later, they arrived at Mama's Diner, a hole-in-the-wall restaurant in a 1950s-style railroad car. Mama was known throughout the area for her homestyle fried chicken. The lunch crowd was just starting to fill the room. They took a corner booth.

After a waitress took their order, Charlotte removed an envelope from her briefcase and slid it across the table. "A letter for you," she said. "From Frank." Emily opened the envelope. The sight of familiar writing—a left-slanted hybrid cursive-print—started an ache in Emily's heart. She missed him so much.

Dear Emi,

If you're reading this letter, and obviously you are <smile>, then I've moved on from this life. I'm sorry that we won't have more time to explore the wonders this world has offered us.

My apologies for putting you through the reading of the will fiasco. That was done to benefit other family members; I needed a way to remove them from the equation without leaving you in the middle of a long legal battle.

For what it's worth, and such as I am able, I'll be watching over you "from that undiscover'd country from whose bourn no traveler returns."

Your loving Uncle Frank

Emily blinked away her tears and read through the letter twice. She hoped he would watch over her and that she'd make him proud. Something about the letter nagged at her. Something he wrote? She was quiet for a moment. "So, what happens next?" she asked Charlotte.

"We'll go back to the house where Daniels will read the actual will. Only family members receiving an inheritance are invited. Congratulations." Charlotte smiled. "Your uncle was quite the character. I'm going to miss him."

Emily opened the envelope once more and studied the letter. There. It was obvious. "I need to make a couple of phone calls, Charlotte. Can you excuse me for a few minutes?"

All but five chairs had been removed from the dining room. Daniels glanced up from his work, placed a finger to his lips, and gestured toward the chair with Emily's name on it. The other chairs were labeled: Dixie, Malcolm, Alice, and Charlotte. Why Charlotte? Emily wondered, as her friend took the seat next to her.

The others arrived with five minutes to spare.

As the grandfather clock in the hall struck the hour, Daniels stood. He placed a folder on the lectern and opened it. In his slow, careful voice, he began to read.

"Now that we've dispensed with the rabble that is our extended family, let's get to my actual last will and testament. Alice, you've served this family for over thirty years. You've acted as manager, advocate, and sounding board. You've kept our confidences and been a true friend. You have a life lease on the Point Cottage and may stay there rent free, if you like, for the rest of your life. In addition, a stipend of fifteen thousand dollars will be deposited into your account each month until your death. Thank you for your service.

"Next, I'd like to introduce Charlotte Llewellyn. Yes, yes, I know you all know her. What you don't know is that she is my biological daughter, the result of an all-too-brief romance.

"Charlotte, your mother and I kept our relationship secret; it was her wish to protect you from the storm that would have resulted had our tryst become public before our deaths. I've honored her wishes. But I've always loved you and wanted to be more involved in your life. A quarter of my estate has been placed in a trust for your benefit until you turn thirty-five, at which point, you'll be granted access to it. Daniels is a good friend and will help run it as trustee."

Charlotte's fingers brushed her lips and tears brimmed in her eyes. "I had no idea," she said. She reached into her bag for a tissue.

Emily squeezed her hand. They'd been close at school, good friends. But all along, they'd been cousins. Her uncle's secret.

"Emily, our photo adventures were the few times I could relax and enjoy spending time with someone who had no ulterior motive. For both that and your support during my treatments, I thank you. My beloved camera collection is now yours; I know they're in the best hands. Use them however you wish. I hope you'll document the world and remember me sometimes. To that end, I've placed another quarter of my estate in trust for your benefit. What I said for Charlotte goes for you too.

"Now." Daniels paused, turned the page, and looked at Dixie and Mal, "Dixie, as my beloved wife, you're entitled to half the estate. My assets have been placed in a trust for your support. Daniels has the details. After Mary died, you threw me a lifeline, and I've been in your debt since. You're too young to be a widow. Find a good partner and have a happy life. I love you.

"Malcolm, my son. You'll receive what you've always wanted, control of Morgan Enterprises. In many ways, you're a conniving scoundrel, probably just what the company needs to take it to the next level. I'm leaving it in your capable hands." Daniels smiled and shook his head as he continued to read. "Lastly, I hope I haven't been a burden to any of you during my final weeks. I've tried to accept my mortality, something all of us need to do when faced with a cancer diagnosis. I hear kidney failure is a not unpleasant way to go. My doctor has described it as a gift to mankind. I hope she's right."

Daniels closed the folder. He laid it on the desk, laced his fingers together on the lectern.

"God damn, him; he was dying, and he didn't tell us!" Malcolm appeared shaken. Shoulders hunched, elbows resting on his thighs, he pressed his palms into his temples.

Dixie put her arms around him, murmuring, "It's going to be all right. You couldn't know."

The doorbell rang, and Alice left to answer it. She came back with Sheriff Taylor, followed by two deputies. "Good afternoon, folks," he said. "We're going to take another look at Frank's study." He nodded at Emily.

"What are you talking about?" Malcolm asked. "There's nothing in the study." He looked at Dixie, who shrugged.

"Some new information has come to light. Where's that suicide note he left?"

"I have it," Alice said. She went into the kitchen and came back with the note in a Ziploc bag. "I haven't touched it." The sheriff handed it to one of the deputies, who tugged on a pair of gloves and began dusting the note for fingerprints.

The deputy showed both sides of the note to Sheriff Taylor. "That's interesting," the sheriff said.

"Why? What did you find?" Dixie asked.

"Nothing."

She frowned. "So?"

"We'd expect to find Frank's fingerprints." He motioned to the detectives. "Suit up, and scour that room." He turned to the group. "I made a mistake. Frank's death was not a suicide. The evidence says otherwise. He was murdered. He did not write that note. The gun was in his right hand—but Frank was left-handed. Furthermore, the lab ran a quick toxicology screen for me today and found Flunitrazepam in his urine. More than enough to knock him out."

"Flunit...What's that?" Dixie asked.

"Rohypnol," Emily said. "Also known as roofies."

"That's a date-rape drug," Charlotte said. "I'm confused."

"Someone administered it to him, then killed him and staged it to look like suicide," Sheriff Taylor said, "with a faked suicide note. So, I ask, who benefits from his death?"

"They all do," said Daniels, looking around the room at Dixie, Malcolm, Emily, Charlotte, and Alice.

"Don't leave town, people," Sheriff Taylor said. He joined the deputies in the study.

Malcolm was agitated, walking back and forth. "Someone's been playing detective," he said.

"Me," said Emily. "Uncle Frank wrote me a letter, and I remembered how he always curled his left arm around the paper when he wrote, kind of upside-down. He was a leftie. But the gun was in his right hand. And that note—the writing just wasn't his. So, I called the sheriff and convinced him to take another look."

"Whatever. Come on, Dixie, let's get out of here." Malcolm grabbed her hand and they left.

"Those two are a surprise," Emily said.

"Not to me," said Alice." I think I saw his car in the drive yesterday morning. I was in my room over the garage, on the phone. I didn't pay attention, really, because Mal was always here a lot. More than he needed to be, especially when Frank was away."

Emily raised her eyebrows at the implication. "What are you saying, Alice?"

"It broke my heart. I finally had to tell him."

* * *

After her uncle's study was processed, Emily walked into the room, imagining it without the yellow tape surrounding the desk and carpet. She knew the emptiness she felt would lessen over time. She opened the case holding Frank's cameras—now hers—and traced her fingers lightly over them. The Kodak Brownie he'd given her when he introduced her to photography. She smiled, remembering how she'd loved that camera, even sleeping with it early on. A Hasselblad 500C, the camera Ansel Adams used when he photographed "Moon and Half Dome" in 1960. And his newest one, the Blackmagic.

She picked it up; its power cord was attached, and the recording indicator on the back was lit. Odd, she thought. She turned it on; the memory card was full. The display showed that ninety minutes had been recorded.

She opened the last video her uncle had taken and pushed play. He waved to the camera then sat in his desk chair. Mozart's "Clarinet Concerto in A," Frank's favorite music, played in the background and he hummed along. Then he turned to the camera and spoke clearly. "Friday, 6:50 a.m. Malcolm should arrive shortly. I've asked him here, to confront him and Dixie about their affair. I'm recording this to catch them in their lies." He sipped his coffee while scanning some papers. A few minutes passed and he slumped, seeming to fall asleep. Dixie and Malcolm entered the study. Frank didn't react; he was passed out.

"Gotta love that roofie," Malcolm said.

"Yeah, that's the only way you'd ever get another girl in your bed," retorted Dixie.

"Got the note?" Malcolm asked.

"Worked on it all morning," Dixie said, grinning. She slipped a glove onto her hand, pulled a piece of paper out of her pocket, and placed it on the desk. She emptied the coffee cup onto the plant by the window.

"Okay, old man, let's get it done." Malcolm walked over to Frank, took out the Glock, and pushed the barrel under Frank's chin.

No! No, no. Shaken and horrified, Emily stopped the video. She couldn't watch the rest. But Sheriff Taylor would be very interested in it.

The irony, she thought. If they'd only waited.

The Day the Migraine Died
Kerry Peresta

My husband's new turntable and speaker setup blares the Rolling Stones's "Honky Tonk Woman" through the house with the force of a tornado. Gilbert, connoisseur of all things rock, experiences his precious vintage album collection at one volume: *mind-numbingly loud.*

I am amazed he isn't deaf.

Three birthdays in a row, I bought him top-of-the-line headphones, to no avail. He tells me the reason he loves vinyl is for the rich, warm sound of analog recordings. Since the sound is uncompressed, he insists, listening to larger, vintage speakers makes for a heady aural experience.

I'm thinking, *"heady aural experience"*?

And here we are. At each other's throats. Again.

I glare at Gilbert's closed office door. It doesn't mitigate the throbbing bass line that threatens to jump-start another migraine. With a sigh, I stride to the bathroom, jerk out ibuprofen, and toss back three.

I think about past efforts to discreetly "lose" his collection. My latest attempt flashes into my mind.

"Ohmigod, NO!" Gilbert had cried, his face a mask of shock at the realization the seven dusty old boxes being loaded onto the "You Call, We Haul" truck were his albums we'd carted around for decades. "I told you I'd sell them on eBay," he protested.

With a roll of my eyes, I scrutinized the familiar countenance, now weathered and lined. Behind his angst, I saw remnants of the energetic, determined, twenty-five-year-old I married. Stifling a smile, I crossed my arms. This was a war I was determined to win. "After thirty years? Yeah, I'd like to live to see that. Honey, we can't keep *everything*."

The young men loading the truck had fidgeted, waiting and watching. Eventually, they unloaded the boxes and, with winks and smiles, left them on the driveway. Gilbert reached out with gentle reverence to touch his collection of six hundred-plus assorted records. The boxes were so heavy, we'd need a forklift to put them back in the attic, I thought.

"Record players are coming back," Gilbert had insisted, struggling to lift the boxes and hide them from my purview. "I'll pick out the best of the bunch and sell the rest."

I groaned. "You're *never* going to sell them. And quit trying to pick up those boxes! Remember your back. You can tell Alexa to play whatever you want on that expensive new sound system you installed in the den."

He turned basset-hound eyes on me. "That was for the TV, not vinyl. If you'd agree to a subwoofer, I wouldn't feel the need to—"

"How many times do I have to explain that a person prone to migraines does not get along with a damn *subwoofer*?" I screeched. "Isn't it enough that you went out and found those huge, freaking ancient speakers?"

His jaw clenched. His eyes turned to stone. "That was a great find, and a good deal." One by one, he muscled the boxes inside the house. I can still hear the muffled thump-thump-thump of the boxes as Gilbert dragged them up the stairs to his favorite dumping ground for everything he wanted to keep and I wanted to throw away—a room I'd avoided for two years. The dump room.

An old argument.

I hate rock music with a vehemence born of too many

days-long headaches. Early on we had agreed—at least in theory—to compromise. When we were together, we would listen to classical and jazz set to a reasonable volume. When I was out of the house, he could blow up Joe Cocker or Janis Joplin all he wanted, as long as the cats' ears didn't start bleeding. Or cops didn't show up at the door.

As a busy real estate agent, I'd worked fifty, maybe sixty hours a week for many years. But I retired. Both of us needed to adjust to being around each other more. As long as his music was a soft burble in the background, I was fine. But the soft burble had steadily escalated into a hard, long blast.

Behind Gilbert's office door, the music stops, then switches to Joan Jett's "I Love Rock and Roll." My forehead furrows. Has the volume gotten louder?

With a frustrated grunt, I stride to my office on the other side of the house and slam the door behind me. I drop into my chair and try to shut out the noise, which ebbs and flows in the background like a toothache. For years I'd tried to reason with Gilbert about the volume intensity. Why did he persist in ignoring the fact that his wife is prone to migraines?

My hands ball into fists. I jump up from my chair, storm to his office, and slap open the door. "This is ridiculous!" I scream.

Gilbert, sitting at his desk with cell phone pressed to his ear, jumps. He mutes the call and mouths, "What?"

"*What!*" I repeat, incredulous. "What do you think? I thought we agreed about this."

He squints at me. "About what?"

"Ohmigosh how many times do we have to talk about it? Do I have to do life with earbuds every waking hour of the day?" My voice rises to surprising levels. I try to control my breathing. "How on earth can you work on client tax returns with all that noise? How do you concentrate?"

"Anna. Calm down." He points at the cell phone. "I have to take this."

"For God's sake, wait until I'm out of the house to play that godforsaken music!"

Gilbert rolls his eyes. "That's the problem. You're always *in* the house, now."

My head jerks into my neck as though I'd been slapped. My eyes narrow. "I'll work on that," I hiss as I leave.

My temper near the breaking point, I look around for something to hurt, like he'd hurt me. Anything. I grab a pillow from the couch and try to rip it in two. A glimpse of my face in the mirror on the wall reveals a person I don't recognize. The mangled pillow falls from my hands as I walk closer to the mirror. My cheeks are blood red, my eyes spider-webbed with protruding veins, and my bobbed brown hair pokes out at odd angles. My breathing is light and fast. I look like a candidate for a psych evaluation. What the heck is wrong with me? I tell myself to get a life. Move on.

With a sigh, I pick up the pillow, plump it, put it back on the couch. The minute my hand leaves the pillow, Heart's "Barracuda" ramps up and almost knocks me over. My hands fly to my ears. I race upstairs to our bedroom into the en suite bath and slam the door against the noise, tears streaming down my face. He *has* to understand the torment this puts me through after all these years! Why is he doing this? Doesn't he care? Stars dance before my eyes. I feel dizzy. Tunnel vision is next. "No!" I declare, my fingertips pressing against my temples. "No, no!"

My single thought is stopping the pain building behind my eyes, and caffeine works fast. Steeling my nerves, I run downstairs into the kitchen and fix a huge mug of coffee. Like a thirsty urchin in Bangladesh, I kick it back in seconds. I drain a second mug as well. It scalds my throat, but no matter.

The music continues to pound. Stevie Nicks's voice is a drill bit breaching both ears. I walk into the den, close all the blinds, and lie on the couch.

Half an hour later, the music stops, the caffeine has worked its magic, and the sun is now low in the sky. I rise and open the blinds. Is he angry with me? Have I been so absorbed in making money that I've ignored the man I married? Or is he just downright oblivious to anything but his own obsession?

Too emotionally exhausted to confront him again, I stare out a window that overlooks my backyard. The birds sing. Butterflies grace the smattering of rosebushes along the privacy fence. Out there, life is normal and good. Delightful. My eyes slice toward Gilbert's office. In here, though...I think I might go mad if things don't change.

My forehead furrows as I pace through the house. The silence from my husband's office is deafening. I frown. My gaze falls on the photos of our grown children. Enjoyable trips to the beach. Hikes in the mountains around Asheville, where we'd made our home after all the moves for Gilbert's career. Have I missed his midlife crisis? Is he having one now? We'd had a deal. *Compromise is part of marriage*, I reassure myself. This can be fixed.

A tight, steel band of pain squeezes my forehead.

I take more ibuprofen. Walk past Gilbert's office and up the stairs. My cushy, king-size mattress beckons me from our bedroom. But I pause in front of the dump room door.

My subconscious has been whispering to me for weeks. *Open the door.* But the thought makes me uncomfortable. I know what's in there—lots and lots of chaos, but so what? It makes my husband happy to save certain things, and I don't see the harm. I just don't want to have to clean it. Or see it.

And I haven't.

Now, though, the room tugs at me. Insists.

Aerosmith's "Walk This Way" roars through the house at a level no human should have to endure. An instrumental riff invades my skull and scrapes it clean. I put my hand on the doorknob. With a deep breath, I open the door.

My eyes try to adjust to the darkness. I peer at vague, dark shapes that dominate the room, and pat the wall for the light switch, but can't find it. I pull my cell from my back pocket and flick on the flashlight.

A horrified gasp squeaks from my throat.

Waffle-type, foam insulation covers every inch of the walls. A mountain of ancient T-shirts and dress shirts and socks that I thought had been donated a year ago sits in a corner. The smell of mildew is overpowering. I clamber over a pile of towels and hangers in an effort to identify mysterious hulking shapes. Dust flies up my nose, into my mouth, resulting in a coughing fit. After fighting my way across the piles that reach almost to the ceiling, my eyes widen in shock.

Electrical cords snake across the floor, under debris, through narrow aisles. I identify logo after logo. Peavey. *Speakers.* The large dark shapes are dented and scarred, vintage speakers from the 80s that look like they'd been picked up at the dump. I find JBL on receivers, and more. Cassette decks, maybe? As I make my way through the labyrinth of wires, speakers, and stereo equipment, the realization dawns. In a dramatic, rebellious move aimed at my hatred of all things subwoofer or extra-loud, my husband has packed enough aging subwoofers and speakers up here for an all-out Woodstock convention. A chill shivers up my spine. Yes, he tends toward hoarding...but this?

This is a nightmare.

From downstairs, AC/DC's "Highway to Hell" pumps through my brain. I retrace my steps, close the door, and take deep breaths. Numb, I sit atop a mound of discarded sheets and pillowcases, draw my knees into my chest, and huddle into a ball. Should I call someone? This has obviously been going on a long time. Tears trickle down my cheeks. After a few minutes of self-pity, I slap the wet away, straighten my shoulders, and slide off the pile, following the network of electrical cords. They culminate at a series of folding tables covered by dusty sheets. Trembling, I brush off cobwebs, pick up one end of a sheet, and jerk it off the table. Then another, and another.

Turntables. Record players of every age, shape, size, and complexity. A stack of old 45s. A box of replacement needles. I make a slow, 360-degree turn. A kind of bedraggled order falls into place—matching speakers, shoulder to shoulder; smallish subwoofers nestled here and there, along with various receivers of every shape and size.

My heart rams my ribcage.

Downstairs, the previous song gives way to Queen's "We Are the Champions," reduced to a soft babbling due to the acoustic treatment of this room.

Abruptly, the music stops.

A hard knock sounds at the front door. I hear Gilbert's footsteps, the front door open, men murmuring. Then, footfalls up the stairs.

I listen hard, holding my breath.

The footfalls stop. I jump at brisk raps on the dump room door.

But I'm never in here! Why would he search for me in here! Quick as a flash I duck under the tables.

The door squeals open. I hear the faint click of a switch, and the overhead light blazes. Where had that damn light switch been anyway?

"What is all this?" an unfamiliar male voice intones.

"I tried to explain," Gilbert says. "It's hard for me to understand, too."

"So," another voice speculates, "when your neighbors call about the noise, your *wife* is the one with the crazy loud music issue, huh? What about the mess in here? She a hoarder, too?" He sighs. "Look, dude, this is the fourth call. We gotta do something about this."

My husband chuckles. My mind spins. *Fourth call? What on earth?*

"Anna likes to pump that old rock 'n' roll. I've explained that during your previous visits, remember? She's all about the vintage sound. I've tried to talk her off the ledge. She doesn't listen. I assure you, we are dealing with it, officers."

Frowning furiously, I claw my way out from underneath the table. "What. Are. You. *Talking about?*"

"There you are! Anna, are you okay?" His salt-and-pepper

eyebrows are up in his hairline. His face creases in concern. I cannot even remember the last time my husband was concerned about me.

Mind blown, I shake my head in confusion. "Am I okay? No, I am not *okay*. What the heck have you been doing up here?" I fling my arms to each side and stare at him. "And why are they here?" I demand, pointing.

The two cops give each other a knowing look, glance at my husband, then me.

My voice rises two octaves. "What's going on?"

One of the police officers clears his throat. "Ma'am, I'm sure you realize there have been many complaints in the neighborhood about the level of noise coming from this home. We've given your husband here several warnings, but..." he took a couple of tentative steps toward me—eyes soft, one arm outstretched and placating—like I was a danger to myself and others. "He's told us about your...uhh...incredible love of music, ma'am. The neighbors are not happy about the noise level, and we want to address the issue, that's all."

"Address what?" I shout, pointing an imperious finger at Gilbert. "He's the one with the problem! I'm the one with the migraines! I even bought him headphones!"

"I bet," one of the uniforms said to the other. They chuckle. So does my husband. All chummy, like the three musketeers. My temper soars to deadly heights.

I glare at Gilbert. "Tell them you're lying!"

"I'd never lie to the police, honey," he says with a smug smile.

I feel like a trapped animal. My fingers drum the side of my leg. I scan the room for something, anything, to work with, and spy an old pole lamp with a nice, heavy base that would make a fine wrecking ball. Quick as a cat, I leap for it. I grab it by both hands, turn it upside down, and swing as hard as I can into speaker after speaker. Then, smiling at Gilbert, I watch his expression melt into horror as he figures out my next target.

"NO!" he yells, his face growing redder by the second.

The police, caught unaware, start moving toward me. But on their faces, I see confusion. I lift the pole lamp over my head and bash a record box with all my strength.

"STOP! You crazy bitch. What the hell?"

"I won't stop until you tell the truth." My next targets: six remaining boxes of albums, ripe for the bashing. An interesting sense of calm settles upon me as I plunge the base of the pole lamp into those damn records. Over and over and over. Then I start on the subwoofers, my chest heaving with short, angry pants.

The cops pick their way through the morass of discard and are inches from my little tantrum, their demeanor less friendly and more determined. I throw the lamp down and watch them slip and slide across the derelict accumulation. Out of the corner of my eye, I spy a dead mouse in an old shoe, and laugh. It is all too bizarre.

Gilbert sits in an ashen heap on a pile of his old shirts, sobbing.

The cops have seen enough.

The short, beefy older one grips my elbow. "Let's go."

I glance at Gilbert with a frown.

The cop sighs. "We'll get his story, too. In the meantime, *you* have earned yourself a little trip to the station so we can have a chat." My husband rises from the mound of shirts, forlorn and red-eyed and staring at the smashed album collection.

I wave my hand at Gilbert. "What about him?"

The younger, quieter of the two tries and fails to persuade Gilbert to leave the room. "We'd like to separate you both for your protection." Gilbert gives up and trudges into the hallway.

The cop holding my arm uses his free hand as a broom to clear stuff out of the way, then urges me forward. "The situation warrants a mental health professional to sort it out. This kind of hoarding is a fire hazard and can lead to other damage. Normal procedure is recommendation for a professional cleanup and counseling for the person responsible."

"It's *his* stuff," I bark. "As far as I knew, he was supposed to take it to the dump, or donate it."

He shrugs. "As the spouse, you are somewhat complicit."

"What! Why? I didn't even know it was going on! I haven't been in this room for two years."

The two cops share a smile. "Ma'am, you say that like it's completely normal." He clears his throat. "And your actions…uhh…" He shakes his head and breathes out a sigh. "As stated, we'll sort it out at the station. Let's go."

"No!" Gilbert shouts from the hall. "I have to see what I can salvage!"

"We understand, sir," the quiet cop says, attempting to keep his balance as he steps over debris and out of the room. "You and I will talk here, and then I'll be on my way."

"Why don't you tell the nice policemen about the subwoofer issue, honey?" I urge, baiting him.

Gilbert pokes his head in from the hallway. He looks at me like he wants to kill me. "If YOU hadn't been so intent on denying me the pleasure of my music, which is anemic without a *subwoofer*, none of this would've happened! How do you think it's been, living with a woman who demands that I stop what I need like food and water? How do you think that makes me feel? Are you nuts? This was my safe place—my listening room!" He snorts his contempt. "What do you think I am, a child? Asking your permission? You can't tell me what to do or *what to listen to*." His eyes wild and crazy, he looks at the cops. "It's *her* fault. I tried to reason with her, but she wouldn't listen." Desperation penetrates his voice. His eyes dart from one police officer to the other. When he sees no hint of mercy, he sighs and gives the ruined record boxes a final, lingering glance. Then he aims his rage toward me, his pupils dilated with anger. "Why choose *now* to come in here?" he hisses. "I had it under control. It was just another complaint. We would've gotten a warning."

My eyes widen. "We?"

He shrugs.

The police herd us downstairs. The quiet cop directs Gilbert—

lost in his own sad, little world—to the kitchen, and joins him at the table. My cop places me in a vehicle. Relief floods through me like a shot of prednisone. As I listen to police scanner chatter, I think about how nice it will be to have someone *else* court-ordered to muck out that room. And how much stinkin' fun it was to murder those subwoofers.

Especially that.

The older cop doesn't seem in much of a hurry, and as I watch from the back seat, he shakes his head at intervals and chuckles.

"Officer?" I ask, "Will I be interviewed?"

"Yes, ma'am, I believe someone will be assigned to get your version of what happened. On the basis of the findings, we may feel you should stay in a holding cell until we can get a mental health professional in to talk with you." He clears his throat. "For you and your husband's protection, ma'am."

I smile at the thought of all that peace and quiet.

Cautious, I grasp my forehead with one hand and wait.

Nothing. The migraine has vanished. With a contented sigh, I settle into my space in the back of the cruiser and watch the world roll by as we pull away from the house.

Duet
Jennifer Riley

Mountain ridges, snow-capped, distant. Deep crusty snow made walking difficult. With every exhalation, Solomon Locker moved through a cloud of his own breath. He trudged, exhaled, and enveloped himself in clouds. The clouds vanished. He exhaled again. His boots stabbed a fallen log and he stumbled. He regained his balance and trudged on.

When he reached his spruce tree stand, he stopped, overcome by emotion. Five years ago, these trees had soared to the sky, their plentiful branches lush and green. Now they were a horror show of drooping branches, brown needles, rotting wood eaten by bugs. He stepped farther into the stand, climbed over fallen trees. The same. All destroyed by deep cuts through the cambium layer, girdled dead as graveyard markers.

He knew who had killed his trees and why. Now it was time for this old man to extract payment of one kind or another.

He walked on in the deep snow. *Save your strength.* Every tenth step, he stopped, exhausted. He'd have a cup of coffee with Mason, talk things over. Discuss eviction, money owed, long past due. A contentious topic, the reason—if there could ever be a reason—for Mason's destruction of his forest.

The blue sky was threaded with clouds. Behind him, Lockers Ridge, one of the highest ridges in Alaska, receded, lost in mist. He stopped and looked behind him. He could see his boot tracks. No one was following him. He shifted the ski pole over to his other shoulder.

Colder and colder. Trudging. Not much longer now. Solomon's breathing slowed. He rotated his shoulders under his parka. He was almost to Mason's cabin, a two-room cabin built from the dried spruce wood of Solomon's trees. Leased yet never paid for.

Five years ago, Solomon had visited this cabin with the lease contract. He remembered its scant furnishings: a tiny table, skeletal chairs made from fir, balsam, and pine, an oil cloth or old tarp used to cover some ancient motor. They'd had coffee in ancient thick white mugs, built to last, hot steaming coffee stirred with two bent stainless-steel spoons, a community sugar bowl, some powdered milk made liquid with snow melt. Mason had signed the lease, and they'd talked for hours. Mason had played his banjo and added rotgut to their coffee until he passed out.

Mason always saved some hooch in case game wardens got nosy and came by for a chat about hunting licenses, trotter lines, mink lines. Or needing snow plowing. Mason owned the only Deere tractor in sixty square miles. If rangers asked him nicely to plow some snow-choked gap, Mason might invite them in for hooch before he got to work. After plowing, Mason returned, retreated to his bed with his bottle, and the world turned without him for a bender that might last a day or a week. Did he ever intend to pay the rent? Now it didn't matter. He'd been asked to leave. Instead, he had savaged Solomon's trees.

As he approached Mason's cabin, Solomon heard with relief the metallic tinkly sound of a banjo. Mason playing banjo meant he wouldn't be too drunk today. Trudging, ready to knock on the door if need be, Solomon slapped his sleeves to knock off snow. When he reached Mason's cabin, the man was sitting on his porch, picking out "Someday." Solomon knew the words, and sang along in his wavery voice. A duet about death and sorrow—that was bluegrass.

They finished the song together and Mason waved hello. He

looked rough and haggard with a scraggly beard. On a small table in front of him lay a chain saw. Mason had been sharpening the chain.

"Hello, Solomon Locker." Mason ducked his head, furtive. "Heard ya done well on the High Street." He blew imaginary metal filings off the chain, straightened up and said, "Come in."

Solomon removed his gloves but kept hold of the ski pole.

Mason motioned him inside the cabin. He said, "Drink, my friend." He had seen Solomon coming. Two steaming coffee mugs waited on a table. He pushed sugar and cream across the table. "Help yourself. You drink black or sugar?" he asked.

"Black." Solomon thought the man was calm enough, being sociable, but he must know where this is going. He imagined the weight of his arm encircling Mason's neck. As both men took a gulp, the tin cup singed Solomon's lip.

"Need a fortifier?" Mason grabbed his bottle of hooch.

Solomon shook his head, no. "Coffee's enough."

"Heard you made a killing," Mason said. "Or several." His gray teeth showed gaps. He couldn't meet Solomon's eyes.

Solomon nodded.

"No people can do what you do. Well, few people," Mason said. "Far off place, High Street." Mason rubbed a black-nailed thumb over the mug's smooth, thick china handle. "Shavin' mug, just about."

"Just about," Solomon said.

"Word is the High Street is a wild place. Tame, but wild," Mason tried again. "Heard you made a fortune. Nice boots. Store bought or catalog?"

"Can't remember," Solomon said.

This small talk was ramping up his anxiety. Solomon could feel sweat forming between his shoulder blades. He shrugged his shoulders up to his ears, relaxed them, felt tension knotting his muscles. He eyed the cabin door. The silence between them expanded until Mason started swinging the chain from his saw over his head. He lunged, but Solomon ducked, grabbed the door handle, and leapt through it to the porch. Mason followed but Solomon was faster with the ski pole; he stabbed it at Mason's feet, tangling them with a quick sideways jerk. Mason dropped the chain, flailed, and as he fell back, his head hit the edge of the small table. Groaning, he staggered into an antique bear trap that hung from a nail, catching its sharp teeth under his jaw. As he clutched his neck to stop the spurting blood, he fell to his knees and slowly rolled off the porch into the snow.

For long, adrenaline-soaked minutes, Solomon watched without pity. His heart's pounding finally slowed; the trembling of his muscles calmed. He took slow, deep breaths as he realized that Mason was dead. An accident, surely, but his involvement would be questioned.

Solomon stood over the body, listening for anyone coming toward the cabin. Silence. He looked around. The chain lay where Mason dropped it on the porch. None of Solomon's fingerprints were on anything but the mug, and in a minute, he'd set the stage for his alibi: he'd visited; Mason had it in for Solomon and swung the chain he was sharpening at Solomon. Mason was drunk; he fell against the bear trap. Solomon never touched him. It was the truth, anyway. No blood, no fiber, no DNA, no hair. His ski pole left no mark on the table or the floor. He could leave the cabin, leave the body.

But he thought of his dead trees, dropping brown needles, the acres of gray, insect-riddled wood, and knew he wasn't finished.

A few more minutes ticked by. Solomon exhaled. Straightening the corpse out, he grabbed it under the armpits and dragged it across snow. Fifty yards to a ravine, stopping for breath every few feet. It took all his strength.

Solomon judged: "You girdled my spruce trees. Now I'll girdle you." At the edge of the ravine, he scraped his knife around one of the corpse's knuckles. Gasping for breath, he pushed and shoved the corpse with the bear trap still clamped to its jaw over the ravine's edge. "Heavy work, revenge," he breathed. "Killed my spruce forest." Tears running down his face, Solomon watched the corpse tumble to rest at the bottom of the ravine, red-tail hawks judge and jury to his revenge. Scavengers cawed and flapped. The ravine quieted. Predator birds swirled to lower branches. Patient, they waited. They'd strip a corpse clean.

Solomon watched a moment: the corpse didn't move. Solomon heard no sound. He looked up, slowly cutting his eyes to the left. Cut his eyes to the right. Dared to turn around, braced and ready, in case he was tackled. He kicked at his boot tracks on the edge of the cliff. He noted with satisfaction that the corpse dragged through the snow had left a wide swath. He found a broom inside the cabin and used it to sweep snow tracks into oblivion. Heavy dark clouds promised a heavy snowfall to bury tracks, blood, Mason's cold body.

One more time he trudged back to the cabin. He filled the tea kettle, set it on the stove, and waited, as if waiting for a corpse to return. In case anyone came by, his story was he was waiting, too, for the hospitality of the host. The tea kettle sang on the blackened stove. Solomon grabbed two mugs, filled them with chicory, and poured hot water over the rim of each. He drank both, savoring his host's final hospitality. He set down the second mug and contemplated. His woods girdled and dead. Mason, same.

Solomon tossed the chicory outside, scoured the two mugs, and shoveled wood embers and ashes out into the snow. He took whisky off the high shelf, opened it, took a swig, and replaced it on the high shelf.

He would be back. This was his cabin now.

Hound Dog
Jamie Catcher

"You can't just barge into an investigation with your makeshift crime-fighting notebook, trailing that smelly basset hound, and tracking sand and dog slobber all over the place. Are you even listening, Elvie? There are risks."

Elvie twisted away from Wally's blue-clad arm as he attempted to guide her out of the active crime scene. "I do not parade, Wally."

Elvie Davis of Herbie, South Carolina, wasn't always sparring with Lieutenant Wally of the Herbie PD, but it sure felt that way. They'd known each other since they were toddlers and still acted as such around one another.

Elvie crossed her arms and stared Wally down as they stood outside the yellow beach house, surrounded by police cruisers and flashing lights. A white SUV weaseled past and made them teeter away from it for safety. "See?" he said. "Risky."

Elvie scowled. That *makeshift* comment really hacked her off. And her guest check order pad was excellent for notes as it made duplicate copies. And Sherlock was not smelly. Sherlock was a *rose*—the most adorable, sad-eyed, floppy-eared basset hound in Herbie. His keen nose and stubbornness often helped him find trouble, making him her spirit animal, best friend, and partner in crime sleuthing, all in one.

Elvie had rescued the pup from a riptide, and he'd rescued

her from her lonely self. And since she'd been named after Elvis Presley, her dad's favorite singer, she named him Sherlock after Elvis's basset hound. Her late dad, king of Elvis trivia, said Elvis had been mortified to sing his version of the song "Hound Dog" to a disinterested, top hat-wearing basset hound on live television. So, she sang it to Sherlock daily, and he now howled it along with her, minus the top hat.

Wally folded his arms. "Stay out of this. I can't always protect you."

"Protect me? Whatever. I want to help find who killed Beau."

Beau Bailey had been famously loved for hosting shag dance competitions at his beach grill, and now he'd been found dead—face down in a cheese platter, a pineapple-ended knife in his neck. After Elvie saw that knife, she couldn't stop thinking about how the pineapple symbolized hospitality. Had he welcomed his murderer into his home? Served them cheddar, and then—goodbye?

"I know it, Elv. He'll be missed. I loved to hear his welcome announcement. 'The Carolina Shag is a cold beer on a warm night,'" Wally said, his voice trailing off.

"'With a hot date and no plans for tomorrow. Let's dance.'" Elvie finished the old shag dance saying for him.

Wally looked tangled in his thoughts as he tilted his head at Elvie, and a corner of his mouth inched up. A solo dimple appeared on his grizzled cheek before he blinked out of the moment and looked away.

Fine. This not-looking-one-another-in-the-eyes thing was happening again. And to think, under a starry moon, they'd once won the annual shag finals at Beau's to thunderous applause. Elvie tried not to remember being in Wally's arms or her life before it turned disastrous, so she glanced down at her sandy flip-flops for grounding, then up to the blue sky for hoping. Palmetto trees fluttered overhead, and a gusty ocean breeze brought the sound of wind chimes and the smell of a lunch fish fry. Her stomach rumbled. Sherlock looked up at her with pathetic eyes and whined. He rubbed his nose to both his front paws, and then sneezed.

"Whatsa matter, Sherlock? Get something on you?" Elvie saw tiny orange-red specks on his white paw, but when she touched the paw, they fell away.

"Have you eaten today, Elvie?" Wally asked.

Great. He'd heard that empty stomach rumble. Elvie fought off a startle of embarrassment and sucked her stomach in to try and make it hush before it betrayed her again. "I'm fine."

"Uh-huh, sure you are," Wally said, and bent down to give Sherlock an ear rub. "I'm worried about you, Elv."

"I'm none of your business."

"Okay. Except when you are." Wally stood and tapped his badge, his gear jingling as he turned to head back to the crime scene.

"I am a public servant," he called, "and you are a private citizen."

"Yes. I'm aware," she snapped.

Wally smacked her in the heart with that *fact*. She watched the back of him recede into the chaos, and looked down at Sherlock. "I don't care what they think about our amateur sleuthing. We got some good stuff, didn't we, Sherlock? You got some good scents, and I got some good clues. We're going home on the flower path. Don't bark at Beach Cat, okay? He has a right to hang out in his owner's garden."

Sherlock thumped his tail, and Elvie slid her order pad in her pocket. It was note dissection time.

Elvie sank onto the sand to watch the waves roll in and out. She leaned back on her chaise, also known as the large hiking backpack that held all her belongings. "Why would someone kill a beloved beach grill owner? No forced entry, and his family said nothing seemed amiss. He had nothing on his calendar, and we have old-fashioned nothing to go on," she said, and wished for a pillow as she fidgeted uncomfortably. The beach was her temporary home, as rents were high and server tips were low. Friends offered their couches, but they didn't always like her having Sherlock in tow. Elvie couldn't leave him.

"Hey, Sherlock. I have a joke for you. A dog limps into a bar. The bartender says, what'll it be, Dog? Dog says, I'm looking for the man that shot my pa...w," she drawled.

Sherlock stopped licking his paws and looked up at her with gentle, hound-dog eyes that said he listened to her every word.

"Aww, Sherlock, my cutest and only listener. Get it? Pa...paw? So, Beau's business roared with success, according to his posh accountant who blabs all at the diner. But a couple of things stood out at his house: He'd stopped reading his mail and taken up eating a lot of boxed pastries. Did something stress him out? I mean, I have definitely taken a bad day out on a box of Little Debbie Honey Buns. I get that."

Elvie kicked off her shoes, and digging her toes into the white-and-black-flecked sand, smoothly sashayed a one-two, three-four, five-six count, switching from right to left with the waves as her dance partner. The memory of being in Wally's arms kept invading her thoughts, but that dance had been a lifetime ago—or rather, three years ago for her, when she had been a starry-eyed police recruit with another future.

Sherlock barked, and Elvie suddenly felt watched. A white SUV had pulled up in the front row of the beach parking lot. Elvie turned away and pulled up her hood. She threw Sherlock a kibble, the brown kernel skipping on the sand. Sherlock stopped the diligent cleaning of his paws, and dove for it, his long ears flapping back.

"You know, I think you could fly with those ears. And pace yourself, Sherlock. It's a long week until payday, and who knows what kind of tips I'll get."

Sherlock whined, and went back to his dedicated paw-bathing.

As she dug in her overfilled backpack, a group of beach goers walked by, giving her a judgmental look.

"Ignore them, Sherlock. We may look like beach bums, but they don't know us." She pulled out her order pad and recreated the crime scene in her mind. Her memory's attention to detail had landed her in police work beside Wally, and also landed her out of it. She'd remembered the right things about the wrong person.

"I didn't disappear though, did I, Sherlock? I'm still here, putting the puzzle pieces together, even if it is through Wally."

The alarm on her phone buzzed.

"Oh, time for work, Sherlock! We can clean up, charge batteries, and you can hang out in the back room and get treats—if you'll sleep and be quiet, Sherlock. Quiet," she said, emphasizing the word and making Sherlock howl.

"Well, something like that." Elvie laughed, and sang her daily "Hound Dog" to Sherlock as the basset hound bayed along in applause.

"The National Weather Service has issued a hurricane alert. Hazardous conditions in the coming days will…"

The radio whined over the din of the diner's lunch rush. Most of the diners paused in a collective hush to hear Hurricane Hortense updates, but some talked louder over it. The doorbell chimed as another patron arrived, and when Elvie looked up, the air rushed out of her. It was Wally, plain clothed.

Elvie hurried her cart of lunch entrees to her section of customers, and served every order by memory. Wally sat in the last open booth in her section.

She forced herself to take a deep breath before walking over to him. "What'll it be, Lieutenant Wally?"

"Hello to you, too, Elvie. Why do you always call me that?"

"Hey, I'm working. No time to discuss our ancient history," she kidded.

"Yeah, well there's a storm coming, and I'm worried about you. Why are you so stubborn about accepting help?"

"There's always a storm coming. I manage. Now, what'll it be?"

"Usual."

"Andouille sausage shrimp and grits, with a cream cola and a slice of coconut cream pie, coming right up."

"Elvie, can we talk serious?"

From behind her, she heard, "Server? I need a refill. Sweet tea."

"If both of us are ever off duty at the same time, sure," Elvie said. She rushed his order up to the kitchen and returned with the refill pitchers, zipping table to table like a hummingbird.

Wally smiled easy when she set down his steaming plate, the fat, pink shrimp hanging over the bowl's edge by their tails. When she got a chance to get back to his table with the bill, he only nodded as he concentrated on writing in a small black leather book. He stood and put his cash down and then, with a look back from the doorway, left the diner with a gust of storm air sneaking past. She doubted that look back was for her.

Cleaning off his table, she found a generous tip, and a note. She looked out the window; but he was gone, and a white SUV was parked in front. Who was that? Third time today she'd seen that car.

Her hands shook as she opened the note.

Elv, forgive me. Three years, six months, and seven days ago, you did nothing wrong. You told the truth against the wrongdoing of a powerful man, and the truth lost that day, and we lost you. I've never stopped wanting to clear your name and we can. He's gone—resigned in a big mess. They're going to want to go over what you knew three years ago. Come over tonight after work?

Elvie's eyes watered as she shoved the note in her pocket. The rest of the afternoon buzzed by, and no customer unhappy with the crunch of their french fries fazed her as she darted table to table, sometimes giving a little spin as if dancing. Elvie was the happiest she'd been in recent memory.

When her shift ended, she went to the back room with a box of leftovers for Sherlock. She had decided to go right to Wally's and imagined all sorts of happy possibilities. But when she opened the door to the back room, no soppy brown eyes greeted her, no happy *arooo*.

"Sherlock, are you in the storage pantry again? You know you're not supposed to go in there, no matter how good it smells. Sherlock?" She looked everywhere, but the room was empty of her best friend.

The heavy door to the outside was shut tight, and Sherlock certainly hadn't opened that door and closed it back after himself, so someone had either let him out, or taken him. Elvie rushed outside, and called for him until hoarse, but there was no sign of Sherlock.

She told her boss about it in case Sherlock came back, and grabbed her pack, feeling lost as she set off for Wally's house, three blocks over. She whistled for her lost pup along the way, and soon reached Wally's white bungalow with the haint blue shutters and door. All the lights were on, and the shade trees waved over a line of hibiscus that spilled their red blooms over the fence. Frogs croaked, and the scent of gardenias hung in the muggy sea air as Elvie walked up the painted seashell-lined path. She heard beach music as she reached the front porch, where a plaque with a crab on it said, *Pinch Me*.

Elvie lifted the mermaid doorknocker and dropped it. Wally's kitsch. Should she leave her backpack on the porch, or take it inside with her? Wally opened up the door and solved the question as he took it and escorted her inside.

"Hey, Elvie. Come in. Where's the big-eared guy?"

Elvie closed her eyes. "He's gone. When I ended my shift, he was gone from the back room. Someone coaxed him out. He wouldn't leave on his own! I called and called."

Wally rubbed his jaw, looking pensive. "It's such a locals' hangout, and we all know he's your dog. No one would do that to you, would they?"

"Unless someone didn't like me and Sherlock snooping at crime scenes. You made that clear."

Wally shook his head. "Not like that. I was worried about you. Everything came out of my mouth wrong."

"Usually does." She grabbed Wally's forearm as a thought struck. "You saw how Sherlock rubbed his nose after we wandered through Beau's house—well, he kept doing it. I've never seen him clean himself so much. He got something on him, something that upset him, maybe from the murder scene. Hounds are extremely sensitive to smells."

"And the killer watched you and took him."

Elvie shuddered. Had Sherlock been taken by the killer? She remembered the feeling of being watched. "I know there are white SUVs everywhere, but I swear I've seen the same one several times today, just sitting there waiting."

Wally set plates on the table, and then turned to pull a dish from the oven with bright red lobster-claw potholders. "Eagle eye, what all did you pick up on at the crime scene?"

Elvie weighed her answer knowing he might not be sending any answers back her way. She had no need to know, officially. "He hadn't read his mail in a while. It was stacked up. Seems odd for a successful businessman. His calendar was blank for that day although all other days had something written, even if it was just *day off*. Makes me think he had something planned for that day he didn't want to think about. And he'd really been hitting the Little Debbies hard. Wrappers and boxes were all over. Again, that seems odd for him. He was this fit dancer."

Wally scrunched up his face in thought. "So, you're thinking..."

"You think. I'm not the cop here."

"But you should be, Elv. Let me try to get you back. I can do it. The captain had his hands tied back then, and I know he regrets it. There's a way back."

She shrugged, weary of failed promises, but the underlying support for her in his plea made her want to accept. Perhaps she had licked her wounds long enough, from a canine point of view. "Let's get my dog back first, okay? And then we'll talk about trying to get my career back."

"Is it a deal?"

She sucked up a breath, her heart picking up its pace as she nodded. "Yes, it's a deal."

Wally's face lit up, his eyes merry and his smile true, as if a great weight had rolled off him. This was the Wally she missed.

"Why are you such a grump sometimes? This is the Wally I know," she said, wanting to touch his jaw, but holding her hands tightly at her side instead.

Wally looked away. "I'm sorry, Elvie. I guess, I'm ashamed. Sometimes I feel I got to where I am by standing on your badge's corpse."

"It wasn't you specifically, but thank you," Elvie said as she took the bowl of lasagna Wally held out. Homemade. How he had time, she didn't know, but she flushed with warmth and wanted to hug him for it.

"Yeah, well, I stood by and said nothing, so it might as well be. I can't stand what's happened to you since."

She shoved garlic bread in her mouth and forced a chuckle. "You mean how I'm a beach bum who waits tables now?"

Wally nodded. "Your late momma, bless her soul, will haunt me the rest of my life if I don't help fix this."

Elvie smiled at Wally's still-healthy fear of her mother and twisted a long string of mozzarella around her fork. Then the doorbell rang and she thought of the white SUV, and her smile vanished. A fierce protectiveness rose in her, defensive against any more loss.

Wally.

Wally went toward the door but Elvie barged in front of him, and pointed to his holster.

He nodded, and unsnapped it. "I'm sure it's nothing," he whispered, and kissed her softly atop the head.

It didn't feel that way, although now her heart skipped for

other reasons. Wally smoothed a strand hair out of her face, and pulled her behind him as he went to the door.

Wally opened up the door to a familiar face, one that belonged to a wiry, well-dressed man that Elvie recognized from the diner. She placed the familiar face together with a page from her order pad: deviled eggs with extra paprika. The chatty accountant. When he saw Wally, he backed away in hasty retreat and blubbered, "Sorry, wrong house."

"Door-to-door for tax prep?" Wally joked, also recognizing him.

"*Ha.* No, but it's a good idea, Officer. Just looking for a client who lives around here. Sorry to disturb you."

"Really. Being an accountant, I would think you'd know your client's exact address," Wally said, and pointed to the large black numbers next to the dolphin art on his porch.

"*Ha.* Silly me," the accountant said, and then retreated down Wally's brick steps. He banged his head into a wind chime made of seashells, and batted it away in a noisy fit.

Wally shut the door and turned around to Elvie.

"That was Adair. Beau's accountant and a diner regular. Table eight," she whispered.

"My bullcrap meter was redlining at his every word," Wally said.

Elvie opened the shutters and peered out. "He brags about investments all the time. Let's see if he drives a white SUV. No, I don't see one." She closed the shutters with a snap.

"Let's take a closer look at Beau's financials," Wally said. "Maybe Adair was stealing from Beau."

Elvie nodded. "And Beau discovered his money was gone and confronted him."

"I've been trying to remember something, and I think it just clicked. A woman came in a while back and said her accountant stole her money, but then she got a text, and said never mind. She refused to file an official report and hurried out. I swear she said her accountant was named Dolloway. He's Adair Dolloway, right?"

"Yes. Follow the money. Can I leave my pack?"

Elvie walked into the precinct beside Wally as if she belonged there. It was just as she remembered. There was the same smell of coffee and yesterday's curry, a hum of clicking keyboards and voices, the same brown concrete walls and fake ficus plants. She let out a deep breath. Police stations were most people's bad day, but to Elvie, this was home.

The radio spouted the latest storm news. "Hey, the hurricane hunters said Hortense wobbled west," someone said.

Cheers.

"And in four hours, they'll say it wobbled east," someone else chided.

Groans.

She sat by Wally's desk and googled Adair Dolloway on her phone as Wally went into the captain's office. When he returned, she held out her phone. "Lookie-loo. And I hope you are not risking getting fired over me being here. Here is Adair Maximus Dolloway, the Third."

Wally leaned over. "He looks like he weighs eighty pounds soaking wet. Hard to imagine he's Beau's killer." Wally pulled up the crime scene photos on his computer. "Cheese knife? It would take a lot of force, being a duller blade. But small and determined packages can be surprising," Wally said, and looked at her, his right eye giving a slight wink.

Elvie shrugged. "He does seem like a coward dog stealer."

"That he does. Let's see what we have on Dolloway," Wally said, and tapped away at his system, but soon shook his head. "Nothing, nothing. He's so clean, he squeaks when he walks. That's probably why we didn't think anything when that woman wouldn't file a report. By the way, Captain asked Dispatch to issue a BOLO for one lost basset hound named Sherlock."

"He did?"

Wally nodded. "Hold up. Would you look at this! Registration for a white Hyundai SUV to Adair Dolloway." He switched his attention to his phone, and scrolled images. "Here's his model. Palisade. You tell me if it's the one you've seen following you today." Wally turned the screen around to her.

"That's it," Elvie said. She stood, wanting to bolt out the door, find this man, and wring his scrawny neck until he gave up Sherlock. Adair must have watched Beau's house after the murder, spying on the police. He'd seen her and Sherlock, and knew Sherlock's keen nose could track him.

Wally waved her back into the chair. "I know. I want to go get him, too. But we have this thing called due process. Some forensics are still out, and there's rules and orders, and a captain to mind."

Hurricane Hortense's bulletin sounded again, and everyone looked at the windows to see if the sky foretold their weekend plans.

"You do, Officer, but I—a private citizen—do not. I want my dog back." Elvie wrote down the accountant's address from Wally's screen.

"Wait," Wally whispered, though he didn't stop her.

They stared at each other in a battle of wills across Wally's desk. Elvie did not flinch. "The longer we wait, the more likely he'll kill Sherlock," she said.

"Let's get with Forensics and find out what upset Sherlock's nose enough to get him stolen."

"It's paprika. The accountant always orders extra on his deviled eggs." Elvie pulled out her order pad and flipped the carbon pages back, and plopped it down on the desk.

Wally tensed. "Table eight's lunch order doesn't really prove anything."

"But it does. He dropped one of the eggs down his front, and I got him another. The paprika must have been on him when he was at Beau's. That was the paprika on Sherlock and once again, no one believes me."

"Elvie."

Elvie marched toward the exit, and stopped to look at the police emblem on the wall. "*To protect and to serve...*the bureaucratic red tape," she said.

Why had she let him get her hopes up? Nothing had changed.

Elvie raced to Adair Dolloway's address as fast as her flip-flops allowed. Would Sherlock be there? What kind of person would hurt an adorable hound dog? A desperate one, she knew. She came to an avenue of sprawling oaks amid mansions, and when she reached his house number, there it was: the white SUV in the drive.

Thick shrubbery enclosed the backyard. She crept into the bushes and peeked through a chain-link fence, hoping to see a floppy-eared hound dog inside. No Sherlock. Just whispering palm trees, birds, and the quiet hum of expensive air conditioning. Nearby, kids jumped in a pool, and someone grilled hamburgers, evidence of South Carolinians either being storm-numb or wanting to get their weekend in while they could.

"Sherlock, here boy," she called, and imagined him loping up with his ears flapping. She scanned the ground, scared she'd see signs of something newly buried.

Metal rattled nearby and her heart felt like it wound around her throat.

"Sherlock?" Elvie made her way along the fence toward the source of the rattle.

There. A garden shed sat in a corner, its door padlocked, its windows in shadow. "Please be Sherlock," she whispered. She climbed over the chain-link fence and slipped behind the accountant's patio wall for cover, losing a flip-flop somewhere in the process. The windows were too dirty to see through, so she found another way to know if Sherlock was inside that shed.

Low, but true to their ritual, Elvie sang the opening to

"Hound Dog."

An "*arooo*," answered back, followed by barks, whines, and a fierce banging of metal from inside the shed.

"Sherlock!" She left her cover and yanked the shed's padlock. It held.

"You do know curiosity killed the waitress, right?" Her lost flip-flop landed in front of her as Adair Dolloway charged at her wielding a kitchen knife with a cold, determined look in his eyes. Crud! She twisted and dodged his jab at her rib cage, and grabbed his wrist to make him drop the knife.

"Oh, you wish," he whispered, sweat beading on his forehead. With tremendous strength he pushed the knife back at her, diving for the soft notch at the base of her throat. Elvie cried out, fighting back with both arms to deflect his slow stab. This must have been how Beau died, with an outlet charcuterie utensil.

As Elvie knocked him off-balance with a kick, he pushed back, the knife almost at her throat now. She screamed and tried to knee his crotch, but missed.

"Nice try. Now you die," he taunted.

"Everyone loved Beau Bailey, and you talked about him like he was your friend," she said, rattling him, giving her the chance to swerve away from the knife and shove him off-balance with her hips at the same time.

Just then, she heard a bang and a shatter, a thud and a grunt. A wild-with-fury and bleeding Sherlock raced at them. He leapt forward, and with his ears flying back and his jaws wide, firmly attached himself to Adair Dolloway's leg.

He screamed and kicked, but Sherlock stayed put.

In the commotion, Elvie clawed the knife away, and threw it far into the grass. Adair now focused his attack on Sherlock.

"Oh no, you're not," Elvie cried, and jumped on his back. As Sherlock growled and Adair howled, Elvie managed to knock him facedown to the ground. She sat on him, and yanked his arms into a handcuffing wristlock as she had been trained, while he sprayed a bouquet of choice words at her and Sherlock.

Elvie looked around her for witnesses or help. How much longer could she restrain him? He really could kill her in broad daylight. She gulped, and her heart raced as he bucked upward to dislodge her.

Then she heard car doors slam and a police radio. As running footsteps approached, she held her breath, and knew Wally had pulled out all the stops to follow her.

"Thank you, Officer Davis. We'll take it from here. Got caught skimming off the top, huh, Dolloway?" That was not Wally's voice. She recognized that voice though it hadn't spoken to her in years. It was her old captain, a man she had equally loathed and missed.

She didn't let go of Adair until two pairs of arms grabbed both sides of him.

"You okay, Elvie?" Wally asked as he hauled a cuffed Adair Dolloway to his feet.

"We're okay," she said with a wince as she relived the knife at her throat. She pulled Sherlock to her side and inspected his white muzzle spotted with blood from his escape. "So glad to see you again, Sherlock. You found a way to leap through a window, didn't you? I always knew those ears could make you fly."

The captain held out his hand to her, and she shook it. She'd seen him at a distance as she snooped crime scenes, and up close, he looked much the same as when he dismissed her three and a half years ago, only the crinkles at his eyes a little deeper. "I expect to see you back in the precinct tomorrow morning at seven sharp for reinstatement, Officer Davis," he said. "Good work."

Elvie smiled, incredulous, unsure whether her feet still felt the ground under them. *Please don't let it be a dream.*

"Yes, sir, Captain. I'll be there."

"And bring Sherlock if you like. You two make a K-9 unit if I've ever seen one. And there's a very positive letter attached to your record, Officer. With our apologies."

Elvie felt tears burn her eyes, and as she closed them, the last three years of pain, embarrassment, and hard living out of a backpack swirled into her memory like a bad dream, one she hoped would fade.

She nodded. "Thank you, sir. That means everything."

Wally mouthed he'd see her at his house. Elvie nodded. "Lieutenant Wally," she pointedly said.

When Elvie and Sherlock walked back down the avenue of oaks together, passing excited surfers carrying their boards on their heads and joggers stretching their arms out in the breeze, it seemed like any other pre-hurricane day, but it hadn't been. It had been the best day, the day a long-missed friend came home to her, the day a wrong was finally righted, and the day a low-to-the-ground hound learned to fly.

"What a hound dog."

Aroooooo…

"Hound Dog" was written by Jerry Lieber and Mike Stoller and recorded by Big Mama Thornton in 1952.

Lips Don't Lie
Bonnie Wisler

Hannah Morgan pushed her fists deep into her winter parka and walked slowly past massive oak trees, making her way through the aging cemetery to a dark gray headstone in the corner.

Missy Morgan
November 8,1956–January 18, 1990
Rock Star

It was late afternoon, quiet and cold. Like her mother's grave. The chill in the air made the silence palpable. She stood motionless, staring at the headstone, wondering about her mother's short life. Hannah had never understood her mother, unsure if she loved her, or if she was loved. Images of her mother passed out on her bed or of strangers coming and going—images that she could never forget—often fed her conflicted feelings.

It wasn't all bad, she thought, trying to focus on the laughter and good times. Singing and dancing, music throughout the day, at least in the early years. But the pain and heartache of later years, the years when the singing and laughter disappeared and gave way to anger and drug abuse—that time always weighed heavily in Hannah's heart.

Moving in with Granny Morgan after Missy's death was difficult. It broke Granny's heart to talk about Missy, so Hannah tried her best to grieve in silence. But at the tender age of twelve, with no one to talk to about her mother, Hannah tried to act like it didn't matter. She buried her tears and grief deep inside. They soon became haunting shadows.

Rock Star. That's a joke. Maybe in her dreams. Hannah lowered her head and tried to say a prayer for a mother she never understood but often blamed for her own failed marriages and difficulties in life.

Heading back to the car, she made a mental note to drive over to see her mother's brother, Jack, when she had some time off. Summers at Uncle Jack's farm were such a treat when she was young. And it wasn't until she moved in with Granny that she learned her visits to his farm were because her mother was following some rock band or in rehab.

It's just us now, Uncle Jack. We're all that's left of this crazy family, she thought.

Months passed before she could get away. It wasn't until a frantic call from Uncle Jack's housekeeper, Nora Williams, prompted Hannah to hastily pack a few things and start driving, praying all the while that her old car would make it. Large raindrops splashed on the windshield as Hannah drove west out of Raleigh, heading toward a small town south of Asheville. Her cell phone rang again.

"Hi Nora," she answered nervously. "Any news?"

"The ambulance is taking him to the hospital in Asheville. It looks like he had a stroke," replied Nora, her voice breaking. "He's not responsive, hasn't been since I found him on the kitchen floor. I'm so sorry to be the one to tell you this, Hannah, but I believe you need to head straight to the hospital."

"Oh God," Hannah said, trying to quell her growing fear. "I'm on my way but it's raining really hard. I should be there in a few hours. And Nora, I hate to ask this, but can you stay with him until I get there? I don't want him to be there all alone, not knowing what's going on."

"I'll stay, not a problem. Don't want the old boy to wake up in a strange place and wonder what the hell happened!" Nora's laugh eased the nervous tension of the call.

It was evening when Hannah arrived and made her way to Uncle Jack's hospital room. Oxygen and IVs dangled from machines in a cobweb of tubes connected to him. His face looked strained. She watched his chest slowly rise and lower, wondering what was going through his mind. Was he aware she was there with him? Nora said he spoke what sounded like Hannah's name several times before she arrived. The stroke had made it difficult to understand him.

He stirred, and Hannah reached for his hand. "I'm here. Uncle Jack. It's Hannah." She gave his hand a squeeze and felt a light response.

"Stone," he said in an almost unrecognizable whisper. "Stone," he repeated.

Hannah leaned in toward him, trying to catch every word. "What did you say?"

"Stone. Sl...slee." He was trying so hard to communicate something. "Sleef." The sound came out as a soft breath.

Hannah thought back, trying to connect his words to anything about his life that might help her understand what he was trying to say. Those were the happy times, she thought, recalling time at his farm as a child, exploring the nooks and crannies of the old barn and wandering through the apple orchard. It was her safe place, a place to escape the realities of life with her mother. She adored Uncle Jack. He never said much, but he had a great laugh and always treated her as a special person.

The long drive and stress of the day began to catch up to her as she settled into the bedside chair. Exhausted, she wrapped an extra hospital blanket around herself and closed her eyes.

It was almost midnight when Hannah woke. Jack seemed restless so she reached across to gently stroke his forehead and hold his hand. "I'm here, Uncle Jack, it's going to be alright," she said, softly and reassuringly.

A slight movement in her hand indicated that he heard her. It was his last. He became suddenly very still, and his face no longer looked strained. Tears streamed down her face as she realized her beloved Uncle Jack, her last living relative, was dead.

K. STEVENS, Attorney at Law, was lettered on the glass door of an old gas station. Hannah parked in front of the building and tried to calm her nerves. It was a bitterly cold morning, the skies heavy with storm clouds.

Nora Williams was already inside, seated at a long, official-looking table. "Have a seat, Hannah." Nora smiled faintly and motioned to the chair next to her. "You know," she said, "Jack didn't care for many people, but he loved you. I believe he felt responsible for you, what with your mother's issues."

"He was like a father to me. I spent most summers with him at the orchard. But after mother died and Granny took me in, the visits were few. I feel terrible that I didn't visit more often after Granny died...I guess I thought there was always more time."

A professional-looking woman entered, her hand outstretched in a greeting. "Good morning, ladies. I'm Karen Stevens, Jack Morgan's attorney."

Karen proceeded through introductions and went right to work reading the will. It was short and brief; Jack was a man of few words both in life and death. A quite generous amount was set aside for Nora, Jack's longtime friend and housekeeper. "The farm, house, accounts, and all remaining belongings and properties are bequeathed to Hannah V. Morgan, his niece, and only living relative," the lawyer concluded.

"Jack invested quite well; he couldn't resist some Apple stock early on." Karen smiled toward Hannah and slid a financial statement across the desk for her to review. "And, as you can see, you have inherited a sizable estate."

Hannah blinked and refocused her eyes as she reviewed the

statement—a first cursory overview, and a second in disbelief. A sum of over a million dollars took her breath away. Her hands began to shake as she gently placed the statement back on the table.

"And there is this," the lawyer said, handing Hannah an envelope. "Jack said it is the most significant part of your inheritance and to make certain that you were aware of its importance."

The envelope was yellowed with age but sealed. Hannah's name was printed out in Uncle Jack's script. "Shall I open it now?" Hannah asked.

"He didn't indicate that you were to open it in private; however, it's totally up to you." Karen responded. Hannah glanced over at Nora for moral support. She was smiling, so Hannah slowly opened the envelope.

Hannah's laughter broke through the silent anticipation in the room. Uncle Jack loved to play his version of hide and seek with her. Only he would never hide. Instead, he would place clues in notes and hide them around the farm for Hannah to find, giving him time to do his work while keeping Hannah happily entertained. It was their little treasure hunt, oftentimes resulting in toys, money, or, even once, a puppy. Today it was a single clue printed on a small sheet of note paper:

Lips Don't Lie.

She had no idea what it meant.

Jack's funeral was held at a small country church with an adjacent cemetery. Jack never was religious but had a deep belief in God and nature, with a strong trust in both. After the brief service, Hannah followed Nora back to the farm, down back roads that she had never driven. The skies were blue, but there was a January chill that made one shiver thinking of the bitter cold days to come.

The old farm was exactly the way Hannah remembered it— good bones, needing some sprucing up, yet somehow warm and welcoming. A covered porch with two rocking chairs reminded her of summer breezes and happier times.

Nora lit the wood stove in the kitchen. A warm glow and the smell of the oak fire quickly filled the room with a relaxing feel. The kitchen was large with a big window over the sink. Coffee cups sitting on a dish towel lined the deep windowsill. A small wood table sat near the far wall with four straight-backed chairs around it. Next to another window, an inviting overstuffed chair overlooked a stand of white pines and the barn. There were newspapers neatly folded on the bench next to it, just waiting to be read.

"I can't thank you enough for your help this past week, I truly don't know what I would have done without you," Hannah said to Nora.

"It's the least I could do, for Jack and you. I've known him since school. Jack was a good man, but he did not suffer fools. There were folks in town who got on his nerves, and he didn't hide it. But if he liked you, you knew that too. And he really loved this old place," Nora said sitting down at the kitchen table.

"I didn't realize you went to school together." Hannah's curiosity kicked in. Nora might know her family's history.

"He was two years ahead of me and quite the catch! He could have his pick of girls, but he was always so quiet and studied hard. Not at all like his sister."

"You knew my mom, too?" Hannah's heart pounded with excitement.

"Not really, but I knew of her. She was a year or two behind me in school, but I remember she sang at all the high school games and local fairs. She was quite talented."

"I hate to ask this, but is there anything else you remember or heard about her? I could never get her to talk to me about when she was young, or about my father, or much of anything personal. She just refused to go there; she'd clam up or tell me it's too painful to remember, and that was it." Hannah sighed, thinking of those difficult times. "And Granny wasn't any help either.

According to her, all Mom cared about was herself." Hannah shook her head, exhaling deeply. "She had a lot of issues."

Nora reached across the table and patted her hand. "That's a lot of worry for you to carry around. Why don't we talk about that later? Right now, you need to focus on you. And look around. This is your place!" Nora said, trying to lift Hannah's spirits.

"I can't believe Uncle Jack left it to me. It's the answer to my prayers. I love this old place!"

"Have you decided to keep it and stay?" Nora asked hopefully.

"I'm not sure. That's something I'll need to sleep on." Hannah sank into the oversized armchair. "I think so. I really have nothing holding me back in Raleigh. I was working two jobs just to maintain a small apartment and my clunker car. Now I suddenly have a wonderful old farm and orchard in the foothills of the Blue Ridge Mountains!" But, she wondered, winters here can be difficult, and do I really want to be all alone out in the country and worry about maintaining an old farmhouse and orchard?

"I do plan on staying for a week or two to go through everything. Would you be available to help me sort through his clothes and other items?"

"You bet. Nothing exciting keeping me at home all day," Nora said, shaking her head. "And if you do decide to stay and need help with the orchard, my son Austin helped Jack in the past. I'm sure he'd be happy to lend a hand with that. He also owns the garage in town, in case you need any work on that car of yours."

"Great! Then if you are available tomorrow, come on over. I'll be here!" Hannah replied, eager to get started and looking forward to getting better acquainted.

Organization must be a family trait, thought Hannah as she started to go through the rooms of the farmhouse the next day.

Everything was neat and tidy. Jack's clothes were neatly folded in the bedroom drawers, and his shirts and coats hung snugly in the small closets of upstairs rooms. She and Nora could start packing up the clothes first and take them to the nearest charity.

Roaming the house, Hannah's mind flashed back to a scene with her mother. Missy had come to pick up Hannah, but there was an argument between her and Jack. Missy threw Hannah's little red suitcase at Jack and ran back to the car in tears. Hannah ran out after her mother, only to stand there, crying and waving goodbye to her mother as the car quickly backed out of the drive. Where did she go and what were they always arguing about?

It was in the den closet—Hannah's little red suitcase. Old and tattered now, but she remembered it well. She unlatched and opened it, expecting to find a child's summer clothes but instead was surprised to see old papers. Documents, letters, and postcards. Perhaps the answer to his cryptic message—*Lips Don't Lie*—was here.

She settled herself on the floor and began sorting through everything in the case. There was a copy of Jack's will, his birth certificate, insurance papers, medical records, and letters and postcards. Farm stuff in one pile, medical in another, and letters and postcards in a pile of their own. But who were they from? An old girlfriend? Most were signed *M*. Could that be her mother? The script was round and curly, like a teenage girl's. The postcards came from cities up and down the east coast.

'I'm in the band—Watch out Madonna—here I come!' M

'on the tour bus. Livin the dream!' M.

'WOOHOO! Sex, drugs, and rock n' roll!' M

'I'm in love!' Written inside a big heart, the initials *SS&MM...M*.

And then a large manila envelope with pictures inside. A picture of a VW van with her mother and others peering out the windows. Written on the back: *the Boss Rage Gang*. More pictures of band members sitting with guitars, beer bottles, and pizza boxes in the background. And another picture. It was her mother and another woman, holding a baby between them. On the back was scribbled *SS*, *MM*, and *H*. She recognized her mother's long dark hair in the picture. She looked so young. Very pretty. They were standing on a stage, with huge smiles on their faces. Is that me? Hannah wondered. And who is SS? They look like a family

"Knock, knock. Anyone home?" Nora called out from the kitchen.

"I'm in the den, and you won't believe what I just found," Hannah replied excitedly. "This is my suitcase from when I was a little girl, and it's full of letters and postcards from my mother to Uncle Jack. It looks like she really was in a band. She never told me..." her words drifted off as she suddenly began sobbing. She finally had some insight into her mother's life. It was as if the floodgates had opened. Tears she had never been able to shed were now flowing, releasing years of pent-up emotions.

"Oh, Nora," she finally got out through sniffles and shallow breaths. "I'm so sorry to do this in front of you."

"I can't imagine what you are feeling, after all you've been through this past week. I'd be a basket case too." Nora smiled down at Hannah sitting limp on the floor. "Let's get some food into you and then we can get back into sorting through some of this." She helped Hannah from the floor and into the kitchen. "A cup of tea to start, and then if you want to tell me all about it, you can. If not, that's okay too."

Hannah's words came slow at first, and softly: "It's hard to explain what it's like to live with someone with addictions. She loved music; but it wasn't until I was eight or nine that I learned she worked for rock groups as a roadie. But whenever she was in that environment for any length of time, she would get pulled back into the alcohol and drug scene, and I can't begin to tell you how many times she was in and out of rehab. I loved her and hated her at the same time. To experience those extremes as a kid tore me apart. When she was clean, life was pretty good, and we were normal. But if she got stressed about something, especially if I asked any questions about who my father was, she'd explode. And often, after that, she'd drop me at some friend's house for hours or days on end. I soon learned not to ask any questions. I just wish I knew the truth—why she was that way." Hannah stopped speaking for a moment and looked out the window at the barn and woods. "I think Uncle Jack is the one who paid for all her rehab stints too. That's probably what they were arguing about that day she threw my suitcase at him. I'll never forget her screaming at him that 'the day Hannah came along really messed up my life.' Those are words a child should never hear." After a short silence Hannah continued, "I married way too young, and that didn't work; but I just wanted to make my own rules. Granny did her best; but she was old, and it was hard for her to have a teenager in the house. Whenever I cranked up my radio, she'd get angry. I guess it reminded her too much of my mom."

Nora made another pot of tea, and Hannah reminisced about the good times too. About her summers at the orchard with Uncle Jack. How he taught her how to make applesauce and apple pies, and how, to this day, the smell of pastry baking always reminded her of him. But most of all he let her be a kid, and for that she was so grateful.

"So, it wasn't all bad, just so confusing." She sat quietly for a moment stirring her tea and then grinned. "And you know what, Nora? I am going to stay here and try to make a go of the farm. I've decided I can do this. The pain is behind me; it's time I quit chasing ghosts and get on with my life. This place makes me happy. I'd be foolish not to take advantage of this gift." And to her surprise, she felt a weight lift from her shoulders.

With a snowstorm in the forecast, Hannah went to the shed to gather more kindling and wood. After neatly stacking it on the front porch for easy access, she headed to the barn to see if there was anything she might need in case the storm lasted longer than anticipated. The old door creaked as she opened it to a familiar musty smell of hay, apples, and old wood. The table that served as a desk sat at the back of the barn just as she remembered, and from the looks of things, Uncle Jack had been working there recently. Bills lying in a wire basket on the desk were current, prompting Hannah to collect them to take inside. Now, with the decision made to take over the farm, she wanted to honor Uncle Jack and stay in good graces with those businesses. She'd get in touch with each of them this week and let them know of Uncle Jack's passing and her intentions of continuing as a client. A nearby stack of empty apple crates came in handy, and she filled one with his office items.

Taking a final look around to see if there was anything else she needed from the office, her eyes fell on his old turntable and album collection. It now took up several shelves, alphabetized by artist, the albums neatly lined up like soldiers. Thumbing through them reminded her of happy summers at the farm. Music drifting through the rows of trees. He swore his apples grew better with music. And perhaps he had a point. His small farm had families coming from miles around when it opened in the fall as a "u-pick" orchard.

Noticing a few albums lying loose on the bottom shelf she decided to put them back and then realized that these were her mother's favorites. Maybe they were hers? Hannah didn't recall Granny having the record collection; Uncle Jack must have kept them.

As Hannah looked through them, one quickly caught her eye—the bright red tongue and lips on the cover of *Sucking in the Seventies* by the Rolling Stones. *Lips Don't Lie*, Uncle Jack had written. And what was it he had said in the hospital? Stone? Slee? Could this album sleeve hold the clue? She studied it carefully, front and back. Nothing there, other than song titles she remembered from days gone by. Nothing that made sense of his note, but she placed it in the apple crate, along with the bills, to look at later. The sky was dark and heavy with low gray snow clouds when she exited the barn.

Back in the warmth of the kitchen, Hannah placed the basket of bills on the floor and tossed the album on the table. A piece of paper slipped out from the album jacket cover. It looked like the yellowed paper sleeve of the LP, but then she noticed faded print. Sitting at the table, she began to slowly pull items, one by one, from inside the album cover.

The first was an article from the Raleigh newspaper:

...a baby has been kidnapped from a local daycare. Police are looking for two young women for questioning. They were described as hippie-looking, with long hair and wearing baggy clothing. They inquired about a tour of the facility for the one girl, who indicated she was seven months pregnant. Shortly after they left the facility, the daycare owners realized an infant was missing from her crib...

Another small clipping was titled *"Rocker Sunshine Sally Found Dead of Overdose." Sally Atwood, better known as Sunshine Sally, lead singer of the grunge band Boss Rage Gang, was found dead in her hotel room of an apparent overdose...The group is in mourning and has canceled all upcoming events.*

The other paper was an old hospital bill, dated a year before Hannah's birth—addressed to Missy Morgan—for a hysterectomy. Hannah dropped it to the table as though it had scorched her hand. What? This has to be wrong, she thought.

She stood and backed away from the table, shaken to her core, her mind racing trying to piece it all together. "What is this?" Hands trembling, she once again picked up the newspaper article about the stolen child, looking for a date. It was the summer of her birth. The article about Sunshine Sally was dated later that same year. Sunshine Sally. Was she the SS on the postcard and picture? What reason could her mother, or Jack, have for saving these articles except...*Am I that baby?*

"Oh my God," she blurted out. "Why?" Hannah dropped the papers and ran outside, slamming the door. She had to get away from it. Her mind raced with so many crazy thoughts.

"Why would she do such a thing? Why?" she screamed again at the top of her lungs. "Am I that stolen baby?"

The clouds had opened, dusting the trees and yard with snow; lacy white snowflakes clung to Hannah's face, mixing with her tears. Their sting was like an awakening, a cleansing. She stood completely still, listening to the beautiful silence that comes with snowfall, suddenly filling her soul with peace and calm. She blinked a few times and realized her tears were now tears of joy. With arms outstretched, face turned up to the heavens, she twirled and danced, shouting, "Thank you, Uncle Jack! Thank you, thank you, thank you!"

Wiping the tears and snow from her face, Hannah turned and, with a bounce in her step, headed back into the house singing a familiar Rolling Stones tune.

I may not have gotten what I want, but I sure did get what I need. And what I need is to do some digging into the Boss Rage Gang and, most of all, get a DNA test. She was finally in possession of information that would help her discover her truth. Perhaps she wasn't alone after all.

Rock 'n' Roll Never Forgets
Karen McCullough

"I'm not feeling it. Can't find the soul." Trace put down her favorite Fender bass and raked hair out of her eyes. "The bass line's solid. The tune's good. Lyrics are killer. But it isn't working. Something's missing."

SaraLynn Coughlin, who preferred to be known professionally as just SaraLynn, sighed. "I know. It's got all the parts, but the whole's not jelling."

SaraLynn's band, Daylily Warriors, had been working on the song for over a week, ever since their manager had found the tune on an obscure, long-forgotten demo album and brought it to them. None of them had ever heard of Joanie Selford and Grunge Tone Blue, the group that recorded the album—for obvious reasons. The arrangements were blah, the drummer shaky, and the vocals uneven at best, but the potential of this one song stood out. SaraLynn and her group reworked some of the music to enhance the hooks and improve the rhythm, fitted in a nice harmony line, and Dana created a great drum score for it. But they all felt a lack they couldn't identify.

"Maybe if we knew what the song was actually about," Carrie, their lead guitar, said. "I mean, 'You took it all from me.' What does that mean? What is 'all'? Who is the 'you' here? I think that's the problem. We don't really know."

"Carrie's got a point," Trace agreed. "We don't understand

this piece yet."

"How about if I see what I can find out about the writer?" SaraLynn suggested. "I'll make some inquiries. In the meantime, let's work on a couple of the others. We're almost there with the album."

Their manager had learned that performance rights to "You Took It All" were available from one of the agencies, but he knew nothing of the song's writer. SaraLynn called a private detective recommended by a lawyer friend and engaged him to find the author.

It didn't take him long.

"I've got good news and bad news," the private detective told her when he called back two days later. "I've found the person you're looking for. She sold all rights to her music years ago to pay legal fees, so that part shouldn't be complicated."

"And the bad news?"

"Not that it really affects you," he said. "Her name really is Joanie Selford. She's incarcerated at a women's prison in Columbia, South Carolina."

"Wow. What did she do?"

"Killed a man, apparently. Battered him to death with a baseball bat. They convicted her of murder, with some mitigating factors. Gave her twenty-five to forty years. She's served twelve years now. I'll send you all the info I've got, along with my invoice for the balance."

SaraLynn sucked in a deep breath. This might be the emotional edge they were looking for.

Her next call was to their manager. "I've got the information on the song's author. I think it will help us nail it."

"Terrific news. That piece is killer." SaraLynn grimaced at the reference, but of course John couldn't see her, so he continued. "It's going to make your career."

"The career that's going nowhere fast right now?"

"I keep telling you, babe. Have faith. You've got the talent. The group's got the spark. You're doing the work. It'll come."

"We've been doing the club circuit for three years now. I thought we'd broken through with 'Who Knows, Who Cares.'"

"You hit the charts with it," he reminded her. "Both rock and country."

"Yeah, at seventy-eight and seventy-two. For a solid whole week. Trace and Dana are both grumbling about getting real jobs. How can I blame them?"

"Look, just hang in. One more album. It's going to be the one. I feel it."

Not much reassured, SaraLynn went to the piano. Music was her refuge, her solace, her therapy, and her outlet. Staring at her hand-transcription of the music, she searched for any insight the new knowledge would bring to the song. She even listened to the original version of "You Took It All" again.

I wasn't sure what life would bring,
But I planned to give it my all.
My heart to care, my voice to sing,
Trying to hold the world in thrall.

Then I met you, the worst day of my life.

You took it all from me, you took it all,
Gave nothing back, left me empty, raging.
You took it all, you took it all from me.

I thought I knew you through and through.
We had our lives planned out.
I never guessed what you would do,
What you were really all about.

When I met you, the worst day of my life.

You took it all from me, you took it all,
Gave nothing back, left me empty, raging.
You took it all, you took it all from me.

Since I met you, the worst days of my life.

You took it all from me, you took it all,
Gave nothing back, left me empty, raging.
You took it all, you took it all from me.

The song wasn't perfect. But the underlying melody was catchy and the lyrics packed a punch. The first time she'd heard it, she'd listened several times and on the third play-through she'd begun dabbling around with the arrangement. The more she tweaked, the more she grew convinced the song would work for them. When she'd played it for the other women in the group, their initial skepticism turned to enthusiasm.

"There's a lot of ways we can go with this one," Trace said. "Mellow it out for country or rev it up and do it as power pop."

"I think we should stick with our usual pure hard rock take. It's our brand. The backbeat's already baked into the lyrics, and we can really drive the triads on the refrain."

Now she listened again and again, staring at the score she'd written out, trying to find in the music what had driven a woman to murder. Several obvious interpretations jumped out at her. A scorned lover? A woman who'd been abused in some way? Jealousy, outrage? Too many possibilities.

A courier arrived with the detective's report and the invoice. SaraLynn looked through the information the detective had provided, but it was just the bare facts he'd already given her, with dates and places, along with names of arresting officers, prosecutors, judges, and a few other things. None of it helped get to the heart of the song.

She put in another call to the man. "I need to talk to Joanie Selford, the woman who wrote the music I was searching for.

Can you arrange that for me?"

He hesitated. "Are you sure about this? You'll be talking to someone who killed another person."

"I understand, but I need to talk to her."

The detective sighed loudly. "Okay. I'll see if I can arrange a phone call. When?"

"As soon as possible."

The next day he called back to give her a number where she could reach Joanie Selford, who would have to approve any visit. "Better you talk to her on the phone first anyway." He filled her in on the procedures she'd have to go through for the call and then for a visit, if she did go. And, finally, he added the warning, "Please, keep in mind, many criminals can be manipulative. And there are two sides to every story."

"Got it."

SaraLynn pushed in the numbers with a shaky hand. She'd never talked to a prisoner before. She'd never had much contact with jails, prisons, and prisoners, other than the one time her brother got picked up for possession. She'd been mad as hell with him about it. Although it seemed like everyone in the business did booze or drugs, she stayed away. Even Trace and the others occasionally ribbed her for her diet sodas and for being so straitlaced, but she knew too many talented people whose lives ended too early.

It took a while and some waiting on hold before a woman picked up on the other end and said, "This is Joanie. Who's this? They said your name was Sarah Something?" Her voice was deep and rough, with a gritty, throaty rasp. The voice on the recording.

"SaraLynn. I'm a musician. I guess you were one, too. I happened to hear one of your songs, and I wanted to ask you about it."

"Sold my whole list, such as it was, a long time ago to one of those big agencies," she said.

"I know. But there's something about this one song that grabbed me, and I need to know what brought you to write it."

"'You Took It All,'" she said.

"Yes."

"Only thing I ever wrote that was worth anything."

"I get the feeling there's a story behind it."

"Oh, honey, I'll say there's a story behind it. Hell of a story. But I ain't gonna talk about it over the phone."

"I live in Raleigh," SaraLynn said.

A pause and then a harsh laugh. "Well, for sure I ain't coming to you, honey."

"All right."

Two days later she drove to Columbia. After passing through an unnerving array of heavy doors, metal detectors, and searches, she ended up in a seat in front of a glass partition. A few minutes later, a woman was escorted into the room on the other side and sat in the chair opposite. Tall, raw-boned, probably in her early forties, her scraggly dark hair was clipped short around her face, but her most prominent feature was a pair of large, dark eyes that stared back hard at SaraLynn, drinking her in, almost absorbing her. A smile curled her lips in an expression that would never be called pleasant. She nodded to the phone, and SaraLynn picked it up.

"So, hey, honey," the woman said, "Your curiosity brought you here after all."

"I'm SaraLynn," she said. "Joanie?"

"Hell, yeah, Joanie. What instruments you play?"

"Guitar. Sometimes keyboard. I also do most of the lead vocals."

"Your group?"

"Daylily Warriors."

"Never heard of Daylily Warriors. You had any success?"

"Minor. Hoping to make a jump with the next album."

"Don't we all, honey. Did at one time, anyway."

"You were part of a group?" SaraLynn asked.

"Grunge Tone Blue. Garage band that graduated to a local cover band, with hopes of going even further. Till it all hit the fan."

"What happened?"

The woman gave her that strange, twisted, bitter smile. "You sure you want to know? It ain't pretty."

SaraLynn pulled out a pen and pad, two of the few things she'd been allowed to bring into the room. "I want to know. You mind if I take notes?"

"Go ahead." Joanie's voice went oddly flat and cold. "Ben Corbett happened."

SaraLynn raised an eyebrow and waited.

Joanie shook her head. "Bass player. Good, not great. Brought him in when our original bassist quit. Handsome devil. And when I say 'devil' I mean *devil*."

"Hm?"

"It was good at first. He was competent and reliable. Made friends easily. But he developed a crush on me. He wanted me bad. Pursued me. I wasn't really into limiting myself to one guy at that time, but he wouldn't hear that message. So we were together for a while. But he kept wanting more and more from me. More of my time. More of my attention. More of my music. It made me angry. Eventually I had enough and tried to break up with him. He wasn't having it. He raged and cried and argued and stomped around, trying everything he could think of to keep me from leaving him. He spread lies and rumors about me, saying I was mentally ill and violent and abusive. He told the others in the band I'd said bad things about them, and that caused the group to break up. He tried to isolate me from everyone, even my own family. He ruined my life, made it a living hell. That was when I wrote 'You Took It All.'"

She paused. SaraLynn looked up from the notes she was scribbling, waiting. Joanie drew a long, harsh breath and let it out slowly before she added, "But he hadn't taken everything at that point. That came a little later, when I finally told him we were done, once and for all. He got angry." She heaved another breath. "So very angry. Just raging and out of control. He attacked me. Put his hands around my neck and tried to strangle me." Her fingers tightened around the phone. "I fought him off and ran out onto the back porch. He chased after me. I found a baseball bat he'd left out there and whacked him on the side of the head with it. Whacked him until he fell down and quit moving."

She threw her head back and looked at the ceiling. "That's when he took it *all*. Everything. Even my freedom."

"It sounds like self-defense. Didn't your lawyer try to argue for that?"

"Guess he wasn't much of a lawyer. They did say there was some 'mitigating factors,' so they didn't give me the death penalty. Just twenty-five to forty years here. Hell, this ain't exactly living."

The silence that followed got quickly awkward. SaraLynn had no idea how to respond, so she closed the pad and capped the pen.

After a while Joanie shook her head and said, "Now you know the sad story. You sing that song for me. See if you can make it into a hit. Maybe even tell my story with it."

"Thank you for sharing it."

"You go with it, girl."

The next day SaraLynn told the band about the visit and related Joanie's story.

"Okay, that gives us an angle on it," Dana said. "Are we going for the anger? Outrage? Or more pathos?"

"I think it's got to be the anger," Carrie said. "That can drive the beat and we go all in on the refrain to hammer the message. But a shading of sadness, especially on the bridges, would be good."

They worked on the tune for the next several hours. Tweaked it here and there. Changed the emphasis on some words. Adjusted the harmonies. Altered the beat. Tried plugging the emotion into various places at different levels.

Finally Dana rapped the sticks in a long, punishing rattle on the snare followed by a hard clang on the high-hat cymbals. "Dammit," she said over the reverberations.

Trace sighed and shook her head. "Still off. It's wrong somehow. Why? *Why?* We've got the song and the story behind it. What else do we need?" She squeezed her eyes shut while the others looked at SaraLynn.

"I don't know. What else would we need?"

Trace opened her eyes. "The other side of the story. I can't put my finger on it, but something doesn't seem right with Joanie's version."

"The detective did say to remember that there were always two sides to a story," SaraLynn said. "And the jury did convict her."

Carrie snorted. "Yeah, but we all know how too many people feel about uppity women. Especially in the South. Sometimes it seems like it's a crime for any woman to take charge of her own destiny."

"That's true," Dana said.

"I know." Trace swiped a discordant sound across the strings of the bass. "But something's still missing. Maybe you should ask the detective about the other side of the story."

SaraLynn called him again the next day. She started by apologizing for bothering him so much, but he interrupted to say, "You pay for my time, so I'm fine with it. What's on your mind?"

"The other side of the story. You told me to remember there are always two sides. We're trying to get this piece of music whipped into shape, and it's not cooperating. Some of the group think we don't have the whole story yet. How do I get the other side?"

She heard a smile in his voice when he answered, "I hoped you'd want it. I'll do some digging, see if I can talk to one of the prosecutors about the case. But maybe you should talk to the victim's family."

"Joanie's family?"

"No, the murder victim's. Benton Corbett's. I'll see who's still living and willing to talk about it."

He got back to her shortly. "I have a phone appointment tomorrow to talk to the former D.A. who prosecuted the case. I've also got a phone number for the victim's sister. She's agreed to talk to you. I'd suggest you arrange to go and see her, just as you did Joanie."

The next morning SaraLynn drove back to South Carolina, this time to a small town twenty miles west of Columbia. After leaving the highway, she followed a winding back road, then a long, unpaved drive to a small, but snug and well-maintained house.

A woman opened the front door as SaraLynn mounted the three steps to the porch. Her hostess was probably in her late thirties but looked like life had gone at her hard. Still, her smile was cordial and she welcomed SaraLynn, introducing herself as Tina Corbett McKenzie.

"You came to talk about my brother Ben, right?" she asked after SaraLynn had returned the introduction. "That's fine. Have you had lunch?"

When SaraLynn said she had, the woman offered her a glass of iced tea, which she accepted. It was sweet, but not rattle-your-teeth syrupy. Tina poured herself some also and led them into a small, neat living room. They sat and sipped for a moment before she pulled out a pack of cigarettes and lighter. "Mind if I smoke? Even after all this time, talking about Ben is hard for me."

"I'm sorry. I don't want to cause you pain. And, of course, you can smoke." SaraLynn hated breathing secondhand smoke and worried about her throat and her voice, but it was only for a short time. She pulled out her pad and pen and asked Tina if she could take notes.

"Go ahead." After the woman had lit the cigarette, she said, "Benton—we called him Ben—was three years older than me. My big brother. I adored him growing up. He was just about the best brother anyone could have. He took care of me, protected me. He was so nice. Everyone liked him. And he had this real gift for music. He sang wonderfully and he played just about any instrument. He loved the guitar and the bass."

She put the cigarette down in an ashtray, hopped off the chair, and took a picture from a shelf in the corner to show to SaraLynn. "This is him. He was so cute, too."

The picture featured a young man in his late teens or early twenties, tall, dark-haired, and smiling. He was indeed cute, and he wore a grin that bordered on goofy without quite getting there.

Tina replaced the picture and sat down. "He was the strongest, gentlest man. There wasn't a violent bone in his body, despite what *she*'d have you believe. He wasn't perfect, but he seemed like it to me. Anyway, that's not what you want to know about. You want to know about that day. That awful day." Her voice broke on the last word, and it took her a moment to steady herself enough to go on.

"You gotta understand what led to it. Ben was really good at music and loved playing it, so when he heard of this group that was looking for a bass player, he tried out. When they accepted him—" She stopped again, picked up the cigarette, inhaled deeply, and blew out a long curl of smoke. "I don't think I ever saw him that happy. But it didn't take long for the trouble to start. *That woman*—" She knocked ash off the cigarette with a sharp rap. "She was the leader of the group. But he came to find out no one in the group liked her very much. She was a self-centered bully, and it was already starting to fall apart."

"But it got worse. *That woman* took a liking to him. Too much. She kind of pursued him. Well, not really 'kind of.' She kept after him. Chasing him constantly. She would go to his

229

house he rented and bitch and complain about the others and say things like they were the only two decent musicians in the group. And she'd try to get him to sleep with her. And he—well, he was a man, and even though he didn't really like her, sometimes, she'd…get to him."

Tina stopped for another long drag on the cigarette. "Look, I don't know what happened that day. Only she and my brother really do, and he's gone. But I know this. He didn't try to strangle her because she wanted to call things off. No way! Hell, he would've been grateful for it. The others in the group can testify to how she was always after him and that he tried to put her off. He didn't like having people angry with him, so sometimes he went along with things even when he didn't want to. And I know he would be kind of angry at himself when he let her…seduce him. But he never would've tried to hurt her. I'm guessing he was trying to get away from her at the time she attacked him. That was kind of the way it went. Like he just took everything she dished out and went along or let it roll off him until he couldn't stand it anymore and he'd run away. He came to my place more than once when she was at his."

She stabbed out the cigarette in the ashtray, staring down at it for a minute. Then she looked at SaraLynn. "So that's it. Can't prove a thing, but I know what I know. And there must've been some kind of evidence since the jury did convict her."

"You didn't go to the trial?"

"Went for my day to testify, but that was it. I couldn't stand to be there the rest of the time. I won't lie to you. I celebrated when they convicted her. But it won't bring my brother back." A tear rolled down her cheek.

SaraLynn thanked her and left shortly thereafter. On the drive home one phrase from the interview haunted her with its echo of the song itself. *He just took everything she dished out.*

The next day she reported the conversation to the band and added her own thoughts. "That line she said, 'He just took every-thing she dished out,' suggests a whole different way to read the song. But I'm not sure that adds up either. Joanie wrote it. Surely that wasn't what she was trying to say." Her spirits dropped as she considered what else they could do to make the song work.

The others remained quiet, too, until Trace picked out a simple bass run up and down, then stopped in the middle of it. "Maybe. You know how when you're writing a song, and it suddenly starts pouring out of you, and you don't know where it's all coming from? Somewhere deep inside, maybe? But the words gush out and you end up with something on the paper and then you look at it later and wonder if that really came from you. Maybe this was like that. She wrote it, but there was more coming out than she realized. Like her subconscious made it ambiguous, even though she thought it was clear. Heck we thought it was clear until...this."

"I'm not following," Carrie said. "How is the song different?"

"The key is the line about 'You took it all.' The obvious meaning, the one we all saw was that the guy took everything from her—like her heart and her love, but he didn't return it, right? But you could also read it as meaning he took everything— all the crap she dealt out, the lust he didn't want—but he didn't retaliate or give it back. See?"

"Oh yeah," Carrie said. "Same words, different meanings."

Dana nodded. "Kind of like those puzzle drawings where if you stare at it one way it looks like an old woman, but you can also see it as a young woman just by looking at it differently."

"Of course, we don't know for sure, either way," SaraLynn said. "But maybe that's okay. Maybe the ambiguity is the real soul of the song. Not knowing which one is the real victim."

Trace gave her a strange, thoughtful look. "I know who I believe. The one who didn't lie to you."

"What?"

"Read your notes from the interview with Joanie again," Trace suggested. "The part where she talks about her relationship with the dead guy. You said you tried to get that part almost word for word."

SaraLynn got the pad and flipped it open. "Got it mostly word for word, anyway. Joanie said, 'It was good at first. He was competent and reliable. Made friends. But he had a crush on me. Wanted me bad. Pursued me. I wasn't limiting myself to one guy, but he wouldn't hear it. So we were together for a while. But he wanted more from me. More time. More attention. More of my music. Eventually I tried to break up with him. He wasn't having it. He raged and cried and argued and tried everything to keep me from leaving. He spread lies and rumors, said I was mentally ill and violent and abusive. Told the band I'd said bad things about them and that caused the group to break up. He tried to isolate me from everyone, even my own family. Made my life hell. That was when I wrote 'You Took It All.'"

"Yup, that's it," Trace said.

SaraLynn stared at the pad a moment, and then she saw it. She got up and grabbed the demo CD where they'd found the song. "The label says it was recorded by Joanie Selford and Grunge Tone Blue."

Trace nodded. Dana and Carrie still looked confused, so Trace added, "According to Joanie, she wrote the song *after* the band broke up. If that's true, how did she record it with the band?"

"She's lying," SaraLynn said. "Everything she said was a lie."

The others looked stunned and then thoughtful before they got back to work. By changing a few chords to vary the emotional effect on each line, it seemed to come together. After some discussion on where to put a few flourishes and significant pauses, the inner strength emerged. They moved the emphasis in the phrasing of the refrains from "took" to "all" and the rhythm changed in a catchy way. The hooks fell into place.

"That third bridge is key," SaraLynn said. "The move from 'day' to 'days.' It's the climax and we've got to hit it hard. Maybe change the chord behind 'worst days' to a discordant seventh, like this." She played it for them, fingering a major seventh but without the third, then hammering on the minor third to make it ring even more. "Make it hit hard. Then we fall off into a lower, sadder repeat of the last refrain."

By the late afternoon they had a pretty good handle on the arrangement and were getting excited about the emerging sound. They played it through, recording it, and stared at each other in triumph as they finished.

"This is going to work," SaraLynn said.

When she took the rough recording for their manager the next day, he was ecstatic. "You got it. Nailed it. Let's take it to the studio. It's going to be huge."

Six Months Later

"I got an email about the interview with *Rolling Stone*," SaraLynn told the other members of the band. "Lots of congratulations from them on reaching the top of their chart and the Billboard 100 with 'You Took It All.' Plus all the standard questions about us and the band and our backgrounds. And then they want to know about the inspiration for the song."

"We've told the backstory often enough," Trace said. "Maybe we need to emphasize the song's roots and what we owe to both Joanie and Benton. For all her faults, Joanie did write the song, and it was something none of us could've done. It took her particular experience to make it happen."

SaraLynn nodded agreement. "Even if she was writing something deeper and truer than she knew. But it was Ben who became the heart and soul of our version. The events around his death are the real story. I don't want anyone to ever forget that this song is ultimately about the destruction of a young man's hopes and dreams, even his future. By dedicating it to Benton Corbett, we can at least keep his memory alive."

The M and M's Mystery
Noelle Granger

I first met Mildred when she moved into my room at the Rest Easy Retirement Home. My former roommate had died in her sleep, as had many others, which is why we called the place God's Waiting Room. Coughs, whoops, shuffling, wails, music, and TV chatter filled the place every day, overriding discussions by those of us still mentally capable of it.

Two days after my roommate died, Nurse Wretched, an ascetic busybody named Norma, who slinked around in a white uniform and rubber-soled, silent shoes, wheeled in my new roomie, saying, "Isn't this nice! Miriam, this is Mildred Wrightnour. Mildred, this is Miriam Gardner. The sun is shining and it's warm today, so why don't the two of you sit out in the sunroom and get to know each other."

Mildred had to be in her eighties, with a cap of short white hair, a pleasantly round face with a sharp nose, and so thin that two of her could have fit in the wheelchair. She wore a cobalt blue blouse that set off her hair. I wondered what she thought of me, a definite mesomorph with a long white braid, wearing wire-rimmed glasses and sweatpants.

I looked at Mildred with suspicion. She was my third roommate, and I wondered if she were healthy. "Hi, Mildred. Where you from?"

"Just outside of Boston. You?" She smiled.

I liked her immediately. Spare with her words. "A Southie," I replied.

She nodded at my mention of South Boston. Tony, one of two Irish aides who clearly worked out regularly came in and deposited Mildred's suitcases on her freshly made bed. Then he and Norma left us alone.

"Can I help you unpack?" I asked. "That dresser over there is yours." I bit my tongue not to say, *still warm from the last resident.* "You need help in and out of your wheelchair?"

"I'm not that decrepit yet. Just can't walk long distances. Bad hip. I'll be fine." She stood easily and began putting away underwear, nightgowns, and sweaters. She placed three pictures on her dresser along with a comb, brush, and a bag of bathroom necessities. "Not much to show for a lifetime, is it?" she commented.

"Nope, but it keeps things simple." I saw her unpack a Swiss Army knife. "What do you plan to use that for?"

"This? It's really handy—comes with a nail file, scissors, and this..." She pulled out the corkscrew and winked.

"Just the thing. I've been wanting to smuggle in some wine."

Mildred looked puzzled. "How can you do that?"

"Tony. He's bribable."

With the unpacking over, Mildred wheeled herself down the hall to the sunroom, pulling up next to a padded chair where I plopped myself down.

"I hear there's a loudspeaker?" she asked.

"Oh, that bloody thing. It gets us up at seven a.m.—don't think about sleeping in—and announces all meals ten minutes before they serve. Also lights out at ten p.m. It's like a frigging boot camp."

She waved her hand in front of her face. "Good Lord, I feel like I'm in a hothouse in here. Can we go outside to chat?"

"They keep it warm because they're certain we all grew up on the equator. And we need permission to go outside. They have to know where you are at all times."

"Really? How about an escape? Ever made one?"

"All the time, because I'm one of the few truly mobile inmates. That door over there leads to a patio. Let's go." I checked my watch. "Lots of time before lunch to break some rules."

When we got outside, I took a deep breath. "Thank God. Smells like eau de old people and Lysol in there. I can't stand it."

Over the next hour or so, we talked about our past lives—she, an instructor at Boston University and I, a secretary in my husband's law firm. Both of us widowed more than ten years earlier. She told me they were nearly broke when her husband died. She didn't say it, but I got the impression he committed suicide. Her children and grandchildren were the light in her life.

"They visit you much?" I asked.

She looked down. "Not much." Her voice dropped to almost a whisper. Then her face brightened. "One of my granddaughters and I are good buddies, though, and she told me this place is on a bus line, so maybe I'll see her more often. How about you?'

"No kids. Ben never wanted them, selfish bastard."

"I take it you had an unhappy marriage?"

"Only when he was around."

She was quiet for a moment, then asked, "What do you do for fun around here?"

"Eat, read, knit, crochet, play card games, watch TV. An exercise program in the common room every day. And music. Did you hear the noise from room 208 this morning when you came in?"

"*Romeo and Juliet* by Beethoven? That's not noise; it's music!"

"Well, look at you, all classical. That *music* used to go on all day and half the night until we gave Nurse Wretched an ultimatum: either shut it down at a reasonable hour, or we would riot."

She chuckled. "You must mean Norma. So who exactly got shut down?'"

"Mr. Redwine and his roommate, Mr. Massey. Redwine was an orchestra director for some high muckety-muck symphony and he's famous for some orchestral piece that he plays frequently. You'll soon be sick of hearing it. He spends his days directing music from CD recordings. Massey played the violin with the same orchestra and likes to play along. I don't think he knows I instigated the shutdown, and I only hope he doesn't find out."

I thought of what else she might like to know. "There *is* other entertainment, if you can call it that: kids singing carols at Christmas, some fourth-rate comedians trying out their routines, and an old Disney movie in the common room. Wouldn't want to over-stimulate our minds. This place isn't the Ritz, Mildred."

Mildred nodded. "My son William told me that even with my retirement and Social Security, I didn't have enough money coming in to maintain my home. This is what my money gets me, with some help from him. And you?"

"My husband embezzled from the law firm and got fired. Died of a heart attack a month later, before we figured out how we could manage financially. I moved to an apartment while I still worked—the firm didn't fire *me*—then to another place nicer than this when I retired. When my money dwindled and I didn't die, I moved here. Nice ride downhill."

"LUNCH WILL BE SERVED IN TEN MINUTES," the bored, nasal voice blasted from the loudspeaker. Mildred startled. "FISH STICKS AND MACARONI AND CHEESE."

"You'll get used to it," I told her. "At least the desserts are good. Today's Thursday, so apple pie."

We trekked to the dining room to the sound of Mussorgsky's *Night on Bald Mountain* emanating from room 208. A perfect introduction to the meal.

Over the next month, Mildred and I formed a strong bond. She had a wicked sense of humor and, after a time, could mimic almost every one of the other inmates. With her knowledge of classical music, I wasn't surprised to hear her humming some of the pieces Redwine played, including his often-repeated symphony.

Mildred told me her husband had loved it and thought it would make a good movie score. In return, I treated her to some CDs of seventies rock and roll. Occasionally we danced to it, if you want to call moving our arms and hips dancing. But I swear it improved Mildred's mobility.

Then a most exciting thing happened. Someone died. And not from "natural" causes.

We noticed something amiss when Norma counted heads at breakfast and asked, "Has anyone seen Maestro Redwine?" When no one answered, she yelled for Tony and bustled off down the hall. Silence, followed by a scream. The massive Tony immediately appeared, saying, "Everyone stay put. There's nothing to worry about." He left, closing the double doors to the dining room with a solid thump.

Mildred and I returned to our places at the table. "Where's Massey? I don't see him here either," she commented.

I looked around. She was right. He was also missing. Figures Nurse Wretched would only think about the maestro.

Just then we heard sirens and beat everyone to the dining room window. Three police cars pulled up, red and blue lights flashing, and we watched as a bevy of uniformed men got out, looking grim. Then we heard clomping down the hall in the direction of...our room. I looked at Mildred, her face reflecting my surprise. "Something's happened to Redwine or Massey," she whispered.

Our room sat kitty-corner to theirs, and I just had to get a look. "Come on, let's find out what's going on. I can get us into the hallway, but do you think you can look agonized?"

She winked. "Gotcha."

I opened the doors and pushed Mildred into Tony, who stood guard just outside the dining room. "Tony, Mildred needs to use a bathroom. Right now." My roomie assumed a pitiful look and hugged her stomach.

He frowned at us. "Use the one across the hall."

"Can't. She has special equipment in ours."

He paused for a minute, clearly trying to think. "Okay, go, but don't blame me if Norma jumps on you."

As I pushed Mildred down the hall, a woman deputy stood in our way and put up her hand.

"Can't go down there. Sorry."

Mildred groaned and clasped her stomach, looking miserable.

"Look, my roommate here needs to use a bathroom, and only ours has the equipment she needs. We're old, for God's sake."

"Alright, alright." She moved aside and we booked it down the hall, glancing into room 208 as we passed.

Mildred gasped. Redwine lay face down on the floor, blood pooled around him. Someone had stabbed him in the back with a violin bow. Through the crowd around the body, I could just make out Massey's feet on his bed, and we could hear moaning. I pushed Mildred and her wheelchair to our room, opened the door, and shoved her inside.

"Did you see that?" she asked as soon as the door was shut. "Can you really punch a violin bow into someone's back? It's not sharp enough."

"I don't think it'd be that difficult," I replied. "I saw cut-off strings dangling from the visible end. He...or she...would just have to hone the wood down. And know something of anatomy to do it, right?"

"Definitely, to know just where to make the fatal insertion," Mildred replied. "But what about motive? Who here would want to do him in?"

"Well, I don't think it would be Massey. He'd lose his musical director, unless they had a serious argument over a sonata. Did you hear the moaning?"

"Yeah, I bet it was Massey. How can we find out if he's a suspect?"

We looked at each other and said in unison, "Tony!"

After lunch that day—yummy creamed chipped beef on toast,

which I'd heard several of our military veterans call shit on a shingle—we pretended fatigue and asked Tony to wheel Mildred to our room.

You live in this place long enough, you learn everyone's weaknesses. Tony's was Little Debbie Nutty Buddy bars, and a friend of mine had sent me a huge box of Little Debbie products for Christmas. I saw Tony salivating when he first spied the box, so I gave him some. Now I'd use my strategic reserve of Nutty Buddies to get information. I'd deliberately left two packages on my bed before we left for lunch.

"If that's all..." he said, after wheeling Mildred in. His eyes drifted and then stopped like a laser pointer on what lay on my bed.

"Yup, they're for you, Tony, but we need some information in return."

"Ah, Miriam, my girl, you know that could get me in trouble. You're always getting me in trouble." He rolled his Rs, Boston Irish.

Mildred wheeled her chair to face him and I sat down at my desk. "I need you to tell us what went on in Room 208 this morning," I said.

"But you saw everything when you went by the door, didn't you?"

"Not everything," said Mildred. "Tell us, and those Little Debbies are yours."

Tony perched on the side of my bed, scooping up the two packages. "Mr. Redwine got stabbed with Mr. Massey's violin bow. The police think Mr. Massey did it, but he was in no condition to defend himself to them because, the devil take him, he was out of it. I think he'd been drugged. Norma told me to help him get dressed, and the police took him to the hospital. Then the medical examiner showed up, pronounced Redwine dead, and took the body off somewhere."

I made notes as he spoke. "So the bow definitely belonged to Massey?"

"Probably," he answered. "Mr. Massey has a number of bows, I'm not sure even he knows how many. But honestly? I don't think he's got the energy, the mental capacity, or the will to murder Mr. Redwine. Why would he? Music is his whole life, and I've never heard a cross word between them."

I thought for a minute. "Do you know who visits them?"

Tony shook his head. "Both of them have visitors, but I don't know who they are. I can find out, if you have any more of these…?"

Mildred and I nodded vigorously and Tony left, happy and humming.

"Let's go outside to talk," I suggested.

Mildred turned her wheelchair around. "Tally-ho!"

After making sure no one occupied the sunroom, we slipped out the door to the patio and sat, enjoying the warmth of the sun on our backs. "So, are we seriously going to try to find out who killed Redwine?" Mildred asked, turning slightly to get more light on her face. "This could be fun!"

"I'm in if you are, hon. Okay…first we need to find out if anyone living here has a serious grudge against Redwine."

"And just how do we do that?" My friend moved even further into the sun.

"Google."

"Oh, goody."

"We need to make a list of the residents," I said. "I don't know them all."

"Me either. We should probably count out anyone in a wheelchair or using a walker. They wouldn't be strong enough to perpetrate the crime…"

Spoken like a detective. I smiled.

"…and those mostly deaf, because they couldn't hear anyone coming."

"Leaving us with maybe a third of the residents to investigate. We're going to have to cozy up to those we don't know and get their names and room numbers, at the very least."

"Speaking of rooms," Mildred replied, "anyone with a room toward the end of the other hallway would probably not be a candidate. Too far to walk not to be spotted, especially at night."

The Rest Easy was a long, straight building, with wings coming off north and south of a central core consisting of reception, dining room, common room, and sunroom. So I agreed with Mildred's assessment. "Ready to get to work, partner?"

"You bet. What's for dinner?"

Many residents considered meals to be the highlights of the day, and I feared Mildred now fell into that group. "Boiled beef. They use all of the beef allotment on one day."

Over the next week, Mildred and I sat with as many different residents as possible during meals and spent time in the common room, learning names and room numbers and if the residents had any connection to Redwine. Turned out the gossip mill continued to churn merrily, so that last query generated a lot of discussion.

In the midst of this, Nurse Wretched came to the table where I ate lunch, leaned over, and spoke quietly in my ear, "I can see what you and Mildred are doing."

Oh, Lord, we've been caught!

"I think it is extremely nice of you and Mildred to get to know all our residents better. I wish there were more like you."

My stomach descended into place, but I had to wait a minute or so for my heart rate to return to normal. After lunch, I told Mildred what Norma had said to me.

"She told me the same thing. I thought I would die right there with my face in the plate." She laughed. "And we had gravy on the turkey and mashed potatoes!"

"Okay, so Norma is fine with us. Let's take stock of where we are." Over the next hour, we scoured our copious notes and managed to eliminate all but two people. "I almost wish we had a larger suspect pool," Mildred said, as we crossed off the last name.

"We've forgotten the people who work here! Norma, for

example, and the receptionist, the nursing aides, and even Tony."

"Tony? Surely not!"

"Well, think about it. He'd be happy for us to blame anyone other than him, so it would be in his interest to be helpful." I paused at that moment and lucky I did, because right then, Tony appeared at our door with the list of Redwine's and Massey's visitors for the last three months.

"How's your investigation going, ladies?"

"We've managed to winnow down the likely suspects. Thanks for this list, Tony. I hope you didn't have any problems."

Tony smiled, showing dazzling white teeth. "Nah, that receptionist loves me." After a pregnant pause, he asked, "You got any more of those Nutty Buddies?"

"Sure." I went into the closet and pulled out another pack. "There you go, and thanks again."

Tony smiled and left the door ajar as he left the room, this time whistling as he walked down the hall.

"A bad rendition of Mozart's *Concerto for Bassoon*, if I'm right."

"Dang, Mildred, where did you learn all this stuff?"

She just smiled and said, "Over the years. My husband played classical music all the time at home."

Tony's list didn't provide a lot of help—based on the last name, only family members. Two men with the name Redwine, possibly sons, and one woman with the last name of Copper, a married daughter? I added those names to our list. "Time to google."

We began by searching for information on the two residents still on our list: Lorraine Pringle, Room 206, and Joseph Entwhistle, Room 214. Lorraine had played the oboe in an orchestra for musical theater in Boston. Entwhistle had practiced law. While I could see where Redwine's life might have intersected with Lorraine's, I wondered what his connection was to our lawyer.

"What kind of law did Mr. Entwhistle practice?" asked Mildred.

More key tapping. "Looks like personal property and real estate lawsuits."

"Can we look up lawsuits against Redwine if we pay for a search? Maybe Entwhistle was one of the lawyers."

"For just $19.99..." I joked. With Mildred's consent, we subscribed to BackgroundSearch.com and found two lawsuits against Redwine, one for plagiarism and one for property theft. Seems our maestro's life had had its problems. Public records showed Redwine had been sued for stealing a composer's symphony, but the suit had been dismissed. And one of his two sons had sued his father over the distribution of his real estate. Entwhistle figured in neither suit.

Mildred took copious notes as I read off the computer screen.

"From what I know from my work in the law firm," I commented, "suits for musical plagiarism are a dime a dozen. And the person suing almost never wins. Okay, so the suit filed by one of Redwine's sons is our main lead. Let's see if the son won the case." More clicking of keys. "Yup, and the other son has launched an appeal. No love lost there."

I moved on to the widowed Ms. Pringle, finding very little. She'd lived an exemplary life, not even a parking ticket. And no connection to Redwine through her music, so we exonerated her. "How about the visitor list, Mildred? Which one of the sons visited Redwine?"

Mildred glanced at Tony's list. "Both, it seems."

"That's weird."

"DINNER IN 10 MINUTES. TURKEY DELIGHT AND SALAD."

We both groaned.

Next, we used our "getting to know you" approach to gather information on Rest Easy employees. Norma seemed inordinately pleased with our effort and nicknamed us the M and M's. *What a hoot!*

I googled the employees and the female visitor, who turned out to be Massey's daughter. "She's clean," I told Mildred, shutting down the search, "as well as everyone else on our list. Maybe we missed something."

"What about Tony?"

"A dead end. I can't find him anywhere online," I replied. "It's like he doesn't exist. No driver's license, no address or birth date. He's a nonperson."

"Well, buck up, cream puff. We've still got three likely murderers. The two sons and Tony. Funny that the sons would visit their father if they're all suing each other. So where do we go from here?"

"Tony told me the sons will come to pick up their father's belongings tomorrow. Maybe we could approach them then?"

We hung around in our room the following morning, peering out our half-opened door. Around eleven, Tony came down the hall, whistling another classical tune, key in hand. He opened the door to room 208 for the two men who followed on his heels and left, luckily for us, without shutting the door.

Mildred wheeled quietly across the hall and I followed.

"I miss him, the old bugger," we heard a tenor voice say.

"Me, too." After a pause, this deeper voice said, "I'm sorry for the lawsuit, Mason. I should have just sat down with you and Dad at the outset and not assumed the worst."

"Well, you *did* sit down with us, so at least our last few times together with him are happy memories. We both forgave you..."

"Should we go in?" I whispered to Mildred. "Sounds like any reason for murdering their father has evaporated."

"Maybe one of them is lying," she whispered back.

I gave Mildred a thumbs-up and we entered the room, finding the two men sitting side by side on one bed. They both had their father's high forehead and weak chin, and they stared at us, puzzled.

"Hello, I'm Miriam Gardner and this is Mildred Wrightnour. We live across the hall. We wanted to offer our condolences."

"Yes, we do miss his lovely music," Mildred added.

Both men stood. "Thank you," said the tenor voice. "I'm Mason Redwine. This is my brother Barry."

"Have the police made any progress in finding your father's killer?" I asked. "We certainly don't feel safe here anymore."

"You know we can't lock our doors at night," Mildred said, arranging her face into a look of concern.

Mason shrugged. "The police are as clueless as we are, ladies. I just can't imagine who would want to do something so brutal to our father. I'm truly sorry you feel unsafe."

"Is there anyone from his past life or even someone here, at Rest Easy, who would wish him harm?" Mildred asked.

Mason and Barry looked at each other and then shook their heads. "No, he didn't have an unkind word to say about anyone here," Barry replied, "except the people who forced a curfew on his music. But he never discovered who instigated it."

Thank heavens for that. I had dreaded the thought of facing Redwine. Mildred and I repeated our sympathy and retreated to our room.

"Well, that's it, damn," she said. "It has to be Tony. I say we confront him."

"Why? He's just going to deny it."

"But there are little tells that lying people have. I learned all about them from *Forensic Files.*"

"Like what?" I asked her, plopping down on the bed.

"Their lips tighten, their eyes dart around, and they blink. Right-handed people look up and to the right...or is it down and to the left?" She demonstrated. "Anyway, with both of us looking right at him, he's bound to give something away."

I thought for a minute. "Okay. Let's try it. I'll offer him another package of Little Debbies for...what?"

"Information on Nurse Wretched. She must yell for him twenty times a day."

I gave Tony the eyeball at breakfast the next morning, and when he came over, I told him what we wanted. He came to our room a few minutes later.

"Norma? I can give you a lot of dirt on Norma." He hadn't failed to notice the Little Debbies in Mildred's hands.

"We really want to talk to you about something else. Sit down, please," I said, as sternly as I could muster.

"I need to get back."

"Sit down or I'll scream," Mildred said. He immediately sat, and we both faced him. "You know we've been trying to figure out who killed Redwine."

"Yeah, and you haven't gotten anywhere."

"We *have* gotten somewhere. We think you did it," I said.

Tony stared at us. He didn't blink, didn't look down or up or right or left, and his face remained frozen in a pleasant neutral. Then he laughed, a loud, snorting guffaw. "Me? Why would you think that?"

We focused on his face as I said, "We googled you and you're a ghost. No address, no driver's license, no history. What are you, an assassin? In witness protection?"

"You two are batshit crazy if you think I had anything to do with Mr. Redwine's murder. Why would I want to kill him? You can't prove I did it, because I didn't. Look, if there's nothing else, I have a lot to do this morning." He stood, winked at us, and left, but not without taking the Little Debbies.

"Hardly what I expected," Mildred commented. "Did you see any tells? Do you think he lied?"

"I didn't see a smidgen of a response. Not a blink, a twitch, or an eye roll. But I still think he did it. What about you?"

"Me, too, but I give up, Miriam. We got nothing and he's not going to tell us anything. I can't think of where to go from here. And if it's not Tony, the murderer may still be here."

Mildred's word chilled me, and we put a chair under the doorknob at night.

Two months elapsed, and Redwine's murder remained unsolved. The police had interviewed everyone and finally stopped coming around with questions. Tony, bless his soul, still thought our suspicion of him was hilarious and apparently forgave us, because he remained as nice as ever.

We didn't stop trying to find something, anything about him, slyly probing Norma to no avail and making a failed, middle-of-the-night attempt to get a look at employee files.

More deaths occurred, but only the usual from natural causes. Mildred and I stayed healthy, until she didn't. She developed a wracking cough and a high fever, and Norma called an ambulance. After the attendants lifted her onto a gurney and wrapped her in blankets, she asked them to wait outside, she needed to tell me something in private.

They left our room, and she began coughing again, exhausted from the effort. I took her hand, and looked down at her, feeling indescribable grief. I leaned down to hear her weak voice.

"Living with you has been the most fun I've had in years, Miriam," she said. "I'm pretty sure I'm not coming back, and I need to tell you something."

"That we're eventually going to meet up again in a place better than this?"

Mildred smiled and shook her head, coughing.

By now tears streamed down my cheeks. "I love you, kiddo. My life will be empty with you gone. You'd better get well."

"Buck up, cream puff," she said. "I need to tell you something. You know those lawsuits against Redwine? Follow up on that composer. The one who lost his lawsuit."

The attendants came back in the room. "Love you, too," Mildred rasped as they wheeled her out.

I collapsed in our chair by the window, drained and crying, and only roused when Norma insisted that I come to lunch. I don't remember what I ate. I only knew Mildred wasn't in the seat beside me.

I dragged through the next two days, asking Norma over and over if she'd heard anything from the hospital. To her credit, she did call and ask, but had nothing to report. On the third day, she came to my room before breakfast. I knew the minute she entered what she would say.

The next day, my emotions more in control, I sat down at the desk and turned on the computer, then pulled out the notes Mildred had taken in her neat handwriting. Seeing them, my tears started again. I found and googled the name of the composer who had sued Redwine: Shaunessey, first name Patrick. *Found him.* I decided to search Wikipedia and his obituary. According to Wikipedia, he was indeed a classical music composer of some renown, who had bankrupted himself suing Redwine for stealing one of his pieces. It was entitled *The Red Herring Sonata.*

I skipped over his early life and the family connections and moved on to the obituary. There I discovered what Mildred wanted me to know: Patrick X. Shaunessey, beloved of his wife Mildred, nee Wrightnour, professor emerita of biology at Boston University.

That night I used the corkscrew on the Swiss Army knife Mildred had given me and opened a bottle of unoaked Chardonnay, her favorite wine. A gift from Tony. I poured myself a good snort-full and toasted Mildred.

To my fellow sleuth, dearest friend, and secret-keeper extraordinaire. How did you do it?

The Sound of Murder
Marni Graff

Even in death, the young woman looked beautiful: creamy light skin, eyelashes splayed across pale cheeks, brunette hair contrasted against a stark white pillow. A large cross on a leather thong had been arranged on top of a sheet tucked under her pointed chin. Disconnected hospital equipment mocked medicine's efforts.

Beside the bed, tears cascaded down her mother's cheeks, while her sister looked bewildered. "Sweetheart," her mother said, "remember when I took you girls to Jones Beach and you lost your bikini top—"

The corpse gave a shuddering breath.

"Cut!" the director's voice boomed.

Callie Lawton sat up, leaned on her elbows, and hummed "I Am Sixteen Going on Seventeen."

Her "mother" scowled. "Do you have any idea how much menthol tear stick I had to use to cry like that?" Susan Ward snapped. "I stink, and for what?"

"Poor you, having to smell like Vicks instead of shedding real tears." Callie pouted and threw a wink to me, her coconspirator behind Camera Two.

My name is Trudy Genova, RN, medical consultant for this scene in the drama *Knight's Castle*. Callie and I had worked together closely; this was her last episode. I'd miss her.

The soundstage door slammed. Ron Dowling, Napoleon of television directors, flew onto the set from the control booth. Black socks with Birkenstocks reinforced his gnome image as he scurried over.

I'd wondered how Dowling expected Callie not to breathe through Susan's soliloquy and waited for him to make it my issue. I had a healthy dislike of misogynists, and Dowling led my list.

"You ruined that shot, Callie," Dowling said. "Dead daughters don't breathe."

"But I'm not dead," Callie shot back. "I can't hold my breath while Susan spews her Emmy histrionics over my body for three full minutes. That's called unrealistic expectations, Ronnie."

"That's called acting." Susan smirked. "Not that you'd recognize the technique."

"Is that what it is, Susan? I forgot because you're so filled with hot air you don't breathe like a normal person."

A snicker ran around the crew. Jill Davis, who played Callie's sister, let slip a *whoop* of laughter.

Callie had recently been cast as Liesl in a Broadway rock-and-roll version of *The Sound of Music*. Susan, desperate for another Emmy, counted on Callie's decision to leave *Knight's Castle* to provide it. Nothing screams winner like crying over your dead daughter.

"Ladies, no bickering." Dowling pretended to think.

I say pretended because I'd worked with Dowling before, and his obtuse brain worked one speed: slow. When he snapped his fingers, he surprised me by having an original thought.

"Got it." He turned to the cameramen. "Camera One, start a long shot of the room and all three women, then tighten on Callie. Camera Two, start with Susan and Jill, then rise to Susan's face." He clapped his hands. "We'll alternate cameras, so Callie's chest isn't continuously in the shot."

Dowling had worked with these men for years but had yet to

learn their names. I sighed because it was my turn to come under his scrutiny. In three, two, one—

"Trudy, figure out how to let Callie know when to breathe—in four minutes."

Luckily I had run across this problem on a soap opera. I ran to the props room and asked Barney for string.

The props manager rummaged in a drawer and found a paddle of kite cord. "This work?"

"Perfect. It won't be seen." Strict union rules meant if the string was a prop, a union member had to bring it on set.

Barney waved me off. "See you at lunch, Trudy."

Clutching my prize, I hurried back, unwinding the paddle. "Try this, Callie." She was still singing, slightly off-key. I loosened the covers nearest me, tied one end around her big toe, then ran the string under the sheet to the foot of the bed and smoothed the blanket. I explained my plan and we exchanged smiles.

Holding the paddle, I sat on the floor under Camera One, Hank, where I could see Camera Two. "All set," I told Dowling.

Camera Two, Jimmy, gave Callie a thumbs-up.

"Camera blocking, no tears, Susan. Just recite your lines." Dowling consulted his watch. "If this works, we'll break for lunch, tape after."

I saluted him, which he pretended not to notice. Callie settled down, Susan dipped her head, and Jill reclaimed her seat. Dowling's voice loomed over us.

"Places—a-a-a-n-d action!"

As the cameras rolled, I tugged the string and Callie held her breath. When the light went on in Camera Two, meaning her chest wasn't in the shot, I jerked the string again to tell Callie to breathe. When I pulled again, she held her breath. It worked perfectly through Susan's speech to her dead daughter, with Jill's consoling hand on her mother's shoulder. Once Susan added tears, most viewers would be moved.

"And cut! Lunch. Taping one thirty sharp."

I left my medical kit under Jimmy's camera, stood and dusted off my jeans, then flipped the covers back to untie Callie's toe. A huge perk of this job was wearing comfortable clothes. No more uniforms. No thanks from Dowling, either, but that was an acceptable trade-off.

Jimmy high fived Callie before leaving for lunch. Callie smiled, showing perfect white teeth and a dimple, before turning my way. "That was inspired, Trudy." Small wonder she'd been cast as Liesl, considering how she glowed.

"Consider it a going-away present." As happy as I was for Callie, I'd miss our banter. She'd made coming to work fun. When she'd announced she would leave the show, the writers killed off her character. Suddenly, a disease acquired on a missionary trip returned, and before you could say "Emmy Award Performance," Lily Knight declined and died, and here we were.

I waited for traffic to slow before I crossed to the commissary. It was a lovely brisk autumn day, and I was thrilled to be out and about in Manhattan. The studio was a block from Lincoln Center, near my boyfriend's precinct. Occasionally I met NYPD Detective Ned O'Malley for lunch.

But not today. Instead, I gathered my auburn hair in a scrunchie as I ascended the escalator, where thick columns and glass railings lent the commissary a modern vibe, and bigwigs ate alongside lowly employees like me. I saw Dowling with two men when I took my tray to Barney's table. The older man hated eating alone. We watched Callie and Jill avoid Susan's table and settle together, yakking away. Susan ate with her husband, Steve, a retired English professor—handsome, if you liked men in tweeds. His booming laugh reached across the tables.

"I'm hungry." Barney wolfed down a meatball hero with gusto.

"So I see." I eyed Barney's meatballs with desire while failing to summon up the same enthusiasm for my Cobb salad. Since

Ned and I started sleeping together, I'd become more conscious of my curves, but those meatballs seemed far more attractive than my diet. Who knew meatball lust was a thing?

Barney wiped sauce off his chin. "Nice to see Callie and Jill aren't letting Liesl ruin their friendship."

"You mean because Callie's hitting the bright lights of Broadway, and Jill isn't?" Barney always heard news I didn't, as I only worked on set for medical scenes. Other days I worked from home, correcting medical bits in scripts sent from many studios. These days on set were enjoyable, getting to know the players like Callie outside their roles, Dowling notwithstanding.

Barney nodded. "They both tried out for Liesl, but Callie was cast, while I hear Jill is understudy for a few roles, including two abbey nuns. That's why she didn't give up *Knight's Castle*."

"Ouch." I thought back to the Julie Andrews movie. "But those nuns are much older and tiny parts."

"Bingo. And Jill's only an understudy. Not enough exposure or salary to leave TV like Callie is banking on."

I knew television actors often did Broadway and kept their TV roles, but sometimes the lure of live theater beckoned, and off they went, salary and security be damned, hoping for a bridge to Hollywood. I felt uneasy for Callie. If she wasn't a hit, she'd have nothing to fall back on.

Soon Susan and Steve left, followed by Callie and Jill. The women would visit hair and makeup while I had coffee and Barney ate the dessert I avoided, since I hoped to see Ned tonight, though criminals often seemed to know when to disrupt our plans.

Barney and I walked back to the studio where I signed in right beneath Steve Ward's signature. Nice that he'd stayed for Susan's big scene. I headed into the cold soundstage, stepping over cables for lights and sound, and pulled my fleece closer. The Kleig lights made sets quite warm; the rest of the soundstage was kept cool to offset the carbon arc lights' intensity.

I thought I'd be the first one back, but Callie was already

under the sheet, her cross arranged on top, eyes closed. I didn't speak to her as she concentrated on losing touch with noises so she wouldn't react. Playing dead was harder than it looked, she'd confided that morning. I hoped she didn't doze off and ruin our string scheme.

Voices came from the soundstage door as Susan strolled in with Steve, her hair even stiffer with spray. They were followed by the cameramen and Jill. Steve took a chair and brought out his phone for a few snaps of Susan's epic cry.

Susan and Jill took their places at the bedside. I'd left the paddle on the bed and drew the covers back while the cameramen took their places. Callie's foot felt cool as I tied the string to her big toe. I had the creepy image of tying a toe tag to a corpse at a morgue, when I noticed her toenail was blue.

I stepped up to Callie's head and scrutinized her, shocked to see circumoral cyanosis—a blue color around her lips. "Callie— wake up!" Nothing. I leaned forward to feel for breaths as I took her pulse.

Susan and Jill stood. "What's wrong with Callie?" Steve called.

No rush of air from Callie's nostrils. No pulse. Holy crap! I made eye contact with Jimmy. "She's not breathing. Call 911 and get my kit." I raised Callie's eyelid and saw paleness and petechiae, the little hemorrhagic bursts that denote asphyxiation.

"Got it." Jimmy handed me my kit, and I took out my stethoscope while Steve yelled, "I'm calling—wait, no bars."

Susan screeched: "No connectivity in here, you idiot! Go outside."

While I listened to Callie's chest, Steve left, hopping over cables. The stage door slammed.

Susan picked up Callie's hand. "She's so cold…"

I resisted saying *because she's dead*, and concentrated on trying to hear a heartbeat. With a resounding thump, I walloped Callie's chest, then started compressions—the song "Stayin' Alive" helping me keep the rhythm—even as my own heartbeat sped up. This could not be happening. *Come on, Callie,* I prayed. *Fight like I'm fighting for you.*

People rushed onto the soundstage. Jill burst into tears, sniveling, and her tears started Susan crying.

Dowling yelled, "What's going on?"

I glanced up for a second to see him run his hands though his wiry hair, making it stand on end. Steve returned and herded Susan and Jill out of my way as I pumped and prayed my litany. Now that I had the rhythm, I wouldn't stop until the EMTs arrived unless someone relieved me.

"What the hell happened?" Dowling's voice squeaked in anxiety.

I finally answered him. "I found her unresponsive." My compressions had pulled the sheet away from Callie's neck, and as I glanced at it now, I saw the thin red line, and every symptom made horrific sense. "I think she's been strangled."

Over two hours later, after the paramedics declared Callie dead, her body was sent to the morgue and her family in Iowa was notified. A forensic team clustered around the bed, dusting for fingerprints, while anyone who had touched the bed had theirs taken. Uniformed officers had cordoned off the soundstage. No one who had been in the studio had been allowed to leave until Ned had shown up forty minutes ago with his team member, Lizzie Damon.

What a way to see my boyfriend. We were supposed to go to my place tonight to eat pizza and watch the Yankees. Instead, we'd probably be here for hours, while Ned searched for answers, and I struggled with my emotions. I hadn't been able to save Callie, and felt a mixture of guilt and sadness.

Ned explained my findings to his medical examiner friend, while Lizzie shepherded me, Dowling, Jill, Susan, Steve, and the two cameramen to a restaurant set on the soundstage. We took chairs around a rectangular table as Ned approached.

Jill consulted her watch. "Will this take long? I have an appointment, and I want to call Callie's family."

So much for being the grieving pal, but I supposed calling Callie's family softened her callousness.

Ned's frown made Jill busy herself with a text as I thrust my hands under my thighs. The adrenaline rush had left me feeling shaky, and I was angry, too. Callie might have been snarky to Dowling, but she hadn't deserved to die at the hands of a murderer. A chill of fear ran through me.

Lizzie readied her notebook, while Ned looked at us in turn. I knew he excluded me, but it was clear he'd decided someone at this table was a murderer. I watched Ned settle down to business. "Let's get the timeline down," Ned said. "Take it from noon, when everyone last saw Callie alive."

"I saw her in the commissary with Jill," I offered. "They left before Barney—the props manager—and I had to. When I arrived around one fifteen, Callie was in bed, but already, um...gone."

"Did you see anyone else in the studio at that time?"

I gave it careful thought. "Just the lobby guard where we sign in. Everyone else was downstairs."

Ned turned to Dowling. "Mr. Dowling?"

"I ate with another director and the show's producer, and came back here about one twenty. The guard told me someone had called 911 and I ran in." He threw me an accusatory look. "I blame Trudy Genova."

Of course you do. I rolled my eyes.

"Why would you say that, sir?" Ned remained professional. It wasn't common knowledge at the studio that we were dating.

"Because she was here when two other deaths occurred, and now this is the third!" he sputtered. "She's a bad penny, brings horrible luck wherever she goes."

What nerve! I did seem like a magnet for death at times, but I certainly hadn't had anything to do with any murders, previous or present. In fact, I'd helped bring the other murderers to justice, despite the danger to myself. Maybe Dowling shouldn't keep hiring psychopaths. I ground my teeth to keep from erupting.

Ned said, "Mr. Dowling, might I point out that you were the director at each of those previous cases, and now at today's death? I'd hardly call you a four-leaf clover."

I bit my cheek, pleased by Ned's defense. Steve guffawed loudly until Susan elbowed him.

"But I was at the commissary after Callie left, and I returned here after she was found," Dowling said. "I was the last one to sign in. Check the log."

"I just did, so you can be excused." Ned turned to Lizzie. "You have Mr. Dowling's contact information?"

Dowling looked upset. "I don't mind staying. You may have other questions." God forbid he be left out of the loop.

Ned stood. "Not unless you saw something pertinent. Do you need Detective Damon to show you the way out?"

"Don't be ridiculous." With a nasty look around the table, Dowling left, stalking his way to the door he let slam behind him.

A sigh of relief ran around the table. "Thank you, Detective. That man is highly annoying." Susan leaned in to Steve, who put his arm around her. "As for me, Steve met me at the commissary. We came back for my hair and makeup retouch, then up to the set. Callie was already in bed when the sh—when the commotion started."

"And you were together the entire time?"

I saw Susan hesitate and knew Ned noticed it, too.

Steve squeezed Susan's arm. "Yes, except for when she visited the little girls' room."

Ugh. I hated the demeaning term.

Jimmy spoke up next. "Hank and me went up the block to the hot dog stand. Two with chili each. Came back to the soundstage right behind the others."

Jill nodded. "He's right. I saw them."

Ned asked the cameramen, "Did either of you have a personal relationship with Miss Lawton?"

Jimmy shook his head. "We liked to kibitz, maybe flirt a bit, but I'm married."

"I'm on loan from *Law and Order: SVU*," Hank said. "Didn't know her before today."

Ned allowed Hank to leave but not Jimmy. I guessed being married wouldn't rule him out.

"Callie and I ate together," Jill said. "When we came back, I went downstairs to makeup, but she went on set to get in character. She hardly needed much makeup to play a corpse." She gulped and pulled a tissue from her pocket. "And now she is one." Her tears fell copiously.

They were either close friends, or she was a great method actor. Then I remembered that she and Callie had been roommates and typed a text to Ned. My phone was muted, but Ned's dinged with the incoming message, and he glanced down as he gave Jill time to compose herself.

"And how long were you downstairs?" he asked.

"Until we were supposed to start filming." She sniffed and looked at Susan and Steve. "I came up just behind them, and Jimmy and Hank were right behind me."

"Miss Davis, I understand you and the victim used to be roommates?"

"What of it?" A bit of Jill's toughness came through, a quality we shared. Women often needed to be tough in this business, or else they got pushed around.

"What changed that situation?"

"Callie started a relationship about six months ago and said she needed more privacy." Jill lifted one shoulder gracefully. "I found a new roommate on Craigslist."

"And was this a continuing relationship?"

"I believe so."

Ned raised his chin to Lizzie, who got up and left, probably to call the doorman at Callie's building for a description of her new guy.

"You ever meet this boyfriend?"

"No, Callie wanted to keep him to herself until it became a more cemented relationship. And she didn't call him her boyfriend, but her lover."

Whoa. Who knew? I'd known Callie liked to flirt, but this was new. But then I didn't advertise my relationship with Ned, either.

Ned pressed on. "Can any of you think of anyone, for any reason, who wanted Callie Lawton dead?"

Heads shook around the table, even mine. Callie was fun and sociable with almost everyone. A wave of sorrow washed over me as I mentally promised Callie I'd find her murderer.

Lizzie returned and whispered to Ned. "Let's take a five-minute break," he said.

The detectives left to confer out of earshot from us. I sat across from the others, while Jill excused herself to use the restroom; at least she hadn't called it the little girls' room. Steve brought Susan a bottle of water, and they stood talking quietly.

With Callie's character ill, I'd worked *Knight's Castle* frequently this past month, and had grown close to Callie. I'd also seen Susan clash often with both younger women, who had received Emmy nominations last year while Susan hadn't. I suppose as the "matriarch" on the show, she felt slighted. Not for the first time was I happy to be an outsider to the roiling emotions of actors and their roles.

That got me thinking. I had industry friends who might have information that could help solve this case. I sent a text, seeking gossip about Callie and her lover, or other news that would help me see the forest for the trees. I received an answer almost immediately from an actor I'd recently worked with: *Let me ask around.*

Exactly what I'd hoped. The others returned and took their seats. Ned avoided my gaze, which told me something was up. I'd bet tonight's pizza that Callie's doorman gave a description of her lover. Would Ned have to use it?

"Let's move on." Ned said. "Miss Davis, you never met this

lover of Callie's, but did she mention his name or call him in your presence? Perhaps he picked her up after work?"

Jill wrinkled her brow. "She kept the relationship under wraps. But this one time"—we all leaned forward—"I heard her end a call with an endearment, 'Chuckles.'"

The reaction was swift and startling. Susan slapped Steve so hard his head snapped back. "Chuckles! That's our private nickname, you goddamned lying son of a bitch!" She pulled her arm back for round two, but Lizzie grabbed her hand.

Callie was sleeping with Susan's husband? My first reaction after this surprise was disappointment. I guess I didn't know Callie as well as I'd thought.

"Let's get you two separated." Lizzie tugged on Susan's arm and moved her to my side of the table, but not before Susan gave Steve's chair a vicious kick.

Susan was on a rant. "Working on your novel late, my ass! You were working on that sleazy slut!"

I was happy a chair separated us. Rage came off Susan in waves. Ned pointed Lizzie to the empty seat between us.

Steve took his hand from his face; his wife's handprint stood out on his cheek in dark red. He looked down without speaking.

"Is there any truth to this, Mr. Ward?" Ned asked. "And do you need ice?"

Steve cleared his throat. "No ice, thanks. Callie and I met at a cast party for *Knight's Castle* last year. Our relationship just...escalated." He looked at Susan. "She had warmth to her, not like this frigid cow."

Susan started to rise out of her chair, but Lizzie pulled her down. Ned capitalized on the situation.

"You two still maintain you weren't apart downstairs?"

"He's a liar!" Susan shouted. "When I came back from the 'little girls' room"—she made air quotes—"I had to hunt him down."

"Where were you, Mr. Ward?"

"You're not going to pin this on me. You took an awfully

long time taking a leak, Susan. I was talking to the makeup gal, Li. Ask her if you don't believe me."

Ned nodded to Lizzie, who left, probably to check Steve's alibi. "Mrs. Ward? Were you in the restroom an inordinate time?"

Susan smirked. "I was gearing up for my scene and needed total concentration. He killed Callie so I wouldn't find out about them."

Steve held his hands out in a gesture of supplication. "Why would I kill the one person who'd shown me love and affection in months?"

"And sex, Steve." Susan sneered. "Don't forget sex. I hardly think she called you her lover otherwise."

"Do you even remember what sex is, Susan?" he asked forlornly.

I pictured him living with a woman whose next plastic surgical procedure or award nomination was what she lived for. For a moment, I almost felt sorry for the guy. Almost.

Ned's phone pinged with a missed call just as Lizzie returned and whispered in his ear. "I need to return this call. Can you two keep yourselves under control?" He looked at both Wards.

Lizzie sat down and wrapped a foot around the leg of Susan's chair so she couldn't push away. An awkward quiet fell that Steve broke.

"I wonder how they'll end today's episode, now that Callie's really dead." He looked upset.

"When we were being fingerprinted, I heard Dowling talking with the producers," Jill said. "They're going to use the dress rehearsal tape and cut just before Callie's breath."

Susan slapped the table. "But I didn't get to the end of my soliloquy!"

"That's right, Susan," Steve said. "A young woman's dead, but you're upset you didn't get all your lines out. You're a piece of work."

Jimmy met my eyes and shook his head. The soundstage door closed as Ned returned.

"At least I wasn't a piece of ass like Callie," Susan said.

I saw Steve try to bite back a retort, but he couldn't help himself. "That young woman had more talent in her little finger than you have in your entire body." This time tears sprang to his eyes.

Susan inhaled to respond, but Ned interrupted her.

"Mr. Ward, we haven't been able to reach Li, so we can't confirm your alibi yet." Ned eyed the suspects at the table. "But I was able to speak to the medical examiner. He's done a visual examination on Callie and agrees that she was strangled, apparently with the leather thong that held the cross her character wore. We'll be able to get partial fingerprints from it."

Now the silence that fell over the table was ominous. Jill, Susan, Jimmy, and Steve looked everywhere but at each other. Who was guilty? Could Callie have had a dalliance with Jimmy that Steve uncovered, enraging him? Was Susan really shocked at Steve's unfaithfulness? Was Jimmy angry that Callie was moving on to a new job—leaving him behind? Heck, was Jill angry for the same reason?

That was when my answer text arrived, and I read quickly through the information until something made me raise my eyebrows. "If I might throw in a question, Detective O'Malley?"

Ned raised an eyebrow. "Of course."

I looked at the four suspects. "You just heard that the fingerprints lifted from the leather around Callie's neck will be compared with those taken earlier. We'll know who the killer is soon enough." I knew partials needed a tedious computer analysis but opened my eyes wide at Ned: *Go with me here.* "Detective, if a person took responsibility now, confessed before those results came in, would a judge take that into account?"

He nodded. "Usually."

I looked across the table, hoping my hunch paid off, but aware that it would be a hollow victory—it wouldn't bring Callie back. Still, it would mean justice for her. "You're an understudy in the revival of *The Sound of Music* for several roles, Jill?"

She shifted in her seat. "Yeah. So what?"

"Including for the role of Liesl, Callie's part?"

"You didn't tell anyone that." Susan frowned. "With Callie dead, you'd automatically step into her role."

"And your career on Broadway would be set," Steve pointed out.

Jill ran her eyes around the table, looking for sympathy she didn't find. If I were correct, she was cornered, and she knew it.

Jill slumped back in her seat. "Have you ever heard Callie sing? That role is supposed to go to a young gal like me who can pass for sixteen going on seventeen. Callie could never do that part justice." Jill sighed. "At lunch I reminded her that she'd left me with a huge lease when she moved out abruptly. I struggled for months until I found a new roommate. Callie owed me, so I asked her to consider letting me have the role for a few months as payback. She promised she'd think it over because she felt badly."

"Like that would have happened." Susan sniffed.

Ned silenced her with a look. "Go on, Miss Davis."

"I believed her, and I ran upstairs to thank her again for considering it. Maybe grease the wheels a little, too. That's when Callie said not to get my hopes up as she couldn't see herself giving up the role for even one night." Jill's face flushed. "She hadn't felt bad for me. It had all been a lie. I just saw red. She always took what she wanted and didn't care who she hurt. Look at Susan and Steve." She rested her forehead on one hand, exhausted by her explanation. "Callie pulled the sheet up, took out that stupid cross, then closed her eyes and started to hum that damn 'Sixteen Going on Seventeen' song. I couldn't bear it. The next thing I knew, I'd twisted that leather thong around her neck until she finally shut up." Her lip trembled.

For a moment everyone froze in disbelief.

Ned stood. "The rest of you are dismissed." He nodded to Lizzie.

Lizzie stepped forward, helped Jill rise, and handcuffed her.

"I'm truly sorry," Jill said, and left with her head hanging down.

"The sound of music became the sound of murder," Susan said as she stood up. "Who would have guessed?" She stalked out, ignoring Steve, who trailed several feet behind her. It seemed that marriage had gasped its last breath.

I shivered and snapped my fleece closed. "I can't believe two people I thought I knew could have such hidden sides. Callie, so callous. And Jill, so...deadly."

Ned put his arm around me and kissed my forehead. "I'll have to book her and get Lizzie to take a formal statement. I might be a while."

"That's okay. We can do pizza and the Yankees later. I DVR'd it." It felt good to know Ned was someone I could count on. Someone who was just how he seemed.

"I'm in," Ned said. "As long as we don't have to watch *The Sound of Music*."

Soundtrack to a Death
Kate Parker

That day there had been five of us squeezed into Anne's Mustang along with our sleeping bags, wine, pot, and barbeque sandwiches. When the Beach Boys or Jan and Dean came on WOBS-AM, we sang along at the tops of our lungs. We crossed the low, two-lane bridge to the island and drove down the narrow asphalt road for a few miles, until we were sure we were far enough away from anywhere so we could party in safety.

That was exactly fifty years ago today. There had been no houses then, no stores, just sand dunes and the five of us. College girls out for a good time. Five sorority sisters full of life. At the beach that night, we were celebrating the end of our university days and the beginning of adult life.

Four of us were friends, and then there was Sophia. I didn't know who she'd tricked into inviting her on this trip. Sophia had become our sorority president the way she did everything: by walking over people. She was going to graduate school with the scholarship that should have been mine. She was leaving with the man who had been engaged to marry Beth immediately after graduation, their wedding already planned. She'd won accolades for the senior architecture project she had stolen from Anne. She had started the rumors of plagiarism aimed at Debbie, costing her the honor and the cash from the university English prize.

I never learned who invited Sophia on this trip, or why, after all the vicious things she did to us. We had all blessed her heart many times by then, having been trained that young ladies don't curse or become abusive.

She may have come along uninvited. She'd done so before. It appeared to be true that blonds had more fun. Or at least always got their way.

That may have explained why we were all willing to join in the pact all those years ago. It was a joke, wasn't it? A straw, quickly selected while we waited for Sophia to come out of the gas station toilet. We tried to be gay and ignore the reality of what we pretended to choose to do while the radio played "I Can't Get Next to You."

We threw out our straws without seeing what each other had drawn. It didn't matter. Not at all.

The sun was setting over the mainland when Anne pulled off the road at a break in the dunes and we began to unpack the car for our celebration before graduation. One night of freedom, one night without cares, one night of childhood before adult life pushed us into our responsibilities. Sophia turned on her transistor radio, blasting "Pinball Wizard," and we danced our sleeping bags and portable grill and charcoal around the dunes and down to the beach. The coolers and grocery bags came next. If anyone had been watching, it would have looked like the emptying of a clown car from the circus.

It was midweek. Nobody was around to watch. Not one car passed us. That was the whole point.

It was the time of year when the night is short and the rising sun would wake us early. One night in which we could be young and free and we had plenty to do before dawn.

We ate sitting on the sand around the little portable grill in our swimsuits and coverups. We hadn't had to worry about insects that night, since the breeze off the ocean was keeping them away. And with my young body, I don't remember being cold unless I had my feet in the surf.

Beth, with her long, straight dark hair and big dark eyes, had been pale and touchy since March. Since that cold night when her fiancé, Robert, stood her up and went out with Sophia. I wasn't surprised that she was the first to say what she was thinking. "I suppose you'll announce your engagement to Robert any day."

Sophia braided her long blond hair into one loose braid and laughed as if she hadn't a care. "Oh, I don't know. Should I be tied down by a fiancé while I'm in graduate school? Oh, and thanks for telling me about that scholarship, Jill. I can't decide if I'll use it or not, but I have all summer to think about it."

How that had burned. I find I'm holding the steering wheel of my Honda so tightly my knuckles are white. I loosen my grip as the memory fades. The car grows warm with the engine off and the windows up. I climb out, put on my floppy, wide-brimmed hat, and walk along the path between the buildings toward the pool and the beach.

The noonday sun shines above me in a cloudless sky. This is now my home. Buying a condo in this development had been a smart move. It makes a terrific retirement place. Even if it means I live close to what they refer to in detective fiction as the scene of the crime. The parking lot now sits where we made camp all those years ago. Where we ate our barbecue sandwiches and drank bottle after bottle of wine while the sun set and the sky grew dark.

I swat a bug that lands on my arm as I walk into the enclosure around the oceanside pool. I take a towel off the cart and stretch out on a chaise lounge, my big beach bag next to me, and slather on sunscreen. I don't remember burning fifty years ago. Children play in the pool, screaming with delight. It's right for the beach to be this way. Joyful. Noisy. Not the way it was that night.

Being dumped by Robert for someone as indifferent as Sophia

must have hurt Beth badly, because she began to really guzzle the wine. I was determined to keep a clear head.

We frolicked in the cold surf for a while before going back to the short grill and toasting s'mores. "This is nice," Debbie said. "Not as nice as winning the university English prize, but nice." Debbie had a round face, curly, light brown hair, and her nose in a book. When we reached the beach, we made her put away the Jane Austen she'd brought with her.

"The university must have seen some similarities to listen to the plagiarism rumors," Sophia said, lighting a joint.

"Odd how the first people to hear those rumors were our sorority sisters before the election for president was held. Long before anyone in the English department heard." Debbie was glaring at Sophia.

"But you made it to graduation. I'm proud of you," Sophia said.

"Who invited you on this trip?" Anne asked, her red curls in a short cap around her head. She stared at Sophia with loathing.

"You all did." Sophia passed the joint to Debbie, never glancing at Anne.

"You told me Jill did," Anne said.

I believed her. Anne had a mind for details. "Oh, no. Not me." I put my hands up, palms forward. I wanted to make that clear to my friends. Sophia had used this same trick one too many times.

Elvis's "Suspicious Minds" began to play on the radio just as Beth said, "I certainly didn't invite her."

We all stared at Sophia. Debbie handed Beth the joint. "Have a drag on the peace pipe."

Beth moved to hand it to Anne, but Anne shook her head. In a firm tone, she said, "I've been used once too often. Once we get back tomorrow, I never want to see you again, Sophia."

I was surprised at how cold Anne sounded.

"We've been sisters since the day four years ago when we pledged Alpha Beta. We pledged our sisterhood forever. Or have you forgotten?" Sophia said. When Anne didn't respond, Sophia added, "I thought not."

Four of us sat there, looking uncomfortable, not meeting each other's gaze. Sophia looked smug by the light of the grill. The radio began to play "Bad Moon Rising," and I couldn't help smiling. It fit. Fifty years on, that memory still makes me smile.

"I have something for each of you," Sophia said. She pulled a paper sack out of her beach bag and handed us each a thin gold chain with a medallion hanging from it. The medallion had the emblem of Alpha Beta on it. "Graduation present."

"From National," Debbie said. She had run against Sophia for president last spring and there wasn't anything she didn't know about how the sorority worked. She would have been a better officer. Until the rumor about plagiarism started and ruined her chances.

"I never said it was from me," Sophia said. How I hated that smug tone of hers. All these years later, I can still hear it.

Sophia handed out her gifts and waited as we reluctantly put on our necklaces. We were silent. Debbie shed a few tears. Beth hugged Sophia quickly and then walked away, down the beach. We probably all felt anger. Fury that there would be no retribution for the wounds Sophia inflicted.

No one knew who had drawn the short straw or if they would act. But wasn't that just a joke?

Sometime after two, the portable grill down to dying charcoal, Beth poured the last of a bottle of wine down her throat and fell over backwards. We dragged her into her sleeping bag, her long, dark ponytail full of sand. Debbie mumbled something and crawled into her blankets.

"Three of us left to finish the wine and the weed," Sophia said. She helped herself while Anne and I watched her with growing revulsion. Even blasted out of her mind, she was gorgeous. Tall, thin, straight blond hair, blue eyes. The image of the perfect sorority girl in 1971. That's what everyone else saw when they looked at her. The four of us had learned differently as we each lost something precious.

In the moonlight, she delivered a lecture to us on how to get ahead, "except you girls aren't exceptional enough. Red head. Mud brown curls. Chubby. Short legs." The real Sophia was coming out in her slurred speech. Then she staggered off to use the ocean as a toilet.

Anne and I turned off the radio, lay down in our sleeping bags, grumbled good night, and went to sleep under the stars.

It was after four in the morning by my watch when I had to go down to the shoreline to pee. I left my watch in my sleeping bag so as not to lose it or get it wet and tiptoed a little way down the beach. The sun wasn't up yet, but the sky was beginning to show rosy tints.

I saw a lump lying half in the water of the retreating tide, just a darker area against the sand. As I grew closer in the faint light, I could make out arms, legs, long blond hair in a braid. By the time I was standing over her, I could see one hand in a fist, clutching a thin chain.

Her own Alpha Beta locket was still around her neck. Whose locket did she hold? We'd each received a locket with the Alpha Beta insignia from Sophia just hours before. If she'd grasped one while in a catfight, someone would be in deep trouble. It would be just like Sophia to create a mess from the other side. But I was determined Sophia had caused her last bit of mischief.

I couldn't open her hand to retrieve the necklace, so I decided to remove her own chain and medallion from her neck. The pull of the waves helped me turn her to do my gruesome task. The body was cold, and I still remember my awful queasiness as I unclasped the chain. Her eyes were closed. Her braid kept her hair mostly out of the way as the ends fanned out like a sea creature. Clutching the chain and medallion in my fist, I ran up the shoreline and got sick.

When I returned to my sleeping bag, I sat down and slipped

the necklace next to my watch as I looked around. Anne lifted her head and whispered, "Are you all right?"

"I am. Sophia's not. She's down by the water. Dead."

Her eyes widened. "You're kidding. One of us really did it?"

"No one else drew straws to kill her."

"Oh, Jill. We'll have to call the police. But let's not mention drawing straws." Anne stood and hurried down to the shoreline.

I followed at a slower pace. Together we dragged Sophia up the beach so the tide wouldn't carry her body away. Then Anne slipped on a pair of cutoffs and a T-shirt and drove down the beach road to the phone booth by the bridge. I sat on my sleeping bag, waiting, as the sky lightened.

Our voices had awakened the other two. When I told them Sophia was dead, Beth grew hysterical. She was determined to tell the police about our drawing straws.

I grabbed her by the shoulders. "Do you want the police to look into all of our motives? Our opportunities? What would Robert think if he found out you were a murder suspect?"

She grew quiet, her eyes wide with terror as she said, "But I didn't kill her."

"None of us did. We aren't killers. She walked down the beach alone. Anything might have happened to her. Anyone might have found her. Or she could have fallen or tripped and drowned. None of us were sober," I said. It sounded sensible.

Beth looked at Debbie, who nodded. "We were stupid to come out here, drinking, smoking weed, and Sophia paid the price."

Anne returned and took charge as she often did. "The cops are on the way. Nobody mentions the straws. It was just a joke, a way to blow off steam, but the police would probably take it seriously and then we'd all be in trouble. Any weed left? Dump it in the ocean. We went to sleep and didn't see anything. Agreed?"

We all nodded, glad someone had a plan. Then Beth ran into the ocean. I could see her retching. She was having a good cry when the police arrived. They left her alone, apparently deciding it was easier to talk to calm girls. We were ordered to pack up our stuff and follow a squad car back to the mainland to the police station. Meanwhile, the police took all of Sophia's belongings.

I put the necklace and watch in my beach bag. We didn't dance our bags and grill back to the Mustang. We didn't turn on the car radio when we started back down the asphalt road. For a change, we didn't talk.

The police questioned us separately. They decided the lockets were identical and worth no more notice. They asked repeatedly if we'd seen anyone. Beth thought she'd seen some lights. Debbie thought she'd heard voices. I said I thought I'd heard a motor, but I couldn't tell from where the sound had come. Anne asked if they'd found anyone lurking about our campsite.

Anne and I both said that when we'd last seen her going down to the shore that she was under the influence, trashed, wasted. Anything might have happened.

The police finally told us the preliminary investigation showed she'd died of asphyxiation, drowned in water and sand. Then the questioning began again.

We had nothing to add. And they had no reason, no evidence, to suspect any one of us or anyone else.

We were finally allowed to leave the tiny police station on the mainland about dinnertime, after we'd given our parents' names and addresses and heard a lecture on staying safe at the beach. We stayed silent on the ride back to the university, stopping at a fast-food joint on the way. I realized then I hadn't eaten all day and I was ravenous. "Everyday People" was blasting out of the speakers in the burger place. Somehow, it seemed unreal.

Sophia's funeral was three days after graduation. We all attended, along with the entire Alpha Beta chapter, and it was the last time the four of us ever saw each other as a group. Too much guilt, I guessed, wondering if one of us killed her. Did each of us wonder, which one of us was it? Who drew the short straw?

* * *

I went to Beth and Robert's wedding a year later. They had two children and divorced after twenty years. Two years after that, Beth died, alone, of an overdose. It was ruled accidental, but Beth's Christmas cards and letters had always talked about Robert. The way she had focused on him all through university.

Anne won awards for her architectural designs and married old money. She led a charmed life up until the day the family jet went down in a thunderstorm.

Debbie was a proud homemaker with four children, seven grandchildren, and a loving husband, all of whom surrounded her as she breathed her last in a hospice two months ago. She and I were the only two to reach our seventieth birthdays.

I went to graduate school on the scholarship that should have been mine to begin with. I lost my wonderful husband too soon. Our only child, a daughter, is my delight. She's given me two adorable grandchildren, now teenagers. They think sororities are a waste of time.

They could be right.

I stretch on the lounge chair like a cat in the sun and give a purr. I'm the only one left now, and I can finally be certain the secret is safe. It gave me a moment's worry at the time, but I was fortunate to have the presence of mind to take Sophia's necklace. After all, she had mine.

Fickle Mistress
Lawrence Kelter

1968

With the crash of a cymbal Fickle Mistress's world tour came to an end—six months of crisscrossing the globe, over and done. And this final show, four hours of jamming and solos, had left them and the audience exhausted, physically and emotionally annihilated.

All told, Rory, Derek, and Stack had performed eighty shows and played to more than three million fans. Billed as rock's first supergroup, Fickle Mistress had only been together three years, but in that short time had been acclaimed the best of the best, a musical explosion like no other, an unparalleled blues-rock renaissance.

The finale didn't come a moment too soon.

The arena thundered with applause as Derek placed his Stratocaster on the guitar stand, and Stack unplugged his bass from the amp. Rory stepped from behind his drum kit, the tattoos on his naked upper body awash in sweat. He began to stagger on his way to meeting his bandmates center stage. His face etched in agony, he clutched his chest and pulled a cymbal stand down with him as he collapsed.

Rory was a genuine rock-and-roll bad boy with a reputation for alcohol, drugs, and mayhem. During the six-month tour, he'd left any number of trashed hotel rooms in his wake. Coffee tables dusted with cocaine had become his calling card. He often taunted the fans with pranks, preying on their emotions.

Tonight, they slowly caught on. It was yet another of the drummer's antics. They loved his practical jokes and had come to expect them.

But he didn't move.

Not after a minute.

Not after three.

Stack moseyed over and prodded Rory's leg with his boot. "Come on, mate. The birds are freaking out."

"Enough is enough," Derek said. "Stop milking it."

Rory's son Jonah stood offstage, absentmindedly flipping a butterfly knife, when he began to suspect that something was wrong. He hurried to where his father was lying. "Dad? Are you finished having your fun yet?" He jostled Rory's shoulder but he didn't move. Panic gnawed at the boy's chest as he knelt next to his father and felt for a pulse. "Call 999. Someone call 999."

As the stage filled with technicians and roadies, the audience's collective gasp became so voluminous as to evacuate all the air from the immense stadium.

Offstage, Dr. Robert, the band's physician, was in the can flipping through a scandal sheet when he heard his name being screamed. He tore the seam of his pants yanking them up as he burst from the bathroom stall. "*What?* What's going on?"

"It's Rory, Doc," Desmond, a stagehand, said, already breaking into a run. "Come quick. He's flat on his face. Bloody well dropped like a rock right after the second encore. Don't think he's acting this time."

"Oh hell." The rotund doctor scuttled as fast as his short legs could carry him. Panting, he hit the stage, which was jammed with bodies. He couldn't see the fallen musician, only those surrounding him. "Let me through," he bellowed as he began his clumsy charge forward. "I'm a doctor."

Molly Jones, one of the backup singers, pirouetted on her

stiletto heels and fainted in front of Dr. Robert as he lumbered by. He tripped on her boot-clad legs and went ass over teakettle, landing on top of the fallen drummer, his face wedged in the apex of Rory's leather britches. Despite his heft, the doc was quickly back in play, pouring perspiration as he rolled Rory onto his back and initiated chest compressions.

"Stand back," he shouted. "Give him room."

Those nearby withdrew, but the stage continued to fill. The gravity of the situation settled on the audience. Fans wept. Some prayed for a miracle. Wailing in misery, the volume of the lament built to an ear-shattering crescendo as they waited, hoping their icon would come around.

A woman in the audience screamed, "He's dead. Oh my God, he's dead."

"I think she's right," a gent standing nearby agreed. "Rory's gone tits-up."

Like cancer, the rumor ate throughout the building until pandemonium reigned. Security personnel fanned out, doing their best to control the situation but, like fingers in a crumbling dike, were woefully inadequate. The dam breached, a tsunami of emotion swept over the crowd, drowning every last soul. With heavy hearts they seemed to accept the report: Rory Panadero, legendary rock star and the greatest drummer of all time, was dead.

Earlier that day

The backstage area had been a calamitous mess, a cacophony of drunks, musicians, and toadies. Most had followed the band for months, some from the beginning of the tour, and were hoping for a few minutes alone with one of the boys, a brief encounter when some of their genius might rub off on them.

Jonah was in the practice room honing his craft on his dad's backup drum kit. The teenager trained relentlessly. With every bone in his body, he ached to make his father proud, to show him that the apple had landed at the very base of the tree. Rory's drumming was hailed as unique. Modern rock was rife with oversimplified backbeat rhythms that bored Rory to death. Instead, he'd improvise with fills that made the group's songs monumentally better. Jonah was determined to become not just a great drummer, but a great drummer in his father's tradition. He was practicing double-stroke rolls when Rory staggered into the room with a bottle of Jack Daniel's in one hand and a redhead hanging on his shoulder.

"What is that racket you're making?" Rory said. "It's all wrong."

The sticks froze in Jonah's hands. "Double-stroke—"

"Yeah, yeah, yeah. I bloody well know what it's supposed to be, but the way you're playing them, mate, it sounds like that cocked-up Austin-Healey I had to scrap, like there's a spud lodged in the exhaust pipe. Come on, Jonah, surely you can play better than that piss."

The boy grew tense but fought past his nerves. He went at it again. "Better?"

"Again!"

He obliged, then looked at his father for acknowledgment.

"Too slow. Faster, mate, *faster*."

Jonah pounded away, unremittingly and unerringly slamming the drumheads like a machine stuck in high gear.

Rory blurted, "Is that all you can do? It's bloody tiresome. Run it backward then switch into a bolero. I'm yawning over here." Groping the groupie's butt, he brought the bottle of whisky to his lips.

Derek looked on disapprovingly. "Riding the lad a bit hard, don't you think, Rory?"

"Hard, my arse. Do you think I got to where I am today being a slacker? Why I worked my fingers to the bone honing my craft."

"The boy looks knackered," Stack said. "Wouldn't hurt you to show him an ounce of warmth. He's absolutely gobsmacked over you, and you treat him like dirt."

Derek and Stack had seen Rory like this far too often, in one city after another, knocking the boy down every time he stood up, cutting him off at the knees for not measuring up to his expectations.

"Rubbish!" Rory said. "At the rate he's progressing he's got no future except playing five-and-dime gigs at weddings and children's birthday parties."

Stack looked over at Jonah and saw the boy stooped over the drums, demoralized, utterly defeated.

Rory was about to take another swig when Derek snatched the bottle and pointed to the groupie. "You can have as much of the ginger as you can handle, but you've had enough of the hooch. Last performance, Rory, it's balls to the wall tonight. You've got to be in top form, and you're positively legless. Lie down and sober up, mate."

Rory wrestled the bottle away from Derek, "Bah! I can down ten of these and still outplay any drummer in London." He fired one last volley at his son. "Play like you mean it. No one needs another stinkin' also-ran." He towed the woman from the room.

"Fool!" Derek grumbled.

Stack shook his head. "Bleedin' nutter."

They walked over to the browbeaten boy.

"That was the alcohol talking," Derek said. "Don't pay him any mind."

Jonah choked back tears. "He's always coming at me. Nothing I do is good enough."

"Your dad...well, he's old school. He thinks this is what he has to do to make you the best."

"Well, it's not, and I'm getting damn tired of him chewing me out all the time."

"That's because you're the oldest, Jonah. You're the heir apparent. When Rory puts down his sticks once and for all, he expects you to pick 'em up."

Derek tried to comfort the boy, but Jonah flinched when he

placed a hand on his shoulder. "Sorry. What's that about?"

"Just got me a tattoo. Sisyphus, like Dad's."

Derek nodded. He understood how much Jonah craved his father's acceptance. "Why that one?"

"Because life's hard—man's eternal struggle and all that. Isn't that what you're saying about Dad pushing me so hard?"

"That's not why Rory got the tattoo, lad. Cheating death twice was why Sisyphus had to push that great stone uphill for eternity. It was his punishment. Your dad almost died two times, the heart attack and..."

Stack cut him off. The bandmates had made a pact to never mention Rory's near-fatal overdose.

"What was the other?" Jonah asked.

"It's in the past," Stack said. "What's important is that I started off on the drum kit before picking up the bass and, believe you me, I wasn't half as good as you are now, my boy."

"I hate him," Jonah swore. "I wish he were—"

"Don't say it." Derek saw how much anger Jonah was holding in. "Once it's out there's no taking it back."

The word never left Jonah's mouth, but he had cursed his father all the same.

Days after Rory's death

Derek and Stack were walking across the parking lot to the Church of Saint Mary the Virgin in Lewisham, London. The fifteenth-century structure was similar to many houses of worship built during that period—dignified but drab, the grounds unremarkable. Without warning, Dr. Robert sprang from his car. "Please pardon the impertinence, gents. Can I have a minute?"

Dr. Robert hemmed and hawed before Derek finally lost his cool. "Oh come on, man, out with it. We're supposed to be paying our respects."

"There..." Dr. Robert began, "there was quite an incident."

"Well, what is it?" Stack asked. "We don't have all day."

"Rory...I mean, *the body*...it's been—"

Derek glared furiously. "What? It's been what?"

Dr. Robert gritted his teeth. "It's been *desecrated*."

"*What?*" Derek blurted. "Mate, are you screwing with us?"

"I only wish I was," he sighed. "Someone broke into the mortuary and flayed his chest with a knife."

Stack covered his mouth. "I'm going to be sick."

"Rory ran with a goddamn wild crowd, but this is beyond crazy," Derek said. "Who would do something like that?"

"I remember a bleedin' nutter what copied every last one of Rory's tats, and he wasn't alone. Half the wannabes in Soho were running around with tattoos of Sisyphus."

Derek spotted a paparazzi lurking behind the hedges. He whispered, "Is Rory in the goddamn casket?"

"All the wounds are on the torso. The mortician said they wouldn't show."

"Thank God," Derek said. "Fucking Rory Panadero—as if twice cheating death wasn't enough, he almost wiggled out of his own bleedin' funeral."

The return concert—two years later

Fickle Mistress was back, their tour beginning on the same stage where the last one had ended. This one was going to be bigger than the last. Forty cities, 130 shows—all sold out. There was a new recording contract in place, as well as fresh endorsement deals following the release of new back-to-back number one singles.

The kickoff concert was the most eagerly anticipated event of the year. Before the band even walked onstage, the arena thundered for an hour as the fans stomped their feet and screamed. Tickets for the much-ballyhooed return of the world's greatest hard rock band were nearly impossible to obtain.

The three mates formed a circle in the dressing room, arms around one another.

"Are you ready?" Derek asked.

"Ready!"

"Then let's do it."

They charged out of their dressing room, down a long corridor, and onto the stage. The crowd went wild as they took their places and launched into their latest chart-topping hit without so much as a word of introduction.

Seeing Jonah at the drum kit where his father once presided evoked magic that Derek and Stack hadn't felt in years.

It was Jonah's first major-venue performance, and he was playing perfectly, seamlessly. He'd recommitted himself to the drums during the band's two-year hiatus. He'd learned from the best and had become the best. Critics would come to say that he had surpassed his father, his speed quicker, his timing flawless, and his fills more explosive.

Watching Jonah work, Derek felt his heart swell. The boy had come such a long way. He'd mastered his craft, grown confident, and overcome an abusive father who'd pushed him and tortured him relentlessly. "Do it faster. Do it better. Do it again. And again!" In Rory's eyes, Jonah would never be good enough. Seeing Jonah sitting at the drums was more than rewarding. It was just.

Derek glanced at Stack, who was admiring the band's new drummer and winked at him. Stack freed a hand for a quick thumbs-up.

They cued Jonah for his solo, and he launched into an explosive roll on the snare, beating the batter head until it seemed it would burst.

The skin stretched over the snare and held taut by the counter hoop had been bleached and treated, but with every smack of the drumstick, the body art refused to stay buried—Sisyphus struggling beneath the weight of the massive boulder. The one-of-a-kind membrane would take the brutal punishment for as long as Jonah cared to dish it out. And he would, without mercy.

* * *

Note: Introduced in 1966, the British trio Cream was widely acclaimed as rock's first "supergroup." It consisted of guitarist Eric Clapton, bassist Jack Bruce, and drummer Ginger Baker. Baker was regarded as one of the greatest drummers of all time, and his son Kofi Baker is also considered an outstanding percussionist. Ginger Baker was notoriously ornery and had a challenging and often estranged relationship with his son.

Past Connections
E. J. Murray

"That's odd."

Tel O'Brien, vocalist of the rock band Sea Wind, opened his eyes without moving from his comfortable sprawl across the sofa. "What's odd, Tano?"

His guitarist, Saul "Lontano" Ryan, hoisted the partially dismantled stringed instrument he'd been working to restore. He had a puzzled expression on his elfin face. "Come look."

Tel heaved a sigh and rolled onto his feet. One hand scrubbed at his ginger mop of hair, standing it on end. "I can't believe you're tearing that lute apart. Doesn't look fun at all."

"I enjoy restoring old instruments. This one needed me. And it's a mandolin. Not enough strings to be a lute."

"Whatever." Tel bent over the elderly desk Lontano was using as a worktable, squinting a bit in the darkening hotel room. "Lights: fifty percent! What time is it, anyhow?"

Lontano glanced at his wrist link as the overhead lights brightened. "Half past five. Here, look."

Tel frowned down at his friend. Lontano's dark hair flopped forward, almost hiding his gray eyes. His long fingers, dusted with flecks of old varnish, held out what looked like the front half of the lute...or mandolin.

Taking the proffered wooden neck, Tel peered at the underside. "An envelope?"

"Glued inside of the body, yes. What do you think?"

"A mystery!" Tel dropped to a seat in the chair next to Lontano's, his thumb already prying at the brittle paper.

"Careful." Lontano tugged Tel's hand away and retrieved his project. "It's old."

Tel's bright green eyes sparkled with excitement. "Probably the deed to a mansion. Or a long-lost will."

Lontano's brow furrowed. "There's only one way to find out." He reached for the bottle of solvent he'd been using.

Tel yawned and propped his chin on one hand. After a few minutes watching Lontano's slow, careful movements, he shoved back to his feet and padded into the kitchen alcove. Shortly, the scent of freshly brewed coffee wafted into the sitting room. Tel shuffled behind the odor, a filled mug in each hand.

Lontano took the proffered drink in one hand and sipped as he dabbed at the glue with his other. "Nearly there," he murmured, testing the paper with his own thumbnail.

"About time." Tel set his mug down on the corner of the desk. "Careful, it's brittle."

Lontano shot his friend the side-eye but kept up his careful tugging at the envelope. After a long moment, the paper separated from the moistened glue with a loud crackle. Tel and Lontano both winced, but the envelope appeared unharmed.

"'Ethel,'" Lontano read.

"What's inside?"

"Patience." Lontano tentatively pried at the flap. "I don't think I can get this loose without it tearing." Tel handed him the razor blade he'd been scraping varnish with. Lontano slit the envelope and gently tugged a sheet of paper free.

"Imagine how long it's been since that paper saw daylight," Tel whispered, his eyes wide.

"It still hasn't. The sun went down half an hour ago."

Tel elbowed his friend. "Well, are you going to read it or not?"

Lontano set the envelope beside his mug and carefully unfolded the paper. Tel winced as it crackled again. He leaned over

Lontano's shoulder and read aloud.

"'Ethel, we're in someone's attic. I'll leave the lute where we was going to meet up. Schmidt will rat us out now the cops nabbed him. I stashed the loot in Old Lady Traver's bathroom, like how we used to hide our money from Pa. If the cops ask, you ain't seen me, and you got no idea where we are. I'll get word to you on the new meeting place. Tommy.'"

"Hardly proper English," Lontano murmured, examining the back of the paper for more writing. It was blank.

"Never mind the English, you know what this means?"

"Tommy stole this mandolin?"

Tel elbowed his guitarist again. "It's a treasure map."

Lontano shot his friend a narrow-eyed glare. "What treasure?"

"You need to watch more crime dramas, pal. Look here, Tommy says he hid the loot in some woman's bathroom. Bet it's still there, too."

"Ah. So all we have to do to find this 'loot' is..."

"Find Old Lady Traver's bathroom, yeah." Tel's face fell. "We don't even know who Old Lady Traver is. Where'd you get this thing anyhow?"

Lontano rose and pulled his chair over to the computer station. "An estate sale. Maybe we can find Old Lady Traver."

His fingers flew across the keyboard. Tel brightened again. He carried his own chair to the station, then fetched the coffee mugs.

Lontano glanced up. "If I enter all of the names from the letter," he said, "as well as the term 'loot,' we should find...ah!"

Tel leaned forward. "Old newspapers. Hell, from the 1930s? 'Thieves Strike Merrick House: Orchestral Recital Interrupted by Bandits.' Hey, it's here in New York."

"Stands to reason," said Lontano, his eyes on the screen. "I did find the mandolin here. 'Halsted Gang Strikes Again.' I'll start with this one."

Tel reached for his tablet. "I'll check the first one, then."

They read in silence for a few moments, then Tel spoke. "So,

Tommy was the leader. Says the police couldn't ever pin a crime on him, though. Always had a rock-hard alibi. Like for this crime, he was invited to the party. He let the gang in the back while everybody was listening to the music. Got away with nearly fifty thousand dollars' worth of jewelry and a lot of cash."

"And that was in the 1930s." Lontano pulled up a second tab. "In today's money, that would be around eight hundred thousand dollars."

"Jaysus," Tel breathed reverently. "We can make that album. And buy the condo."

"My article says he had a sister named Ethel. The police questioned her but she never said where the loot was."

"'Coz she never saw the lute."

"Mandolin. That Schmidt fellow did name the others."

"But they ran for it. Nobody ever found the jewelry, Tano. Think of all that money."

"Assuming we can find it. Wait, here's one that says Tommy was killed in a shoot-out, along with another member of the gang."

Tel's face fell. "Poor Ethel. If she'd only looked in the...er, mandolin."

"Why would anyone look inside a mandolin?" Lontano scrolled further down the screen. "The last two gang members were caught trying to board a ship to Europe. They claimed Tommy said only that Ethel must look for the loot."

"How could she look for the loot when the letter was...Jaysus, Mary, and Joseph!" Tel's palm thumped against this forehead. "Don't you see? Look for the loot—look for the L-U-T-E."

Lontano frowned. "It's a mandolin."

Tel punched his shoulder. "Maybe they didn't know that, okay? Maybe they weren't bloody guitar geniuses like you."

Lontano rubbed the sting out of his shoulder and kept scrolling. "Here's something. The police investigated Ethel. She was a housekeeper for Mrs. Victoria Traver. It gives the street.

Let me see if I can get a number for the house. Yes, here it is."

Tel snapped a screenshot. "Wonder if it's anywhere close to the hotel. We could nip over and check out their bathroom."

"I doubt they'd let us just walk in and tear up their bathroom." Lontano returned to his mandolin, picking up the rounded backpiece.

Tel downed the last of his coffee. "No time for that," he said. "I need some dinner if I'm going to come up with a scheme."

A group text to the other three band members gathered everyone in the hotel lobby. Tel let out a groan when he saw that the others were accompanied by their manager's latest idea: their own personal journalist. Ethan Morris was two decades older than they were, which made him middle-aged and thus, a drag. Even with the band just standing around, the man kept snapping photos. He used an actual camera, too.

Tel leaned toward Lontano. "Does he have to document our every waking moment?" he muttered.

"Exposure," Lontano replied, clapping the vocalist on the shoulder.

Tel slumped across the lobby to join the others. He gave Morris a wide berth as they filed into the restaurant. As they ate, though, a crafty look came into Tel's green eyes. His forehead wrinkled and he stared at the photographer across the table.

"Do I have something in my teeth?" the man finally asked.

"How'd you like a real scoop?" Tel countered.

Morris chuckled. "Besides you youngsters? What'd you have in mind?"

"An absolutely true mystery. From the 1930s. There's treasure."

"All right, you've caught my interest. Keep talking."

"C'mon up to the suite, then." Tel thumbed the payment screen and shoved to his feet.

The rest of the band trailed along, curiosity evident on their faces. When Morris saw the aged letter, a dimple creased his cheek. "That's more like it." He set up a portable tripod for his camera.

"And you found an address for this old lady?" he asked, snapping shot after shot of the mandolin's interior, the glue-covered envelope, and the letter itself.

Tel read off the address. Morris nodded brusquely. "That's over in Brooklyn."

"Tano and I are going to get up early tomorrow and go out there."

Lontano's eyebrows rose but he said nothing.

Morris finally put the camera down. "Want some company?"

Tel grinned. "I was thinking how most people jump at the chance to get their picture in the paper."

Morris lifted an eyebrow. "If you do find something, it'll be bigger than that."

"Tano will be rich, for one thing."

"I believe stolen goods must be returned to their rightful owners," said the guitarist.

"Probably a sizable reward," Morris said. "Maybe some TV appearances."

"More exposure," said Lontano.

Tel rubbed his hands together. "*America's Most Wanted.*"

Morris checked the time on his wrist link. "What's 'early' to you fellows anyway?"

Tel scratched his head. They generally slept in, but the band wasn't on tonight's lineup. "Let's say we meet up for breakfast at eight a.m.?"

The other band members winced. "Count me out," said the drummer, shaking his head.

When the keyboardist and bassist agreed, Tel glanced at Lontano.

"I'll go," the guitarist said with a grin. "After all, it's my mandolin."

"Well, if we're going to get moving at the crack of dawn, you and I better not stay out all night partying." Tel eyed the other three band members.

"Another reason not to go," said the bassist with no sign of remorse. The three filed back out, noisily debating which bar might provide the liveliest Friday night. Tel shook his head and closed the door behind them.

"Now," he said, pulling out a chair for Morris, "we need a grand scheme to get us inside that house."

"Couldn't we just tell the truth?" Lontano frowned at the mandolin. "We could split the reward if they help us find the treasure."

Tel winced. "Why do I see our money dribbling away?"

The next morning, following a bit more computer work, Morris drove a rental sedan to the residential district in Brooklyn, eventually locating an empty parking spot on the proper street.

"That's it," said Morris, stepping out and pointing. "Three houses back."

"The one with the jungle instead of a garden?" Tel asked, tipping his sunglasses up for a better look. He'd disguised himself with a fedora over his bright copper locks and a suit instead of his usual T-shirt and jeans. Lontano, on the other hand, had opted for a sweatshirt and khaki trousers, with a stocking cap pulled low over his forehead. Even Morris had to agree the two looked markedly different from their onstage personas.

The photographer sported a shoulder bag packed with lenses and external flash attachments. His suit looked as if he didn't own a clothes hanger, and his shoes had scuffs on their scuffs. He led the way up the sidewalk to the house in question, which resembled him a good deal in appearance. The wood siding, once a cheerful yellow, had faded to gray with only the occasional hint of color in a protected corner. Bits of gingerbread had fallen from the second-floor roofline.

Tel mounted the steps and rapped on the peeling green door. Within a few minutes, they heard the clomp of boots approaching over a wooden floor. The door swung open to reveal a woman a little older than Morris, with gray beginning to salt her short dark hair. She was dressed in paint-spattered overalls and an Inhaler T-shirt, with sturdy work boots on her large feet.

She eyed the trio on her doorstep skeptically. "Yes?"

Morris stepped forward, hefting the camera around his neck. "Ethan Morris, ma'am. Freelance. I'd like to talk about your house."

The woman gave him a wry smile. "If you're thinking of a before-and-after shoot, you'll have to wait until I win the lottery and get it registered."

"As a historic house?" Morris shared a look with Tel and Lontano. "That does have a bearing on what we'd like to talk about."

She studied them for a long moment, then shrugged. "Well, it's broad daylight, and you don't look like serial killers. C'mon, I just turned the coffeemaker on. Name's Jess Brooks."

Tel gave her their names. He wasn't surprised they didn't trigger a reaction. Their fans were usually quite a bit younger than Jess. He and his guitarist followed Jess and Morris down a short hallway into a kitchen that had the photographer whistling in surprise. "Those appliances…"

"Are older than I am, yeah," the woman finished. She rummaged in a leaf-green cabinet, coming up with five mismatched mugs. "Cream?"

Tel and Morris raised their hands and Jess pulled a carton from a refrigerator matching the cabinets. Setting that on the table, she poked her head back into the hall. "Sam! Coffee and company."

Tel glanced up at the thud of more boots on the stairs. Another woman, perhaps a decade younger than Jess, trotted into the kitchen, wiping paint-spattered hands on a faded towel. She studied their guests, her blue eyes sparkling with curiosity. Her gaze may have lingered on Lontano a bit, but she detoured to fill the mugs with dark brew.

Jess introduced them, then jerked a thumb at the chairs

surrounding the battered old table. "Let's hear it, then."

Once they were seated, Morris cleared his throat and tugged the yellowed envelope from his bag. "Have you ever heard of a lady named Victoria Traver?"

Jess chuckled. "Sure. My great-grandmother. Lived in this very house until she died. Grandma grew up here. Mom never appreciated the old place, so Grandma saddled me with it."

She patted the table affectionately. "Sam and I moved in when Grandma started needing help. Now she's gone, we've been trying to fix it up, get them to register it."

"Did your grandma ever talk about Ethel Bleeker?" Tel asked, leaning forward to rest his elbows on the tabletop. "She would have been your great-grandma's housekeeper."

Jess's eyes widened. "Man, that's digging deep. Is this about that old jewel robbery?"

"It is," said Lontano. He explained how he'd found the envelope. Jess and Sam studied the brittle paper as he spoke.

"What are you proposing?" Jess finally asked. She gave Lontano a skeptical look.

"A fifty-fifty split of the reward. We looked it up this morning on the FBI website." Lontano pulled out his tablet, showed it to Jess and Sam, who whistled appreciatively.

"What's to stop us from tossing you three out on your ears and taking it all?" Jess asked. Tel thought a twinkle might have sparked deep within her brown eyes, but he wasn't certain.

Sam elbowed her partner. "Fifty percent is more than we have now. That'd replace the roof. And they did find the letter."

"Letter schmetter. It's not their house the loot is hidden in."

"But we'd never have known to look for it."

"Damn it, that stuff's in the house somewhere. How long would it take us to dig it out?"

Lontano leaned forward to retrieve the letter. "Statistically speaking, it might take years. Or you might never find it. If it weren't well hidden, someone else would have done so already."

"Besides," Tel added with a wink, "you said you wanted to

fix the place up, not tear it to the ground."

Jess frowned, staring into her half-empty coffee mug. No one spoke for several minutes. "Hell," she muttered finally. "Probably have to rip out every wall to find the damn stuff."

She held out a hand to Lontano. "Fifty-fifty and no tricks, all right?"

Morris pulled another paper from his bag. "We wrote up a contract to make sure. Even split between you and Mr. Ryan here."

Jess and Sam read the page, their heads together. Jess shot Lontano a grin. "Straightforward. Just as I like 'em." She pulled a pen from her overall pocket and signed, passing pen and paper across the table. Lontano signed below Jess's scrawl.

"Now for us witnesses," Morris said, scribbling his own signature.

Once all had signed, Lontano handed over the original letter. Jess studied the age-darkened paper for a moment, then unfolded it and read aloud. She and Sam looked at one another. "The bathroom?" they said together. Sam's shocked expression mirrored her partner's.

"Tell me you didn't remodel it," Tel begged, his hands folded before his face.

"No," Jess said slowly, "but there's no place to hide anything in there. The style back then was to have everything open. Here, I'll show you."

She rose, and everyone followed. The bathroom was on the second floor, between the two larger bedrooms, one of which sported tarpaulin over the wooden floors and fresh yellow paint on one wall. Like the kitchen, the bathroom fixtures were pastel, in this case a pale peach.

"See?" Jess crossed her arms, leaning against the doorway. "Nothing. Afraid you've wasted all our time."

Tel stared around the room. Jess was right: there really wasn't a good place to hide fifty thousand dollars in jewelry. The sink didn't even have a cabinet underneath, and towels were stacked on a set of bare shelves inset into the wall beside it. The toilet was the old-fashioned sort with the tank near the ceiling rather than just above the seat. No good way to get up there and hide a bag of jewelry—and besides, wouldn't they have shown up in the toilet bowl sooner or later?

"Where should we start?" he mused aloud.

"See if any of the walls sound hollow," Morris replied, rapping near the window with his knuckles.

After a solid minute of everyone in the room knocking at the surface nearest them, Tel called for a rethink. "Too much noise. Morris, keep checking the walls. Lontano, try those shelves. There could be a compartment behind them. Sam and Jess, what about the plumbing? Any way Tommy might have installed a double pipe or something?"

The two looked at one another for a moment. Jess shrugged and bent to tap the pipe beneath the sink. "They look like normal-sized pipes to me. I guess we could check it out, though. Sam, shut the water off, would you?"

They both trotted back downstairs. Shortly, Jess returned with a toolkit, then they heard Sam's shout from the yard. Jess pulled a monkey wrench from the kit and removed the trap from beneath the sink. A thin stream of water poured onto the floor but Jess ignored it in favor of the pipe.

"Nope," she said, handing the trap to Tel. "Just a normal iron pipe. Looks like it's about to rust through, though. Another thing to replace."

Tel studied the trap. She was right: it was solid, if rusting. Nowhere to hide even an earring, much less the rest of the jewelry. Jess had gotten a flashlight and was peering into the other pipes exposed beneath the sink.

"Anything?" Tel asked hopefully, setting the trap on the floor.

"Plain old everyday pipes, I'm afraid."

Morris was still working his way around the room, rapping knuckles against every inch of wall. Tel, Jess, and a recently arrived Sam looked at Lontano, who shook his head. "I've taken all the linens out, and the shelving. Sounds like solid wall behind them and I don't think Tommy had time for carpentry."

Tel sighed, ran a hand through his hair again. "Probably not. But he said it was in the bathroom."

Morris turned from his examination of the wall over the bathtub. "If anyone had found the jewelry, it'd have been a big deal. I'm betting it's still in here somewhere."

Tel flung his hands up. "But where?"

Lontano perched on the edge of the big tub. "I wonder."

"What?" Tel squatted down, looked in the direction Lontano's eyes were pointed. "What are you looking at?"

"Those." Lontano reached out to thump a fingernail on the metal legs of the sink. "If they're hollow, they're certainly big enough to hide a lot of things."

Tel grasped the nearest leg and twisted. He grimaced. "Not budging, here. Maybe it needs oil."

"Let me try." Lontano put out both hands.

Together, the two twisted. A loud metallic screech had them all clapping hands to their ears.

"Jaysus, that's worse than chalk on a blackboard," muttered Tel. He winced as Lontano twisted the leg once again, then it was loose enough to turn easily.

"We'll need something to hold this," Lontano said, peering inside of the leg.

Jess trotted to the bedroom, returning with an empty dresser drawer. Lontano tipped the leg upside down. Everyone in the room sucked in a reflexive breath. A beam of sunlight flashed fire from the gemstones sliding from the hollow metal leg. Diamond and emerald rings, gaudy earrings and bracelets, necklaces of every imaginable shape and color. They poured from the hollow pipe like a rainbow, seemingly without end.

Morris bent close. His camera flashed like a lightning storm. Tel plucked a ruby necklace from atop the pile, holding it up to the sun. "Can you imagine wearing something like this?"

Jess snorted. "I can imagine all the good that money could have done, instead of draping some old woman's neck."

Sam elbowed her partner. "It's lovely," she said, stirring the pile with one finger. "I've never seen so much jewelry."

Tel gave her a wink. "We could open a store."

Lontano screwed the sink leg back into place. "I think we need to report this."

"Let's check the other leg," said Jess, putting a hand out. This one came loose after only a little twisting. Jess tipped it up over the drawer. Something rustled, but nothing fell out. She peered into the leg, then looked up, her eyes wide.

"It's full of cash," she whispered.

Tel slid his hand into the opening and tugged. He came up with a handful of paper bills. "Looks fake to me."

Lontano plucked a fifty-dollar bill from Tel's fist. "They're just old, I think."

Jess was already pulling wads of paper from the leg, then tipping it up to shake the rest of the bills loose. They fluttered down over the jewelry, filling the rest of the drawer.

"Man, those people had fat wallets," Tel muttered, flipping through the paper money in his hand. "Over a thousand dollars I'm holding."

"No credit cards back then," Lontano said, handing the fifty back. "Too bad we can't just keep it."

"Who says we can't?" Tel pulled the stack of cash closer to his chest.

Lontano gave him the eye. "It's stolen. The FBI would just ask what we did with it."

"Imagine poor Ethel working the rest of her days here," Sam said, stirring the fortune in the drawer with a finger. "She'd have been set for life."

"Too bad she didn't look in the lute," Tel said with a grin.

"Mandolin," Lontano corrected.

Jess hefted the drawer and headed downstairs. Sam and Morris trotted after. Tel and Lontano restored the bathroom to its original condition before joining the others in the kitchen.

Morris had already set up his lights and was putting together a small plastic box. "Portable studio," he explained, placing an emerald ring within the box. He took several photos of the ring, in different positions, before replacing it with a matching bracelet and starting over.

"Good thing I brought extra memory disks," he muttered, adjusting one of his lights.

"Where's the FBI contact number?" Jess asked. "May as well get that over with." She sighed as Lontano passed over his tablet. "We could totally restore the house."

"We can't keep all this money in a drawer all weekend," Sam said, shoving to her feet. "I'll go pick up a safe at Ace."

Morris looked up from the ruby earrings he was photographing. "We'll need pictures of all of you, too. We can come back later for that."

"Yeah," Jess muttered, looking at her paint-stained hands. "Don't want posterity seeing me in this state."

"Why don't you start counting that cash, Tel," Morris ordered. "Lontano, get us some more information on Tommy and his gang. We'll want to jump on a book deal before anyone else thinks of it."

"Who died and made you boss?" Tel muttered, reaching for the drawer.

The FBI showed up Monday afternoon. Sea Wind had crowded into the hotel suite for an impromptu practice session. They were scheduled for a three-day battle-of-the-bands contest later in the week. Tel heard a knock at the door during their break. It sounded like the knock of a visitor who'd been at it for a while. Tel swung the door wide.

A black-suited man held up a badge. "Agent Finley."

Tel allowed him in, showed him the mandolin pieces, gave him the lowdown along with Jess and Sam's address. Finley said he'd meet them there. The whole band wanted to see the jewelry, so Morris drove the rental car again. He was still miffed that Agent Finley had refused to be photographed. An offer of entry into the official press conference had somewhat mollified the photographer, but he was still sulking when they opened the safe.

Everyone except the agent drew in a deep breath at the sight. The drummer reached for a bracelet. Finley tugged the heavy box away and closed it again. The case he'd carried inside, once opened and set on the table, proved to be lined with velvet pockets. Finley pulled out a tablet, swung the safe door open again.

"If you'll bear with me a little while," he said, "I'll just inventory everything."

As he began snapping pictures, Jess flipped the coffeepot on. The three band members found seats at the kitchen table, their wide eyes on the gleaming jewelry. The other civilians poured coffee and retreated to the parlor to read over what Morris had written for the upcoming book. Nearly an hour later, the clunk of the safe closing brought them back to the kitchen doorway.

"Looks like everything is here," Finley said, hefting his case in one hand. He transmitted his office link number to Lontano and Jess. "I'll notify you when you can go public with your find. We'll hold a press conference. You'll be allowed to tell your side of the story then."

Jess and Sam exchanged a glance. Their free hands met, entwined.

"There's our historic significance," Jess said softly, a dimple appearing in her cheek. "Now we just need the reward money."

"When will we get the reward?" Tel wanted to know. He nudged his guitarist with a broad wink.

"Once everything is officially catalogued, you'll receive a check."

"Which we will then split," Lontano said with a nod to Jess.

"Agreed," she replied. "If you young whippersnappers are

out of town, we'll wire you your half."

Sam elbowed her partner. "If it weren't for these whipper-snappers, we'd never have found that jewelry. Did you know those legs screwed off?"

Jess shook her head with a smile. They trooped to the front door to watch Finley climb into his black sedan and pull into the street.

Tel clapped Lontano on the back. "You know, I kind of like solving mysteries."

"'The Mystery of the Old Mandolin,'" said Jess with a grin. "Shades of Nancy Drew."

At Tel's blank look, she sighed. "Before your time. Grandma taught me to read on those books."

"Before I forget," Lontano said, pulling the yellowed envelope from his jacket. "You should frame the letters."

"Yep," said Sam. "Going to display them in the hallway. Right beside the signed photo of Sea Wind you're going to get me."

At Tel's startled look, she gave them a wink, then frowned. "You boys just better win this weekend. I've got money riding on it."

Lontano gave Tel an odd look. "You need a lot of money for a historic house, don't you?"

Jess snorted. "You ain't kidding."

"Can I see our agreement?" Lontano asked, pulling out his copy of the contract.

With a puzzled expression, Jess handed over her copy. She gasped as Lontano ripped both pages into confetti. She reached out for Sam's hand and squeezed it hard.

"You need it more than I do," Lontano said.

"What?" Tel yelped. "We're not rich."

"We have what we need," said Lontano with a smile. "We can strike it rich with the next album."

Tel's lower lip stuck out. "A reward would have been nice." Then, he shrugged. "If we're going to make it on the rock circuit, we need to get back and practice."

They shook hands with a stunned Jess and Sam. Tel took a last look at the old house. Maybe he was imagining it, but the place looked grateful. It would be a grand site once it was restored.

As they drove away, the photographer pointed out a sign in front of another old home. "Look, an estate sale."

"Hell, no!" said Tel.

A Funny Face
Karen Pullen

Seven little girls in black leotards and pink tights. Blond black cinnamon hair screwed into pony tails, neat pigtails, hanging loose, curly frizzy shiny straight not-very-clean. A little-girl funk fills the room as they wiggle and twist, distracted by their mirror images, only half listening to the curvaceous instructor who admonishes "pay attention, second position," and slides her right foot to the side, opens her arms parallel to the floor. Seven little girls imitate, working themselves into wobbly seconds.

Sam watches through the one-way mirror as her daughter's arms sag out of second. Leah wanted to take hip-hop, not ballet, but Carter said it was lazy dancing, trashy; she'd take ballet or nothing. Sam went along like she always goes along.

Sam herself had started in the dance studio when she was three; by high school, two hours a day, classical Russian. Hard, hard work until perspiration and chronic starvation landed her a position in the North Carolina Ballet at the age of eighteen, principal dancer at twenty-two. Dance was her life for nine more years until a sprained ankle—grade three, torn ligaments—required surgery. As she lay on an examining table, the capable hands of Dr. Carter Fish, an extremely attractive surgical resident, manipulated her foot and her ankle and came to rest on her thigh. "You won't dance again," he'd said, "but would you have dinner with me?"

So, she quit ballet. Retired at thirty-one. No tears; she was tired of the jealousy, competition, favoritism. She wanted real health insurance and her own place. Carter was exactly the ticket. They married six months later.

Leah yawns. Is she having a good time? She has the body for ballet—long legs, short waist—but four-year-olds have the attention span of a fruit fly. Sam sighs and looks at her watch. Four thirty. Time for a swallow. She doesn't even feel the last drink, the one she had before leaving home; it might as well have been water. Sam unscrews the top of her stainless-steel water bottle and takes a goodly sip. Vodka, grapefruit juice, and plenty of ice. Perfect. Sam leans against the wall, enjoying the way her head feels, a bit of a buzzy spin going there.

A half hour later, Leah saunters out of class surrounded by the pack of girls. Ballet at this age is all about the social. Sam leads Leah out to the Audi, moving deliberately. It has begun to rain, and a gust of wind pushes her off-balance. Oh man, this drive is not going to be easy, but it's only a few miles to home, they will make it fine. Leah buckles herself into her car seat, and Sam starts the car. The wipers aren't really keeping up with the torrents of water, and it's hard to see, so she drives very slowly toward the parking lot exit. She looks left and sees headlights a good ways off. Plenty of time. She accelerates but nothing happens, the car doesn't move. She mashes the gas pedal again, and again, then realizes the car is in neutral. She puts it in drive and finally the car shoots forward and with a loud bang, smashes directly into the side of a small SUV. The SUV had been going at a good clip, and the physics of the collision send it into a spin before it comes to a stop heading the wrong way. The Audi is parked in the middle of the highway, the front end all smashed to hell. She tries the gas pedal again but nothing happens. Oh shit. She twists in her seat to check on Leah, who is frowning.

"What happened, Mommy?" Leah asks.

"Accident, sweetie. We're okay." She feels quite nervous about being parked in the middle of the highway, but traffic has stopped in both directions. A man is getting out of the SUV. At least he doesn't seem to be hurt, but he sure looks pissed as hell. She feels dizzy, and the rain, the headlights, brake lights are blinding. She blinks and rubs her eyes. Leah starts to cry. A siren and blue flashing lights. Oh shit.

Even though it's not yet bedtime, Leah wears her Tinkerbell nightgown. She lounges on the floor beside the big brown chair in the living room with her favorite toys: a red-haired ballerina doll named Judy, a white bear with no eyes (Orvie), and Horsie. They play Castle and Escape and Birthday Party. Leah tells stories and acts them out, taking on the part of each character. A lot of talking, in different voices for the different characters. Sometimes they fight or cry and get loud.

Mommy sits in the brown chair, tinkling the ice in her glass. Leah looks up at her; Mommy's eyes are closed. "I'm getting a headache, darling. Go play in your room," she says. Leah doesn't mind, she likes being in her room with her toys where no one tells her to be quiet.

Ponch follows her. He's a Chihuahua. He trembles because he's afraid of thunder, and an incoming summer storm has sent him into near-seizures. Leah tries to comfort him, whispers everything will be all right. Her hands mash down his ear flaps, and she talks softly and sings in a crooning voice as she tries to cover the noise of the thunder. But Ponch's tiny being senses the distant percussive explosions and vibrates with distress. Leah can't calm or comfort him.

Mommy has pills that will calm Ponch. Leah wraps the quivering dog in a blanket and carries him down the stairs, through the living room, through the kitchen, past Daddy's office (he is listening to music and must not be disturbed). Oh no. Mommy's in bed. There's no light coming from under the bedroom door. She mustn't disturb Mommy who needs her sleep.

Maybe Daddy will help. She opens his door an inch and puts

her mouth to the opening. Music blasts at her, the loud booming music Daddy likes. It hurts her face. "Daddy? Daddy, are you busy?"

He's mad about something, she can tell. His face is red and frowny. "Get out," he says. She takes a step back and shuts the door, shuts out the music though it's still so loud through the door.

BOOM! Lightning crashes nearby. Ponch whimpers and half leaps out of her arms. Leah has to do something. She opens the drawer in the bathroom where Mommy keeps her pills. There are so many bottles. Which one would calm her little doggie? BOOM! She decides on the blue pills. Those are the bedtime pills. It will do him good to sleep.

She goes to the kitchen and gets a piece of cheese, tears it into pieces and wraps the pill in cheese. Ponch gobbles it, he loves cheese.

At night, the big window in the living room is like a mirror. Leah is admiring her reflection in the Tinkerbell nightgown when a giant CRACK-BOOM of lightning makes Ponch give a little doggie scream. He's stopped shaking but is drooling out of his mouth. Ugh. Leah puts him down on the sofa and tucks the blanket around him. The now-dark window rattles from a gust of wind. Outside, tall pines sway against the gray sky.

A flash of lightning lights up the outside like daytime, and Leah sees a person outside. A woman, looking into the house, looking at her. Leah stands very still. The woman's black bangs drip into surprised eyes like Dora the Explorer's and her lips are puffy like the lips of Rainbow Fish. Because the woman looks like a cartoon, Leah isn't afraid. She presses against the window, trying to see the cartoon woman better. A palmetto bug scuttles across the windowsill and Leah jumps back, watching it crawl down the wall and under the sofa. Ponch's eyes are closed but he isn't sleeping; he pants like he's been running. His soggy spit turns the white sofa cover dark and yellowish. At least he isn't trembling anymore.

Another CRACK-BOOM. The cartoon woman has come

close. She flattens her face against the glass and the smashed features frighten Leah, imprint on her memory. (The memory will haunt her for years, triggered by gusting wind, by lightning, by palmetto bugs.) She collects Ponch's hot little body, Horsie, Orvie, and Judy. Scoots up the stairs to her bedroom, slams the door. Darts into her closet. Stumbles over shoes to the far end where Mommy's long dresses hang, and slips behind their perfumed silks. Her heart pounds, her breath rasps in her chest, and, unable to hold it in any longer, she pees. The warm gush soaks her nightgown and stings her legs. Clutching her dog and toys tight, she curls into a ball.

Jackhammers stab Sam's skull, one over each ear. Mouth full of cinders. A horrible noise, a jingle, a brisk tinkly Scott Joplin tune. Over and over. Stop stop stop. The call finally goes to voice mail. Sam grinds her teeth and opens her eyes. Ouch. Shuts them as her head spins.

"Mommy?" Leah's breath is warm in Sam's ear. "I'm really really really really hungry. Are you going to get up?"

"Sure." But Sam isn't sure; she feels quite ill. How much did she drink last night? She remembers the afternoon vodka coolers, opening a bottle of Cab. There would've been cocktails, more wine at dinner, and brandy after, but really, no memory of the evening. A sudden urge to vomit propels her out of bed and into the bathroom where she retches into the toilet. Man oh man. Not good. Alka Seltzer, stat. She drops two tablets into water and sips the fizzy concoction. Gags a little but it stays down. I have to cut back, she thinks, hating the hangover. She's not quite ready to blame herself for last night's accident. There was a problem with the Audi's transmission. And the SUV was speeding, she is sure of that. Partly his fault.

Leah has dressed herself in a pink Cinderella ballgown, decorated here and there with green marker. Her fine pale hair is matted, and she smells like urine. When Sam feels more human, she'll get Leah into the bathtub. There was no bath last night, Sam is pretty sure. And Carter didn't turn off his radio. Operatic shrieks are making their way from his office speakers to her eardrums, not helping her stomach cramps or her head. She has no memory of seeing him last night, though surely they had dinner together, from the looks of the kitchen. Is he still here? He usually leaves before six, for surgery. On noses, chins, ears. Boobs, butts. Plumping, lifting, injecting, shaping.

Sam pours milk into a bowl of Frosted Flakes, makes coffee, fills the dog bowl. Usually Ponch is scrabbling underfoot, gobbling his food. "Leah, have you seen Ponch?"

Her daughter pauses her spoon in midair and shakes her head, no, whispers into Orvie's ear. That eyeless bear is creepy. Sam sips coffee, decides the Cab is what made her so sick. She'll switch to Chardonnay. White wine is a social drink, and there's a case in the garage, not too oaky. She tries not to think about the Audi's crumpled front end, the tow truck, the ticket, insurance points, the many long hours in this day. Where is the dog? Why is Met opera bellowing from Carter's speakers?

"Leah, have you seen Daddy?"

The child widens her eyes, shrugs. A soggy cereal flake adheres to her chin.

"What does that mean? Yes, you saw him?"

Leah shakes her head, no.

Detective Homer Greely pulls on gloves and punches off the radio, source of the loud, pulsing migraine that is Wagnerian opera, so that he can hear Brenda, the lead Forensics tech.

"We've got shoe prints," Brenda says. "Someone stood outside the big window, in the rain, came in the back door through the house to this office. Stood right there"—she points to the taped-off shoe prints—"then turned and left. Has to be the shooter. We'll compare the prints to the database but off the top of my head looks like a woman's size eight. A little bigger than my size seven."

"A woman. The plot thickens," Homer says.

"She dripped. See where it's evaporated? So maybe during that downpour last night, around eight, eight thirty. She rode a bicycle. There's tread marks up to the window and mud tracks on the driveway."

Shoe and bike tire prints will help but aren't enough to convict. He turns to the body. Homer has seen plenty of dead bodies, and this one isn't special. A single gunshot between the eyes has ended the life of Dr. Carter Fish, knocking him backward, toppling his desk chair onto the floor. What *is* special is the magnificent home—exclusive Southport address fronting the Cape Fear River—and the wife, a waif-like creature with eighty-proof breath and perfect posture.

He meets with her in the kitchen, an acre of tile and marble, strewn with dirty dishes and pots with caked-on food. The back door, the most likely point of entry, is unlocked. Shoe prints are taped off here also.

Mrs. Fish has been crying, and her eyes are red. A child sits by her mother's feet (clearly smaller than a women's eight), clutching stuffed animals. Mrs. Fish combs the child's tangled hair with her fingers. "I have no memory of anything last night," she says. "I had a car accident around six and then came home with Leah in an Uber. Then nothing."

"Blackout. It's happened before?" he asks gently. In his sixth year of sobriety, Homer is quite familiar with ethanol's effect on the brain.

She sighs.

"Did you see your husband last night?"

She pulls her knees up, hunches over them to hide her face. "What I said. Don't remember."

They walk through the house to see if anything's out of place. It goes on forever, room after room. There's even a pool table, game room, and hot tub. Leah trails. In her room, the bed is made up. Mrs. Fish frowns. "Where did you sleep last night?"

Leah points to her closet. Mrs. Fish opens the door and immediately closes it. She staggers out of the room to the bathroom and they hear sounds of vomiting. Homer peeks. There's a dead dog, a strong smell of urine. Jesus.

Leah's big eyes are trained on Homer, who thinks this young child is too composed and watchful. Well, maybe she was paying attention last night. Put herself to bed in the closet. Peed herself. Why?

He picks up the eyeless bear. "What's his name?" he asks.

"Orvie," she whispers.

"Orvie, did something scare you last night?" he asks.

"The cartoon lady." Leah mashes her hand against her mouth and nose, opens her eyes wide.

"That's a funny face," Homer says. "Did the cartoon lady come in the house?"

Leah shrugs, hands out. "I hid." She points to the closet.

When Mrs. Fish emerges shakily from the bathroom, Homer asks, "Why would someone do this? Did your husband have any enemies?"

"He received a threatening letter last week. Anonymous, from an unhappy patient. He kept it. I'll show it to you."

"Are there many of those? Unhappy patients, I mean."

"Well, he just won three lawsuits. They didn't get a penny." She puts her arms around Leah. "Phew. You need a bath."

A conversation with a lawyer from Dr. Fish's malpractice insurance company yields three names.

"Dr. Fish has been murdered? Sorry not sorry." Hazel Ransome's smile doesn't reach her eyes. She's about thirty-five, dressed in baggy sweats. Her skin is boiled-egg perfect, pore-free, but bears evidence of injections: a shiny forehead, weirdly puffy lips. Two children in diapers cling to her legs, their mouths plugged with pacifiers. "Come on in, pardon the mess," she says. Homer steps gingerly through a landscape of plastic.

"You were a patient. You sued him recently," Homer says.

"Hell, yeah I sued. They're hard as Granny Smith apples. Want to see?" Hazel grabs her sweater and raises it up. Homer looks away but not quickly enough to avoid seeing her breasts. The larger one points at him like a rocket, the smaller one angles off to the side. It's also higher on her chest. Wow.

"Dr. Fish redid them," she says. "Twice. After that I didn't have any money left to get them fixed. So, I sued."

"You gave him three chances?"

Hazel flushes purple. "That's what his lawyer said. My choice, elective, blah blah. The jury agreed."

The boy toddler lets go of Hazel's right leg and hands Homer his pacifier. "Hey, thanks," Homer says, gingerly accepting the wet offering. He wonders if Hazel's angry enough, over the edge, and cuts to the chase. "Do you own a gun?"

"When my husband left me, I got one for security. But I didn't go out last night. Who would watch these two?"

Homer feels a surge of sympathy. Single mom, butchered boob job, broke. Still, quite a motive. "You ever ride a bike?" he asks.

She shakes her head, no, brushes her dark bangs out of her eyes. "I push a double stroller, though. Want to see it?"

Kris Donner opens her apartment door wearing a surgical mask. Bangs cover her forehead, so all Homer can see of her face are limpid sea-blue eyes with dark lashes. So, it's difficult to tell how she's reacting to the news of Carter Fish's death. Her eyes blink and she mumbles something he can't understand.

"Sorry, what's that?" he asks.

She pulls the mask off and he tries not to recoil from the sight of her nose, which is largely missing. It's barely a nub, with two holes. "'He had it coming' is what I said," she says. There's something off about the rest of her face too. Her cheeks are lopsided; one is a blob down near her mouth and the other is sunken. "Quite a look, isn't it, Detective?" she asks. "Wouldn't you sue?"

"Mmmm," Homer says, unable to imagine any circumstance that would allow someone to cut up his face.

"Come on in," she says. She motions him to the couch. "Move over, you two." A pair of golden retrievers unwind themselves and slide onto the floor.

Homer sits, knowing his charcoal gray slacks, creased sharp and fresh from a dry cleaner's bag, will be coated with golden hair. "You didn't win, I heard."

"Before the surgery, Dr. Fish gave me a thirty-page book about risks. The jury got a copy. Then they said because I knew what could happen, I didn't deserve a penny." Kris rocks back and forth, rubbing her hands on her muscular thighs. Homer can see weights and exercise bands piled in a corner behind an exercise bike. She notices where he's looking. "Yeah, I work out here. Can't go to the gym looking like this. But some body part has to compensate for my face."

"Ever do any cycling outside?"

"Only at night. When there's a new moon and it's dark."

Phases of the moon. Relevant? "Dark like last night?"

"The moon was full last night, Officer."

"But overcast, stormy."

"That's right." She doesn't avert her gaze, seeming to challenge him to look at her. Her eyes are beautiful, mesmerizing. Tragic.

He looks away, down at the carpet matted with golden hair. Her bare feet. Average-sized bare feet.

Miranda Degraff agrees to meet him in the evening. "My house, OK? I don't go out in public."

The house is another mansion, waterfront like Dr. Fish's. Midnight-blue Jaguar sedan in the driveway. Out back, the

Cape Fear River, a dock, a boat, a pool illuminated with under-water lights. Nice. In early spring, Homer fishes around here for mullet. Smoked, they're tasty.

She keeps the lights low but Homer can still see the results of Carter Fish's handiwork with a scalpel: eyebrows nearly to her hair line, leaving her forehead looking like a Neanderthal's, cheeks pulled back to her ears so that her puffy lips are perpetually parted. Wow.

"I want to cry great choking buckets every time I look in the mirror. But I can't cry—something happened to my tear ducts," she says. In the dim light it's impossible to tell her age, her face shiny like an eggplant. But her eyes are a deep well of misery.

"You sued him," Homer says.

"How could anyone see this face and deny my claim? But those insurance companies, man. Their lawyers are ugly people. Uglier than me on the inside." She screws up her face a little and makes crying noises.

"You must be angry. Want to get even, somehow," Homer says.

"He won't do this to anyone now. The world should be grateful. To whoever killed him. You know."

"Do you ever ride a bicycle, Ms. Degraff?"

She shrugs. "Yes. To firm up my butt. The only body part he didn't ruin."

"At night? Last night?"

"There was a terrible storm and I'm scared of lightning. Would you like a drink, Officer?" She kicks off her slippers and tucks her feet under her firm butt, tips her head. She might be trying to smile. The slippers look like giant fluffy cats. They could be any size.

"Do you own a gun?" Homer asks.

"I might. Do you have a search warrant?"

He did not. No judge would issue a search warrant on this property just because a woman's tear ducts don't work. He needs more.

* * *

Homer ponders this case. People must be unhappy with the results of their plastic surgery all the time. They sue. They lose, because juries aren't sympathetic. But do they seek the ultimate revenge? He's never heard of a case like that. Something else is going on with this killer. He reminds himself that there was an eyewitness.

Sam feels better about herself—Leah's had a bath, her hair's in tidy braids, and she smells like soap instead of urine—and Sam herself has washed up nicely. She doesn't smell like booze. She's been drinking water by the gallon which surely has flushed out her liver by now. She also feels a million times worse, since drinkies have always been her happy place. Without them, she's unmoored, plagued by her awful feelings.

Carter is dead. *Someone came into our house and shot him in the head.* That's a terrible reality she can't look at yet. And Ponch. Their sweet little dog that never barked, lived only for cuddles and treats. His death has floored her. Chardonnay, forgetting, won't bring him back. She needs to grieve the dog's death. Her fault.

A curious little withdrawal tremor has taken over her body, accompanied by a whirring in her brain. *What I deserve.* She tries to focus on the detective. She's forgotten his name. He has questions for Leah, he says.

Leah twirls around the room in her blue taffeta Elsa costume.

"That's a pretty dress," the detective says.

"Ponch died," Leah says. "He was sick. Want to watch me dance?" She hands Sam the eyeless bear, red-haired Judy, and Horsie. She raises her arms overhead, then leaps across the room and back again. If Sam could allow herself to feel anything, she'd be proud of her little girl, for being social, for being brave enough to dance. But feelings will break her. She grips her water bottle tightly.

"Tell me about your friends here," the detective says to Leah. "Did Horsie see the cartoon lady?"

Leah shakes her head, no. She pushes the Judy doll into the detective's face.

He takes the doll. "The lady was scary, wasn't she, honey?"

Leah nods.

"Why? Did she make a mean face?"

Leah presses her hands over her face. Peers at the detective through her fingers. "Like this." She grabs her toys and burrows into Sam's lap. "Why are you shaking, Mommy?"

Sam can't answer. Fifty shades of terrible.

Homer goes outside and stands in front of the large window, not close, being careful not to disturb the killer's footprints, the bicycle tread marks. He pushes aside the branches of a prickly hedge. There, about five and a half feet off the ground, on the window. There's an impression of a face. She had pressed her face against the window. They'd been so focused on the footprints and bicycle tire treads that they overlooked the window.

He knows who the killer is now.

He takes a few pictures, and heads to the office to get a search warrant for DNA, bicycle, gun, and shoes.

Homer warns the deputies before they knock on the door. "Don't react to her face. Keep it professional."

It takes less than an hour to collect what they came for, and to swab inside Kris Donner's lopsided cheek. She's quiet and cooperative. He decides not to cuff her, but recites her Miranda rights as he leads her to his car. "You were at Dr. Fish's house last night, and we'll be able to prove those were your shoe prints, your bicycle tire prints, a bullet fired from your gun. Your DNA will be found in the face print on the window. So, I know you killed him. You'll go to prison for years. Is revenge worth it?"

"Not revenge." She begins to explain.

Homer Greeley has been a homicide detective for eleven years, and he thinks he's heard every stupid reason people give for murdering someone: gang pressure, money, rejection, abuse, revenge, blackmail, greed. But he's never heard anything like Kris's motive.

"I'm in love with my lawyer," she says. "I retained him to sue the pants off Dr. Fish. I fell in love with him, and wanted to move in with him and let him take care of me for the rest of my life."

Her damaged face turns to Homer. "It's unrealistic. He's married, a nice guy. Can't hardly look at me. But the only time I'm happy is when he's driving me to depositions or court. It's the leather seats of his Jag, or his cologne—something sends me into a rare state. After we lost my lawsuit, I wanted more time with him."

"So, you committed murder?"

She shrugs. She's not going to confess yet. "I want to talk to my lawyer."

Two days later, in the afternoon, there's a memorial reception at Carter's office. They've organized everything. People offer condolences, saying things about Carter that make Sam wonder whether they ever met him. His patients are unmistakable, with their slick foreheads and wide-open eyes, tight necks, plump lips, and boobs like balloons. Sam gets through it with a sweaty grip on her water bottle. *Get through it*, the mantra of the moment. Surprisingly, it works. People's expectations are low.

Sam doesn't want to think about the last time she saw Carter, lying dead behind his desk. She tries to think instead about

Ponch. She finds a photo of the dog on her phone, and prints it out. Fastens it to the refrigerator, surrounded by Leah's drawings, assorted magnets, and takeout menus.

"Give yourself a break, Mrs. Fish," the detective tells Sam. (She still can't remember his name.) "If you hadn't passed out, you might have been killed too. Or Leah."

"I guess that's one way to look at it." Sam laughs, for the first time in three days. She is still shattered. She's even turned on the Met broadcast, because the faint operatic shrieking anchors her attention outside her own head. She can hum along. Be in the moment. Do what needs to be done: make the bed, wash the dishes, drive Leah to preschool. Pour every bit of booze in the house, entire cases of wine, down the drain. Walk walk walk for hours until her blisters have blisters.

"I brought Leah a present, for helping to solve the case," he says, handing her a gift bag. Inside is a stuffed dog, super-soft, tan and white. Like Ponch.

"She will love that." Tears prick her eyes. His kindness is overwhelming. Carter was never kind.

"And something for you," he says. It's a flyer for the South-port AA meetings.

Sam takes the flyer. She's seen it before, online. When she was toying with the idea of stopping for the hundredth time, she researched rehabs and AA, Day One blogs, and Soberistas. "Gosh, there's a meeting every day."

"I go at six p.m.," he says. "Let me know if you want a sponsor."

It's a lifeline. She hasn't had a drink in three days, but her willpower feels tender, like it wouldn't take much to crumple it. "I do. I do want a sponsor, Detective."

"Call me Homer," he says.

They shake hands. His hand is warm and gentle. "See you at six," he says.

After he leaves, she closes the door and leans against it, suddenly aware how a soprano's warbly shriek makes her feel stabby. She goes into Carter's office—not looking at his desk—and unplugs the speakers. The silence is lovely. Different. Something has ended. It's the oddest feeling.

Falling Star
Jacy Sellers

Mismatched chimes, accompanied by blinking lights from the busty teal mermaid slot machine, mock me. This is not my resort. Is it? I have no idea what time it is. My heels wobble as I cross the purple-patterned carpet of the casino. The wild design hurts my head, and I close my eyes while staggering into a very tall mustached man.

"Watch it," he says. "Hey! I know you! Gaby! Loved your song the other night on the show. I voted for you!" He reeks of a cheap cigar and soured alcohol.

"Sorry," I mumble, backing up, fighting a wave of nausea.

The guy is wearing a Vegas T-shirt, carrying an absurdly large beer. Is it morning? This is the city of lights, but no one ever sleeps here. Within seconds, he aims his phone at me. "Can we get a selfie? I can tag *Sin City Star* in my post. Hashtag SinCityStar."

He slams his cheek into me, and I stumble, a few flashes, until I lose my balance. My backside smacks into the floor, a shot of pain erupts through my muscles, and I'm buried in billows of white satin ruffles. My vision blurs into streaks of aqua and lights.

Legs and slurred phrases from different voices bounce all around me.

"Sing for us, Gaby!"

"Love you!"

"Hashtag Falling Star."

"Sick! What's on her dress?"

"It *is* Vegas."

A pair of gold Louboutin heels catch my attention, and I pat them to make sure they're real. An arm pulls me to my feet. Olivia.

"I don't feel so good," I whine to her false eyelashes and solemn face.

Despite her frozen Botox face, she's a welcome relief in her usual black jumpsuit and sleek ponytail. Olivia shoves an oversized hoodie and sunglasses onto me.

"I've been looking for you." She clutches my arm, her cheetah-print nails digging into my skin. "We have to go, now."

The crowd is a sea of phones. Among them is our crew member Josh with his video lens aimed at me. How long has he been filming me? He's wearing a *Sin City Star* embroidered hat pulled down as if trying to hide. The showrunner of *Sin City Star* had assigned Olivia as my producer and Josh as my cameraman when I made it into the top ten. Every competitor has their own crew who films them both on and off the stage. I've gotten used to them.

Olivia drags me through the wall of people, knocking into shoulder after shoulder. Josh's camera moves with us. We pause in a corner, wedged between two open slot machines.

"I don't know what's happening. I feel sick." I grip Olivia's wrists. Did my words slur? My brain is scrambled, and the flashing lights aren't helping.

"Gabrielle. We've got to get out of here." Her voice is high-pitched and anxious.

But her use of my full name sends shivers down my spine.

"Why did you leave your room? Where's Kevin?" Her questions rattle my aching head.

White satin dress. Last night.

Elvis.

Vows.

Wedding bells.

Rings.

Where is Kevin?

My new husband?

Oh, God. My new husband.

A queasy feeling rolls through my stomach.

Two guys ogle us with phones out as I fumble to pull the sweatshirt down over itchy lace and crinoline ruffles. One comes in for a close-up. Olivia huffs and slaps his arm, causing him to drop his phone. Josh catches everything on film.

Like always.

"Bitch! We wanted a selfie with a star," the other man snaps. "Her voice may be a good mix of folk and pop, but she's a disaster."

"We don't need reminders of any disasters." Olivia smirks, turning to Josh. "You'll have to edit this."

"It's too late," I mumble. Someone probably already posted it on social media.

The curly-haired man pulls out his phone, walking backward, snapping more pics. "By the way, your hoodie doesn't hide all the blood on that wedding dress," he hollers.

I gaze down. "Blood? Is that blood?"

"Forget it. Let's go," Olivia says, pulling me to the lobby and outside the casino into the blaring sun. I can't see a damn thing, so I put on my sunglasses. The enormous sign for the Burning Love Resort floods me with memories of last night. Here, I married Kevin in the Elvis chapel. The film crew produced the ceremony. The other competitors were guests, and our families watched on video stream. We had a reception, drank too much, went to our room, and then what? My memory fails until I woke up just now, wandering the casino.

A sleek car with tinted windows waits, and the driver holds the door for us. Before I crawl in, I glimpse a lighted billboard across the street. Kevin is holding me in his arms, and the headline reads, *MURDERED SIN(GING) CITY STAR*.

"Kevin was murdered? When? Where?" I'm shouting. A small crowd gathers, many holding phones. Josh cuts off his camera and climbs into the car.

"Hush!" Olivia snaps, putting a hand on top of my head and shoving me down into the car.

Tears sting my eyes. I plop onto the sleek leather, and that's when I notice saturated red stains across the skirt of my white dress.

"Liv?" My legs shake. "Liv, it's all over me."

"It'll be fine. Here. Sniff this." She opens a vial of eucalyptus essential oil.

My heart pounds. I snatch the vial and huff, letting the scent weave through me.

Olivia cracks the car window, letting in a steamy gust of pot-filled Vegas air before lighting a cigarette. She offers me a drag. The temporary cure I need after a blackout morning, a sham wedding, and now, a murder? Kevin has been murdered? I can't. And the blood on my skirt worries me. A lot.

"Gaby." She shifts toward me. "I'm here for you. We will find out what happened together."

I really hope so. Olivia has always been in my corner. When we met, we easily fell into a routine of iced coffees, calendar checks, wardrobe approvals, and song rehearsals. She had already been following me from my trends on TikTok. I trust her.

The car's every turn nauseates me. I grab a bottle of water from the cup holder and drink it down. I'm parched. "Where are we going?"

"The police station," Josh says.

Olivia snaps her fingers at him, and he mechanically readies the camera. She never likes Josh speaking to me.

"Why? I don't remember anything. Why *did* I leave the room? I can't believe he's dead. Someone killed Kevin?"

The driver glances at us through the rearview mirror at my outburst. Olivia pushes a button and rolls up the privacy window.

No one answers. The nausea tumbles inside me. I touch my wedding ring, studying it, trying to picture the ceremony and anything afterward. A sour taste rises in my throat.

"It will be fine, sweetie. That's why I'm here." Olivia reaches to squeeze my hand. Her brown eyes twinkle. The car screeches to a stop.

"Let's go," Olivia leads me out of the car while Josh follows us.

We're standing in front of a big stone building. The letters are fuzzy, but I can read them okay: *Las Vegas Metropolitan Police Department.*

"No. I can't do this!" I push against Olivia to get back into the car, bumping Josh.

She pulls me back, slams the car door shut, and the driver takes off, leaving us on the sidewalk to meet my fate.

"It's our civic duty. The police want to talk to you," she states. "There's enough gossip and news out there. We need to set things right."

"How am I supposed to do that?"

"Hey!" She shakes me, not hard, but enough for nausea to kick back in. "You've got to get it together. Tell them what you know. This is your chance to start that conversation. This isn't going to be easy, but I'm here for you. The whole world is here for you."

She eyes the camera and gives me a swift hug then steers us toward the massive compound of a building. A barbed wire fence surrounds a section of an outdoor yard. I wonder if I get to leave today or if they'll suit me up in orange.

Inside the building, the claustrophobic lobby is crowded. My heart pounds. I step to the front desk with Olivia as all eyes follow us, and the conversations die down.

I keep the hoodie drawn behind the sunglasses, and tug at the scratchy fabric of the dress I want to rip off. "Dammit. Why couldn't I change before we got here?" Or more importantly, why didn't Olivia encourage me to change first? She always insists that I look my best, not my worst.

A uniformed man steps out from behind the front desk. "Come with me. Uh. The camera needs to be outside."

Olivia nods at Josh, who grimaces at me before he leaves.

A petite woman with a tight blond bun stands in the middle of the chaos like a statue in a tailored navy suit. She steps closer to us. Her badge flashes from her waist.

"Gabrielle Perrin?" she asks in a firm monotone.

"Yes," I gulp, toying with my gaudy wedding ring.

"I'm Detective Stanton. I just have a few questions." She spins on her black heel and walks away from us as a signal to follow her. Usually, I had the followers, especially the thousands on my social media accounts.

Then she stops and eyes Olivia. "You may wait in the lobby."

"Hold on. Our lawyer is on the way." Olivia pulls out her phone.

"No need. She's not a suspect," the woman says curtly and walks on again.

I'm not?

Olivia reluctantly nods for me to follow.

A couple of gawkers whisper as we walk past them with their cell phones out. I hope Olivia will bust theirs too.

The detective pauses in front of a metal detector. "Remove everything from your pockets. You will retrieve it after we chat."

I pat myself. "I don't have any—" A bulge on my hip. This wedding dress has pockets! My phone. I pull it out and place it into the collection bowl.

Detective Stanton steps toward a table with a small black box. "We'll take your fingerprints here."

I don't question her instruction, and afterward she takes me to a stark, chilled room with a scratched-up wood table and two metal chairs. "Sit," she commands.

Rude. I'm not used to it.

I plop onto the hard chair on the other side. My skirt billows all around. The windowless room only has a large mirror, probably one of those two-way kinds. Wonder who's on the other side, watching?

The woman closes the door and sits across from me. "I'm the lead investigator in this case. I have a few questions for you about the death of Kevin Stewart." She hands me a bottle of water.

"Um. Maybe I should wait for my lawyer or something?" My head starts to clear. I open the water bottle and take a gulp. "I don't know what happened." I cough.

"I haven't asked you any questions yet." She takes a notepad and pen from her jacket pocket.

My lips tighten. This tiny woman intimidates me more than an arena filled with hundreds of fans screaming for my songs. But I won't let her get the best of me.

"Tell me everything, starting with last night," she says.

I take a deep breath. "Let's see," I strum my fingers on the table, expelling anxious energy. "I got married? To Kevin. Yes. We left the chapel and found ourselves in the hotel room. Then, I don't know. Did we have sex?" A bubble crawls up my throat. I suppress a tiny burp, tasting of sharp lime.

Lime. I had a drink? More than one?

"Drop the act. This isn't going to be viewed by your fans." Her face is cold and expressionless.

I blink back to the hotel room. We toasted our sham marriage with champagne. Then, I blacked out. I don't even remember walking into the casino, but that's where Olivia found me.

"C-c-can I have one of those tests? Like a drug test?" Sweat pops from my temples. Either it's hot in here, or the hangover has kicked in. Vomit stacks itself in my throat. "I need a..."

Before I can say *trash can*, I barf all over the floor next to me. The relief expels fragments of stress. My stomach untwists. I wipe my mouth and glance at the detective. She frowns, but hardly reacts. She's definitely had experience with others like me.

"Yes. We will do a drug test. and let me remind you, my job is to reveal the truth. Raw and unedited. Unlike your so-called reality TV show," she says without an ounce of sympathy.

"You know how this looks, right? The two of you go to bed. He's stabbed to death, and you walk out covered in blood. Give me one good reason to let you out of here?"

I burst into sobs. She already thinks I'm acting; I might as well turn on the faucet for her. I don't remember Kevin covered in blood. Where is the lawyer Olivia mentioned?

"I didn't do anything," I sniffle.

"Then why did you leave the room? Not call for help?" she asks without emotion. Apparently, empathy isn't in her blood.

"I don't know." I wipe my nose with the hoodie sleeve.

Detective Stanton scribbles in her pad. "What else can you tell me?"

"That's all I know."

She tosses a business card onto the table in front of me. "Contact me when you remember anything else."

"Can I go?"

"You are welcome to leave. I wasn't keeping you. In fact, you came here voluntarily."

"It was the right thing to do." I stand.

"Confessions are always the right thing to do." Detective Stanton doesn't crack a smile. She has an amazing poker face. "Now, I'll need that wedding dress, to enter it into evidence."

I follow her to a bathroom area and trade my bloodied dress for a Vegas tourist T-shirt and a pair of adjustable waist pants. I even leave the hoodie behind. I pee in a cup and turn that in too. After I get my phone back, I meet Olivia in the lobby.

"What did she ask you? And what did you say? What the hell are you wearing?" Olivia points at my shirt, "It says, *This is my hangover shirt.*"

"Just take me back to my room." I pull at the tight clothes and adjust my sunglasses against the sun's glare.

"What did you tell her?" she presses.

"The truth." As much as I knew.

A sleek black car pulls up to the curb, and Olivia opens the door for me. We climb inside just as a small group of fans runs up, swinging their phones. Silence. Olivia stares out the window.

"What's wrong, Liv?"

"While you were busy entertaining that cop, I've been on the phone with the producers. Trying to save your career." She pauses. "They want to run with it."

"Run with what?"

"Kevin's death. If we air the show, we're being transparent with our fans. They'd want to know the truth."

"The truth?" I sink into the seat, wishing it would swallow me whole. "I don't even know the truth. What will Kevin's family think? Shouldn't they have a say?" Kevin has been dead for twenty-four hours and we're already talking about how we can best satisfy our fans?

Sometimes, I really hate this life.

The car turns several more times before landing at my hotel, the Sand Mirage Resort. A man and a woman dressed in jeans and black T-shirts wait for me on the curb. They're part of *Sin City Star*'s security team.

"You don't even know his family," she says. "Besides, this could be a good opportunity for you. Maybe to tell your side of the story."

As I process, she wraps her arm around me and hugs me tight. What is my side of the story? I don't have one. I smell her rose perfume, and my nerves smooth out. Olivia has a way of calming me. If it wasn't for her friendship or her access to the best fruit smoothies in Vegas, I'd be a hot mess on *Sin City Star*.

"Do you want to come in?" I ask, getting out of the car.

Olivia offers me a half grin and doesn't move.

"Not now. I've got more calls to make." She takes out her phone and starts tapping away like she always does. "Security will be in the hall for you. You need to read for the show tonight."

A show. Tonight? I completely forgot. "Are you sure I should go on—I mean...after...after everything?"

She blinks at me for a moment. "We can't cancel a live show. Plus, they're making it a tribute to Kevin."

A tribute. That's good. Great, actually.

For the first time, my shoulders relax. Olivia's right. The show must go on, and I trust she'd help me fix this no matter what the risk. I mean, sure, technically, it's her job to do that, but it's more than just work with her.

She's my closest friend.

And in this business, friends are hard to come by.

She tucks herself back into the car. I drag myself down the back alley and up the service elevator to my seventy-fourth-floor hotel room. The clock reads 10:02 a.m. As I undress for a shower, I slip off the diamond wedding ring with its halo setting and place it on the counter.

The producers had planned for me and Kevin to live together at *Sin City Star*'s staged mansion. What did they expect to film? Our life together while I either won or lost the competition? God. Am I now considered a widow? No. It was fake. Made up. Olivia told me a couple weeks ago that we were losing viewers to other shows like *Cosplay Singer* and *Hotel Hook-Up*. The producers wanted rich content, so they fabricated stories among the competitors filled with grief, drama, and romance.

And now, murder? That was not fabricated.

After a steamy shower where I try to clear my mind, I slip into leggings and a tank before picking up my phone. Two voice messages. One from Olivia and the second from LVPD. I ignore them. There are several texts from the other contestants and the stage crew. And calendar reminders for rehearsals, photos, and interviews, most lined up in advance of last night. One stands out. *Backstage Pass for Lacey Layne at Sand Castle Resort*. I forgot about this until now—a scheduled event for me to admire a successful musician. Each of the contestants received one for different shows in Las Vegas.

Without a second thought, I apply makeup and change into what the producers call plain clothes. I crack open the hotel door, and security is right there. The woman raises her eyebrows at me.

"I have a pass," I say.

"Yes. Olivia mentioned that. We'll accompany you," said the security man.

We take an elevator down to the underground service corridor, connecting to the resort's sister property, the Sand Castle Resort. Within ten minutes, I'm sitting in the designated backstage viewing area, alone. The security team stands nearby. Gold twinkles within the rolling fabric panels onstage. A glamour of bling and lights, similar to the theme on *Sin City Star*. I blink back to the first song I performed.

Honey, you're looking at the truthful deceit
But that mistake still cuts me deep
I need something real, something true, make me feel
An everlasting love 'til dawn

From behind the scenes, I watch Lacey sing. She's everything I want to be. Confident and captivating. Her sold-out shows every night are proof of her success. So often I've dreamt of having a music residency in Vegas after the *Sin City Star* finale.

Lacey comes off the stage, high from her performance. Her eyes glitter as bright as her dress.

As she walks past me, I blurt, "You're incredible! I hope to be like you someday."

She stops to stare at me, and her eyes darken. That stage high fizzles away.

"Not likely. Murder is bad for a career," Lacey says.

My cheeks erupt into flames. "Ex...excuse me?"

"Then again..." She tosses her silky hair. "I suppose it also depends how the producers twist the story."

I'm sinking with shaky legs.

She motions behind me. I spin to face the lens of Josh's camera. Of course he's here. How long has he been filming me?

Sweat clams up my skin, and this backstage area seems to be getting narrower. More crew members crowd around us as they prepare for the next show.

"La-Lacey?" I try to get her attention. I want to salvage the small hope of impressing my idol, but a sharp pain deep in my throat swallows my words.

She walks away, disappearing into her dressing room. I check my phone that I'd turned off during the performance. It displays thirteen missed calls and a string of texts from Olivia.

Hey Im here.

Im in your room

Where R U???

Pick up ur phone!

I need to talk to u

That cop is coming to ur hotel room

Meet me in lobby now

"Shit!" I fly out the backstage door. Josh runs after me with the camera as I knock into a couple of trash cans before jumping into an elevator. I lost security somewhere.

"How long have you been filming me?" I ask him.

"Long enough," he mutters.

The moment the elevator doors open, I rush into the ultra-modern lobby to meet Olivia. Hundreds of police cars are outside, surrounding the Sand Mirage Resort. Okay, maybe more like three, but the flashing lights and uniforms are suffocating me. Two cops give me sideways glances. I furrow my brow at them and they turn their backs. My phone vibrates. Olivia.

Turn around, the text reads.

Olivia balances two iced coffees between her hands and her phone. She wobbles on her too-high heels, sloshing the coffees.

"Ah! Thank you!" I reach, but she pulls back.

"I'm not even sure I should give you one after you ignored my texts and calls."

"I had my phone off during Lacey's show." I pout. "Pretty please?"

She rolls her eyes and hands one to me. "It's almost over. I lined up a news interview so you can tell your side of the story."

I finish half of the coffee. The caffeine smacks my nerves and ignites my mind. "What's my side of the story?"

"Sadness," she says. "You're devastated about the whole

thing. You can fake that, right?"

It won't take much acting.

It was complicated between Kevin and me, but I never expected it to end this way.

A news crew from LV18 stands nearby. The red-haired reporter touches up her caked-on foundation, while the videographer adjusts his camera stand. Olivia guides me closer. Out of the corner of my eye, I see Josh filming everything. Detective Stanton walks toward us, followed by two uniformed officers. Are they going to arrest me? On TV?

Olivia heads them off as the reporter goes live. "I'm here with Gaby from *Sin City Star*. Last night, she married her love, Kevin Stewart, also a contestant from the show. But this morning, he was discovered dead inside their honeymoon suite. Gaby, I'm so sorry. We're all heartbroken. How are you doing?" the reporter asks in a semi-sympathetic tone.

I speak into her eyes slowly. "Shocked. Scared."

Olivia motions for me to cry. I blink at her instead. Fake crying isn't easy. She knows that. Why is she pressuring me on top of everything else?

"I can't even imagine. But I supposed that's one less competitor for you, right?" the reporter asks.

"Huh?" I glance at Olivia for guidance, but her back is turned, she's arguing with the detective.

"Sources say they found the murder weapon with your prints. Are you worried?"

"I-I...don't know." My knees go weak, and I stagger into Josh. Interview over.

Josh points to my cup. "Did Olivia put something in your coffee?" he loudly whispers. "I saw her doctor your champagne last night."

Detective Stanton has heard. "Tell me," she says to Josh.

He tilts his camera to the detective and pushes a couple buttons. I crane my neck, but as if on cue, my stomach rolls. I'm getting sick again. Why am I sick again? I've barely eaten or drunk anything except that iced coffee.

Wait. *Was* it the iced coffee?

The crowd in the lobby inflates. More gawkers with phones. The flashes escalate. Pressure slips behind my eyes. Cameras are weapons. They share what we want them to. The walls close in, the wallpaper patterns of fish and seahorses multiply as a new wave of nausea and lightheadedness consumes me. I wobble, sinking to the floor.

Detective Stanton kneels beside me. "You okay? Deep breaths."

I comply. In through the nose, out through the mouth. The nausea passes, I feel better. I look up. The uniforms are cuffing Olivia. What the hell? A surge of adrenaline and confusion clears my head.

"Liv? What's going on?"

"I'll tell you what's going on." She tries to wrestle her wrists away from the cops, but is unsuccessful, then glares at me. "*You* took my last chance in this competition. *You* didn't need this with your industry connections."

"What? No! I earned my spot." I furrow my brows. Olivia has no clue how hard I worked.

"So, they gave me a pity job as your producer. And it was my job, *my job*, to control your narrative. I hated pretending to be your friend." Olivia chuckles with scorn. "But isn't that what this show is all about? A fabrication?"

"I guess everything really *is* rigged." I shake my head. "But why are they arresting you? What...what did you do?"

"Someone decided to catch the falling star." She cuts her eyes to Josh.

An officer carts Olivia out as Detective Stanton takes out her phone and scrolls to show me an email. "The lab matched ketamine traces in the champagne bottle with your and Kevin's drug screens. The hotel's security camera footage shows Olivia going in your room around midnight, after you and Kevin. With Josh's footage of her doctoring the champagne, we have enough evidence to arrest her for murder."

An enormous wave of relief washes over me. "This is good news." I pause. "For me. But I don't get it. Why would Olivia murder Kevin?"

Stanton shrugs. "Looks like she was trying to frame you."

"Not gonna happen with you on the job, Detective."

She smiles for the first time. I decide that I like her.

One of our security guys joins us. "That's enough for now. We'll bring her to the station tomorrow with a lawyer. She's got to prepare for tonight's show."

The detective nods and leaves.

I inhale a sharp breath, then exhale shakily. I can get past this. After a large glass of cucumber water and a power bar, I'm changed by wardrobe, hair, and makeup from a murder suspect into the first *Sin City Star*.

Black heels.

Silver sheath dress.

I pull out my lyric journal, flipping through the pages until I land on the song I'd been writing since my audition. Each of us had an opportunity, but I feel more ready now than ever.

I step into darkness, trying to focus in the shadows, while creeping closer to the front of the stage.

There's a live audience before me. Nine microphones circle tall stools. The rustle and breaths of the other contestants, waiting for their turn after I go first in this round.

A spotlight blasts over me.

I maintain composure.

Applause erupts in the theater.

I cup the microphone and sing:

Here's my side, my story, my truth
Standing alone but I'm stronger than you
That time we dined, you fell hard for a star
As I brightened, the world grew below my glow
I rose high but you fell low
You made a wish and it never came true
You lost your chance, your all, with me

My glow fed your envy
The pain all but stabbed me
Now, it's my turn, baby
It's my turn, baby

The Day the Music Died
Pamela Raymond

While he mulled over the best way to do the worst thing, a voice rang out followed by a bare-knuckle rap on the front door. "Hey Dave! You home?" A cupped palm pressed into the block glass window to the left of the door. "It's me. Mason!" Mason never had great timing, but he could not be ignored.

"Cool it, will ya? I'm coming." Dave stood up and shuffled from the kitchen to the foyer. He wiped a smear of dried blood from his left thumb to his ink-blue *Rick and Morty* T-shirt and checked his nails for any lingering specks. Glimpsing Mason's shadowy figure on the other side of the opaque window, Dave opened the door as if it were a normal Wednesday evening.

"Hey, Mason. What's up?"

The wheezy neighbor paced in front of him. Sweaty, corn-blond bangs framed Mason's square face. His coat hanger frame sported surprisingly fresh jeans and a pullover green slicker, the bottom wide, the drawstring undrawn. *Wonder if he just swam into that thing.* The thought hidden behind Dave's eyes.

"Oh, hey, Dave. Sorry to bother you." Mason looked anything but sorry to bother Dave. "Ah, are you finished with the chain saw yet? I kinda..." His voice trailed off, but his eyes finished the sentence.

"Yep, yep." Dave took a breath. *Calm down, dummy.*

"Seriously, Dave. How long does it take to cut down a few

twigs?"

"However long it takes." *Deep breaths, man, keep it loose.* "Listen, I'll bring it by tomorrow morning. Would that work?"

Mason stared, then relaxed his shoulders. "Okay. I can live with that. But first thing in the morning, okay?"

"Yeah, buddy. Sure thing."

Wandering down the hall, back to the kitchen, Dave assessed the damage. The dinette table resting on its side sported a jagged peg where a wooden leg used to be. Shards of brown beer bottles in a plastic dustpan next to the recycling bin. *Don't forget to toss the dustpan with that.* The last item on his to-do list. It had taken hours to check off the others—sort Gary's body parts into black plastic bags and tape them up, bleach the ever-loving fuck out of the bathtub, and...*This is no time to start a mental trip down the yellow brick road, idiot.* Dave needed to focus.

Things had spiraled out of hand, and Dave was still processing it. Processing it and believing that "do unto others before they do unto you" was the new golden rule.

Gary and Dave were casual enough drug buddies by the end of sophomore year, right before Carly Rae Jepsen's "Call Me Maybe" became the soundtrack of the summer. They'd hit the underside of the football bleachers to toke a few joints after skipping fifth period. It would start with chants of "Home of the free. Home of the brave. Home of the lit!" and descend into fits of hysterical laughter, the metal stairs above them rattling in tandem.

Back in the days of pom-poms and pop quizzes, this passed for a genuine friendship. On some occasions, they would daydream about the future. Dave would create the next HAL 9000, thank you very much, and Gary would take his hand-me-down guitar on tour in Europe. Life was simpler and dreams bigger when you still lived with your parents.

As the years passed, Dave watched as hard luck hit Gary upside the head. He could strum his way around a Gibson knockoff alright, but Gary would never be the next Slash. Didn't have the looks or charisma to supplement his immense talent. Lumpy and awkward were Gary's most glowing qualities. Gary's "big time" amounted to spotty gigs at raunchy frat houses or low-rent bars followed by couch surfing to keep a roof over his head. After running into Gary at the corner of Randolph Street and Depression, Dave offered him a place to stay for a few days. Those few days turned into a jam session that would flip Dave's fortunes for good.

That first night, Gary laid out a harmony on his guitar, loaded with unstable and wild chords that transitioned into a smooth interval. Between a succession of notes punctuated by gloomy silences, Gary would nerd out on the academics of death metal's connection to Beethoven.

"Hey, bro, what do you think of this?" Gary plucked a coarse riff that made no sense but was infused with undeniable magic. From his perch upon the barstool, Dave tilted an affirming nod in Gary's direction. Gary balanced the guitar on his paunch and busied himself fingering the strings to start on another cord. The front of his mullet dangled in his eyes, the jet-black mop swaying as he looked from the neck of the guitar to the body. He fiddled for a few minutes, frustration creeping up around the corners of his mouth until he spotted inspiration, the keyboard straddling two milk crates in the corner of the living room. "Dude, get that thing over here!" He pointed a chunky finger at the instrument that Dave hadn't turned on since last summer's barbecue.

The barbecue that started as a celebration of Dave's new gig at Veulent Technologies and finished with Jessica ending their three-month relationship. Her parting words started with, *"It's definitely you, not me,"* sandwiched between a few disparaging words about his keyboard skills and something about embarrassing her in front of her friends with his awful rendition of "Every Rose Has Its Thorn." Dave was unaware of it at the time, but his own hard-luck story had just begun.

"Man, you remember Mrs. Tichenor's class in junior year?" A softness came over Dave as he recalled Mrs. T and her steady encouragement as he sat at her upright piano, cracked pages of *Teaching Little Fingers to Play*, guiding his journey. A journey cut short by a father who felt nurturing an artistic side was meaningless, the sentiment reinforced with the back of his hand. Formal lessons with Mrs. T ended, and Dave was self-taught after that. "I'm a bit rusty, but...what the hell."

Dave scooted down to the stained beige carpet, leaning back on his hands. He watched. He listened.

Has Gary always been this good? Nah. Maybe?

Dave allowed Gary's taut rhythm to drown out his lack of success at work, his lack of success finding another Jessica, his father's brutal lack of inspiration. Joining in on the synth keyboard, Dave felt alive but bitter.

Gary's unsolicited deconstruction of Dave's playing, *"You're off tempo, bro,"* and general critique of his skill level, *"Don't quit your day job,"* irritated Dave to the core. His brain pushed beyond the haze of self-loathing and sheer annoyance and settled on a very selfish thought. He could enter the company-wide contest for a music score to launch the newest game at Veulent, using his old stoner friend's music.

This was the second time Veulent had run an internal contest, and it had done wonders for the first winner, Mara, from the production department. The suits treated Mara's catchy tunes for the *Osumare Serpent* series like the Second Coming. Now she led her own team. Dave salivated at the thought of getting in on that action.

A steady supply of hoppy beers and organic weed proved to be the right lubricant to get Gary to produce. But Dave needed him to finish this magnum opus. He needed a win.

"Hey, Gar, maybe I can pass this along to the suits. I mean, hell, they're looking for some dark moody shit to play in the background of *Aganjú Force* coming out this fall." Lies work better when seasoned with a few granules of truth, so Dave salted to taste, and Gary ate it up.

"Aw, man, that would be so tight! I mean, it's not *Call of Duty*, no offense, but *Aganjú Force* would be great. Yeah, man, hook it up."

With deliberate and quiet intent, Dave decided that when a door closes, a window opens, and, as luck would have it, Gary crawled through.

Thus, the deceit began. And it ended with a broken table and a lot of blood.

The rush was unexpected and instant. The praise heaped on this mosh pit of musical chords was intoxicating. Before he could help himself, Dave owned the praises that didn't belong to him, basked in the affirmation of a breakthrough that wasn't his, pocketing a ten-thousand-dollar bonus for his winning non-efforts. As far as Dave was concerned, once the execs noticed him, all his work would be forged in genius.

Dave spent weeks avoiding Gary from whatever prepaid cell phone his guitar hero friend could get his hands on. What started as a casual check in, *"Which way is the wind blowing with the suits, anyways?"* became a daily ratcheting up of inquiring minds want to know. An agitated Gary would not be easy to shake. Especially when he showed up at Dave's door.

Dave delivered the lie, as breezy as the air floating up a skirt. "I've been putting this off, man," a sigh to give the moment gravitas, "the suits didn't go for it. Thought it was trying too hard. Not the right 'image'"—in bent finger air quotes—"for their market. Sorry dude." Dave let his critique sink in.

Gary's tears melted, becoming slick pools. He raised his shoulders, in that aw-shucks sort of way that disappointment brings, and extended his hand and broken dreams to Dave, thanking him again for trying. Dave watched Gary as he crossed the lawn on his way to the bus stop a few blocks away at the corner of Lexington and Poor Sap.

* * *

Shaggy-haired employees peppered the Veulent Technologies hallways, their paychecks containing the kind of zeros their parents could only dream of. Since the announcement of his win, Dave's ego swelled within those halls. The daily barrage of congratulations became normalized and expected. But Dave knew today was different when the meeting popped up on his calendar.

Dave entered the conference room with the swagger of a Disney villain. *I'll finally get my own team and some respect around here.* He stopped short, confused. Suits unfamiliar to him populated faux leather chairs circling the buffed wooden table. Some with arms crossed, some with elbows planted on the mahogany, all of them stone-faced and humorless. *What in the world?*

Clearing his throat with authority, Oren, the neophyte CEO, barked, "Take a seat, Dave." Dave heeded the request.

Dave sat opposite from Oren, his hands in his lap, then rubbing the thighs of his denim. One of the nameless suits broke the quiet.

"Dave, I'm with the legal department here at Veulent. We—" Lawyer Guy motioned around the table, "—need clarification on the music you created for *Aganjú Force*. We're hoping you can answer some questions."

Dave's thoughts raced in hot and heavy, the temperature in his cheeks keeping pace. "Yeah, sure. What's up?" His voice took on a boyish octave.

"So," Lawyer Guy's tone as measured as a cobra winding out of a basket, "just to be clear. *You* created this music, right?"

Dave responded, "Yes, sir," followed by a weighty swallow. "Yeah, the melody came to me out of nowhere, and I ran with it." That was close to the truth given Gary pulled it out of nowhere during what Dave would later christen *The Lost Weekend*.

"There seems to be a bit of a problem, Dave. A copyright infringement lawsuit was leveled against Veulent for the use of the music you created. It's one of those nuisance lawsuits, but we must address it. All we need from you is your creative notes and all your recordings. You know, an origin story of what you did, so we can counter the allegations."

The churning knots in Dave's belly threatened to bend him over like a folding table. He leaned forward, rubbing his hands on his legs once more, and picked up a glass of cool water from the mirrored tray, the one probably reserved for the damned. Then popped it like a tequila shot. "I, I, um, did it all at home."

Lawyer Guy's expression had not changed since Dave walked in the room. Cobra-like to the end. But Dave sensed an imperceptible glint in his eye.

"Dave, the company is aware you don't have any documentation on your work laptop. That's why we are asking for the paper trail."

His legs felt like Jell-O on a roller coaster, his eyes strained and unblinking. *They searched my computer? What the fudgesicle?* Dave reached for the water glass only to find it bone dry. "Uh, okay." Concentrating on this ever-expanding nightmare became more challenging by the second, but Dave willed himself to keep his head on straight. Time to get crafty. He had to find out more about what Lawyer Guy knew.

"So what if some loser says it was a, what did you call it, copyright infringement? Don't *they* have to prove it? I mean, I stand by my work, no problem."

An amused, quizzical look came over Lawyer Guy. The kind Dave imagined a cheetah might have when eyeing up a gazelle gliding through the Serengeti. "Dave, not to get too legalese on you, but you're sort of correct. The claimant does have to prove two things: access and substantial similarity. Access hinges on if the claimant can prove you have heard the claimant's music at some point before creating yours. Substantial similarity is more esoteric. It hinges on whether an average listener can tell that one song is a copy of another or hears enough elements to believe that it is."

Dave's mind calculated the answers to both questions. *Yes, and yes.*

"Regardless, Dave, we need to respond, and you need to help us."

Dave's focus disintegrated into a one-word response. "Oh."

"Can you get back to us by tomorrow morning? Need to move fast to quell this opportunist." Lawyer Guy followed up with the zinger that Dave knew was the real reason for this tribunal. "Is there anything to be worried about, Dave?" And there it was.

"Of course not!" Dave heard his false indignity ring out like a high-pitched death knell.

"Okay. Email me what you have by nine a.m." Lawyer Guy conjured up a crisp white business card from his breast pocket. The card moved from one suit's hand to another on the way to Dave. A furtive scan of the table did little to bolster his outlook on this situation.

Oren leaned into his chair. The subtle repositioning caused a loud, squeaky hum, almost fart-like in nature, against the artificial leather. The entire room pretended not to notice. "Alright. Thanks, Dave." Oren motioned toward the door.

On the walk back to his cubicle, Dave fingered the white rectangle as if it were misted in acid while *Holy crap!* echoed in his mind on repeat.

It was the release of *Aganjú Force* that forced, pun intended, the dam to burst on Dave's duplicity. Gary showed up at Dave's house again, but this time it wasn't the laid-back version of Gary, but the cat-on-a-hot-tin-roof version knocking at the door. Dave guessed Gary might not have regular access to room and board, but he must have regular access to the internet, which was full of hype about the *Aganjú Force* launch, lauded for its fiery composition and its tonal balance of mood and story.

Dave let Gary in without a game plan. Civil words were exchanged, at first. The discussion escalated to more of an outdoor voice than an indoor voice situation, and Dave was not prepared.

"Bro, you lied to me. You lied like a dog! My shit was primo, and you straight up stole it like it was nothing!" Gary's stale breath was desperate, inches from Dave's face.

"Dude, I had to! You don't know what it's like. All Cutthroat Island out here!" Dave's adrenaline kicked in. "And you coming around here after that stunt you pulled with the lawsuit. That bullshit play isn't going to help either of us!"

"What lawsuit? Is this some more of your spun sugar fairy dust?" Gary's portly physique was looking more menacing by the minute. "Look, that's your problem. What matters to me, right now, is getting my due. What matters is YOU telling THEM what you did and get me some credit, bro. And some skrilla for my troubles."

"What? How much money do you want? I only got a five-grand bonus." The half truth slipped easily from Dave's lips. "Around four grand after taxes."

"I want credit on the game and, just to show I'm willing to work with you on this, I'll take three grand. The rest is yours as a finder's fee."

Dave's mind went into stealth mode. He had to think quickly because giving any credit—creative, coinage, or otherwise—to old buddy, old pal Gary was not going to happen.

"I can do the money but not the credit. I could lose my job, and I need this job."

"No can do, bro, I need both. Get my career started for real this time." Gary leaned into Dave, fists clinched, a hard but hopeful stare in his eyes.

Dave lowered his gaze. He needed to stall a bit longer. *The Grand Canyon would be easier to cross than getting out of this mess.*

Tensions were running at high tide. Dave could never really be sure what triggered the fateful events but trigger they did. Emotions flooded Dave's brain and he went into fight-or-flight mode when the scuffle broke out.

The odds were not in Dave's favor.

Gary had the scrappiness of a part-time street urchin and outweighed Dave by about a toddler. However, Gary didn't leverage that extra weight to his advantage. Going down, head hard on the sharp edge of the counter, Gary toppled the table, breaking the right wooden leg like a crispy bread stick.

While mulling over the best way to make excuses for the worst thing he'd ever done, Dave recounted during his sentencing the revisionist history that brought him to this point. *No, no, Your Honor and kind members of the jury, it was never my intent to keep the glory for myself, only to borrow it. Yes, yes, Your Honor, I might have coopted the music, but I certainly had the right to protect my person from this unruly, quite gifted maniac of a man!*

All facades of hope fell away when Veulent head honchos testified that their internal investigation did not uncover Dave's fraud. The suits were unaware that Dave was not the author of the music. As for the lawsuit that led to this predicament, it disappeared as soon as Veulent served the other party with a countersuit. An intimidation tactic of corporate America.

Dave was clueless to the fact that these kinds of copyright infringement lawsuits rarely go to trial and are notoriously hard to prove. In the end, even if Gary had had the gumption to sue, he would have likely lost. Dave had no idea that carving up his high school pal was unnecessary. And quite unpleasant, in retrospect.

The disturbing headline of Gary's pieces floating in garbage bags in the Chiswick River caught the jury's attention, and Dave's fingerprints on the bags did not help his self-defense plea. Mason's neighborly account, which placed the chain saw in Dave's capable hands, kept the eight men and four women in the jury box riveted throughout his two days of testimony.

Luminol on the stoneware kitchen tile told the story, the buried guitar in the far corner of the backyard was the epilogue, a silent confession of guilt that the jury hung their hats on.

Strapped to a gurney in his best prison whites, Dave considered his fate another stroke of bad luck. He often thought how being unemployed would not have been such a bad deal after all.

Dave closed his eyes, his arms prickled with the panic of knowing his final moments were here and now. *This really is the day the music died.*

ACKNOWLEDGMENTS

Rock, Roll, and Ruin is the natural segue from the Triangle Sisters in Crime's first two anthologies, written around the themes of sex (Carolina Crimes: 19 Tales of *Lust, Love, and Longing*) and drugs (Carolina Crimes: 21 Tales of *Need, Greed and Dirty Deeds*). Sex, drugs, rock 'n' roll—a classic trilogy abounding in opportunities for mayhem.

Submissions were open to chapter members and SinC members who live in the Carolinas. They submitted original, never-before-published stories around a musical theme. A blind judging selected the finalists.

Rock, Roll, and Ruin is a group project. Triangle SinC chapter members who donated time and expertise include Sara Johnson, Diane Kelly, Caroline Taylor, Toni Goodyear, and Gina Schmidt. Hank Phillippi Ryan, a past president of the national Sisters in Crime organization, generously agreed to write an introduction. *Rock, Roll, and Ruin* could not have been produced without their significant contributions.

The greatest thanks are due to the twenty-seven authors. Inspired by musical memories and fired by imagination, they harnessed their creative energies and wrote very different stories about characters—some musicians, some not—whose lives are impacted, for better or for worse, by musical influences in their lives.

ABOUT THE AUTHORS

JAMIE CATCHER writes from her home in Aiken, South Carolina with a fluffy collie at her side. She is the author of the short stories "Riley & The Sand Demon," published in *Carolina Crimes: 19 Tales of Lust, Love, and Longing*, and "A Calceologist Has a Bad Day," published in *Carolina Crimes: 21 Tales of Need, Greed and Dirty Deeds*. She has written seven manuscripts, and counting.

Mystery writer **E. B. DAVIS** lives in Frisco, North Carolina where she enjoys island life. Her short stories have appeared online and in print. *Carolina Crimes: 19 Tales of Lust, Love, and Longing* contained her story "Ice Cream Allure." "The Pearl Necklace" was chosen for *The Fish That Got Away* anthology. She serves as the Education Coordinator for the SinC Guppy Chapter and interviews authors at writerswhokill.blogspot.com.

JUDY FOWLER lives in Virginia Beach. She's a member of two SinC chapters and has stories forthcoming in two anthologies. She's publishing her first novel, about murders in a jail. She has a master's degree in Forensic Psychology from John Jay College of Criminal Justice, and she used to sing opera.

DAVID GOLDSTON splits his time between Chapel Hill and Boone. In addition to being an avid reader, he enjoys hiking in the North Carolina mountains and dabbling in photography. This is his first published fiction. Thanks to Karen Pullen and Toni Goodyear for their support.

TONI GOODYEAR's short stories have been published in the popular anthology series *The Killer Wore Cranberry*, *Kings River Life*, Bouchercon's *Murder Under the Oaks*, *Day of the Dark* by Wildside Press, *Fish or Cut Bait*, and the first two volumes of Triangle Sisters in Crime's trilogy of sex, drugs, and rock 'n' roll. Toni is retired and lives in Chapel Hill, NC.

MARNI GRAFF is the award-winning author of the Nora Tierney English Mysteries and the Trudy Genova Manhattan Mysteries. Her story "Quiche Alain" appears in the Agatha-winning Malice Domestic Anthology, *Murder Most Edible*. Managing Editor of Bridle Path Press, she's a member of Sisters in Crime, Mavens of Mayhem SinC, and Triangle SinC. Graff was a longlist judge for the 2020 International Association of Crime Writers Dashiell Hammett Award.

NOELLE GRANGER is a Professor Emerita at the University of North Carolina School of Medicine. After forty years of research and teaching, plus earning her EMT license, she decided to use her knowledge of human anatomy and emergency medicine to write the Rhe Brewster mystery series and a historical fiction novel, *The Last Pilgrim*, about the oldest surviving passenger on the *Mayflower*. She blogs at saylingaway.wordpress.com.

KATHY HEADY is the author of four mystery novels featuring Nara Blake, a young woman who investigates lost and stolen art for a British museum. Kathy lives in North Carolina with her husband and two cats, Tang and Sirius Black. Her house looks out on Carolina woods, almost fulfilling her childhood dream of living in a tree house. Learn more at KathleenHeady.com.

ABOUT THE AUTHORS

POLLY IYER is the Amazon-bestselling author of one novella and ten novels including the Diana Racine Psychic Suspense series. Polly's a retired illustrator who translates her fantasies into stories of excitement and romance. One reviewer describes her characters as "…making heroes out of damaged people." Check out her website at PollyIyer.com.

LAWRENCE KELTER has published thirty novels, including *Back to Brooklyn*, the studio-authorized sequel to the hit film *My Cousin Vinny*. Literary icon Nelson DeMille assisted with his early work. Before saying, "Lawrence Kelter is an exciting novelist, who reminds me of an early Robert Ludlum," he said, "Kid, your work needs editing, but that's a hell of a lot better than not having talent. Keep it up!"

GINA LEA's first book, *Defining Destiny*, was called "an ideal, frothy beach book" by Kirkus Reviews. She is editing the second book in her mystery series, as well as editing her first YA novel about a magical library. Her story "The Windmill" was published in *Carolina Crimes: 21 Tales of Need, Greed and Dirty Deeds*. Gina Lea lives in North Carolina with her best critics, her husband Rob and peke-pug, Zuzu.

JENNIFER LOWRY is from Maxton, North Carolina and loves the small-town life. She is a fan of all things horror and UFC. When she isn't literacy coaching, publishing, or homeschooling her son, she can be found sharing the author journey online or hiding behind the pages of a new book. She's published over thirty books. Grab a pumpkin coffee, and a Reese's cup, and check her out at JenLowryWrites.com.

KAREN MCCULLOUGH is the author of more than two dozen novels in the mystery, romance, fantasy, and paranormal genres, including the Market Center Mysteries series and three books in the No Brides Club romance series. She's a member of Mystery

Writers of America and Sisters in Crime, and a past president of the Southeast chapter of MWA. She invites you to visit and learn more at her website, KMcCullough.com.

JAMES MICHAEL MCGUFFEY was introduced to reading at an early age by his mother. This included mysteries starting with Arthur Conan Doyle and on through Agatha Christie and current favorites Michael Connelly and James Lee Burke. He has always imagined stories running through his head. Once he retired, his wife, the writer Liz McGuffey, encouraged him to put pen to paper. He will soon finish a draft of his first novel.

RUTH MOOSE was on the creative writing faculty at UNC-Chapel Hill for fifteen years. She published four collections of short stories and two novels. *Doing It at the Dixie Dew* won the 2014 Malice Domestic award from St. Martin's Press. She recently moved back to Albemarle, North Carolina where she grew up.

E. J. MURRAY lives in Greenville in a little house filled with books and photographs. She has been telling stories since she realized it was a great way to become the center of attention. When she's not off in her own little world, she can usually be found with a camera in one hand. E. J. has published several short stories in small magazines and anthologies. This is her first crime story.

BONNIE OLSEN lives in Chapel Hill where she mostly writes historical fiction, but sometimes she churns out a short story or two.

When *USA Today*-bestselling author **KATE PARKER** found she was unable to build a time machine in her backyard, she began to research and write historical mysteries as a means to time travel.

She is the author of fourteen novels and seven novellas. Visit her at KateParkerBooks.com.

KERRY PERESTA spent twenty-five years in advertising as an account manager, creative director, and copywriter before she began writing full-time. She is currently writing the second book in the Olivia Callahan Suspense series, available in 2022 from Level Best Books. Kerry is past chapter president of Maryland Writers' Association and a member of Lowcountry Sisters in Crime. Kerry lives in Hilton Head Island, South Carolina. Discover more about Kerry at KerryPeresta.net.

KAREN PULLEN has published two mystery novels, *Cold Feet* and *Cold Heart*, and a short story collection, *Restless Dreams*. She edited the first Triangle Chapter's anthology, *Carolina Crimes: 19 Tales of Lust, Love, and Longing*, which was nominated for an Anthony award. She has an MFA from Stonecoast at the University of Southern Maine, and lives in Chapel Hill, North Carolina.

PAMELA RAYMOND is a native of New Orleans, Louisiana but calls Raleigh, North Carolina home. Her first writing love is horror, but she is game for trying cozy mysteries on for size. Her fiction focuses on her love of the Big Easy and bringing diverse characters to life. Pamela was a 2019 semifinalist for the Golden Donut Award. "The Day the Music Died" is her first published fiction work.

When **JENNIFER RILEY** isn't writing short stories, ebooks, and novels, she's pursuing beekeeping, making soap, permaculture, and sustainable building. She hopes to build her own writer's retreat someday. Her story "Rolla," about young love and rivalry in southern Kentucky, was included in the Triangle Chapter's second anthology, *Carolina Crimes: 21 Tales of Need, Greed and Dirty Deeds*.

JACY SELLERS is president of the Queen City Suspects chapter of Sisters in Crime. Her stories can be found in anthologies and web collections. She's part of an author duo for a young adult fantasy series, The Jadesin Journals. Jacy lives in Charlotte, North Carolina. Visit her at JacySellers.com

E SENTEIO is a writer of crime and horror fiction. E grew up in a shadow-filled attic, rummaging through hope chests overflowing with mystery magazines and spinning stories from cobwebs.

CAROLINE TAYLOR is the author of five mystery novels, one short story collection, and a nonfiction book. Her story, "Intervention," was published in *Carolina Crimes: 21 Tales of Need, Greed and Dirty Deeds*. She's deeply indebted to Dwight Mason, whose tales of diplomatic service abroad inspired "Morocco Rococo." Visit her at CarolineStories.com.

KARI WAINWRIGHT has several mystery short stories published in anthologies and belongs to three Sisters in Crime chapters, as well as a local writers' group. She resides in Arizona with her husband Tom, son Travis, Shih Tzu Oscar Wilde, and her Kindle full of books.

BONNIE WISLER writes stories of the heart flavored with a dash of mystery. Her first novel, *Count a Hundred Stars*, received a five-star rating from *ForeWord Clarion Review*, and her short story "Boomerang" was included in the anthology *Carolina Crimes: 19 Tales of Lust, Love, and Longing*. Bonnie lives in Durham, North Carolina, along with her four-legged rescue, and enjoys long walks, good reads, and great British Tele.

On the following pages are a few
more great titles from the
Down & Out Books publishing family.

For a complete list of books and to
sign up for our newsletter,
go to DownAndOutBooks.com.

Swing Gang
A Vince McNulty Thriller
Colin Campbell

Down & Out Books
June 2022
978-1-64396-268-9

Titanic Productions has moved to Hollywood but the producer's problems don't stop with the cost of location services.

When McNulty finds a runaway girl hiding at the Hollywood Boulevard location during a night shoot e takes the girl under his wing but she runs away again.

Between the drug cartel that wants her back and a hitman who wants her dead, McNulty must find her again before California wildfires race towards her hiding place.

White Out
A Penns River Crime Novel
Dana King

Down & Out Books
July 2022
978-1-64396-269-6

A tough winter gets worse when a Black Penns River cop kills a white supremacist. A leader of the movement decides to set an example while creating a martyr for the cause.

Meanwhile, a poker tournament offering a million-dollar cash prize combines with a once in a decade snow storm to stretch the Penns River police to the breaking point.

Snake Slayer
Rob Pierce

Down & Out Books
August 2022
978-1-64396-271-9

Three criminals on the run, not just from the law but from other criminals. Two of them are lovers, the third her former lover. Where does love lie, except in the grave?

If you liked Pierce's *Vern in the Heat*, you're going to love *Snake Slayer*. And if you didn't read that one, strap in for the ride.

Moonlight Gets Schooled
A Dick Moonlight PI Thriller
Vincent Zandri

Down & Out Books
August 2022
978-1-64396-284-9

When Dick Moonlight PI is called in by the APD to look into a beautiful blond woman by the name of Virginia Gamble who teaches English at a prestigious private boy's school and who's allegedly sleeping with her underage students, he finds himself snared in a trap of illicit sex and violence.

He also comes face to face with Gamble's angry Mexican Cartel drug dealing boyfriend who's vowed to kill every man and boy the teacher has slept with. Including Moonlight.